Snifter of Death

Bloodstone Series
Book 2

Chris Karlsen

Excerpt from Snifter of Death

Graciela stood on the top stair of the chapel cursing her luck when a man's disturbingly familiar laugh interrupted her thoughts. She took a quick step to the left and flattened herself against one of the portico pillars. The horrible laugh rippled over from close by. It sounded like Detective Bloodstone's from the morning she'd bailed out Addy. He'd said something that sent the shine boy scampering away and had all the detectives snickering, including Bloodstone.

Taking a deep breath, she peered around the edge of the pillar expecting to see the detective. His presence would've been the perfect end to this entire St. Jude's Chapel mission-turned-catastrophe. To her great relief, it came from a carriage driver. She hadn't noticed a group of them gathered at the corner waiting to be hired. *Graciela, you had no reason to be frightened. You'd done nothing wrong. Stop being such a ninny.*

She left the church and headed home. Zachary would be getting up from her nap soon. The whole way home she questioned her luck. A dozen people are murdered every day in London.

How hard can it be to kill someone?

Look for Chris Karlsen's other titles

The Bloodstone Series
Silk
Knights in Time Series
Heroes Live Forever
Journey in Time
Knight Blindness
Dangerous Waters Series
Golden Chariot
Byzantine Gold

ISBN-13:978-1545211090

ISBN-10:1545211094

:

Chapter One

London, 1889
Metropolitan Police-Holborn Station

Graciela had just opened the door to the station when she was slammed against the doorframe. A struggling mass of constable and resisting arrestee crushed the breath out of her. Another constable rushed to the aid of the first. The officers bumped and jostled her more as they stumbled into the lobby finally bringing the reluctant arrestee under control.

Graciela caught her breath, straightened her clothes, and not for the first time wondered whether she really wanted to go through with her plan. Uncertain if she'd find the courage to proceed down the road if she hesitated now, she took a deep breath and pushed her way into the station.

She tugged the wide brim of her hat down as much as possible and stepped up to the lobby's desk. "Sergeant, I'm here to bail out a prisoner. His name is Newt Addy." She handed over the five pounds bail money, almost all her savings for the past six months. "Will he be released immediately?"

The sergeant nodded, put the money in an envelope made a notation on it, and then placed it in a drawer. "He will." The sergeant looked her up and down with a curious expression. "Is he your husband? You don't seem the type to associate with his sort, if you don't mind my saying."

"My relationship with Mr. Addy is none of your affair, sergeant. Can we dispense with the chit-chat? I'd like to get on with the business at hand." The longer she stood in the station lobby, the better the chances of some Peeler remembering her face. The odds of the police connecting her to what she planned were few, but Graciela wasn't taking any unnecessary risks.

The sergeant huffed and glared at her before he signed the bail form. He handed it to a chinless officer who looked barely past school age. "Bring Addy out."

Graciela watched an endless flow of police officers hauling men in various stages of resistance toward the lockup. She pulled a perfumed handkerchief from her reticule and held it to her nose as the combination of sour alcohol, sweat, and unwashed bodies hung in the air like London's famous fog.

In an adjacent room, the detective bureau according to the sign, a tall, attractive, and compared to the other plainclothes detectives there, better-dressed man waggled a warning finger at a shoeshine boy. Whatever he said sent the lad scampering off and had the men at the nearby desks laughing.

"I don't know if you'll ever make an honest creature of that little bugger, Bloodstone," said one.

Bloodstone. Graciela recognized the name. Rudyard Bloodstone was the detective who solved the British Museum murders last year. She remembered because it was all everyone talked about for weeks. She wondered if he was the detective handling the Addy case. Not that it mattered; her contact with Addy would be limited.

"Who bailed me?"

She turned toward the clipped east end accent.

"She did." The sergeant nodded her direction.

"What? Why?" Addy looked from the sergeant to Graciela and back to the policeman. "I've never seen that bit of muslin in my life."

The sergeant shrugged.

Graciela came over. "You don't know me, but I've business I'd like to discuss with you. I prefer to talk to you outside."

Addy didn't move.

"Either come outside or I will take my bail money back and you can sit in jail. Your choice, Mr. Addy. I haven't all day."

"Let's go. It's your finny."

Graciela led the way and didn't stop until they were a block from the stationhouse. "What do you mean, 'it's my finny?'" She feared it was a vulgar sexual reference that would make her regret going anywhere with him.

"A finny is five pounds, what it cost to bail me."

"Oh. I can't talk on the street. I can't take the likes of you into a decent tearoom where I'd normally go. Is there a pub you know of that is not too foul?"

"Follow me."

She'd have paid for a trolley ride if he'd told her his choice of pub was off an Oxford Circus mews. It was a strange pub with no sign outside, dimly lit, the darkness hid what Graciela suspected was filth. But no one paid them any attention when they entered and Addy led them to a small table in the back, ordering two pints on the way.

"What's this about then?" he asked, pulling a chair out, not bothering to pull out hers.

A man who'd had his nose buried in his tankard lifted his head and looked her up and down. Graciela sat but kept one hand tight on her reticule nestled in her lap. "How long have you been a burglar?"

"Hey, I'm not admitting to nothin'."

"Please, let's not mince words. I'm not the prosecutor. I need to know how experienced you are as a burglar."

The beers came and Addy waited until the barman left before he answered. "Been at it since I was nine, been caught three times, twice before I was twelve and then this last time. I wouldn't have been caught this time if it wasn't for bad luck. I know the routes and times all the Peelers pass by on the patch I'm working. Here I was coming out of the window with my goods in a sack when a Peeler comes out the backdoor of the neighbors and sees me. Apparently, their cook was sweet on him and had the copper in for tea." He took a deep swallow of beer. "Bloody bad luck I tell you."

He took another deep swallow, stared hard at Graciela over the rim of the tankard, then put it down. "You haven't answered my question. What's this about?"

"I assume from your experience you can pick locks."

"There isn't a lock made I can't pick."

"I want you to teach me how to pick locks."

Addy sat back, eyeing her like a rabbit eyes a cobra. He shook his head. "No. I know what you're doing. This is something to do with you and them Peelers. You're ginning up some kind of case where I take the fall. Oh no."

He stood and started to leave, but she grabbed his arm. "Please don't go. I swear this isn't what you think. I truly want to learn. I can't tell you why. It's personal, very personal. It has nothing to do with the police. Nothing could be farther from the truth."

"I don't need competition."

"I won't be competing. I'm not, how you say, *working* your neck of the woods, so to speak, your domain. My goal has strict limitations."

He nodded. "I don't even know your name."

"What's your favorite name for a lady?"

Addy grinned, revealing a short row of bottom teeth. "Molly. My mum's name was Molly."

"Call me Molly."

For the first time since entering the police station, Graciela relaxed a bit. Addy would come around to helping her, she could tell. She took her first swallow of beer. Beer wasn't her favorite choice of alcoholic drink. She liked cognac better and kept a small bottle secreted in her room. The maids never came into her room to clean. Since she was a paid companion, not family, she was expected to tidy up after herself, which Graciela preferred. She didn't need the maids snooping into what few personal items she had, including her wee bottle of cognac. If Mrs. Zachary found out about the alcohol, she'd get sacked. The old bat was a strict teetotaler who blamed all society's ills on demon rum. Even if she wasn't death on drink, she kept a tight fist on her money. Zachary would cut her meager salary. Cognac was expensive. Graciela bought the least expensive and restricted herself to a snifter a week and only on Saturdays.

"If I agree, would you be willing to pay me for teaching you, Molly?"

"No. I haven't that kind of money. I just spent five pounds on your bail. As for teaching, you'll have to make yourself available on Mondays. I only have that time free."

"I can, but it will take a long time for you to be an expert at a number of different locks if that's your intention. Can't you find more time?"

If she was really careful, she could get past the staff and out for an hour after Mrs. Zachary went to bed. The maids and cook would be playing cards and talking in the kitchen. It'd be good practice in case she had to slip past the staff of Bartholomew Cross.

"How can I get in touch with you?" she asked.

"Ask at the bar for Kip. He's the landlord here and knows where to find me. Leave a message with him." Addy took another swallow of beer, eyeing her over the edge of his tankard. "I don't know what your game is, Molly, and I don't want to know," he said, setting the tankard down. "Crime is not your bailiwick that's for certain. Your kind tend to get caught or killed. For your own sake, do some exploration before we meet again. Check out the property. You need to know how many doors and lower floor windows the building has. Are you looking to enter a business or residence? Are windows left open? See if you can tell how many people come and go during the day and what times. Whatever your *game* my dear, you can't steal nothin' if you can't escape the building."

"I'll try to find out as much as I can." Graciela left enough to pay for their beers and said goodbye.

She walked down Oxford Street thinking about what she needed to do for her reconnaissance.

My game, Mr. Addy, is murder.

Chapter Two

Rudyard pulled the letter from his pocket and set it down then removed his coat and hung it over the back of his chair. He poured himself a cup of tea from a kettle the detectives kept on a sideboard and took turns keeping hot. He returned to his desk and thought about the lady who'd sent the letter. The rosy scent of her perfume on the stationery drifted up, which surprised him. He'd have thought after spending several days crossing the Atlantic in the cargo hold of a ship and more days in a mail coach from Southampton, the floral reminder would've faded completely. He used his thumb to pop the envelope open and began to read what his former lady friend had to say.

"What are you reading?" Archie, his partner asked, taking his coat off and hanging it over his chair back.

"A letter from Evangeline."

"Is she coming home?"

"Not from the sound of it. She's inviting me to come visit her in New York. Apparently, she's doing quite well at a place called Lord and Taylor."

"Sounds religious."

Ruddy shook his head and continued to read.

"They're a fancy emporium on something called *the Ladies' Mile*. She wants to show me the sights in New York," he said, looking up.

"You should go."

New York, America. Ruddy grunted at the thought. He'd seen Buffalo Bill's Wild West Show in '87 when it came to London. He suspected beneath their city clothes most New Yorkers were still a bunch of Buffalo Bills, all bluster and brass. "I see no reason to go all the way to America."

"Why not? Although, I doubt there are many sights to see. It's America for heaven's sake, barely out of colonial nappies. But you'd be going to see Evangeline."

"That's the only reason I'd go and the reason I won't." Archie cocked his head and gave him a quizzical look. "I am fond of Evangeline but I don't love her. I don't want her to think there's more to what I feel than there is. If she'd stayed, maybe my feelings would've grown into love. I don't know. But I don't want to hurt her by misleading her."

"I take your point."

The rest of the letter was filled with general family information about her sister and nephew and her sister's new husband. Ruddy skimmed it and put the letter back into the envelope and tucked both into his jacket pocket.

"Detective Bloodstone, Detective Holbrook." Constable Northam approached with an arm around a young woman supporting her as he walked toward the detectives' desks.

An attractive woman, she looked to be in her

13

twenties. Her bonnet was askew and she held a handkerchief with lavender flowers embroidered on it over her mouth like she was trying to stop herself from bursting into tears.

Ruddy and Archie both jumped to their feet. Archie, more fatherly than Northam and Ruddy, slid his arm around the lady's waist, relieving Northam of that duty. Ruddy brought a chair over and Archie eased her into it. Ruddy had turned the chair so she faced Ruddy's desk and not the lobby. They didn't need to speculate. Both had been in law enforcement long enough to recognize how victims responded to certain types of crimes. From the looks of the woman, they figured a sex crime was involved.

Archie knelt on one knee. He gently brought her hand from her face down to her lap and keeping his much larger hand wrapped around hers said, "I'm Detective Holbrook. What's your name?"

"She told me—" Northam started to say. Ruddy put a quick finger to his lips and gave a tiny shake of his head.

"You were about to tell me your name," Archie said.

"Ivy. Ivy Janes."

"Well, Miss Janes, you're safe now. Whatever's happened, you're going to be fine. I think a cup of tea would be good. Would you like that?"

She nodded.

"Milk or lemon?"

"Milk, please."

"Clive, you heard the lady," Archie said without taking his eyes off Janes. After Northam left, he told her, "We'll just be quiet a moment while you catch your breath. I can feel your heart fluttering like a bird's through your gloves."

Ruddy admired Archie's manner with traumatized victims. He was the best of all the men in the detective bureau. It was a special talent. Ruddy tried to cultivate a little of the personable warmth that flowed from Arch. His attempt never quite translated the same.

Ruddy joined Archie and squatted so he was eye-level, too. "I'm Detective Bloodstone, Miss Janes. Once we have your tea, if you wish, we'll relocate to the interview room. It's private. Would you prefer to talk to us there?"

"Yes, please."

Clive returned with the tea. Archie helped the victim to her feet and led her to the interview room. Ruddy grabbed a notepad, his pen, a soft lead pencil, and his drawing pad, and followed.

He freshened his tea on the way and closed the door to the room after the other three took their seats. They went through the details of getting her age, address, and the best place and time to contact her. She sipped her tea, then looked at Ruddy and a faint smile briefly touched her lips.

"Are you ready to tell us what happened or do you need a few more minutes?" Ruddy asked unsure of how deep the calm ran.

"I'm better now."

"Start whenever you're ready."

"I was walking to work on Ormond Street."

"What time was this?" Archie asked. Turning to

Clive, he instructed, "That's your patch. Make note of where and when she saw the suspect."

"It was half-seven. I'm an embroiderer for Dobson's Haberdashers. All the ladies who do detail work buttons, embroidery, monograms and the like start early."

"Go on," Ruddy said.

"I'd just crossed Powis Place when a hideous man jumped out from a doorway with a knife, waving it in my face. He forced me around the back of the building and into the mews—said he'd cut me ear-to-ear if I didn't go." She dropped her head and her hands began to tremble. Archie immediately eased her through the fearful memory with soft reassurances.

While he talked to the victim Ruddy wondered how no one saw anything. At half-seven the sun is up and there's a good amount of foot traffic. "You walk this beat. How could someone not see him accosting her in this mews?" he asked Clive.

"It's a dark and narrow alley with piles of rubbish stacked about, sir. Not fit for wagons even, all the deliveries are done by handcarts."

The victim took a deep breath, let it out slow, and then turned back to Ruddy. "I'm ready to go on. Once he got me in the mews, he had me step behind a smelly stack of broken wood pieces. 'Lean against the wall,' he said, and I did. 'Don't move or I'll cut you.' Then, he got on his knees, raised my skirt and laid his cheek on my thigh and began to rub, up and down, back and forth—this thigh." She tapped her left thigh with her finger and shuddered. "Can you imagine how disgusted I was detective?"

"I can. Then what did he do?"

"He switched and did the same to my other thigh. After he finished rubbing his filthy face over me, he...he...unfastened my stockings, took them off me, sniffed them, and pocketed them. Then, without a word more, he stowed the knife behind his back and dashed off to I don't know where. I ran to the mouth of the alley, but he was out of sight already. I screamed and the young officer here came right away. Together we searched but the bugger was nowhere to be found." She gave a short gasp and clamped a hand onto Ruddy's wrist. "Now that he's seen me, do you think he'll come after me again?"

Ruddy gently unwound her fingers. "No. He's a twisted sort that's for certain, but I believe he was only after your stockings. However, it wouldn't hurt to take a different route to and from your work."

Ruddy set aside his report forms, picked up his soft pencil and opened his drawing pad. Archie had a way with making victims comfortable. Ruddy had a way with art. "Describe him for me."

She locked on him with fearful doe-like brown eyes. "I can't. I don't want to think on his face so close to mine, that knife so near to me."

"You don't have to do anything you don't want to do," Ruddy explained. "But it would help immensely to know what he looks like."

"He'll likely hurt another, won't he?" she asked.

"Probably."

Her gaze fell to Ruddy's hands on the sketch pad. She kept her head down for several minutes. Long enough for Ruddy to think they weren't going to get much more out of her. Then she reached over and ran a finger across the monogram on his shirt. "Fine work. RCB, what's the RC for?"

"Rudyard Cerdic."

"Cerdic. A Welshman."

"Yes."

"My people are from Ireland. They came over during the famine." She pulled her hand away and said, "He wore a tweed woolen cap with a tattered bill. He never took it off, but from what I could see, his hair was ginger."

She continued and Ruddy quickly started drawing. She did a fine job considering how traumatized she'd been. The problem was the suspect looked like ten-thousand other scruffy men of middle age and middle height and weight in London. Just once, Ruddy wished he'd get a suspect with all gold teeth in the front or a skull and crossbones tattooed over his face or warts in the shape of a boot on his cheek. Something that made you say, "You're him," with one look.

Ruddy showed her the sketch. "Is there anything else I should add?"

She shook her head and grew very quiet. She sat still as stone for a minute and then slammed both hands on the table and shot forward. All three officers jerked back. "The bounder stole my stockings. My new, not a snag in them, stockings. Cost me two bob. When you catch him, I believe I'm owed a free kick. One kick, in the naughty bits, fair is fair."

Ruddy avoided eye contact with Archie. If he looked at Archie, he'd surely laugh. From the corner of his eye, he'd seen Archie's mutton chop whiskers twitch from trying to stifle a giggle. "Actually Miss Janes, you're not entitled to a revenge kick."

She tipped her head and tilted her chin. She didn't bat her eyelashes but blinked slowly in an odd way as though she was thought it seductive. "Are you sure, Detective Bloodstone?"

"Flirting with me will not earn you a free kick, Miss Janes," Ruddy said and smiled. "But we're all sympathetic to your cause. If there's nothing else, Officer Northam here will escort you to your work."

Ruddy tore the sketch from the pad and gave it to Northam. "When you're done escorting Miss Janes, show this picture around to the other officers that border your patch and to the shopkeepers. See if anyone recognizes him."

"Sir...a word." Northam stood and stepped outside the room and out of earshot of Miss Janes and Archie.

Ruddy joined him.

"I wondered why you let her go off, and well, natter on about your monogram instead of the crime. Why let her be distracted from the matter at hand?"

Northam hoped to be a detective one day and was enthusiastic to learn from Ruddy and Archie. He sat in on as many interrogations and interviews as he could and often asked questions after.

"If a victim is hysterical, then you must do whatever it takes to calm them down," Ruddy explained. "A victim making no sense is no help. She wasn't hysterical but terribly distressed. You have to let her find a sense of normalcy again. Stitchery is part of her normal, daily life. It's a touchstone for her. That's what she needed to help her move forward."

"I see. What of her sudden anger?"

"Anger is often the other side of fear."

"Thank you. The pretty thing was flirting too, sir," he said even softer with a wink.

Ruddy pulled Northam into the corner. "Heed this warning, Clive. Never socialize with the females on a case. I know you know to avoid suspects but avoid the victims too. If the defense discovers it, they'll cast a shadow over your involvement in the case in court. They'll suggest your relationship influenced your handling of the case and tainted your professionalism. Trust me. Don't do it. Now go."

Northam offered Miss Janes his hand and escorted her from the station.

Ruddy and Archie returned to their desks to find Geoffrey Marsden, a reporter for the London Gazette, sitting where Miss Janes had. Marsden puffed on a pipe engulfing the area around the desks in a giant smoke cloud. The smoke didn't bother Ruddy. A constant haze filled the Boot and Bayonet, his favorite pub. Most of the soldiers he'd served with smoked pipes or cigars. He'd even smoked a pipe for a short time when he first joined the army. He quit because he didn't like the taste it left in his mouth. The problem with Marsden's smoking was the tobacco he used. Ruddy wasn't sure where he bought it or what brand he favored but it had to be the cheapest in London. It smelled worse than what most soldiers smoked, like it was mixed with dried horse shit. Ruddy'd bet a quid it was part manure of some kind.

"Why are you here?" Archie asked, waving the smoke cloud from his desk.

Marsden removed his pipe and blew out a stream of smoke. "You know me. I like to check in and see what's up with you fellows. Not that I don't trust you to share a ripe story with me should one occur—but I don't."

"Rightfully so, as we've no obligation to share any story with you, ripe or not," Ruddy told him. "Take your arse and equally stinky pipe out of here, Marsden."

"Come on, Bloodstone. Don't be like that. I'll bet there's a press-worthy story about that woman who just left. I was heading this way when Officer Northam brought her to the station. I saw you take her into a private room to talk. What's going on? Is there a rapist in the neighborhood?"

The glee in the reporter's voice at the possibility of a serial rapist on the loose set Ruddy's teeth on edge. "What happened to the lady is none of your business. There's no rapist running around. And if you think to bribe Seamus, the shine boy again into tattling what he overhears from the detectives, I'll ban him and you from the station until one of us dies of old age. Now get out."

"You're not being fair, Bloodstone. When the whole city was trashing the police for their failure to capture the Ripper last fall, I made you and Holbrook look good for your work on the museum murders and the Viscount Everhard case, which I wasn't obligated to do."

Ruddy had had enough. He snatched the still lit

pipe from Marsden's hand and flung it into his trash can. "Bull's balls, you're a lying dog and that's an insult to all dogs. We looked good because we did a good job."

"My pipe!"

Marsden's eyes widened and he pulled back as Ruddy pressed close, spitting his words. "Speaking of obligations, you only got those stories because you used shady means to position yourself and the paper to extort the department into giving you an exclusive. How you managed to stretch that into weaseling another exclusive out of us this past spring, I don't know. But, as far as I'm concerned we're done."

Marsden slid his chair back a few inches. "See here, Bloodstone, we can work together." He pulled a handkerchief that might have been white once but was grey now from his frock coat pocket and wiped a thin line of sweat that trailed down his temple. "Your lot can use some decent press. It wouldn't hurt to have us on your side. The police still haven't recovered from the Ripper debacle."

Ruddy thought about the different forms of harm he'd like to do to Marsden and what discipline each would bring.

Archie recognized the look in his eyes and slipped a hand under Marsden's arm, lifting him from the chair. "It's best for you to go now. Believe me."

"Just think about what I said. A joint effort all around benefits everyone."

"Leave." Archie made a shooing motion. Marsden gave one last begging look Ruddy's way and left.

"You shouldn't let him stir you up like that.

He'll find a way to be a barnacle on us again, you know that don't you?" Archie poured the remnants of his tea on the small fire Marsden's pipe had started in Ruddy's trashcan. He poured another cup of tea and sat at his desk. "What do you think of our stocking thief? I'm hoping since she's never seen him before that this might be a one-time thrill seeking caper."

"It would be nice if you're right but I think he's just getting started. He enjoyed the exchange too much for it to be a one-time event." Ruddy then started to recreate another copy of the suspect's face on his sketch pad.

Chapter Three

Graciela took advantage of Mrs. Zachary's Tuesday and Thursday afternoon naps to slip from the house. She used Tuesday's free time to acquire the nondescript clothing she'd need when she researched details of Cross's home and business. A woman alone without parcels or visible purpose, tarrying in the area, was bound to be noticed. She was unknown in the neighborhood. Sooner or later someone would ask about the strange woman loitering about.

A walk through her neighborhood observing who people paid the least attention to gave her some ideas. She settled on a newsboy. They went everywhere and no one looked twice. She kept looking until she found a boy about fourteen who was her size. "How much for your clothes?" she asked.

"What?"

"How much for your knickers and shirt?"

"Blimey." The boy laughed and then nudged a shine boy sitting on the curb next him and pointed to her. "The mad cow wants me clothes."

Graciela grabbed him by the arm and started to pull him away from the foot traffic on the sidewalk.

"Lemme go, you mad cow," he said almost yelling now.

"Hush up, you little guttersnipe. I'm going to offer you a shilling for your clothes but you'll get a swift kick and nothing else if you don't stifle yourself."

The boy stopped yelling but jerked his arm out of her grasp. "What do you want with my clothes?"

"None of your business. Are you wearing drawers?" She waved her hand dismissively. "Never mind. I don't care what you've on under your knickers. Do you want a shilling or not?"

"Show me your money first. I'm not convinced you're not barmy."

Keeping a tight hold on her reticule, Graciela took a shilling out and showed him.

"Right then, I'll sell you my knickers and shirt."

"I want your hat, too."

"I should charge you another tuppence for that."

"It's stained. Include the hat or the deal is off."

He nodded his agreement.

"Here." She handed him a tapestry knitting bag. "Go in the alley and put your clothes in this bag. Don't dawdle."

She waited for him at the mouth of the alley. He returned a couple minutes later wearing a too small undershirt, torn drawers, and scuffed boots. He didn't appear at all embarrassed by the lack of clothing. She'd ask but if he didn't care, why should she?

When she finished with the exchange, she bought a pair of black high-top shoes and socks. After a thorough washing, she stored the clothing in a small valise and stored the valise in an upper nook of Zachary's carriage house.

On Thursday she spent two tiresome hours going over archived articles in the London Times Financial Pages. Bartholomew Cross would be in there somewhere. His type went into law or banking or finance in some way. Her theory proved right but the blurb she found didn't relate to him professionally. The small entry was an announcement of his mother's passing away last year. *Anne Cross, mother of Bartholomew Cross, Senior Financial Advisor at Kingman and Kingman, has passed away after a long illness. Services will be held at St. Jude's Church, Kensington, 21 August, 10:00.*

Rather than go further back into the archives and waste more tedious hours, she headed for St. Jude's. The residence would be listed on the mourner's guest book. He'd take that book home. She'd need to see the church's records.

Once there, she realized what a mistake running off without a plan was. She stood in the middle of a lovely medieval chapel with no idea of where to find the funeral records.

"Daft ninny."

"Can I help you, Miss?" a charwoman sitting up on her knees in the corner asked.

Graciela jumped and turned. "Ah..." was all she managed until her heart stopped pounding and dropped from her throat to her chest. "I didn't see you there."

"Didn't mean to give you such a fright. I thought you were speaking to me."

"No, I was just speaking my thoughts aloud."

"Lovely day to you, Miss. I'll get back to my work."

Graciela wandered along the main aisle of the nave trying to figure a way to get a look at the records. There had to be a way to talk the vicar into giving the information on Cross. Then the penny fell. She'd use Mrs. Zachary. Zachary never came this way. The odds of her coming into contact with the vicar and finding out about the ruse were slim to none. But since she was the widow of a respected former secretary to one of Mr. Disraeli's cabinet members, it made sense she'd know someone like Cross.

Graciela hurried back to the charwoman. "I can use your help after all. Can you direct me to the Vicar's office?"

"Out this side door, past the cloister and rose garden, there's a small cottage with a green door. That's his office and residence."

"Thank you."

Graciela knocked and the housekeeper answered and led her to his office. What a dark, intimidating space his office was with books piled on the floor and desk. Blood red wool drapes were pulled closed over the windows blocking out the sun. Black oak and brown leather chairs were set one behind the desk and one in front. She imagined it was how the Inquisition's Priests' rooms looked. One oil lamp burned and it cast the Vicar's face in a weird shadow that deepened the hollows of his cheeks, lit the cheekbones and forehead, and hid his eyes under the overhang of his brows. The brightest spot in the room was the man's bald head, which gleamed in the lamplight.

By contrast the unflattering impression was forgotten when the rich smell of roast cooking hit Graciela. Her stomach rumbled loud and long. "Thank you for seeing me. Please excuse the unladylike roar of my hungry stomach. If you'll pardon the obvious nature of my compliment, but your lunch smells heavenly, Vicar."

"Yes, cook is a treasure. Now, how can I help you?"

He didn't offer her a seat, which meant she hadn't long to make her case. "I'm Esther Zachary's friend, Calvin Zachary's widow."

"I know of her. We met many years ago."

"We've been living abroad and only recently returned. She's learned of Mrs. Cross's death and wanted to send her condolences to the family. She's not sure if they still reside at the last address she has for them. We thought you might have the information in the church records, having handled the funeral services."

From his inscrutable expression he didn't believe a word of what she said. If she had a fingernail of hope that he did, it vanished with his hard-eyed scrutiny. He eyed with disdain her bonnet with the faded ribbon, the cheap wool dress, the lace gloves she'd carefully repaired where they'd torn. "What address do you show for the Cross family?" he asked.

Her mind went completely blank. She knew many streets in several fashionable neighborhoods. She and Mrs. Zachary often took carriage rides around

Hyde and Regents Park. Why couldn't she think of one street? Finally, she blurted the only one that came to her, which was no doubt wrong. "Park Lane."

The Vicar smirked. Not smiled. Smirked. That meant it had to be wrong.

"I suggest you start there. In the meantime, I will have my housekeeper escort you out. I don't know what you're playing at but I don't care for mischief. You'll do your soul a good turn to drop a coin in the poor box on your way to the street." He rang a small bell on his desk and the housekeeper came. "See this lady out."

Graciela stood on the top stair of the chapel cursing her luck when a man's disturbingly familiar laugh interrupted her thoughts. She took a quick step to the left and flattened herself against one of the portico pillars. The horrible laugh rippled over from close by. It sounded like Detective Bloodstone's from the morning she'd bailed out Addy. He'd said something that sent the shine boy scampering away and had all the detectives snickering, including Bloodstone.

Taking a deep breath, she peered around the edge of the pillar expecting to see the detective. His presence would've been the perfect end to this entire St. Jude's Chapel mission-turned-catastrophe. To her great relief, it came from a carriage driver. She hadn't noticed a group of them gathered at the corner waiting to be hired. *Graciela, you had no reason to be frightened. You'd done nothing wrong. Stop being such a ninny.*

She left the church and headed home. Zachary

would be getting up from her nap soon. The whole way home she questioned her luck. A dozen people are murdered every day in London.

How hard can it be to kill someone?

Chapter Four

"Nothing yet, Superintendent," Ruddy told Henry Jameson, the head of Holborn Station. "I made several drawings of the suspect and handed them out to the constables who worked the area around where the crime occurred. He didn't look familiar to them or the shopkeepers."

"Maybe we'll get lucky and this unpleasant stocking business will turn out to be an isolated event."

"Hate to be the bearer of bad tidings, sir, but King's Cross station also had a case. These perverts rarely stop at one attack."

"Same fellow?" Jameson asked.

Ruddy nodded. "I made a few drawings for their men to show but no one can identify the man."

"Keep trying. You both can leave."

Archie and Ruddy left and returned to the bureau.

Ruddy took two steps and momentarily stopped short. "As I live and breathe..." Hurrying to his desk, he wrapped his brother in a tight bear hug. "I thought we'd lost you to the sub-continent forever."

"India might be the 'jewel in the Queen's crown' and I'm happy to take her majesty's coin to stay there, but I had to come home for a wee time," Will said when they broke apart.

"Let me introduce my partner, Archie," Ruddy said. "Archie, this is my brother, Will." The two men shook hands. "Let me get you a cup of tea and a chair."

Ruddy brought both over to his desk. "How long will you be here?"

"I'll only be in London a few days. Then I plan to head on home. I'll stay on there for a couple of weeks before I go back. I wondered if I might stay with you. If you've a spare blanket and pillow, I can stretch out on the floor. I'm trying to save my blunt for when I'm home. I'd also like to buy mum a hat while I'm in London."

"Of course you can stay with me. Don't be silly. You'll not sleep on the floor. You'll sleep in my bed while you're here. I've a perfectly fine stuffed chair and ottoman I can make a bed out of."

"No—"

"Stop. No arguing. As for the hat, I happen to know of a hat maker who might give you a nice discount."

"Really?" Will looked from Ruddy to Archie and back. "Anything you want to share about this hat maker?"

"We saw each other socially for a brief time last year. She was widowed then. We parted friends and she's since remarried. Nothing more."

Archie pointed to the insignia on Will's uniform sleeve. "I know most of the army's ranking insignias but I've never seen that one. What's your rank, if you don't mind me asking?"

"I just got promoted. I'm a Sergeant-Major."

"Sounds impressive," Archie said.

"It's about as high up as a non-commissioned officer can go," Ruddy told him. "Congratulations Will. Well done."

"Still not a Victoria Cross." Will turned to Archie. "You know my brother has a V.C.?"

"More tea?" Ruddy asked, trying to change the subject.

"I know about the V.C. but he won't discuss the details much," Archie told Will.

Archie was one of Ruddy's favorite people in the whole world. A police partnership resembled a marriage partnership but neither closeness meant you didn't consider strangling the other person once in a while. Archie using Will to pry information out of Ruddy about the medal was borderline justifiable homicide.

"Ruddy, why won't you talk about it? That's the biggest honor you can receive from the Queen for your military service," Will asked.

"Because it's not something I wish to boast about, if that's all right with the two of you. I am not especially proud of getting the V.C. nor am I not proud. It's something I received for doing what needed to be done."

"Which was?" Will said, prodding.

"Which was?" Archie joined in.

Ruddy shot Will an unblinking, hard-eyed stare he saved for uncooperative prisoners.

"Go on then," Will blithely said.

Ruddy sighed. "I was in hospital. The Zulus

attacked and set the hospital on fire. We all helped each other get out. End of story."

Will shook his head and added, "No. There's more. You were in hospital being treated for yellow fever. You did what you did while in a debilitated state."

"How do you know that? I never told Mum and Dad the story behind the medal. Who told you?"

"The Home Secretary knew you had a brother in the military. He told your Commanding Officer who wrote a letter to mine with the details of the award."

"Sirs." Constable Northam came over. "We might have a lead on the stocking man."

"Do tell," Ruddy said, eagerly waving the young bobby over.

"A shopkeeper on my patch has a man who just purchased a stack of stockings, different patterns and different colors."

Ruddy didn't see how that was suspicious. "So? The man has a wife who likes variety."

"I said the same thing," Northam said. "The shopkeeper told me the man bought the largest size he sells."

"Again, so?" Ruddy wasn't seeing the issue. "He has a voluptuous wife."

"A few minutes later the shopkeeper caught a glimpse of the man taking a pair of the stockings from the box and holding them up to his face and then against his own leg. The shop man thought that odd. I must say, sir, I do too."

Archie looked to Ruddy, wiggled his brows and said, "It is weird. I've never messed about with my

Meg's stockings...not in that way, if you catch my drift."
He turned to Northam. "Did you ask if the fellow looks
like our suspect?"

"I did. That's the rub. The shop man said he
doesn't. But as we haven't had anyone else to look at, I
thought he was worth having a chat with anyway,"
Northam said with a shrug.

"Does the shopkeeper know where the man
lives?" Ruddy asked.

"He does. After the man came from behind the
shop, he climbed into a carriage at the curb in front and
the shop man heard the address he gave the driver."

"Let's pay the stocking lover a visit," Ruddy said
and stood.

"Can I come?" Will asked. "Sounds like it might
be a bit of fun."

"You mind?" Ruddy asked Archie.

"Fine with me."

****

Northam used his nightstick and knocked hard
on the door. "Open up, police." He waited a couple of
beats and raised his stick to knock again when the door
opened a crack.

A middle-aged man peered out. He kept one
hand at his throat clutched to whatever he was wearing.

"What do you want?" he asked, eyeing the four
of them and giving Will a second look.

Ruddy pushed his way in followed by Archie
then Northam and Will. "Close the door and search his
things," he instructed Northam.

The man's face flushed nearly as bright as the
red cabbage roses on the silk lady's dressing gown he

wore over the ribbon-trimmed chemise and silk lady's drawers. Beneath the drawers he wore the embroidered stockings the shopkeeper said he sold him, which were held up with lace garters. He'd finished off the boudoir attire with pink satin slippers with gold tone buckles. "How dare you force your way in here. I shall register a complaint with your supervisor." He shot a curious glance Will's way. "Why's the military here?"

Ruddy was briefly distracted by the thought of where the man bought garments the size he needed for his hobby. The man was almost as tall as Ruddy, which made both of them much taller than most women.

Ruddy tipped his head toward his brother. "You needn't pay him any mind, he's only an observer. We're here on official police business. What's your name?" Ruddy asked, knowing in his heart he wasn't the fellow who rubbed his face over Miss Jane's thighs. This man wanted to be a woman, not be with a woman.

The man planted his hands on his hips. "I'm not answering your questions. You've no right to question me."

Archie busied himself taking notes next to Ruddy. Will stepped up to the other side of him and held up a framed, sepia-toned photo of what at first appeared to be a woman. The woman was sitting in a fan-backed wicker chair next to a large potted fern. The stylized pose had become popular in the last year. As photography had grown in popularity, more and more Londoners were having their picture taken with various props. Exotic plants and Indian-looking furniture was the current rage. Will handed the picture to Ruddy.

Ruddy took a quick look and then set it down.

In it the man in front of them wore a terrible blonde wig made up of fat girlish curls and a frothy, frilled frock.

"Based on this photo, I doubt you'll be registering a complaint with anyone," Ruddy said with confidence. "I'll ask once more. What's your name?"

The man flopped down in a stuffed chair and began to cry. "I haven't done anything wrong."

"Then you've nothing to worry about. Your name. Now," Ruddy said. "And for all our sakes, stop blubbering."

After another loud sob, the man composed himself and dabbed at his eyes with the back of his hand. "Innis Cuthbert."

Archie wrote the name down and asked, "How is it you're home during the day and not at work?"

"I own a public house."

Archie leaned over and whispered to Ruddy. "A pub owner would be on the street early like our victim. He'd want to be available for his deliveries."

Ruddy half-shrugged in agreement. He still didn't see Cuthbert as good for their crime.

"What's the name of your place and where is it?" Ruddy asked.

Cuthbert clasped his hands together like a man in prayer. "Please don't make me tell you. Please. Any cloud on my name can cause me trouble. I can't afford to lose my license."

"If I arrest you, you'll lose it for sure. That may happen yet if you continue to stonewall us. Answer me." Northam came from the bedroom with a stack of stockings as Ruddy was issuing the warning. He put his hand up to stop Northam from giving them to him. He'd let the younger officer handle the man's delicates. "Well, your pub?"

"The Raven's Nest on Wharfdale."

"Where were you last Tuesday morning at approximately half-seven?" Ruddy asked.

"Here, getting ready to go to the pub to sign for the days deliveries."

"Can anyone vouch for you, confirm you were here at that time?"

Cuthbert shook his head. "I don't think so. There's only my landlady and her daughter in the other flat. I didn't see them on my way out."

"You're going to have to come with us. Northam find something to put those in, a pillow cover or something similar. Stay with him while he dresses in normal clothes," Ruddy said.

Wide-eyed Cuthbert said, "You are arresting me."

"Not formally. Not yet. We're taking you in to see if the victim identifies you," Ruddy explained. "If she says—"

"You'll arrest me for...for being what I am." Tears rolled down Cuthbert's cheeks. "I didn't hurt anybody. I didn't attack anyone. I like pretty clothes is all."

"We're not formally arresting you yet. Just hurry and get dressed. If you're innocent as you say, then you've nothing to worry about." Ruddy made a shooing motion. "Get on with it."

"Are all your suspects so weepy?" Will asked low. "I thought there'd be more excitement. I thought there'd be fisticuffs."

"Usually are. This one is a whole other breed," Ruddy said. "Let's get him hooked up and out of here," he ordered Northam.

****

A constable had just arrived with Miss Janes. Ruddy was in the process of explaining how she'd view the suspect. Northam would keep the man secured at the far side of the interview room while Ruddy and Archie would stand on each side of her. She could take as long as she liked and if she couldn't say whether he was the man or not, that was fine. Better to say she didn't know than to wrongly accuse anyone.

At that point, another constable came over to Archie's desk. "I've a new victim of the stocking thief, sirs."

"When did this happen?" Archie asked.

"Just a few minutes ago. I was on my patch on Clerkenwell and heard a woman screaming. I ran and the lady told me she had left a green grocery down the road moments earlier when a man approached her with a knife. He forced her into an alley where he made her remove her stockings and—"

"Slow down constable," Archie told him. "Where's the woman now?"

"Here. She's at the front desk."

"Send her back."

"I'll tell Northam to release Cuthbert," Ruddy said.

"Can I still see him?" Miss Janes asked.

"If you want." Ruddy waved Northam and

Cuthbert out of the interview room and explained to them that he was releasing Cuthbert based on new information.

After Cuthbert went by her, Miss Janes told Ruddy, "He wasn't the man. Didn't look anything like him."

"I know. But, I had to show him to you anyway as we had other evidence at the time that could've had some bearing on your case. Thank you for coming in, Miss Janes. I'll have a constable walk you back to the haberdasher's."

"May I stay for a bit? I'm mostly through with my work for the day."

Ruddy thought it an odd request. What woman wanted to stay around a nasty police station? He couldn't see the harm though. "If you wish but sit over there." He pointed to an empty chair by the table with the tea tray.

Archie brought the new victim straight to the interview room. Ruddy joined them with his sketch pad and soft pencil. The second victim told the same basic story. After obtaining her stockings, the suspect rubbed his face on her thighs but didn't interfere with her sexually in any other way. He ran off and disappeared by the time the constable arrived. Her description of the suspect matched that of Miss Jane's. She was able to add bushy eyebrows and pockmarks on his nose.

When they finished, he walked out and saw exactly what he didn't want to see, Will and Miss Janes, heads together, deep in conversation, laughing and smiling, enjoying themselves way too much. In his mind, he thought Will would busy himself talking with the other detectives, not the crime victim. Time for Miss Janes to go.

"Thank you Will for entertaining Miss Janes but don't you want to get on over to my flat and change?" He smiled at Janes. "Surely, Miss Janes you have someplace you'd rather be," Ruddy said.

"Wait here a moment," Will told Janes who smiled and nodded. He stood and walked a few feet away and indicated he wanted Ruddy to follow with a single tip of his head.

Bloody hell. His brother hadn't been in town a day and was already giving him a headache.

Ruddy went over and started before Will got a word out. "I'd rather you didn't go or do whatever it is you wish to with Miss Janes. First of all, she's a flirt. She flirted with me when we met. Beyond that, she's my victim. You're here for a brief time. After that, it's off you go and I'm left with a weepy woman on my hands one I am bound to see again due to my criminal case. Not to mention socializing with ladies costs money and you said but a short time ago you were trying to save your blunt for when you went home."

"Ruddy, do I have to tell you what it's like being stationed in Mysore for years and years? It is not a hive of pleasant social activity. I'm only here for a few days. Let me have some fun. I'll only see her for a day or two at most and spend the rest of the time meeting your friends."

How does one keep from killing a sibling? A question for the ages. "Seeing her for only a day or two is not a solution. I am still left with a weeping woman, you soft-minded sod."

"No you'll see. I promise to be a perfect gentleman. I will be on my best behavior. It shall be a night or two of lovely dinners and a bit of music hall fun. Swear on my sergeant's stripes."

He knew Will to be a man of his word. "Fine." Ruddy dug his key from his pocket and wrote his address down on a piece of paper. "This is my address and the key to my flat. Tell my landlady, Mrs. Goodge you're my brother and she'll arrange for the neighbor boy to bring water up for a bath for you. I have a tub in my place."

"Thank you. You're a good brother."

"My dog's name is Winky. He'll bark but be your friend forever if you give him a bite of biscuit. I keep a dish of his treats on top of my dresser." Ruddy took out five quid and handed it to his brother. "Here."

"You don't have to give me money. I'll just be a little short going home," Will said.

"You don't come home often enough to be short. Take it."

"Don't wait up." Will winked and slid his arm through Miss Janes' and escorted her out of the station.

"Bloody hell," Ruddy said, watching them leave.

****

At home Ruddy walked Winky, stopped by the kitchen for a large bowl of fish stew and biscuits from Mrs. Goodge and went up to his room. He'd been regaled briefly by his landlady's commentary on Will.

"What a handsome brother you have, Mr. Bloodstone. So distinguished. He could pass for one of Mr. Cecil's cabinet members, he could." This was followed with a blush and her tittering like a young girl.

"You mustn't tell him I said that."

"Don't worry. I won't," he assured her as he started up the stairs. He'd rather run naked through a snowbank than tell his brother he was setting hearts fluttering. There are some things one simply doesn't tell a brother.

Ruddy shared his dinner with Winky while he drew several updated portraits of the stocking thief. The new ones included the bushy eyebrows and pockmarks on the nose.

Finished, he put Winky on a leash and went down to the Boot and Bayonet. The pub was owned by his good friend Morris and catered to soldiers, both active and veterans. Enlisted and non-commissioned officers made up the crowd. Morris discouraged officers drinking there. A veteran of the Crimean War who lost his right arm in the Charge of the Light Brigade, Morris had little regard for ranking officers. An opinion Ruddy shared. According to Morris, "The British Empire could've been established with nothing more than sergeants heading her army."

Again, Ruddy agreed. Thanks to his own sharp tongue and quick temper, in eight years of service, he never rose higher than corporal. When he was promoted, it rarely lasted. Sooner or later, an opinion on a lieutenant or captain's order made too loud got him quickly demoted back to private. A punishment he shrugged off.

Morris brought two beers and set one in front of Ruddy, joining him at the table. "Working any interesting cases?" He took a long pull of beer from his tankard.

Ruddy told him about the attack on Ivy Janes.

A frown crept into Morris's bland expression as he listened to the details of the crime. "Strange. He only took her stockings. He didn't do anything else, anything worse, you know…"

"No real physical harm, no."

"I don't understand this stocking thief of yours. By menacing innocent women with a knife, he's running the risk of going to prison. All for silly stockings. Why not pay an East End trollop a few pence and get your stockings that way? No worries."

"The stockings aren't his whole goal. He wants to see the spark of fear the knife generates in the eyes of his victims. He enjoys their terror. He also wants that skin-to-skin contact when he rubs himself on them."

Morris's frown morphed into a grimace of disgust. "Let's hope he remains happy with touching and taking and nothing more."

"It's a problem for certain. I worry he'll escalate."

"Your dog is lapping up spilled beer from under that table." Morris pointed.

"Winky come here."

The dog trotted over and hopped up next to Ruddy. Covered in beer foam, Winky's black-button nose was now the same shade of white as his wiry hair.

"For mercy sake, look at you." Ruddy used the cuff of his shirt to wipe the foam away. Winky burped. "Ugh. Winky!" Ruddy flapped at the stink of stale fish stew and beer it carried.

"Did your dog burp?" Morris asked.

"Yes and a foul smelling thing it is too."

"Rudyard," a familiar voice called out.

"Oh, there's my brother." Ruddy waved.

"I thought you said he was out with your victim."

"He was."

Will grabbed a stool and joined Ruddy and Morris. "Evening." He turned to Morris and seeing his injury extended his left hand. "I'm Will, Ruddy's brother but I'm sure he told you that already."

"Morris Thornley." Morris shook with his left hand. "I'm the owner-proprietor here. He gave Will's uniform insignia a nod. "Ruddy said you were recently promoted to sergeant-major. Congratulations. I left a mere sergeant," he said with a smile. "Let me get you a drink. A bitter good with you?"

"Bitter, lager, ale, I'm happy with whatever you have," Will said.

Morris flagged down his granddaughter. "A tankard of our best bitter."

"What happened with you and Miss Janes?" Ruddy asked Will.

"She's husband hunting and I'm not wife hunting. She started asking lots of questions about being the wife of a soldier in a colony like India."

"I wouldn't have considered marriage while serving in Africa," Ruddy said. "But we were moving around a lot. You've been in the Mysore for years. It's pretty settled."

"Still one hesitates. Although Cawnpore was years ago, the memory of the slaughtered colony keeps many of the men from starting a family."

Morris tipped his head toward to a table with two grey-bearded men playing cards. "They're veterans from that Cawnpore regiment. Every once in a while, when they're foxed, they speak of the massacre, the bloody sight of the men's wives and children cut to ribbons. It's a sight that will always be with them."

"Did either of them lose a wife or child?" Ruddy asked, thinking what a gruesome memory to live with.

"I don't know," Morris said. "I've never wished to know, if you take my meaning."

Both Ruddy and Will nodded.

"The worry over similar insurgency lingers. There's never been real trust between us and the colonials since. Plus, life in an outpost like India is not easy on a woman. I don't want to drag any woman I love from her home to a place where everything is strange to her. It's blistering hot all day, every day, except for when the rains come. Then it's wet and hot. There's fever and disease like nothing we've ever seen here. Other than me, there'd be nothing of England for her. Would you bring someone you love to such a place?" Will asked Morris.

"No."

"I want to put four more years in and then I'll retire. After that, if the mood strikes, I'll think about marriage." Will eyed Morris's granddaughter.

He poked Ruddy in the arm. "On the subject of women, while Miss Janes and I were at the music hall, we saw the star singer. You and I need to go tomorrow night. She's a fine filly. Round on top, nipped at the waist," Will made the shape of a figure eight with his hands. "Red hair she dared to wear loose, alabaster skin, sang like an angel. If I were staying in London, I'd be on that like a bird on a worm."

"She's probably married," Ruddy said.

"Wasn't wearing a ring. I looked."

"What's her name?"

"Honeysuckle Flowers."

Ruddy smiled. "Honeysuckle Flowers…there's an actressie name if I ever heard one. I like actresses. They're not too toffee-nosed to object to a bit of slap and tickle."

"My thought exactly." Will raised his tankard in toast.

Chapter Five

Jameson, Ruddy, and Archie sat tilting their heads side to side contemplating which two officers to pick. They'd chosen five of the shortest, slimmest men with the lightest beards in the district. They lined the unhappy five up in their undershirts by Ruddy and Archie's desks.

Jameson was sitting at Ruddy and Archie's desks when the suggestion to put two officers in dresses came up. "They should work the neighborhoods where the crimes occurred," Ruddy said. "We can have two undercover officers in plain clothes trailing them."

"I say, let's try it," Jameson said. "We haven't any other avenues to work. We'll want young officers you have full confidence in, should they need to fend off the assailant before his support team arrives."

With those words, Northam, who stood by in the bureau listening suddenly paled to the color of a dead swan.

Ruddy leaned over and whispered to Jameson, "Northam thinks we're going to make him do it. Look at him."

Archie heard and both he and Jameson glanced over. "Northam, come here lad," Archie said. "Let me feel your face."

Northam gave a quick panicked look behind him as if by some miracle he'd see another Northam standing there. He came over and stopped by Archie's desk, standing at attention with his hands at his sides.

"Bend down, lad," Archie said.

Northam did and Archie ran the back of his fingers along one cheek and then the other. "Oh, very soft. You should have a feel, Superintendent."

"I'd like that," Jameson said, lips twitching as he stifled a laugh. "Come here, Northam."

Northam stood ramrod straight in front of the Superintendent and bent from waist in a perfect hinge-like move. Jameson took his face in both his hands and rubbed his cheeks. "Look at these rosy cheeks." He gave them a light pat, dropped his hands, he sighed and said, "Close to perfect, but don't worry, Northam we're not using you."

Ruddy would've sworn Northam lost an inch in height he sagged so much in relief.

Ruddy, Archie, and Jameson had a good laugh. "Really Northam, on my worst night, under the influence of the worst drink, I'd not look twice at you were you in a dress," Jameson told him.

"Now back to the business at hand. Who do you prefer?" Jameson asked. "I think the blond chap on the end suits and the ginger-haired lad in the middle. You two, step forward."

Ruddy, Archie, and Jameson stood to take a closer look at the two the Superintendent selected. "Well?" Jameson shrugged one shoulder. "I say they're as good as we're going to get."

"I agree. From a distance, they'll be fine. They don't have to be kissable," Archie said.

"Ugh, sir. The deed is disgusting enough without the added visual," the blonde officer said.

"Where will we find the clothes?" Ruddy asked. Most women he knew wouldn't be inclined to loan out dresses. Most didn't have that many spare dresses to begin with.

"This isn't common knowledge but HQ provides each district with a small slush fund. Mrs. Jameson won't involve herself in any sordid police business." Jameson turned to Archie. "Holbrook, would it be possible for you to talk your Meg into coming over today and taking the measure of the lads here and sewing a couple of frocks?"

"She'd be happy to help. Northam, you know where I live. Dash over and bring my lady wife back."

"Sir." Northam rushed off.

"You other three are dismissed. Get dressed and get back on your beats," Jameson ordered the two remaining officers over. "I know you fellows hate this assignment but we are here to protect those who cannot protect themselves. We serve the law. What you do is for the greater good. As humiliated as you may be walking around out there in such garb, bear your noble purpose in mind."

Not what Ruddy would term the finest inspirational speech. Not the worst either. Although, if asked, he couldn't come up with anything better himself. Inspirational talks weren't his strong suit.

In the military, he admired the colour sergeant in his regiment who had a special knack for raising the men's spirits. The broad-chested sergeant would pace in front of the ranks bellowing out how they'd fight shoulder-to-shoulder. "A Martini-Henry rifle and a bayonet with some English mettle behind it and we'll defeat any savage on any given day," he used to say. Ruddy smiled to himself at the memory.

Ruddy had lied about his age to get into the military. At his young age, when he'd first gone in, all of the sergeants frightened the pants off him. Once he stopped being afraid of them, it was, as his brother said, only his own sharp tongue that got him into trouble.

As supervisors went, he liked Jameson over others he'd met. Like most folks, Jameson had his favorites. But when it came to enforcing the rules or punishment for violating the rules, Jameson didn't play favorites. As a Superintendent, he'd defend his men against general complaints and accusations. But Jameson was also a political animal and wouldn't risk his position. He wouldn't face down HQ. If pressed, he'd bend to any ill political wind from Whitehall.

Like Ruddy, the Holbrooks lived within walking distance of the station. Margaret Holbrook was the picture-perfect woman you'd put with Archie. Archie had just turned thirty-six. A man of medium height with light brown hair, he kept himself from running to fat by playing rugby twice a month. Even with his rugby outings, Arch leaned toward the stout side and had a chubby face, which looked chubbier because of his beloved muttonchops.

On her tiptoes Margaret maybe came to his chin. She had dark brown hair she wore in a tidy knot at the nape of her neck and a sweet spray of freckles dotted her nose and cheeks. Whenever she took Ruddy's hand in hers, his were bear claws by comparison. He found the lady a delight on most occasions other than when she was trying to introduce him to available women friends who'd make wonderful wives.

She arrived a short time later and led the two young officers into the interview room to measure them.

"She was very kind, sir, she was quick about it and never teased either of us," Eustace Higgins, one of the undercover officers said.

Ruddy fully expected the whistles and comments to come with unrelenting fervor once the undercover men were in the dresses. "That kindness won't last with your mates here. You know that, don't you?"

"Sadly." Both young men hung their heads knowing the harassment was inevitable.

"Mrs. Holbrook," Jameson came out of his office as she was about to leave and asked, "How long do you think it will take you to make the dresses?"

"I'm a fine seamstress, if I say so myself. Me mum was, as was my grandmother. It's in the blood. Give me three days."

Jameson clasped her hand in his. "Choose two colors that you like to wear. When this is done, I'll see about those frocks going to you." He gave her hand a pat and said, "Thank you again, Mrs. Holbrook for doing this. You're a treasure."

Jameson came back to where Ruddy and Archie

52

sat and gestured with his hands for them to come closer.

"I'm letting you know ahead of time so this doesn't turn into a Battle Royale in case things go from bad to worse. But if we get a third victim of this stocking thief, I'm bringing that reporter, Marsden, in to do a short story for the broadsheets."

"Please, Superintendent. No," Ruddy pleaded.

"Sir, he's bloody awful difficult to get on with," Archie added.

"You two will have to figure out a way to get along if it becomes necessary. A third victim and we have to warn women in the area and have one of your drawings put alongside the story." Jameson patted Archie's shoulder. "Perhaps we'll get lucky and it will end with this last victim or perhaps one of our fake fair maidens will lure him into custody," he said and walked away.

"Why do I feel like it won't end here?" Archie asked, watching Jameson's back.

"Because it won't," Ruddy said, sadly certain he was right.

Chris Karlsen

Chapter Six

After the Vicar sent her away, Graciela returned to the drudgery of searching the London newspaper archives. Only this time, she didn't search the financial sections, she searched the society pages. At least some of the non-useful information might be more interesting, and it was. She liked reading about the royal family the best. It was an article about a royal cousin that led her to the information she wanted. The cousin was a patron of the Royal Historical Society as was Bartholomew Cross. In the paper was an announcement of a charity fundraiser he and his sister hosted at his home Montague Place. Montague Place was a stone's throw from the museum and nowhere near Park Lane. No wonder the vicar knew she was lying.

Graciela didn't wait for her day off. "Don't need to be a newsboy yet. Sunday clothes will do."

She crept out at first light on the following Sunday morning, long before she'd be attending church with Mrs. Zachary. If she walked fast and took a cab part of the way home, she could get there and back in time. She estimated it would only take a few minutes to get a good look at the door locks front and rear. She'd draw them as best she could for Newt Addy and what she missed on paper she'd describe. The man was a burglar for mercy's sake, he should have some clue without her having to go into enormous detail.

She slowed her pace as she entered Cross's street, seeing the lamplighters putting out the lights on his block. She tugged her bonnet down and tightened the bow.

"Morning, Miss," the man on the corner said as she passed. "You're out early. Careful as you walk, the cobbles are damp and slippery yet."

"Good morning to you as well. Thank you, I'll take care." She continued to the corner of the next block and turned. Then she swung around and headed toward the alley behind Cross's townhouse. She figured by the time she came round to the front again, the lamplighter would be down the street and out of sight.

Cross's backyard wasn't fenced. The light was on in the kitchen, which was expected. At this hour, only the cook preparing the servants' breakfast and the maid lighting the morning fires would be up. The same as Zachary's household. Graciela stayed close to the tall hedges that had been planted for privacy. Light from the kitchen window shone on the doorknob and it was easy to see the knobs were the same as Zachary's only his were shiny brass and hers were pewter.

She hurried through the gangway to the edge of the house and peered both ways to see if the lamplighter had left. Behind her a first floor window was thrown open and someone, a man, began to make a trilling sound.

Trilling? Graciela shrank into the hedgerow and watched the window.

Small birds began to land on the windowsill as a man's hand, a man she couldn't see yet, sprinkled bread crumbs. The trilling crumb man began to mix his birdsong with a variety of light sounds. Then she saw him. Cross. *What the devil was he doing up at this hour?*

A white scrawny cat with black ears and eyes like a furry masked highwayman slunk out of the shrubbery. The skinny animal pounced, nearly catching a sparrow on the ground eating fallen crumbs.

"Beast." Cross threw an expensive crystal snifter at it, striking it hard in the shoulder. "Get. I'll have you poisoned."

The cat hissed and leapt toward its hiding spot.

"Bastard," Graciela whispered.

"Ugh." Cross rocked back and forth a few times as he spread his crumbs and twice clasped the window frame to steady himself.

Graciela thought he might fall out the window. *He's foxed. There's good information. He likes his drink.*

He stepped away and Graciela took advantage of his absence to run to the front. From there she had a decent view of the entry door locks. As she suspected, they were the same as those on Zachary's house. Satisfied, she started for home but stopped after a few feet. She couldn't help wondering how badly hurt the poor cat was. The animal's backbone had stuck out and looked full grown but tiny; probably small from malnourishment. It wouldn't last long on the street. The last thing she needed was a pet. Would Mrs. Zachary even let her keep the wee one? She did have a cat of her own, Shadow, a sweet grey.

She snuck back and dropped to her knees at the end of the hedgerow and whispered, "Puss, puss." To her surprise, the little thing trusted another human and limped out of the shrubbery.

She turned the cat over. "Good, you're a girl. So is Shadow. All Zachary can do is say no," Graciela told the hurt kitten as she walked. She bundled the cat into the crook of her arm. When it purred, instead of sounding like *meow*, it sounded like *me-too*. Graciela stroked her foundling. "I shall call you Me-too."

She talked to Me-too as she walked through the park. No one was around to think her mad or ask if the cat spoke the Queen's English. They were mid-conversation when Graciela paused, kissed its furry head and said, "Thank you, Me-too. You've given me an elegant idea."

Poison. I shall use poison.

Chapter Seven

Graciela wasn't ashamed to admit the rough looking patrons at Addy's no-name pub made her leery. He told her to wait for him outside the entrance but she said no and demanded he meet her at the south end of Oxford Circus.

"They're not as dangerous as you think," he said, joining her.

"Please, I've never laid eyes on a scruffier, shabbier lot. I'm sure most would sell their mothers for a bottle of gin and pair of new boots."

"The vast majority of them are laborers from the immediate area. They're chimney sweeps, window washers, stone masons and the like. You've seen men like them a hundred times. You just never got that close to them. Don't want to have that skin-to-skin contact with the working class, eh?" He stepped back and eyed her up and down. "Although looking at you, I don't see why you'd be so toffee-nosed acting, clearly you're far from upper class."

"No, I'm not a toff. I've a job."

"What kind of job? Let me guess, you're a governess?"

"No. I'd rather not say. Can we leave off the

subject?"

"I don't want to...Molly, who's name that really isn't. I've the five quid it cost to bail me so I can repay you. You won't have that saber to rattle over my head. If you want my help, you'll tell me more about yourself. I'm curious. What's your job?"

Graciela hadn't expected rebellion. Where in the world had Addy come up with the money? She quickly answered her own question. He burglarized someplace and fenced the loot. With no leverage over Addy, it came down to how much was Cross worth to her? The questions wouldn't stop with this one and now Addy had the advantage. She needed his expertise.

She sighed and chose to surrender. "I'm a lady's companion."

"You poor creature."

"What do you mean by that?"

"You walk in two worlds with a foot in neither. You sit in the parlor and play cards with the old lady, I assume it's an old lady, it usually is. Or, you engage in some other entertainment with her so she puts you up in the main part of the house, close at hand and not below the stairs with the maids and such. You can sleep upstairs, but you can't eat in the dining room with the family because you're not family. Nor can you eat with staff because you're not truly one of them. When you travel with her, you go in First Class like she does, not in the third class carriage like staff. You're living luggage that keeps her from being lonely or bored. You're of her world but not part of it and you're not part of theirs."

"It's a good position, I would never complain."

Both were true but Addy was right. She was neither fish nor fowl. She ate in her room every morning and night. The staff treated her with courtesy but none were friendly. She wasn't invited to their private celebrations. She wasn't part of their gift exchanges at the holidays. Only she and Mrs. Zachary gave each other one gift. When the old woman died, she'd be out of a job. The prospect terrified her.

"We're here. Time to hold your nose, Molly." Addy opened the pub door for her.

"Thank you." She took two steps and stopped to let her eyes adjust to the dim light. Then the stink hit her. The warm weather and their hard-labor sweat were a knock-back punch to the senses. "Ugh."

"Breathe through your mouth. There's a table in the corner. Follow me," Addy said.

Graciela took a gulp of air, hiked her skirt up a couple of inches, not trusting when or if the floors were last cleaned, and trailed behind him as he cleared a path through the crowd of men. On the way, he grabbed the elbow of a passing barmaid. "Two tankards of beer. We'll be at that table."

They sat in silence until the beer came. After the barmaid left, Graciela asked, "Are you familiar with the townhouses in Belgrave Square, Mayfair, and Regent's Park?"

"Of course. No point in my burglarizing poor neighborhoods now, is there?"

Heat flushed her cheeks. She was smarter than the common burglar and should've known better than to ask such a silly question. "I want you to show me how to break into one of those locks. I notice they tend to be similar."

"They are. I've yet to see one that's extraordinary beyond the standard means of unlocking with simple tools."

"Is it hard to learn?"

He shrugged. "Are you stupid?"

"No."

"Then no. When do you want me to show you?"

She hadn't thought her timeframe all the way through. She wouldn't admit it to Addy but she was a little afraid of having too much time between learning how to break into the lock and choosing her poison. She hadn't decided which poison to use yet. She needed to research which one served her best.

"Molly?"

"I'm thinking. I have to do some research first."

"Research?"

"There's more to my plan than just breaking into a townhouse."

"Still don't want to share your plan?" He took a long pull of beer, swallowed, and wiped his mouth with his shirt sleeve. "Never mind, I don't want to know. I'd rather not share the scaffold with you. A Peeler catching me out as a burglar gets me Newgate Prison. I don't fancy getting caught doing anything more."

"You assume I'm up to something worse."

"Drink your beer. When you're ready to learn about locks, you know how to get in touch. We'll meet somewhere else, somewhere we won't be seen and where you can practice on a few."

She finished her beer and he led her through the throng of drinkers and out of the pub where they said their goodbyes. "Have any idea when you think you'll want to meet?" he asked as she started away.

"A week or so."

"Good. Till then."

She started off again when he called out. "Molly."

Graciela turned. "Whatever you're planning, think hard. I've seen men hang. It's a gruesome business. If they don't do it right, you'll kick and twist in the wind and piss yourself. There'll be no forgiveness for your sex. The government doesn't care if you're a woman."

What gave this criminal the right to speak so boldly to her? "Why are you telling me this? Who are you to speak to me about such things? You're not family. You're not even a friend."

"I'm not a fool either. I know you plan to break into a rich man's home and it's not to steal anything. You don't ask about how to fence goods or what items carry the most value. No, you're going in for another nefarious reason. I fear, Molly that you'll get yourself caught. If that happens, I worry you'll resort to a terrible drastic action to defend yourself and that may get you hanged."

"Shut your mouth. What I do has nothing to do with you." She whirled around and rushed down the alley toward Oxford Street.

You'll kick and twist in the wind.

A wretched keening came from somewhere close. She stopped and slumped against a building wall, realizing it came from her.

You'll piss yourself.

Beer and what was left in her stomach from breakfast spewed from her. She moved away from the offensive leavings, grateful she hadn't embarrassed herself on Oxford Street. She looked behind her to see if Addy had seen. Thankfully, he was gone. Back inside the pub no doubt.

She wiped her mouth with a handkerchief she kept in her reticule and took a moment to compose herself. A spray of vomit dotted the hem of her dress. Her other everyday dress was in the laundry. She'd have to wash this one tonight and hang it out the window and hope it dried by morning. "Drat."

When she felt calm enough to continue on she made her way to a tram for home. One thought stayed with her all the way.

I'm not going to hang because I'm not going to get caught. And I will not let any man terrorize me again, not you Mr. Addy, and certainly not you again, Mr. Cross.

Chapter Eight

"Let's take a tram. A sunny day like this is perfect for sitting on the top deck," Ruddy said to Archie.

After a short wait, the tram they needed came by and he and Archie boarded.

"You want a face-to-face because you think Napier will lie to us?" Archie asked once they were seated.

"I think he might, yes."

"I'm not defending him, but it is understandable from his point of view considering the way we cut him out of the Everhard case."

"Sounds like you're defending him. Be honest, you know we did the right thing. He'd have made a cake of the whole thing. If we brought him along, he'd have turned the whole arrest into a tangle involving protocol because of Everhard's status. Lord knows what he'd have done once the shooting started."

Two young boys with fishing poles followed by an older man climbed to the top deck. Once the tram passed Whitehall it would stop at the Thames crossing. They were probably headed there. The threesome brought a smile and memory of home to Ruddy. On

Sundays, after church when the weather was good, his father took him and his brothers fishing. In a family of ten children, any catch was mighty welcome.

"That's our stop up ahead," Ruddy said.

Archie tugged the wire, signaling the conductor.

"Good fishing, boys," Ruddy said as he passed them.

City of London police headquarters was located in one of the city's large old guildhalls. What was originally a big meeting hall for workers, had easily been walled off into sections. The largest area was for the lobby where citizens were met by several desk officers and a supervising sergeant. This was also where constables brought arrestees past and into the lockup and booking area. Similar to Holborn Station, the detective bureau adjoined the lobby but had a partition that was half-wall and half-glass. Unlike Holborn, the guildhall's high ceiling allowed for an upper floor with wrought iron railings and leaded glass windows that provided storage for case files. At Holborn, storage was down in a damp, rat infested basement.

"I can't help being envious when we come here," Archie said. "They have so much room."

"I know." Ruddy shared his envy. At Holborn, they were packed in tight. Here each detective unit had their own tea cart and coat tree. "Better hurry. It looks like Napier is getting ready to leave." Napier was a senior Detective Inspector and Ruddy's counterpart with the City. He started with the City shortly after Ruddy signed on with London Metropolitan Police.

"If it isn't Bloody Ruddy Bloodstone, what brings you here?" Napier asked, buttoning and smoothing the front of his frock coat. "You can't possibly want information from me."

Ruddy expected the supercilious "Bloody Ruddy Bloodstone" greeting from Napier. They'd disliked each other from the first. The Bloody part was a snide reference to Ruddy's military past.

"Not exactly. We're here to share information." Ruddy laid his leather folio on Napier's desk and removed two of the drawings he made of the stocking suspect. He explained about the two crimes that occurred in Holborn's jurisdiction. "This is a drawing we made from the victim's description. We don't think these are the first attacks for this suspect. But we haven't any other reports from Metropolitan districts. We thought to ask if you had any similiars."

"You do want information from me. If we did have similar crimes, what good would it do for us to share what we know with you? Last time I got tossed aside after you were ordered to keep me included in all your activities."

"The crimes were our jurisdiction and as we explained then, we had to act fast. We had reason to believe Everhard might leave the country." Ruddy pushed a drawing closer to Napier. "Now, can we return to the topic at hand? Does this man fit the suspect description for any sexual crime you have?"

Another detective came over. "Hey, that looks—"

Napier looked up and loudly cleared his throat. The other detective glanced at Napier then said. "I'll wait for you in the lobby."

Napier's boss, Chief Superintendent Effingham

came out of his office and over to Napier's desk. The ranking system between the two agencies had only slight differences. As a Chief Superintendent, Effingham held a higher position than Jameson. An advantage he'd wielded in the past.

"Detective Bloodstone, Detective Holbrook, what brings you here?" Effingham asked.

"We wanted to drop off a drawing of a sex criminal who's been working our district and might cross over into your jurisdiction," Archie explained.

Effingham looked down briefly, sniffed and paid no more attention to the drawing. Opening a tin of sweets he had in his hand, he removed a candy and popped it in his mouth. He extended the tin to Ruddy and Archie. "Lemon drop?"

"No, thank you," they both declined.

Effingham shrugged and turned to Napier. "Are you ready, Nathaniel?"

"I am."

"Perhaps you should invite the Metro lads here to watch you work out in the ring." He turned and gave Ruddy the thin-lipped smile usually reserved for snake oil salesmen. "Might do you good, Bloodstone, to see how a fight should go when done properly by the rules."

"No offense, sir, but you think these bludgers and footpads we get into it with in the street fight by the rules?" Ruddy asked, making an effort to temper his tone.

Effingham drew on his candy with a wet obscene sucking that ended in a series of quick tongue clicks. He shot Napier an oily smile that Napier returned in kind. "Don't be ridiculous. One does whatever is necessary with street ruffians. I am thinking down the road we might have a competition between our departments. It wouldn't be fair unless everyone knew and fought by the rules."

The penny dropped for Ruddy. *He's itching for a fight because he had a certain winner in his toadie, Napier.* Napier was the City of London's department boxing champion three years running. The hostility between Napier and Ruddy was common knowledge and Effingham's comment about a competition between agencies was a cover for what he intended. The penny had dropped for Archie as well, judging from his expression. From the smug exchange between Effingham and Napier, neither thought Ruddy and Archie knew of Napier's status as boxing champion. That distinction wasn't news shared among the two agencies. Ruddy only heard through a source at Scotland Yard when he happened to be there on a routine matter.

"Well, you coming to my practice or not?" Napier asked.

"Now you mean?" Ruddy assumed the invitation was meant for a future visit.

Napier nodded.

Ruddy thought why not? "Sure. We've some time to spare." He laid two copies of his drawings on Napier's desk. "I'll leave a couple drawings of our suspect. I'd appreciate it if you'd show them to some of your patrol officers."

Effingham had his own carriage and driver, which he ordered brought round. The boxing ring was walking distance to the station but according to Napier they rode to avoid a sweaty and unpleasant return walk.

Never a boxing enthusiast, Ruddy had only heard the gossip that they drew a rough crowd. No surprise there. The rings were dirty and often located in back alleys and stunk of sweat, blood and vomit from injured combatants. Nothing about watching the business of two men beating the snot out of each other appealed to him. When they entered Kelly's Athletic Club, Ruddy expected the worst sort of place.

"This is rather nice, considering what it's for." He couldn't help but comment seeing spectator stands, a host/proprietor stand where guests placed their bets, and a special section set off for the fighters. In the middle was the actual ring. It smelled of men and sweat but nothing like he imagined or been told. No blood or vomit on the floor, although a black man with a mop and bucket stood by in the corner.

The fighters and their coaches nodded as Napier entered. The host came over to greet both Napier and Effingham. Effingham introduced Ruddy and Archie and they all took seats in the stands while Napier disappeared into another room to change.

"The ring is larger than I thought it would be. I'd heard they vary in size." Ruddy was showing his ignorance about the sport but he was curious. If he wound up fighting Napier down the road, he wanted to know all he could about the rules restrictions.

"This is a 24-foot ring—the true size a ring should be," Effingham explained.

"Who does Napier spar with?" Archie asked. "There's quite an array of men here size-wise."

"Nathaniel will hop in the ring and whoever volunteers, that's who he'll spar with. Since this is practice, they'll only go about five or six rounds. In a real fight, they'd go twelve unless there's a knockout, of course."

"How long is a round?" Ruddy asked, thinking this had the potential to drag on quite a while.

"Three minutes."

Three minutes. Ruddy'd been in enough fights to know that kind of time can go either way. It flies when you're winning and is an eternity when you're losing and he'd been on both sides of that ticking clock.

Napier came out. He was bare chested wearing only white knicker-like drawers and soft-soled black leather shoes. A man hurried over with a pair of brown leather gloves and helped get them on and tied over Napier's hands. Gloves helped the hands but were hell on the face. Ruddy made quick notes since he'd only ever seen him in street clothes. The shorter Napier had about a stone, maybe a stone-and-a-half on him in weight and from the look of him when he flexed his biceps and forearms, it was all muscle weight. Good to know. *I'm still going to knock you on your arse, though.*

"That's Nathaniel's coach," Effingham said, pointing to the man helping Napier.

The two sparring men in the ring finished after a few minutes and Napier stepped into the ring. His coach stood with him and asked for a volunteer sparring partner. A barrel-chested, bearded man with short thick arms slipped between two ropes. His legs were like his arms—thick as tree trunks. In a heavy

Russian accent he said he'd do it.

A third man who'd been in the ring with the two previous men had remained. He wore a loose fitting shirt with the sleeves rolled up to the elbows, knickers similar to the fighting men and soft shoes like theirs but he didn't fight. He circled the men as they sparred, watching, occasionally barking orders.

"I assume he's a referee," Ruddy said to Effingham.

"Yes. He referees the official matches as well."

Ruddy questioned the man's ability to stay neutral. Surely he'd begin to favor certain men after a while. It's human nature.

Napier's coach moved to a corner just outside the ring. A bell rang and the Russian and Napier began sparring. Napier bobbed and the Russian missed landing a hard roundhouse, instead just grazing the side of Napier's temple.

Napier countered with a quick left jab that knocked the Russian back into the ropes. Napier followed with another left and then a right cross.

"That's some left Napier's got," Archie said.

Ruddy nodded. "Interesting since he writes with his right. I'd have thought that his dominant hand."

The Russian gave as good as he got but Napier had him on the ropes a number of times. Ruddy kept a close eye out for weaknesses on his part. The few he caught were hard to judge as to whether they were overall weaknesses or just faults the Russian knew how to bring out. He'd like to see Napier sparring with other fighters but couldn't figure how to go about arranging that. He wasn't a member of this club and had no intention of joining. Napier and Effingham would prevent him even if he tried.

"Napier's better than I thought," Archie whispered. "But if this is his best, I still think you can polish him off."

"This isn't his best. He's not foolish. He won't let us see his best. He'll save that for our day." Ruddy's mind was spinning. Who could he get to be a mole and finagle a way into this club to spy? Where was Napier weakest? In a street fight knowing a man's weaknesses weren't that important. Hit wherever you could land a punch and hope to knock him down or out. Here he'd be hampered by rules and time. He had to make every punch count.

Ruddy gave Napier and Effingham a few more minutes to relish showing off before he pulled out his watch. "We need to get back to the stationhouse. It's been entertaining. Thank you for the invitation, Chief Superintendent." He stood.

"I'll be in touch with Henry about a possible match," Effingham said, referring to Jameson. "Nothing like sport between men to stir the blood. It'll be fun."

"Fun indeed. Let's go, Arch." Ruddy hopped down to the floor.

****

On the way back Ruddy and Archie briefly discussed who they might slip into the athletic club. They eliminated any constables from Holborn as they might be recognized. Archie suggested Seamus.

"What need does anyone there have for a shine boy?" Ruddy asked.

"None," Archie replied. "It was a desperate suggestion because I'm out of ideas."

They rode the tram the rest of the way in silence.

"I don't suppose it's ever crossed your mind if you did fight, you might lose," Archie said, settling down at his desk. "Napier's experience worries me plus he knows all their piddling rules too."

Of course it crossed Ruddy's mind. The man who thinks he can't lose a fight is delusional. Doesn't matter how big or strong or well-trained you are, you have to assume there's always someone bigger and stronger and better trained. But Archie didn't need to know of his doubts. "Just because he's their boxing champ doesn't mean he can't be thrashed."

Between the army and police work, Ruddy had his fair share of fights. He'd delivered far more thumps than he'd taken. All were street fights. Having experience operating within the rules gave Napier a big advantage.

"That, right there," Ruddy said, jabbing the air and driving home his objection with his finger. "The ridiculousness of including rules is what offends me. If you're going to fight, then by God, fight. All this nonsense about you can't do this and you can't do that, then it's not a fight anymore. That's just two men rough dancing with each other."

"Are wagers being made yet?" came Freddie Coopersmith's cheery voice from behind Archie.

Ruddy leaned to the left so he had a better view of Coopersmith as Archie turned in his chair. "What are you talking about?" Archie asked.

"Ruddy's going to fight Napier, right? We all hate that arrogant bugger. Our money is on you, Bloodstone," Coopersmith said far too loudly for Ruddy.

Ben, Coopersmith's partner, nodded his agreement and left his desk and half sat on Freddie's, a cup of tea in his hand. "Don't pick a ring in the City's jurisdiction. Doesn't matter the match is between Peelers, I don't trust their lot to not put the fix in with the referees. We need a place that's neutral. If it's not one in their jurisdiction, it automatically puts it in ours, but we choose one that's not in our district. That's fair.

The other detectives had stopped what they were doing to listen. "Someone neutral should hold the money," another added.

"Jameson will do," Ben said.

Ruddy's hands shot up. "Wait, wait, wait. I haven't agreed to fight Napier or anyone. I've not been approached. Arch and I are having a hypothetical discussion. Nothing more."

Freddie eyed him with the same suspicion he reserved for cutpurses and footpads. "You said you don't like the rules but know he'd demand using them and whatnot. Why talk like that unless you're planning on a fight?"

"We saw Napier about a case. Every time he sees me, he likes to poke the bear. He's spoiling for a fight. In the past Effingham has intervened. Today, Napier wasn't his usual irritating self and Effingham mentioned a future boxing competition between our agencies. Just to clarify, my name was not specifically mentioned as a participant."

"Doesn't matter, he made his intent obvious," Freddie said.

Ruddy knew too well Effingham would enjoy seeing him humiliated. He never told Archie or anyone at the station of the brief history he and the Chief Superintendent had. When he received his V.C., General Chelmsford asked what his plans were after his requested discharge. Ruddy had said he wanted to go into law enforcement. He wanted to work a city department, preferably London. Chelmsford made some innocuous comment and moved along. Ruddy didn't think any more on it.

When the time came he applied with the London Metropolitan Police Service but not with the City of London. The City department was too small an agency. He preferred to be with an agency that had the bigger population and more activity. He was anxious to handle every kind of crime. He might see and do all that with the City but it would take longer than he wished.

To his astonishment, while examination process with London Metro, he received a letter from Effingham, who was only a Commander at the time. Effingham offered him a post, no examination needed. He guaranteed Ruddy rapid rise within the ranks. Apparently, Chelmsford had interceded without Ruddy's wanting or asking and contacted Effingham. Ruddy had turned the offer down and Effingham never forgave him.

"You'd let us know if you were going to fight, wouldn't you?" Freddie asked. "It'd be wrong to keep that to yourself."

"After Arch and me, you all will be the first to know."

Freddie and Ben had a quick exchange and then Freddie scooted his chair closer to Ruddy's desk. He said in a low voice that had Ruddy and Archie straining, "Being an unmarried man, should this fight become a reality, I'd suggest you avoid feminine companionship for at least a week prior. As a married man myself, I can attest to the fact attending to a lady's physical needs can exhaust a man." He made fists and flexed. "Rubbery legs and arms..." He relaxed and pressed closer, looking straight at Ruddy. "You understand what I mean," he said and winked.

Good Lord. Bad enough Freddie Coopersmith was giving him risqué advice. But twice a year the station had social events that involved wives and special lady friends, the summer picnic and the Christmas party. Now, when he saw Mrs. Coopersmith, he'd have to contend with the image of Freddie tending to her "needs." And that was not a picture he ever wanted to conjure. He'd seen Freddie without a shirt. The man would make an unshorn ram envious. Thanks to Freddie, the sight was fresh in his mind all over again and had his poor wife attached to it now.

"Thank you for the sage advice," Ruddy said. "Let's go, Arch. I need some air."

"Where to?"

"I'd like to stroll by the Odeon Music Hall. Will says there's a lovely singer there I should see. I'm hoping they have a poster out front. I might go tonight."

Chapter Nine

The Odeon was one of the newer theatres in the city. The owners, a consortium of men who owned several small breweries, built it on a lot that formerly housed a burned out factory. They'd spared no expense. Long bars made of imported teak wood from Southeast Asia lined the side walls. Glass shelves were filled with bottles of Caribbean rum, whiskey from Ireland and Scotland, exotics from the Continent like Absinthe and anise-flavored Raki from Turkey. Light from the gas lamp chandeliers glittered off gold-veined mirrors that hung on the walls. Housed beneath the bar were the more common drinks like beer, ale, and the occasional bucket of champagne for the man with high hopes for the evening's end.

The main floor was like most every other music hall, simple straight-back wooden chairs arranged around wooden, linen-less tables that sat either two or four. The owners weren't so silly as to waste money on fine chairs and tables. Not when at least one night a month, and more often than not, two or three nights, a donnybrook over some real or imagined nonsense was bound to occur. Above the main floor were two more tiers for standing room only customers. Waiters attended to them from simple service bars at the rear of each tier.

Chris Karlsen

A music hall admirer, Ruddy had been to several in the city. The Odeon had the best stage with a sizeable pit so they had a big orchestra who made even mediocre singers sound good.

"Would you rather sit or stand?" Ruddy asked Will.

"I'd rather stand at the bar. This end of the bar gives us a direct line of sight with the dressing rooms."

"Are you going to try and talk to Miss Flowers?"

Will quickly eyed himself in the mirror behind the bar. "Would you blame me?"

"No."

They took two open spots at the end of the bar that gave them a perfect view of both the stage and the path to the dressing room. Ruddy raised his hand to get the bartender's attention. "Two beers and two Irish whiskey chasers please," he ordered, when the bartender looked up. "I don't know what good it does since you're leaving in a couple days."

"If I talk to her, which I'm not really planning on, it will be on your behalf. I told you last night, you should chat her up."

From the artist's rendition of her on the theatre poster, the lady was as attractive as Will said. Ruddy hadn't decided whether he'd attempt much of a conversation with her. A lovely entertainer, men probably attempted to charm and seduce her all the time. She may find their efforts, his included, tiresome. Slathered in flattery for who knows how long, she might be an unpleasant creature, snippety or vinegary, not worth chatting up.

That said, Ruddy liked the idea of having one

special lady in his life. Not a wife, necessarily, but a special lady. If the relationship deepened into a love match, he'd welcome family life.

A stagehand came out and lit the gas lamp footlights as the orchestra entered and took their seats. Another stagehand tied back the outer heavy red velvet draperies. A second set of red velvet drapes remained closed.

Then the interior drapes opened and the tuxedoed Master of Ceremonies walked out onto center stage. A dozen men and women entered and made up the chorus. Miss Flowers wasn't in the group. Above them, a canvas painting of Queen Victoria dropped down. The music started with the popular music hall tune, *Oh! The Fairies.* Every audience loved the song and sang along. Ruddy and Will joined in singing loud like their nuns back in Brecon's stone church classroom taught them. After the people finished the short tune, the Master of Ceremonies declared, "God save the Queen."

The audience stood and repeated the blessing and sang along while the orchestra played the National Anthem. The men in uniform, like Will, stood at attention.

The Queen's picture was pulled from view and the chorus darted off stage. The inside curtains closed again and the Master of Ceremonies stayed and read a list of the evening's entertainment. Then he introduced the next act, a ventriloquist. A man dressed in white tie and tails, top hat included came out from the opposite side of the stage with a puppet dressed the same. He brought a chair with him and sat, putting the puppet on his knee. A political discussion between the two ensued.

The puppet made some observations about the Prime Minister that were as funny as they were harsh and astute. "I didn't think I was going to like this fellow. I mean a man talking to a puppet, I thought, how silly. But he's got the P.M. down to a gnat's bottom," Ruddy said, chuckling.

A glow of light in Ruddy's peripheral vision caught his attention and he turned. It came from Flower's dressing room. The star exited and closed the door. She smiled as she walked toward them, wearing a lavender dress of lace-covered silk with a sheer silky material over her shoulders to her throat. She smiled and walked past the short stairs to the stage and over to Will.

"You were here yesterday. You sat there." She pointed to a table for two in the front row.

Ruddy had never seen his brother at a loss for words. If only a moment could be bronzed in time.

"I'm gobsmacked you remember me," Will said at last.

"What lady doesn't remember a fine example of a man in service to her majesty?"

"You flatter me."

"Are you with the Queen's Guards here at the palace?" she asked.

"No. I'm just on leave in London. I'm deployed in India."

Honeysuckle turned to Ruddy. She looked from him back to Will and then to Ruddy again. "You're brothers?"

"Yes. And he does live here in London," Will rushed to add.

She peered over her shoulder in a coquettish way that women do. "Is he mute?"

Ruddy hoped Will read his I'm going to kill you look. "No, he is not," Ruddy jumped in with. "But he does have an irksome brother who blathers on unnecessarily before I can get a word out. I know from your poster outside that you're the star, Honeysuckle Flowers. I'm Rudyard Bloodstone and the vexing man to your right is my brother Will."

She gave each a warm smile accompanied by a slight feminine tip of her head. When she smiled and tipped her head Ruddy's way, she kept her eyes up and on him. If he knew her even a little better, he'd have pulled her behind the curtain and kissed her. He knew a little about heat between a man and a woman and there was heat in those pretty green eyes she'd locked on him.

"May I buy you a drink?" he asked.

"No thank you, detective. Not before the show. But afterward, I'd love to share a bottle of champagne with your brother and you."

A stunned Ruddy asked, "How did you know I was a detective?"

She put her forefingers to her temples. "Read it in the leaves of my afternoon tea."

She'd said it with a straight face. Ruddy's heart sank. The woman was mad as Mr. Carroll's hatter. Or worse, she was part gypsy. He hated dealing with gypsies and their alleged metaphysical abilities. Whether it was reading tea leaves, or the Tarot, or

81

crystal balls, they were all nothing but tricks to part a hard working person from their money.

Flowers burst into a laugh and then said with a tiny push to his chest, "You should see your face. You believed every word." She turned to Will. "You did too, didn't you?"

"In our defense you said it with such a serious face," Will said, sounding haughtier than their upbringing justified.

"I *am* an actress." She turned back to Ruddy. "I saw you and another gentleman this afternoon looking at the theatre posters. You pointed to something and your jacket moved and exposed your shield. I'm not one to delve into fortune telling of any kind."

"That's a relief," Ruddy said and meant it.

"Are you with the City or London Metropolitan?"

"London Metro."

"My uncle is a constable in Norfolk."

Another pleasant surprise. His profession caused the demise of his relationship with Allegra the year before. "Oh. Norfolk's a lovely area to work."

"There's the emcee. I'm next," Honeysuckle said. "I've another show in an hour and then I'll be free to join you gentlemen. I sing new tunes but some old favorites as well. You must sing along with the favorites. I'll be watching from the stage." She raised her skirt high enough to scandalously show a shapely ankle and bit of leg as she climbed the stage stairs.

On stage the curtains parted to show a backdrop that was painted to look like a city park with a promenade. Honeysuckle opened with the popular melody, *When I Take My Morning Promenade*. Members of the chorus joined her on stage, the ladies carried ruffled parasols that they twirled and danced around. The men dressed in morning coats and high hats served mainly as dancing props for the women.

To Ruddy's delight, twice while she danced she came over with a flounce that flashed those lovely ankles again.

Chapter Ten

"What are you doing down here?"

Graciela nearly jumped out of her skin at the sound of the cook's voice. She thought she'd be able to get in and out of the kitchen before the cook was done outside in the ice house.

"I wondered if we had any rat poison. I thought I saw a mouse," she lied to the cook.

"Yes, I keep a box on hand." She laid a ham leg she brought from the ice house on her work table. "Where did you spot the vermin?"

"Maybe it was a mouse I saw. I'm not sure. It happened so fast. It was more a brown flash of something outside the front door."

"You go on. I'll take care of putting out any poison. We use strychnine and if milady's beloved Shadow accidentally gets into it and dies, it will be the death of my job as well."

Graciela expected Zachary's staff kept strychnine on the premises, most homes in the city did. It was a common form of pest control. She originally planned to steal some but changed her mind. Rethinking her plan, she figured she ought to research the effects of different poisons, see how long it took for them to work, how much did she need to use, and what condition was the victim in while on the brink of death? She was about to do that when the cook caught her.

Graciela pinned her hat on, kissed a curled up Me-too on the head and left for the British Museum's library.

After three tram rides, she had an aggravating, bordering-on-unpleasant exchange with the Chief Librarian over whether she, a woman, should be granted an entrance ticket to the domed Reading Room.

"This is a place of serious study," he said. "There's nothing of womanly interest here."

After lying and telling him she was doing research for her fiancé, Graciela was finally admitted. She wouldn't have been half as irritated if he hadn't been right. If she wasn't in need of information on poison, she'd never set foot in the place. She couldn't imagine anything of interest to her there.

Most of the men were too engrossed in the material before them to notice her but several she passed by raised their heads to eyeball the female invader. She quickly found the book she needed and sat at a table in the back as far out of sight as possible.

The four easiest poisons for her to acquire were: cyanide, strychnine, belladonna, and arsenic. She eliminated cyanide straight away. Although it was used in a number of ordinary everyday things like paints and wallpaper, she wasn't certain how to administer it. She needed a system that would fool Cross.

She'd never personally killed any pest with strychnine and hadn't seen the effects. According to the book, the victim died from asphyxiation. First they frothed at the mouth and had muscle spasms, which grew in intensity until the neural pathways, whatever they were became paralyzed.

"I don't know about that," she whispered, thinking aloud. "Sounds dodgy, how long do they flop around?"

She moved onto belladonna. Also known as deadly nightshade, the poison came in berry form, which would be impossible for her to administer. Reading on, there was a case where a spy put it in a drink that retained the sweet taste of a fermented beverage. Cross was drinking cognac the night she saw him. Would he drink a sweet drink? She shook her head. Too risky.

Finally, she settled on the King of Poisons, arsenic. "Perfect. Odorless, colorless, tasteless, and only a few grains needed to kill a man." She looked around to make sure no one might have heard the last.

She returned the book and waited until the Chief Librarian was busy before she left. He had a box on his desk for visitors to drop their passes into when they exited. She kept hers in case she wanted to return. If she did, she'd wait until he was out of sight and use today's pass to gain entry.

On the way home, she stopped at the no name pub and left a message with the bartender for Addy. She was ready to have him show her how to pick a lock. She also stopped at a chemist on Oxford Street to buy a bottle of arsenic. The chemist on Oxford wouldn't know her like the one in Belgrave Square. Not that the authorities would ever track the poison back to her if they even discovered Cross was poisoned, but why take any unnecessary chances?

****

"Here? We're going to work out in the open where everyone can see us?" an appalled Graciela asked. Addy had brought out a table from the pub with a standard black metal door lock on it. In front of him were a couple of simple looking tools along with a tankard of beer.

"Yes. No one will bother us. You should know by now the pub's patrons have no interest in what anyone else is getting up to. We'll start whenever you're ready."

"I'd like to get a Pimm's Cup first."

Addy kicked the empty chair her way. "Sit. You can have a drink when we're done. This won't take long to learn or it shouldn't if you have your wits about you, which is why I say no drinks for you."

"Fine." Graciela sat.

Addy put the lock between them and turned it so the locking mechanism showed instead of the knob and keyhole. "This uses a lever lock system. It's a simple system to defeat, for which I am grateful," he added with a smile. He picked up a small, multi-use knife the kind Graciela had seen carpenters and other tradesmen carry. "Insert the knife here and push." He inserted it into a hole in the back plate. "If you listen close, you can hear the spring clip release. Once it releases you'll have access to the bolt you need to move out of your way." Addy then used what she'd call a tiny pry bar. "With the bolt moved, use this to feel for the groove in the mechanism that secures the lock. Give it a push and you're done."

"How can I find a little groove I can't see?" For a man like Addy who'd done this sort of thing for years, picking the lock was something he could do blindfolded. Graciela's plan hinged on her sneaking into Cross's home. After Addy's demonstration, she saw slim hope of achieving that.

"You can't miss the groove. It's a deep notch. I see worry written across your brow. You'll master it in no time. Go ahead. You try now."

She'd been at it for what felt like forever. She'd succeeded in opening the lock several times over but Addy kept making her do it again and again. "Can I have that Pimm's now? I've done this a thousand times," Graciela asked.

Addy pulled out a gold pocket watch with someone else's initials on it. Graciela wondered who the original owner was.

"Ten minutes to the hour. Keep practicing for another ten minutes and then you can quit. You've done quite well. I told you that you'd master it."

"I have. Why must I keep it up for another try?"

He shrugged. "Then don't. Doesn't matter to me. I'm not the one who'll go to prison if you're caught."

"Do be quiet." She picked up the utility knife and worked the spring lock one last time.

Chapter Eleven

Archie waved the desk sergeant over as Mrs. Holbrook walked into the lobby. "My Meg's here."

Archie hurried to meet his wife and help her with the bulky tapestry bag she carried from her.

"Please have one of the constables walk our latest victim home and have someone find Constables Young and Flanders. Tell them to report to the bureau," Ruddy told the sergeant Archie waved over.

"I'll send someone straight away. If you'll follow me," the sergeant instructed the victim, "we'll have you escorted home shortly."

"I take it the dresses are finished?" Ruddy asked Margaret Holbrook.

"I'll put them in the interview room and get Jameson," Archie said and headed that way.

Mrs. Holbrook nodded, then giggled and sheepishly admitted, "I'm anxious to see them on the fellows and not just to check the fit. Is that awful of me?"

"We're all keen to see them all done up. You're not alone in your awfulness," Ruddy said. "I'll get you a cup of tea while we wait."

Jameson and Archie came from his office. Jameson carried a sack in his hand. "Mrs. Holbrook, you look lovely." He pulled two hats from the bag. "I managed to lay my hands on two bonnets with wide brims. Should cover their faces well enough to fool our thief into coming close."

Ruddy returned with the tea. "Did you want one, Superintendent?"

"I'm pouring one for myself, I'll get you one too, sir," Archie said, joining them again.

Jameson looked at the latest drawing of the stocking thief and asked Ruddy, "The woman here earlier, that's number three for the thief. Where did he grab this last one?"

"Great Ormond Street again," Ruddy said, putting the final touches on this drawing. "This victim noticed the thief was missing all but the front six of his bottom teeth.

Ruddy put his art materials away. "At first I thought we might concentrate both teams in the Ormond Street vicinity since he's struck there twice now but that may be a tactical mistake."

Brows high, Archie handed a cup of tea to Jameson and asked, "What? Why is that a mistake?"

"My thought exactly. I was going to make the same suggestion. We should concentrate our teams around Great Ormond," Jameson said.

"The second crime occurred on Guilford Place. I have a feeling the suspect may go back there next, if there is a next time."

Ruddy got up and removed the district map from the wall and laid it out on his desk. "If he doesn't return to Ormond or Guildford, I believe he'll hit along here." He marked out a rectangle-shaped area that incorporated the two crime scenes and expanded to include the immediate vicinity. "I have a feeling he's working this corridor and not likely to venture too far out. It explains why other Metro districts or the City haven't had similiars."

"You think he's comfortable in this area and that's why he'll stay in it?" Jameson asked.

"I do."

"If he's comfortable, I'd say it's because he works somewhere nearby. From the description of him, I can't see him having the money to live in the area," Archie said.

The constables working as the decoys arrived along with four men acting as their support teams.

"Everyone to the interview room," Jameson ordered. "Except you, Mrs. Holbrook. If you'd please wait here while the constables change out of uniform and into their..." he glanced at the glum-faced Young and Flanders, the undercover constables and back to Margaret Holbrook. "Their costumes. I'll call you when we're ready to have you come in for any final touches."

"Certainly."

The undercover group, Ruddy, Archie, and Jameson all relocated to the interview room. The support teams made no effort to maintain any proper decorum, crumbling into laughter as soon as Young and Flanders had the dresses on and all but buttoned. Ruddy didn't dare look at Archie or Jameson or the three of them would fall out too.

Ruddy buttoned Young and Archie buttoned Flanders while Jameson called Margaret Holbrook into the room. "Can you breathe?" Ruddy asked Young.

"This is awfully tight across your ribcage."

Young nodded. "I can breathe but just. If I have to defend myself, I'm afraid the dress will rip to shreds though."

Small-boned and thin, Flanders dress fit much better.

"Oh good, you put the right dress on the right man. I meant to tell you who I intended each dress for," Margaret said.

She ran her hand down the back of the bodice on the dress Flanders wore and then down the long sleeves, checking the fit. "With your ginger hair and light eyes, I knew cornflower blue would be perfect for your coloring," she said, tying the bow at the waist.

She went to Young and repeated the same action, sucking in air when she saw how tight the bodice was. "Sorry Constable, I must've been off a bit in my measuring. Do you want me to take it home and make some alterations?" she asked, turning to Jameson.

"Young said he can breathe but doesn't have a lot of freedom of movement," he explained and then asked Young and Flanders, "Can you both flex your arms? You need to be able to defend yourselves even if it means tearing the gown."

Both constables flexed fine. "Don't bother altering the dress, Mrs. Holbrook. I'd rather the men get out into the area of the crimes and start patrolling. You just might lose a dress but let's hope you don't."

"I understand. Well gentlemen, I'm going. I've gardening to do. No need to walk me out, Archibald. I'll see you at dinner."

Jameson, Ruddy, Archie and the undercover group gathered around the district map still laid out on Ruddy's desk. Ruddy told them his theory of the thief working a specific corridor. The two groups split coverage of the corridor and left for their assigned areas.

"Better go see Marsden," Jameson told Ruddy and Archie.

Both groaned in unison. "Must we?" Archie asked.

"I told you after three victims we'd get the press involved. We need to warn the ladies in the area. Don't forget to take a drawing with you for their front page." Jameson pointed at Ruddy but said to Archie, "Don't let him antagonize Marsden."

Ruddy took umbrage to the comment considering any prior quarrels between him and Marsden were instigated by Marsden.

"No worries, Superintendent," Ruddy assured him.

"Good. I'm off to lunch. Come to my office later and let me know how it went."

After Jameson left a sneaky smile crossed Archie's face. He had a devilish glint in his eye and his focus was on Ruddy. People talk about intuition. Some folks have it stronger than others. Ruddy had good intuition, especially when it came to police work, like his feeling about their stocking thief. He also had a weird feeling about that smile and glint.

"I have an idea. You're going to hate it. But hear me out," Archie warned.

"Does this idea have anything to do with me?"

"Yes."

Ruddy stood and put his jacket on. "If you know ahead of time I'm going to hate it, then whatever it is, I'm not going to want to do it. I don't have to hear you out."

"But you do. It's brilliant and as much as you might hate it, you'll see the craftiness behind my plan."

"Fine. What's your idea?"

"Marsden."

Ruddy had no clue what he was talking about other than they were supposed to be en route to tell him about the thief. He shook his head baffled.

"Get Marsden to act as mole in the athletic club. He can spy on Napier and report back."

"You've gone soft. No. I'm not asking that buffoon for a favor."

"He's perfect." Archie's hand gestures grew with each rationalization. He reminded Ruddy of a mutton-chopped defense attorney. "They'll never suspect him. He can go in under the cover story of writing an article on boxing and the club. They'll jump at the chance for good press. No one will suspect his true mission."

Ruddy started to argue but other than his personal dislike of Marsden, there wasn't a good reason for him to say no. It was clever, a perfect cover for a spy. "Damnation Arch, I want to object but I can't. It's wickedly sly. I like it."

"Let's go and talk to him. There is one catch to this," Archie said, donning his bowler.

"I'll be beholden to him."

"No way around it."

****

The London Gazette took up the lower floor of the old brick building that used to house an iron works. The large front windows facing the street were a complete waste in Ruddy's opinion since they were always shuttered closed when he was there. The most unusual thing about the paper was they employed an attractive female secretarial assistant in the newsroom. Very modern of them, he knew of no other newspapers who hired a woman.

"Do any of your male employees pester her?" Ruddy asked, curious as Marsden looked over the reports.

He looked up. "No. That was a condition of her employment. She's not to consort with any of the men and she doesn't. She comes to work, does her job, and goes home. She has children and needs the money. She won't risk her job."

"Just wondered," Ruddy said.

"It's too late for inclusion in the evening edition but I can have the story and the rendering of the suspect in the early edition tomorrow. We'll run them throughout the week," Marsden said and handed the drawing to one of the paper's runners.

He opened his bottom drawer and pulled out a bottle of Glenlivet scotch whiskey, a glass and two teacups. "I realize you'd rather jab a bayonet into your thigh than join me for a proper drink in a pub," he said, looking at Ruddy. He poured three fingers of whiskey into the glass and cups. "So, we can drink to our conspiracy here.

Wanting to get the ugly business of using Marsden as a mole out of the way, Ruddy discussed that matter with him first. Some part of him hoped Marsden would say no, but he also recognized the advantage and hoped he'd agree.

"How desperate you must be to have sunk to requesting my assistance." Marsden smirked in an oily, smarmy way, as though he knew what your sister looked like naked.

Ruddy stood. "Forget it. I don't need to listen to this blather and boast. Our deal is off."

Marsden flapped his hand, gesturing for Ruddy to sit. "Don't get in a twist, detective. You had to know I'd have a bit of fun at your expense after all our squabbles. I won't ask why you want me to be your operative or why this club. I'd be lying if I said I wasn't deeply curious." He took a sip of the liquor. "I especially wish to hear, one day down the road of course, why the detailed sleuthing of this Mr. Napier is desired."

Wish in one hand, spit in the other, see which you get first, Marsden. Ruddy sat again, brought the cup to his lips and then set it down without drinking while he crafted a diplomatic lie. "Perhaps. Suffice it to say that I am grateful you're willing to do this for me. I'll find a way to compensate you." *Not a good lie at all.*

"Don't worry about compensation."

He threw the comment out like he was talking about the weather and not something that already burned like hot coal in Ruddy's chest. "I want to know exactly what you want in return before this agreement is sealed."

"You know how important exclusives are in this competitive business, which is why I appreciate you came to me first with this stocking thief story. I'm sure that there will be a case in your future that I will be in dire need of being the first to break, so to speak. Quid, pro, quo." Marsden relaxed back in his chair and smiled that sly cat smile again.

"We won't do anything that jeopardizes an investigation."

"I wouldn't ask you to. It's information like this, letting us be the first to run a story on a thief running loose. A quick word dashed off to me when you have someone in custody. I'd like to be the first reporter on the scene. That sort of access."

Archie leaned over and whispered to Ruddy, "The deal's not for long. Once you have the details you need on Napier, you'll be done with it."

Ruddy brought the teacup to his lips and threw the whiskey back in one swallow. "Deal."

****

By the time Ruddy and Archie returned to the station and finished their paperwork on the new crime, their shift ended.

"Is Will still here?" Archie asked, tidying his desk.

"No. He left on the midday train today."

"He seemed to be enjoying his visit every time I saw him. Think he'll come back soon?"

"He did have a good time." Ruddy had missed his brother more than he realized. His visit reminded him how much Will made him laugh. "I doubt he'll return before he retires. It's such a long journey from India."

"Too bad." Archie jabbed Ruddy in the ribs.

"You're seeing that fancy singer Miss Flowers tonight, aren't you?"

"I am."

"Where will you take her? Your usual source of entertainment is music halls and that's rather redundant in her case."

The same question plagued Ruddy since the night they met and she agreed to go out with him. Choosing a nice restaurant for dinner was easy. He thought she might like to go dancing. Before she left for America, he and Evangeline had gone several times. She enjoyed it but that didn't mean Honeysuckle did. Desperate for suggestions, he'd sought help.

"I asked the widow at my boarding house where she likes to go for entertainment other than music halls, which I can't picture her going to anyway. She and her widow friend love the ballet when it's in town. She said there's a famous Russian company here now."

"The bell-lay." Archie's Yorkshire accent often crept into his conversation when mockery was his goal. "Have you ever been?"

"Don't be daft. Who knows? Maybe it will be fun. I bought tickets for their program, something called, *The Pharaoh's Daughter.*"

"Maybe."

****

At home Ruddy washed up, shaved again, and put on a freshly cleaned and pressed shirt. Quality tailored suits were a small luxury he allowed himself. The one he'd worn to work would've been fine for the evening but he changed into his newest suit. He added a garnet red tie for a splash of color. It was too bold a color to wear for work but perfect for a night on the town. He took one last look in the mirror and headed downstairs.

The aroma of roast beef, onions, and fresh baked bread hit him like a wall of deliciousness as he entered the ground floor. Mrs. Goodge was preparing dinner for the boarders. An excellent cook, he'd have to say his landlady was as talented as his own mother in the kitchen. And his mother worked miracles managing to feed ten children and a husband from a slim pantry where meat was a luxury.

"Mr. Bloodstone, aren't you the dashing one tonight?" Mrs. Goodge caught him in the foyer on his way out.

"Thank you, Mrs. Goodge. I'm always flattered by the attention of your lovely self."

The stout, older landlady blushed bright pink from her shiny cheeks to her forehead damp with kitchen perspiration. She giggled and fanned her face with the tail of her apron. "Where are you off to? From the look of you, I'd say there's a new lady waiting somewhere."

"Yes, there's a lady waiting this evening."

"Good. We want this one to stay. Get her a nice bouquet. I'm sure you'll make a fine impression just being yourself, but flowers can only help."

Mrs. Goodge had met Evangeline and brought her tea on the few occasions she visited Ruddy at home. Goodge ran a strictly proper boarding house. Visitors of the opposite sex were restricted to sitting in the garden or the parlor. At her New Year's luncheon for the boarders, Goodge asked why she hadn't seen

Chris Karlsen

Evangeline during the holidays. Ruddy explained they'd parted company when Evangeline sought greener pastures.

"I'll do that." He gave her a light buss on the cheek. "Goodnight."

Ruddy didn't get over to Leicester Square terribly often. He wasn't familiar with the St. Martin's Hotel where Honeysuckle said she had a suite.

The main entrance to the hotel was located one door down from Charing Cross Road. White stone, with a dual-pillared elegant Georgian façade, Palladian windows, and the name on a bronze sign attached to one pillar, it wasn't at all what he pictured. In Ruddy's mind, he assumed it would be more like other women-only residence hotels, plain brick with a few oblong windows.

He stepped inside to another surprise. Blue and gold paisley wallpaper decorated the lobby. Normally he wouldn't know the name of the pattern but Margaret Holbrook's dining room had a similar pattern. She said it was the height of current fashion. Oxblood leather wingback chairs were set around tables throughout the room. To the right was a service bar where tuxedoed waiters came and went with trays of drinks for patrons in the lobby. To his greater surprise, men and women were coming and going up and down the stairs. The hotel was clearly open to both genders.

Ruddy stepped up to the desk clerk who was unobtrusively tucked away between two large potted palms. "I'm to meet Miss Flowers. Do you have a runner who can let her know Mr. Bloodstone has arrived?"

"We do have a porter to attend to such things when needed but that won't be necessary. You may go straight to her suite. It's on the third floor. That's our residential floor. She's in Number 333."

As he climbed the stairs, the advantage of seeing a woman who lived in a hotel crossed his mind.

The third floor kept the residents on the quietest level. Noise from busy Charing Cross Road that drifted into the lobby and second floor was reduced to a low muffle. The rooms were laid out in a hopscotch pattern with even ones on the right and odd numbers on the left. Honeysuckle's room was two in from the staircase.

Ruddy knocked and she answered the door with a bright smile and cheery, "Come in." She closed the door and taking his hand led him into the sitting room.

"These are for you." Ruddy handed her the bouquet. He bought the largest and most colorful one the flower vendor had. "You look lovely."

"Thank you. How kind. Please have a seat. Would you like a drink while I put these in water?"

"Yes, please." Ruddy sat in the nearest chair.

She looked better than lovely. She wore a peach-colored silk dress with a lace overlay. Compared to the music hall, the better lighting of her suite showed how bright green her eyes were. Her complexion was smooth and pink as a cameo.

Her suite appeared to be laid out similar to his rooms at the boarding house. The parlor was the main room with a bedroom and bath off to the side. He liked the way her sitting room was decorated-not as flamboyant as the lobby. Showy rooms with fancy wallpaper and fussy, uncomfortable furniture didn't appeal to him.

Honeysuckle went to a built-in cupboard with leaded glass front and opened it. Inside were decanters of various liquors and glassware. She poured him a drink from one decanter and handed it to him. "Irish whiskey. I noticed you were drinking it the other night." Then, she poured a second drink from a different decanter. "I prefer scotch whiskey."

She pulled a vase from the other side of the cupboard and put the bouquet in it, touching it up here and there before setting it on the table. "Very pretty."

"The policeman in me can't resist mentioning concern over the lack of security at the hotel. I came up to your room no questions asked. I worry that any sort of rogue might wander the halls," Ruddy said.

"I've lived here for several weeks with no problem. There's a desk clerk on duty twenty-four hours a day. You may not have seen him, but there's a security officer here twenty-four hours a day too. They stop anyone who looks suspicious, or so I've been told."

"The neighborhood isn't dodgy so that's good." He'd contact the Metro detectives that handled this district and check on criminal activity in the area and problems at the hotel. If he discovered any issues, he'd suggest she relocate.

"Where are we going this evening?" she asked.

"I made reservations at the Criterion for dinner and I have tickets for the ballet after."

"The ballet," she repeated with a surprised lilt to her voice, which he took as a good sign. "I've never been. What a wonderful evening you've planned."

****

Five Hours Later

They weren't nearly as embarrassed as they should've been and began laughing before they hit the exit doors of the theatre. They continued to snicker on the carriage ride back to Honeysuckle's hotel.

Neither Honeysuckle nor Ruddy knew for certain which of them fell asleep first during the performance. The last thing Ruddy remembered were mummies coming to life on stage.

"What's the last thing you remember before dozing off?" Ruddy asked, helping her out of the carriage.

"A lion chasing the daughter. I'd say I'm sorry for falling asleep but since you did too, I don't feel too awfully bad. If you don't mind my asking, why did you choose to go to the ballet tonight? You said you'd never been before so you're not a patron of the art."

"My favorite form of entertainment is music hall but I thought that's the last place you'd want to spend your evening off. I asked a lady in my boarding house where she liked to go and she said the ballet. Who knew it was a cure for insomnia?"

Honeysuckle laid her hands on his chest in a familiar way that pleased him but he wasn't certain how to interpret. "How sweet of you to go to such lengths to impress me. I'm flattered. Honestly, I love music hall entertainment as well. I enjoy nothing more than seeing other performers. I also like dancing and the occasional play."

"What a relief. Next time, music hall it is then." Ruddy slipped her arm through his and escorted her to her room.

"Would you like to come in for a late night cognac?" she asked when they got to her door.

He really didn't know what to make of that. All sorts of hope shot through him. "I'd love to."

Optimism must've shown on his face, since she quickly added, "It's cognac only, Rudyard. For now."

"Did I give myself away? Was there a gleam in my eye or something?"

"Something like that. You shouldn't play cards."

"Fortunately, cards aren't for me, not like lovely ladies are," he said with a wink and a smile. He found both went a long way with women.

Chapter Twelve

The night had finally arrived. For sixteen years Graciela longed for revenge but never dared to hope for it. Now she'd see her wish fulfilled. She'd been patient. She spent her nights off for the last month spying on Cross. She made sure of his habit to drink late into the wee hours of the morning, well after his staff had gone to bed.

Graciela brought the valise with the newsboy's clothes into the house. She waited until Zachary's staff had retired for the night to change into the outfit. Then she pulled a box from the bottom of her dresser drawer where she kept it tucked away. She hadn't looked at the contents for years, not until that day she'd seen Cross.

She sat on the bed, opened the box and removed the stained cotton bloomers, bloomers stained with the evidence of her loss of innocence. She cut a small square brown with old blood and slid it into her pocket. "A little something for you to take to hell with you, Bartholomew."

She didn't want to risk discovery and questioning by any other staff members so she skipped lighting a candle. Instead, she crept downstairs by feeling her way along the walls into the kitchen. That was the trickiest room as she never knew what chairs or other equipment cook left out. She bumped into a utility table hard enough to leave a nasty bruise on her thigh but kept from crying out.

Outside, she avoided the circles of light from the streetlamps and stayed close to the buildings. At this late hour, most of the people out on foot were likely lamplighters or night-watchmen. But there'd also be coppers and you could never predict when a curious one would want to stop and question a person. Worse than running into a copper were the robbers, footpads and others who presented all types of dangerous encounters. All reasons to keep out of sight as much as possible. She could've gotten to Cross's much faster had she not had to keep to the shadows.

Midway the full impact of what she was about to do struck her. Momentarily reeling, she eased round the next corner and rested against the building, breathing as though she'd been running. She fingered the flask of poison in her pocket, stroked it around in between her thumb and forefinger, brought it out and stared at it in the faint light from the streetlamp. Over the years, she'd planned a thousand different ways, ten-thousand ways to find revenge. How she wanted him to suffer the way she suffered. Could she actually watch the life leave his body? She'd never seen anyone die.

The stench from the night soil man's wagon drove her back into the doorway of the building where she'd stopped and rested. The wagon passed and she stepped out into the street. She paused. To the left led to Cross's home. To the right back to Zachary's.

I've waited too long for this. I've come too far

to surrender. She took a deep breath. Let it out, took another and let it out. Then, she turned left.

When she reached his house, she lay in wait watching. If Cross followed his routine, he'd make one last trip to the privy in the rear yard before retiring to his library for cognac. He didn't disappoint. As soon as he left out the kitchen door, Graciela hurried to the front and onto the portico. She worked the lock the way Addy taught her and had it defeated with a barely heard couple of clicks.

She eased inside and into the library where she poured the vial of arsenic into the decanter of cognac. The butler had already drawn the heavy draperies across the larger windows for the night. It was a risk but she wagered Cross, like Zachary, was a creature of habit and always used the same small window to call to the wild birds he liked to feed. She hid behind the larger set of windows and used their draperies for cover and waited. Not long after Cross returned and the butler poured him a snifter of cognac.

"Will that be all, sir?"

"Yes, Desmond. You may go."

"Goodnight, sir."

She'd guessed correctly. Cross went to the same window to call to the birds the night she rescued Me-Too. He opened it and began his trilling thing, calling to his little birds.

Ugh, it's too early for your birds, you buffoon. Just drink your cognac already. Graciela ventured a one-eyed peek around the drapery. It looked like he hadn't touched his drink.

He burped and finally gave up and sat down

again.

Thank you, God. She smiled at her unintentional blasphemy of thanking the Lord for hurrying a man to his murderous death at her hands.

Minutes passed when she assumed he was enjoying his drink. Arsenic acted fast. She wouldn't have long to wait once he drank enough and she'd added a healthy dose of poison to the decanter.

Finally, she heard him choke and groan. Again, she peered around the curtain. He held his hand to his stomach and had his head tipped back, groaning in pain. Sweat beaded his forehead. All signs of arsenic poisoning.

She stepped from behind the drape. "Good evening, Bartholomew."

His head snapped up.

"Don't call out," she ordered. "You've been poisoned. If you call out, I'll run and you'll never receive the antidote in time to save yourself." She gave him a few seconds to debate his next action.

Pain grabbed his insides again, doubling him over before he could respond. Then, he lifted his head slightly and asked in a raspy voice, "Who are you?"

"Oh, we've met but I know you don't remember me so let me introduce myself. I'm Graciela Robson. We met sixteen years ago...well, not met exactly but came together at the will of you and your friends."

He squinted, trying to focus on her. "You're a woman?"

She removed her cap, unpinned her hair and gave it a shake.

He shook his head recognition escaping him as

she knew it would. "I don't know you. I don't care who you are. There's money in the desk drawer. Take it. Just give me the antidote and go."

"Not yet. Soon confusion will set in and you need to remember. Sixteen years ago you and three friends from the Oxford rowing team were coming from practice. You saw a sweet fourteen-year-old local village girl picking flowers along the riverbank. When you saw she was alone, you stopped and formed a circle around her. You touched her hair and cheeks and told her how pretty she was. Still don't recall?"

She moved closer, close enough to see his eyes bounce as he tried to focus, tried to reach for a memory he'd thrown away ages ago. "No. No."

"You said rude things about her among yourselves. You said she was ripe for the plucking and that it would be a shame to waste her on a nothing little farm boy. Coming back to you yet?"

"You're mad," he mumbled and pulled his legs up, curling into a semi-fetal position. He dropped his feet to the floor suddenly and attempted to stand. "My birds. Must feed my birds."

Confusion, another sign of the arsenic's effect.

He staggered back down and begged, "Please help me."

"You argued about who should go first. You won, arguing you were the one pointed me out to them. They took turns holding me down. You were all careful not to tear my clothing. All I had when it was over was the blood of my virginity to show as evidence. You were quick to inform me that even if I showed that to the authorities, no one would believe me over you lot.

People don't believe girls like me over men like you, you said. Money and position will always have the final say." She smiled. "Unless, of course, you're a woman with a flask of arsenic."

He groaned and began to rock violently, nearly falling from the chair.

She knelt in front of him. "Tell me the names of the other three and I'll give you the antidote." She pulled another vial from her pocket and held it up.

"So you can kill them too?"

"They need to know what they did. What are the names?"

"Never...tell...you..."

"Are you willing to die for them?" She wiggled the vial in front of his eyes.

He blinked several times and she thought he'd pass out before speaking. He raised a finger and pointed to his desk. "In my book, Skinner, Lloyd-Birch, and Finch." He made a feeble attempt to snatch the vial from her, grabbing air instead. "Save me now."

"Beg me. Say the words."

"I. Beg. You."

Emotion she hadn't expected swept over her, a thrill astonishing her with its strength at just hearing those words from him. She rocked back on her heels. She had anticipated a sense of accomplishment, anticipated a wave diabolical pleasure but nothing like this searing power that seemed to start at her feet and burn in a wonderful way out every pore on a path upward.

She stood and went to the silver tray with three decanters, wanting a potent drink, a celebratory drink.

Obviously, she couldn't touch his cognac. She sniffed one of the other bottles. *Port. Port is for lady's companions or women with delicate natures, not a resolute, flinty woman.* She sniffed the last decanter. *Whiskey. Yes, whiskey it is. A man's drink...or the drink of someone capable of doing what a man believes only men capable of.*

She poured three fingers full into a glass, drank half and knelt in front of Cross again. "I beg you. I said those same words. But they didn't get me anywhere. Yours won't either." She removed the vial of colored water, the alleged antidote and threw it down her throat. She chased the water with the remaining whiskey.

She eyed the decanter with tainted cognac, debating if she should take it. She wouldn't want one of the staff tempted to tipple to wind up dead. She decided against removing the bottle reasoning that as soon as the maid came in to light the fire in the morning and discovered the body, she'd run for the butler. He'd send for the doctor. The odds were slim any staff might stop to drink under the circumstances. Graciela hoped none would anyway. The thought of an innocent dying as a result of this horrified her. The possibility hadn't occurred to her before now. She pushed the possibility from her mind and turned back to Cross.

When Cross lost consciousness and fell from the chair, she tucked the square of bloody bloomer linen into his palm and wrapped his fingers around it. He took his last breath a short time later. She verified he had no heartbeat and briefly contemplated closing his eyes so he looked less horrified entering the afterlife. But she didn't. She searched his desk for a ledger with the names of his associates, found it, and then left out the front door, shutting it softly behind her.

The entire murder had taken less time than she thought. She'd be home before dawn. Fast business. Arsenic in a massive dose was indeed the King of Poisons. She hugged the ledger close to her chest.

One down, three to go.

Chapter Thirteen

"Don't bother taking your hat and coat off," Archie said as Ruddy walked into the detective bureau. "We've been ordered to look into a suspicious death over on Montague Place."

"What do you mean suspicious? Is the fellow shot, stabbed, hung or not?"

"Details are slim. The desk sergeant said the alleged victim was an important banker and something about his death doesn't look right."

Ruddy had no intention of taking the word of a hysterical wife or other relative that some heinous act had to have occurred. Their grief all too often wouldn't allow them to accept that death has come to a loved one who was otherwise healthy.

"Doesn't look right to whom? Before we go dashing off on a wild goose chase, I'd like to know who the source of this suspicion is and why they've concluded something is amiss." He went over to the desk sergeant. "You must have more information on this death on Montague. Why is this suspicious?"

"I don't. They sent their footman here with a message from the butler that Mr. Bartholomew Cross had died and that there indications that it was under suspicious circumstances. Sorry Ruddy, but the footman wasn't exactly a font of information."

"Bloody hell. All right. Let Jameson know where we went and what's going on."

****

The butler, Desmond, led them to the library. "This is how I found him. I went into his chamber at 7:30 a.m. to wake him. Mr. Cross kept a strict timetable. When I saw his bed was unslept in, I became alarmed and went immediately to the library."

"Why here?" Archie asked.

"It's Mr. Cross's habit to...well...imbibe late into the night. He had trouble falling asleep and often didn't retire to his bed until the wee hours of the morning. He'd stay in here reading and feeding the early birds." The ghost of a sad smile passed the butler's lips. "He had a fondness for wild birds. Some even trusted him enough to land on his offered hand."

"Was this where you saw him last?" Ruddy asked.

"Yes."

Ruddy felt along Cross's arm then along his leg and spine for signs of lingering rigor mortis and found none. He pulled out his pocket watch and checked the time. "What time was that?"

"11:00 p.m., detective. I went to my chamber afterward."

"What about the rest of the staff? Are any of them up and about after you go to bed?" Archie asked. "A valet perhaps?"

Desmond shook his head. "Mr. Cross didn't desire the services of a valet. If needed, I helped him dress. I am also the last of the staff to retire for the night just in case he requires anything."

Other than the usual lividity, Ruddy didn't see any marks on the body. "What makes you think this isn't a simple heart attack?"

"Look at how he's curled up, detective. He's balled up as though in pain, in the fetal position."

Ruddy shrugged. "Sorry but I don't see the significance in that. I'm sure a heart attack is painful. Even if it isn't his heart, it could have come from food poisoning. I've suffered that in the past and can verify that you'll double up in agony quickly enough."

"It couldn't have been food poisoning. We all ate the same food he did. None of us is sick. There are other issues that make me suspect something suspicious happened."

"Go on." Ruddy planned on letting him express all his theories and get it out of his system. It was the best way to handle the problem. Let them talk and then explain how they were wrong and leave.

"The front door was unlocked," Desmond said with some urgency.

"So."

"I never forget to lock the front door."

Ruddy had him now. This he could settle with easy logic. "Everyone makes mistakes, Mr. Desmond, everyone. We all forget things. By some coincidence you happen to have forgotten to lock the door last night."

Desmond shook his head hard. "No. You don't understand. I've been the butler here for two decades. My father was Mr. Cross's father's butler and my grandfather his grandfather's butler. I never, ever forget to secure the doors, never. None of us has ever been remiss in our duties in that way."

"I don't mean to insult you, Mr. Desmond, but it does happen. Let me see the lock. I'll check to see if it's been tampered with," Ruddy said to appease him. They'd come through the front door but neither Ruddy nor Archie had been looking for lock tampering at the time.

Desmond led them to the door and Ruddy inspected it from both sides and saw nothing, no scratches or marks of any kind. "I don't see anything out of the ordinary. I'll admit a good burglar will defeat this type of lock without leaving marks and I suppose if burglary were the criminal intent here, that might have occurred. Have you checked to see if anything is missing?"

Defeat crossed Desmond's face. "I did. Mr. Cross kept a hundred pounds in his desk and it's still here."

"What about family jewels?"

"Mr. Cross's mother lived with him but when she passed her jewelry went to his sister. She lives in Surrey."

"Have you noticed anything else of value missing?"

"I haven't checked but I will and let you know if I discover anything."

"There's no sign of forced entry. No sign of struggle. I have to say, I don't see any evidence of foul play, Mr. Desmond," Ruddy said.

"What about this soiled cloth? I think the stain is dried blood. I've never seen it before. I pulled it from his hand and then replaced it so you could see where it was originally."

Ruddy took it from Cross's hand and examined it. "It does look like an old bloodstain but it might be any number of things." He handed the linen to Archie to examine.

"I'm not saying he was murdered, detectives, but I do believe something extraordinary happened that triggered Mr. Cross's death."

"We understand your intent. Did Mr. Cross belong to any gentlemen's clubs?" Archie asked and wrapped the cloth in a clean piece of paper.

"Yes, Boodles," Desmond told him.

"We'll inquire if he had any outstanding gambling debts that might've brought him into contact with unsavory types," Archie said.

"In the meantime, to put your mind at ease, Mr. Desmond, we'll have a formal autopsy performed to determine cause of death. We'll be taking this bottle of cognac and we'll run tests on it, if for no other reason than to eliminate any possible contamination that might have triggered some kind of food poisoning, as it appears to be the last thing he ingested," Ruddy said.

"You'll keep me informed, won't you?" Desmond asked. "All of us on staff served Mr. Cross for many years."

"We'll inform the family of all the details. What we discuss with the staff will depend on what we discover," Archie said.

"Of course."

Ruddy instructed the constables on the scene to notify the medical examiner to send transport for the body. "One of you bring the decanter. Be careful not to spill any. We need to test the contents. We're taking the glass he drank from to see if we can test what little remains."

"Yes, sir."

Out on the sidewalk, Archie turned to Ruddy. "What do you think? I don't see this as a murder, do you?"

"I think he had a heart attack."

"What about the piece of linen? What do you make of that? It's a weird twist."

"I suspect he was foxed and dug it out. It's some piece of sentimental nonsense and was reliving a memory when he keeled over. Let's get the laboratory to confirm and get Mr. Desmond out of our hair."

Hours later Ruddy munched on an apple as he read over the gambling records Boodles kept on Bartholomew Cross. The proprietor of the club had not been co-operative with them when they asked about Cross's gambling habits. Had he answered their questions when asked, he and Archie would've been on their way. But no, he acted like a puffed-up pigeon and refused to give them any information, choosing instead to give them some silly tripe about protecting the privacy of their clientele.

"Really?" Ruddy had responded. "I'm protecting the rights of one of your members who is a possible victim." Then he walked into the back office where he knew the club kept the books on each individual member. He found the one on Cross and left with it, over the loud objections of the proprietor.

Hot on his and Archie's heels, the proprietor

demanded to see Jameson. The three of them went into the Superintendent's office. Jameson, not being a member of Boodles but a different club didn't give a whit about the man's objections and supported Ruddy and Archie's actions, sending the proprietor packing. Neither Ruddy nor Archie were fooled. Had it been Jameson's club, they'd have surrendered the book and likely been made to apologize.

Ruddy ate and read. As wealthy men go, Cross was a conservative gambler. He never lost more than fifty pounds. If he lost that amount on any game or any given night, he paid his debt and quit. Commendable in Ruddy's view. Conversely, he never won much either. The men he played with were of the same conservative ilk and didn't risk much. Ruddy didn't recognize any of the names of the men Cross regularly played cards with, which surprised him. Boodles was known to have a wealthy membership of men in business and politics.

"Anything?" Archie asked.

"He never over extends or takes a large amount off anyone else. Cross's life looks fairly ordinary. I tell you there's nothing to Desmond's suspicion. Once we have the autopsy and—"

"Detective Holbrook and Detective Bloodstone," it was the runner from the laboratory. "I have your report from this morning." He dropped an envelope on Archie's desk.

"What was the result?" Archie asked.

"Arsenic. A lot of it."

"What?" Both Archie and Ruddy sat upright in their chairs and repeated in unison.

The runner nodded. "The cognac contained a

large quantity of arsenic. Whoever added the poison meant the drinker to die. No antidote would save them if they drank even half a glass. . Everything is in the report." The runner turned and left.

Archie slid an opener under the envelope seal. "Appears like Cross was murdered. I can't believe it. Desmond was right."

Chapter Fourteen

The Medical Examiner was still processing the body when Ruddy and Archie arrived, but he'd finished his toxicology tests on the stomach contents. The tests confirmed death by arsenic poisoning.

"Was it only in the cognac or had the food been tainted as well?" Ruddy asked.

Both detectives stood out of the splash zone as the doctor poured a bucket of water over the autopsy table. A sheet of blood ran off the end into a floor drain.

"Only cognac," the M.E. said, swiping at a pool of blood the water missed.

"Thank you. It's not much but every little bit helps," Archie said. He and Ruddy headed to the Cross residence.

****

"Detectives, please come in," Desmond said, opening the door and gesturing for them to enter. "Are you here with new information on the death of Mr. Cross?"

"We are and we need to interview the staff. Please gather them for us," Ruddy instructed.

The butler's brows lifted a fraction as he closed the door and turned. "Is foul play involved as I suspected? Can you share what you discovered?"

"In part," Archie said, removing his hat. "Turns out, your suspicion was well founded. His cognac was laden with arsenic."

"Dear Lord." Desmond looked sincerely horrified.

Archie continued, "You can understand why your staff are the first folks we wish to talk to."

Without asking, Desmond took Archie's hat from him, no doubt out of force of habit and hung it on a hall tree.

Ruddy wasn't fond of hats and often left his at the station. Because of the warm weather, today was one of those days. He hated how the bowler made his head sweat. He had spent eight years sweltering under a hot helmet serving her majesty in Africa.

He moved past Desmond deeper into the hallway. "How many does Mr. Cross employ?"

"Four, plus the carriage driver's grandson who serves as the stable boy. Mr. Cross preferred to keep his staff small."

That was unusually small for a townhouse this size but went hand-in-hand with Cross's conservative gambling habits.

"Please bring the staff in one by one and show us to a room where we can interview each in private," Ruddy ordered and pulled his notebook and pen from his pocket.

"Yes, yes, of course. This way please." Desmond led them to the parlor. "I'll bring you both some tea and then have the cook come in first."

Archie shot Ruddy a wary glance.

Desmond started to leave but paused in the

doorway. "Are you certain you need to speak to Billy, the stable boy? He's just ten and never allowed in the main part of the house. The lad only comes into the kitchen and staff dining room. The only time he's ever been as far as the parlor is Boxing Day to receive a gift from Mr. Cross. I can't imagine he knows anything about arsenic even if he had access to the Master's cognac."

"I don't know yet if we'll need to talk to him. Probably not, but tell him not to go anywhere," Archie said.

"And we'd actually like to interview you first, Mr. Desmond. If you'll gather everyone and have them wait in the kitchen for now and when you've finished, come back and we'll start with you," Ruddy told him.

"Yes sir."

After Desmond left, Ruddy turned to Archie. "I saw that wary look. I doubt anyone intends to poison us. If our killer is here, they know the station is aware of where we are and it wouldn't do for two detectives to keel over dead in the house."

Archie didn't look a hundred percent convinced but said, "I suppose."

An hour later they'd interviewed three of the four employees excluding Billy. As potential suspects went, none stood out. They had a cook who'd been with the victim since she was a young girl, a butler whose family had served as butlers to the Cross family for three generations, and a carriage driver about to retire after thirty-five years of loyal service.

Desmond brought fresh cups of tea. "We're ready for the maid," Archie said.

"Let's hope she turns out to be a major surprise and looks good for the murder. I'd love to wrap this case up fast," Ruddy said. He went to the door and waved the woman in.

A petite young woman whose mobcap couldn't contain the mass of dark curls that framed her face stood frozen in place. Pale eyes, wide as a startled doe fixed on Ruddy and she gripped the sides of her skirt with clenched fingers. Ruddy stepped aside so she could pass. He also shifted his weight onto the balls of his feet ready to take off after her if she bolted, which he half expected.

"Get along with you, Alice. The detectives haven't all day." It was Desmond. He'd stepped up next to her and gestured open-handed for her to move to the parlor.

She didn't look at him but hurried toward the room, her eyes on the floor. Desmond physically moved her further into the room so he could close the door when he left.

"Sit down, Miss Ferguson, it is Miss Ferguson, right?" Ruddy asked.

"Yes."

"Please, sit. We need to ask you about your relationship with Mr. Cross."

Still standing, staring at a spot on the opposite wall from the detectives, she said, "I'm just the maid, sir. I never had no relationship with himself."

Ruddy had to lean in to catch each word. She spoke softly and a heavy Scottish brogue made understanding her difficult.

"I'll not ask you again, Miss Ferguson. Sit."

Ruddy took her hand and led her to the chair where he put a gentle but firm hand on her shoulder until she sat. She continued to avoid eye contact and he tipped her chin up hoping to get her to look him in the eye but she wouldn't. "We must ask you some personal questions. It's important. Can you look at me, Miss Ferguson?"

She peeked over but turned away again.

Ruddy glanced at Archie whose brows notched up in his typical I'm suspicious reaction. Ferguson's skittishness probably had him thinking along the same lines as Ruddy. That she might have been preyed upon sexually by Cross. It wasn't uncommon among the English upper crust for powerful men to force their will on women like Ferguson who need their jobs. Odd behavior, especially the kind exhibited by Ferguson: the flinching, the shrinking away, her refusal to engage face-to-face, were symptoms Ruddy had often seen in victims of systematic abuse.

Ruddy chose not to force the issue of looking at him with her. "Mr. Desmond tells us you've been in service to Mr. Cross for two years." She nodded. "It's important for you to be totally honest now. At any time in the past did he touch you or take advantage of his position with you?"

"Take advantage?" She continued to avoid eye contact.

Ruddy dipped his head trying for a better angle to see her expression. "Touch you. Do anything inappropriate with you. Ask you to do things for him of a sexual nature?"

Ferguson shook her head hard. "No. Never. I'm

a good girl." She tried to jump up but he stopped her with a firm hand to the shoulder.

"Miss Ferguson—Alice, please don't think to run off. Talk to us. Did he ever say anything unseemly to you?"

She shook her head but not as hard, shrinking away from Ruddy, from his disturbing questions.

Time to turn her over to Archie and hopefully she'd feel less intimidated. Ruddy didn't see anything in his manner of questioning for her to find objection with, which made him highly suspicious. She had to be lying. Why else would she respond so fearfully?

"See what you can get out of her," he whispered to Archie and then left the room to look for Desmond.

The butler, along with the cook, and carriage driver, were sitting at a long prep table in the kitchen drinking tea. "Mr. Desmond, a word." Ruddy tipped his head, indicating he wanted the butler to join him in the hallway.

"Yes, detective," Desmond said, coming next to Ruddy outside the parlor.

Ruddy had left the door open just enough to peek inside. "I have serious reservations about what transpired between Mr. Cross and Miss Ferguson. Every time I ask her a question, she acts like I struck her with a hot poker. Her behavior isn't normal. She acts like she expects to be tortured. Take a look."

Desmond stepped forward, peered inside, watched for a moment while Archie posed a question and then moved back to where Ruddy stood. "She's a queer fish, isn't she? I would never have hired her, but Mr. Cross bypassed me. He said he was doing a favor for a friend in Glasgow." He smiled. "I wouldn't put too much store in Alice's odd behavior, detective. She wouldn't say boo to a ghost. Nor does she look anyone in the eye when she speaks. She never has."

The fact she acted strange with everyone in the house didn't eliminate Cross as a possible abuser. "Do you have any reason to believe Mr. Cross had any sexual contact with her? Please be honest. I understand you wish to remain loyal to the family you've served for generations but remember we are trying to solve his murder. His reputation won't suffer as the information will not be made public." The last was a lie he felt no guilt over. If it turned out Ferguson killed Cross because he was taking advantage of her sexually, that would come out in trial. Cross's reputation would be destroyed. But if a lie was necessary to catch a killer, then so be it.

"Mr. Cross's father had a weakness for pretty female staff members. It was a costly weakness financially and one that broke his mother's heart. Mr. Cross would never bring that type of scandal to his home, not after enduring the gossip from his father's constant foolish dalliances." Desmond stiffened and he pressed his lips together, letting his disapproval show for just a moment. His expression turned neutral and again and he continued, "To my knowledge, Mr. Cross never looked twice at Miss Ferguson. Frankly, they barely crossed paths. When he was upstairs, she busied herself downstairs and she worked upstairs after he left for the bank."

With the staff eliminated, they had zero leads. Something was missing from the victim's story. What were he and Archie missing? There was a reason why the man was murdered. He didn't have a gambling problem. He supposedly had the loyalty and devotion of his staff. No long line of jealous family members looked to inherit large tracts of land and immense amounts of money. This wasn't random. Murderers didn't wander up to a fashionable townhome, pick the lock, poison the resident's cognac, and leave for no reason.

Could this be the act of a jealous lover, a woman scorned perhaps? "Mr. Cross was a bachelor but like most men I assume he had a man's needs," Ruddy spoke frankly to the butler.

Desmond's cheeks colored slightly and he nodded.

"Did he have a special lady friend?"

"No."

"Then how did he satisfy his needs? Did he have women visit him here?"

Desmond's head snapped back slightly as though the suggestion was a slap in the face to the man's dignity. "Certainly not. I told you he refused to bring scandal to his door."

"Enlighten me."

The butler held his finger up, took a quick peek inside the parlor and then said to Ruddy, "Have you heard of a private club called The Pleasure Chest?"

"Of course. Every copper this side of the river has heard of it." Ruddy had never been inside the club and didn't know anyone who had. But he'd heard tales that no desire sought was out of reach at the Pleasure Chest. If a man had the funds, he'd find someone there who'd do it.

"Whatever temptations took Mr. Cross, he satisfied them at the club," Desmond said.

From Desmond's resigned tone, Ruddy had the impression the butler was disappointed by his employer's suffering the same weaknesses as the rest of humanity.

The parlor door opened all the way, and head down, Alice Ferguson scurried out back toward the kitchen. The world's biggest two-legged dormouse. A mean thought but Ruddy couldn't help himself.

"She insists nothing untoward was said or done by Cross," Archie said, joining Ruddy and Desmond.

"I'm not surprised. I told you Mr. Cross was not that sort of man. Now, if that is all detectives, the staff and I have a busy day ahead of us. Mr. Cross's sister and her husband are en route here for the viewing and funeral once the body is released. The staff has to prepare the house for their visit and the viewing."

"We're finished. Thank you for your cooperation. We'll see our own way out." Ruddy and Archie headed for the front door, Archie grabbing his hat as they did.

"Where to now?" Archie asked once they were on the sidewalk, putting on his bowler.

"The Pleasure Chest."

"You jest? The notorious brothel?"

"Technically a private club," Ruddy corrected. "Unless, or until, it is exposed as other than that it will remain designated as such. There are too many well-to-do members for that change to happen."

"Should we tell Jameson we're going?"

Ruddy hoped to avoid involving Jameson until after the fact. The Superintendent would likely want to go. There wasn't a copper at the station who wouldn't be chomping at the bit to go out of curiosity. If he came, Ruddy knew, somehow, some way, he'd muck things up. Because as any copper worth his salt will tell you, that's what supervisors do.

"We should but let's not. I'll take the heat for the decision," he told Archie.

"Balderdash, if we're going to be in the soup, then we'll be in it together. I have to confess, I've never been in any house of ill Fame." He removed a small mustache comb from his coat pocket and ran it over his mutton chops then followed that with an additional finger-smoothing.

Ruddy chuckled, watching the ritual. His partner wasn't a vain man by nature. He'd only seen him preen on the rare occasion Meg was meeting him for a special evening out. "Are you fancying yourself up for the strumpets?"

Archie shoved the mustache comb away. "No. Meg mentioned she might meet me for tea later and I thought I'd tidy up a bit."

"Really?" Not believing him for an instant.

"Shall we take the tram?" Archie asked, ignoring Ruddy's doubting question.

"Sure."

****

They passed the club twice before finally finding it. The Pleasure Chest was located off of Shaftesbury Avenue in Soho. If a person didn't know the exact location, it was easy to miss. At first look anyone would take it for a private home or commercial concern not open to the public. It had a padded red leather front door with heavy metal studs and a lion's head brass knocker. The building was a simple white brick structure consisting of three floors. The long windows were all covered in drapes pulled closed to inquiring eyes. Only a two-foot by two-foot plaque in brass with the club name next to the door identified the building as The Pleasure Chest.

Ruddy knocked. A short, broad-chested, clean-shaven, bald man with biceps the size of an ordinary man's thighs opened the door. He wore all black including a pair of leather fingerless gloves. One eyebrow approached his non-existent hairline. He eyed the two of them briefly, and then said, "This is a private club," and started to shut the door.

Ruddy and Archie brought their shields up for him to see. "Not to us," Ruddy said and pushed against the door, forcing it open. "Who's in charge?"

The man swore under his breath and moved aside. "Mrs. Darling."

"Take us to her." Baldy was clearly one of the club's enforcers in case of trouble and as they followed him Ruddy thought how tough it would be to fight a man like this. Solid, low center of gravity, and possessed of brute strength from the look of him, and ham-fisted—just the type it took a squad of Peelers to bring down if he resisted arrest.

They entered a room that reeked of stale cigar smoke and cloying patchouli. *Whorehouses. They all smell weird.*

The room resembled an oversized parlor filled

with fancy furniture. Scattered all around were expensive inlay tables, velvet settees, chaise lounges, padded chairs and tufted ottomans. Chandeliers were strategically hung to cast the room in sufficient light without shining harshly in any one place. Nothing in it looked suited for a private men's club that catered to the wealthy of London: no leather furnishings, mahogany tables, imported tropical plants, or tuxedoed wait staff.

Across the room, standing in a doorway was a double of the man who answered the door. Twin enforcers. Interesting, Ruddy thought. Different. He counted eight young women in frilly boudoir—style outfits sitting and laying around, some chatting, some reading, and a few staring at him and Archie with bored expressions. One stood in front of an older woman while the woman pulled and tucked at the younger one's lacy corset.

"Pardon me, Mrs. Darling but these detectives wish to speak with you," the muscled servant said as they stopped in front of the sofa where she sat.

She turned to Ruddy and Archie. Darling appeared to be in her mid-fifties. Her eyes were clear, big and blue, but most of what must've been golden blonde hair had gone white. The flesh around her chin sagged only a little and in spite of the overuse of powder and rouge, the vestiges of the beauty she once was remained.

"What could you possibly want with me?" She gave the young woman in front of her a light shove. "Go on."

"We need to talk to you about a member of your

club," Ruddy explained. "Mr. Bartholomew Cross. He's been murdered and we're investigating the case."

"I can't and won't speak of my members to you. Their privacy is of the utmost importance to them. I am honor bound to keep their trust."

Of course you can't. There's nothing *so* precious as the honor and ethics of a Madame. Ruddy kept the thought to himself. He leaned down and whispered to Archie, "Keep talking so her attention is on you."

Ruddy stepped away and casually strolled around the room. He needed a violation to use as leverage against her. She could only hide behind the private club front so much. She ran a brothel and what brothel didn't have something to hide?

In the background Archie told her, "Mrs. Darling, dead men have no expectation of privacy so that excuse doesn't stand."

"You can't make me tell you anything. Besides, I'm not sure what it is you wish to know."

"For starters, who was his favorite lady? Don't most of your members have favorites?" Archie asked.

"Many do, yes. So what?"

"We need to speak to her."

"Why? What's that other detective doing?"

"Stand up," Ruddy ordered an Arabic looking whore who'd been lying on a chaise.

"See here, you can't order my girls around," Darling said, moving off the sofa toward where Ruddy stood.

Ruddy ignored her and swiftly took hold of her wrists, eliciting a squeal of protest from both her and Darling. He turned the girl's hands palm up and wrapped his middle finger and thumbs around her wrist bones. He let go of the girl's hands and took a step back.

She wore a floral print silk robe over flesh-colored tights and a lacy bustier. "Slip the robe off," Ruddy ordered and she did.

Darling lunged for Ruddy but Archie was there to shove her away.

Ruddy eyed her hard from the front and then from the side. Coming face-to-face with her again, he asked, "What's your working name?"

"Scheherazade."

"What's your male name?"

"Don't say anymore," Darling blurted.

"Quiet," Archie hauled her by the arm back to the sofa and pushed on her shoulder until she sat.

"Your male name?" Ruddy repeated.

"Yazid."

"Where are you from?"

"Morocco."

"You can sit down again." He walked over to a young Asian woman sitting ramrod straight, chewing a lip, and watching him from an ottoman. "Stand up."

She shook her head.

"Really? You want to do this the hard way?"

The Asian slowly stood. A hipless, tiny-boned creature, she wore a satin choker three fingers wide that covered most of her neck.

Ruddy slipped his index finger behind the front of the choker. "Swallow."

The whore shot a fearful glance Darling's direction. Darling looked ready to leap off the sofa and tackle Ruddy. Archie must've suspected it crossed her mind and kept his hand on her shoulder.

"Swallow," Ruddy repeated.

The Asian swallowed.

Ruddy pulled his finger from the choker. "What's your working name and your boy name?"

"I go by Jolly, but my given name is Kang."

"Where are you from?

"Hong Kong."

"Sit down." Ruddy went over to where Darling sat. If looks could kill, she'd do what the Zulus had tried to do to him in battle and failed.

Ruddy had his leverage. "Now, we don't care about what you and the lads are getting up to here. We aren't interested in violations of the decency laws, but some people are. One word from us and we can have them here. So you have a decision, Mrs. Darling."

"Cross's favorite is Violet. I'll take you to her."

Darling rose. As she passed, she slapped Kang who yelped and fell onto the ottoman. Darling led Ruddy and Archie down a corridor with red and gold flocked wallpaper. Flocked wallpaper from France had become the rage the last couple years. Mrs. Goodge had said she'd love to redo her parlor in a bright flocked paper. Wait until he told her he saw it in a brothel. That'll put an end to her wanting to line the parlor walls with the garish stuff, Ruddy thought.

They stopped at a room at the end of the hall. Darling didn't bother to knock. "Violet, these are detectives. They want to talk to you about Mr. Cross. Apparently, he's been murdered. Just tell them what they need to know." Darling turned to Ruddy. "Pull the bell cord when you're ready to leave and someone will escort you out."

"Thank you for your cooperation," Archie said.

She snorted and left, closing the door behind her.

Violet sat on a bed with a peach-colored silky coverlet and several pillows trimmed in lace the same shade. She wore a pink corset with a frilly robe she left untied. The corset pushed her breasts to the brink of falling out. She had flesh-colored stockings held up with pink garters and sat cross-legged brushing her hair. What she didn't wear was bloomers.

A beet-faced Archie bent to set a pillow over her private bits. "Cover yourself up. Have some decency."

Violet smirked and gave him a peck on the cheek as he leaned down to place the pillow.

Archie jerked away and wiped at his cheek.

"You're just offended because you don't know where my lips have been," Violet said still smirking.

"Enough of your shenanigans, I'm going to be blunt," Ruddy said, turning his attention to her. "All we really need to know is if Mr. Cross had any unusual preferences sexually. His murder is a puzzle. We're trying to put the pieces of his life together to see why someone would want to kill him."

"Well, I didn't kill him."

"Not saying you did."

"Did you work outside of here? Do you have a gentleman friend who might be jealous of Mr. Cross?"

"No. Mrs. Darling takes care of all our needs. I don't have to work elsewhere. There's no man."

"What did Cross want when he was with you?"

"Rape mostly."

Both Archie and Ruddy exchanged a baffled look. Ruddy thought he'd heard wrong. "Sorry. Did you say, rape?"

She nodded. "He...you know...couldn't keep it going unless I was tied up and pretended to resist." She shrugged off the oddity. "To each their own. As long as they pay, I do what they ask. You want to pretend to rape me. Fine."

Ruddy had to admit he'd seen and heard a lot during his years in the military and the police, but pretend rape struck him as pretty damned strange.

"That it?"

"No. He liked Master and Slave."

"Who is who in that scenario?" Ruddy could guess but best to clarify.

"I wear the collar." She pointed to a thick black leather collar with a silver ring hanging on the wall. "He has me either on a leash on all fours and commands me or on the bed tied to the posts. Then he flogs me at will. There's a selection of whips. See." She pointed to a table Ruddy hadn't noticed when they entered with several whips of different lengths and styles.

She might've been talking about the weather, her tone was so easy and matter of fact. He searched her face for any telltale sign of fear or anger or revulsion at what Cross did. Nothing. She blinked and stared back at him.

Archie snatched the brush from her. "How old are you?"

Startled, she recoiled but recovered fast and

tried to grab her brush from him. "Don't know. What's it to you anyway? Gimme my brush."

Archie paced between the bed and the table of whips.

"Did he ever injure you badly?" Ruddy asked, wondering if Darling could've sent one of the enforcers over as retribution if Cross injured Violet.

"Occasionally."

"What did Darling do?"

"She made him pay extra for every day I missed work. He was good about tipping me extra too. Very generous he was."

Archie came back to the bed and stuck a cat o' nine tails in her face. "And you're all right with being beaten? What is wrong with you?"

She watched him clearly not grasping why he cared, why he was so upset. "It's not so bad. I heal fast enough. I won't always have to do this. I'm not stupid like the others. I save my money. One day I'll have my own place like Mrs. Darling. A few bruises and scars are worth it."

Archie opened his mouth to argue but Ruddy laid a hand on his arm. "It won't help, Arch. You have to walk away from this."

Archie tossed the brush and cat o' nine tails on the bed and stepped back.

Ruddy turned to Violet. "One more question. Did Mrs. Darling ever get angry with what Cross did? Would she send one of her men to speak to him, to warn him to be more careful?"

"No. It's not as though Mr. Cross is the only member who favors whips and slave games. Jolly has a special member who likes her to wear a leather hood and put him on a rack." Violet shrugged again. "Money is money."

"Thank you, Violet. We'll be going now." Ruddy rang the bell and the same man who answered the door led them out.

Ruddy waited a minute to see if Archie would explain why he got so upset with Violet. When he didn't Ruddy said, "You got your feathers ruffled in there with Violet. It's not like you. She's not the first whore we've dealt with."

"Her age bothered me. She's several years older than my girls but when I looked at her young face, I couldn't help thinking of my own sweet daughters. It's easy for you to distance yourself. You don't have children."

"My not having children has nothing to do with it. I distance myself from situations I can't change."

"What a terrible life that girl leads," Archie said as he and Ruddy walked down the street.

"Who knows what kind of life she left. At The Pleasure Chest she has a full belly, a roof over her head and clothes on her back. Whatever she came from, she clearly feels the beatings are a fair trade off, however short-lived the lifestyle may be."

"Pathetic."

"That it is." Ruddy saw a pub sign a block ahead. A drink and meal might help take Archie's mind off Violet's dark world. "I feel like a beer and a bite to eat. How about you?"

"Sounds good."

After choosing a table with no one sitting

nearby and ordering, Archie said, "I know the brothel is our best option for finding a suspect, but I didn't see anyone who really stood out. The twin musclemen are possibilities but what's the motive? Jealousy over Violet? She said she doesn't see men other than customers."

"I agree. From what she said and what we saw, I don't see anyone with a strong motive either."

"Speaking of the whores, how did you know about the Moroccan and the Asian?"

Their beers came and Ruddy took a long pull before answering. "When I was deployed in Africa the brothels there had quite a few men like them from Morocco and Tangiers, men who passed for women. Asians too. All of them tend to be on the small side and can pass for women easier. Most have some masculine physicality that they can't hide though, usually it's thick wrists or an Adam's Apple. The Moroccan had heavy wrists and the Asian had an Adam's apple. I saw it bob even with the choker. I had to be sure, which is why I tested with my finger."

Even with nobody close Archie lowered his voice and leaned across the table. "Did you mean what I think when you said nice tuck? The few times we've dealt with them I never gave any thought to their ways."

"The lads have to fool the folks somehow."

"Sounds bloody uncomfortable."

"I don't care to speculate but prefer to focus on our problem. Who killed our banker?"

"Who indeed?"

Chapter Fifteen

Graciela's next victim, Daniel Skinner, lived in Belgrave Square not far from where she lived with Mrs. Zachary. Which, she thought at first, was pretty convenient—no sneaking around alleys at night. She could get there, do what she needed and get back in a blink.

She conducted her first few reconnoiter sessions in daylight, dressed normally (another convenience.) She walked by numerous times at various hours. No one noticed a woman strolling past. At the corner of Skinner's street sat a teashop where she took tea several times and watched his home. Somewhere in the dark recesses of her mind, she'd believed the next murder would be as easy to execute as Cross's. She drained the last of her bergamot-scented Earl Grey, leaned back in her chair and said with a sigh, "Graciela, you're a fool."

Cross was a bachelor, but Skinner had a wife and a daughter in her teens. Besides the family, he had a much larger staff than Cross. Skinner had a butler, two footmen, a carriage driver, and a cook. She could assume they had a least one house maid if not more.

Mrs. Skinner no doubt had a lady's maid. The daughter probably had one as well. No proper aristocratic Englishwoman went without a lady's maid. A young man in his twenties came and went as well, often bringing along a friend. Graciela's rape occurred sixteen years prior. Skinner and the others were still at Oxford. He wasn't old enough to be the young man's father. She guessed the man might be a nephew or other relative.

"This is a nightmare," Graciela said to herself, watching one of the footmen carrying boxes from the carriage following a mother-daughter shopping trip.

There was no possible way for her to sneak in and locate the library, assuming he had a library. Every townhome she'd been in with Mrs. Zachary did. On the outside chance she managed to break in undiscovered she had to hope he drank. Most men did and even if he didn't, he probably still kept brandy and port handy for visitors. If he did have brandy or drink on hand, how could she keep the young man or one of his friends from drinking the poison? She couldn't. Plain and simple.

"What to do? What to do?" Discouraged, she left the teashop and returned home.

At home in her chamber, she read through the information in Cross's ledger again. Nobody is ever truly safe. If you really want to kill someone, you can find a way—eventually. She glanced at the other two names but it was a momentary distraction. Skinner had to be the next. The others had bigger logistical problems. Harlan Lloyd-Birch lived in Surrey. He'd be last. She'd have to go on holiday to kill him. Nesbit

Finch no longer lived at the address listed in the ledger. She had to research where he moved or worked.

Me-Too hopped onto the bed demanding her attention, walking over the ledger, he pawed at the book.

"Stop, you'll tear the pages." The cat hissed and went into boneless mode when she tried to lift her off. "How do you do that, go as if you've no skeleton at all?" Graciela's pulling up didn't budge the feline. The cat stretched like soft taffy as she lifted. Finally, Graciela won by scooping her hand under the cat's bottom and moving her off the book.

She closed the book and hid it away in the back of a dresser drawer. The only alternative she could think of was to stake out Skinner's law office.

The cat lay on her side with her head and front paws on Graciela's thigh as she sat on the bed, legs straight, back propped against the headboard. Me-Too batted at her leg but stopped when Graciela began to stroke the length of her.

"I need some answers, Me-Too. So no playing for a bit, pay attention. Move your tail back and forth if your answer is no. Flip it up and down for yes. Understand?"

The cat flipped her tail once.

"Skinner is a solicitor. His office is on Chancery Lane and my only choice for the poisoning. Of course, I will scout the location."

Me-Too clamped her front paws around the tip of Graciela's finger and nibbled.

"Chancery is a busy street. I can see the layout of his office and not worry about being noticed. The thing is—what if he has a partner? I'm not a murderer-murderer. You know that. I am not in the business of killing people willy-nilly."

Me-Too stopped nibbling her finger, rolled onto her belly and stared up at Graciela, as though the mention of killing people willy-nilly had her interest.

"Yes, I realize some would classify what I did to Cross as murder. But I'm not that type of murderer. I did not kill him for the usual low-brow reasons people kill. I did it to get the justice that I didn't receive years ago. I couldn't even report what they did. Cross laughed afterward and said no one would believe me and he was right. They were rich young men and I was a simple village girl. And justice always favors the rich."

"I hope he works alone. If Skinner doesn't...Me-Too, it distresses me to my core, but I might wind up accidentally taking an innocent life. It's morally reprehensible I know."

The cat jumped off the bed and onto the window sill.

The more she thought about the possibility, the more she doubted she'd go through with poisoning Skinner. There was no way to justify killing someone who hadn't done anything to her. But, she was getting ahead of herself. Maybe he worked solo.

****

The tram stopped at the corner of Chancery Lane and Fleet Street, steps from the New Law Courts. Graciela had read they'd relocated there. She'd never seen a courthouse and on the ride envisioned a dreary, dirty brick government building, not the fine one before her. She took time to admire the structure with its façade of Portland stone and diverse towers.

She wondered if the interior was as nice. For her, the question would go unanswered since she wasn't a lawyer, a judge, a witness, or a police officer. Females in the spectator section were frowned upon. The only other way to see the inside was as a prisoner. If by some quirk of fate it looked like she might become a suspect for the Cross and other killings, she'd do whatever necessary to avoid arrest. Whatever necessary. Not a worrisome problem though. The odds were slim to none of her ever becoming suspect. There was simply nothing to connect Cross and the others to her.

While she stood in front, several dozen bewigged and black-robed court officials entered, along with numerous citizens. The citizens might've been witnesses, victims, or spectators. The infamous crimes drew large crowds. It occurred to Graciela that Skinner was one of the wigged and robed officials who hurried by her and she missed seeing him. She headed toward his office, which was close to the courthouse, on the off chance he left it open.

"May I help you?"

Graciela jumped and turned at the sound of the voice. She'd been standing in front of Skinner's door studying the lock system. His seemingly impossible lock system. The door had thick glass panes inset with a medieval looking metal drop bar across it. A bar she hadn't the strength to lift without help.

She'd seen Skinner coming and going from his home. This might be his partner, although Skinner's was the only name on a plaque by the door.

"Are you Mr. Skinner?" Graciela asked, pretending she didn't know what he looked like. "I may be in need of a solicitor. What sort of legal work does Mr. Skinner do?"

"No, I'm his clerk. Mr. Skinner is a probate and general family law solicitor. He's not in at the moment. If you'd like to come in and give me your information, I can have him contact you."

What to do? Her panicked mind raced. Going in and seeing the layout of the place would give her a great advantage. But what could she tell the clerk? She'd have to give him false information that was obvious. But when Skinner tried to contact her and discovered the deception, his suspicions would be raised. She didn't need that. It'd be so much better if he were a criminal defense attorney. Their clients and client's families must lie to them all the time. He'd think nothing of another deception.

"Miss?"

"Thank you. I'd love to leave my information." She'd rather take a chance and see the inside. The false details wouldn't lead back to her.

He unlocked the door and needed to set his briefcase down to raise the bar, which took both hands. He held the door for her and she went inside.

The clerk gestured to a chair. "Please have a seat." He set his Gladstone Bag on the one desk in the outer room and removed a bundle of papers from inside.

From what Graciela could tell there were only two rooms to the office but Skinner might share the back office. "Does Mr. Skinner have a partner or associate?"

The clerk shook his head. "No."

At least she had that worry off her plate. Risk of the clerk having a nip shouldn't be a problem. Mrs. Zachary's solicitor was a stickler for propriety. He wasn't the sort to sit around sharing a brandy with an employee. Graciela didn't think a Belgrave Square toff like Skinner was the type either. Conversely, an employee who wanted to keep his job didn't nip into the boss's drink.

"What sort of legal work do you need done?"

"My elderly auntie has a small amount of property and requires a will," Graciela said, resisting the temptation to embellish. She found through personal experience that the more she added to a lie, the harder it was for her to remember every flourish.

"Mr. Skinner will need to meet with your aunt in person, of course."

"Of course."

The clerk went to a file cabinet and pulled out several forms. "Please fill these out with your aunt's information and yours. Mr. Skinner will make arrangements for a meeting. Would you like some tea while you're filling those out?"

"Thank you. That would be lovely."

The clerk went into the other office. Graciela hoped he'd leave the door open so she could sneak a glimpse but he shut it behind him. She skimmed the forms, searching for a question she'd ask clarification for.

She rose and knocked on the other office door. "Sir, I have a problem."

The door opened and she pointed to the line that asked about her aunt's age and state of mind. "I don't know her age for certain. She gives different years for her birthdate. I'm not sure how to explain her state of mind. It's good but she's a hair forgetful. Is that an acceptable answer?"

While she spoke she scanned the room. No rear door but there was a street level window facing the alley. The locking mechanism was an iron bar about a foot long attached to the frame and slid into a steel well in the sill. She'd seen the same type on many French doors. The lock presented possibilities.

In her peripheral vision she saw a decanter with what looked like claret or port in it, but no second decanter for brandy. Claret will do, as long as he drinks it.

She'd seen all she needed. Rather than continue with the charade she told the clerk, "Thank you for the offer of tea. But if you don't mind, I'm going to take the paperwork with me. I'll fill it out and return tomorrow. What hours does Mr. Skinner work?"

"He arrives precisely at 9:00 and has lunch at his club at 1:00. He leaves for the evening at 5:00. I'll check his schedule for tomorrow." The clerk turned the kettle off and came back out to his desk. "If you come at 10:00, he might have a few minutes to speak with you."

"I'll do that. Good day."

She went straight from Skinner's to the pub. She found the owner and sent a message to Addy asking to meet as soon as possible. A messenger came to Mrs. Zachary's midday. Addy would see her later that afternoon. She had to lie about a doctor's appointment to get the time off, which wound up costing her more time. Mrs. Zachary had insisted Graciela use the family carriage and driver if she wasn't feeling well. As a result, Graciela had to tell another lie and say her destination was Harley Street, where most of the decent doctors practiced. The carriage driver let her off in front of a building with several physician's offices.

"You needn't wait for me. I'll find a cab to bring me home."

"Mrs. Zachary will want me to wait."

"Please don't. If I'm feeling better, I may stop for a cup of tea. Please, it will be all right. You can go."

He touched a finger to the brim of his hat and turned pulled from the curb. She lingered in the doorway until the carriage was out of sight and then boarded a tram going the opposite direction toward the pub.

Graciela plopped onto the bench, breathless from her mad dash from the tram stop to the pub.

Addy pulled his stolen watch from his waistcoat pocket. "I was beginning to think you weren't coming."

"I had to work around a time-consuming deception to get away from my employer."

Addy raised his tankard and held up two fingers for the barmaid to see. "Why am here?"

"I've a lock I can't handle." She explained about the bar across the door. "There's a window with a lock I can work if you can show me how to cut glass."

"No worries there." He gave her an odd look over the rim of his tankard before draining what remained and setting it back down. "A bar across the front door. Strange business."

"No, it's—"

"Don't say another word. I don't want to know."

"This coming Monday, midday, in the alley here like before. I'll bring my cutting tools. The beer is on you next time."

She was on her way to revenge number two. She just had to time it so Skinner was there alone. Anticipation brought a smile.

Shouts from workmen outside on Oxford Street broke into her reverie. Her smile faded at the thought of all the foot traffic around Skinner's office. Even with the clerk gone, Skinner only had to yell out and help might come before she got him to drink the arsenic. She needed a means to compel him to remain silent and to drink.

"If you wanted to force someone to do your bidding, how would you go about it?" she asked Addy.

"Other than relying on my vast supply of charm?"

"Yes, a real person not a fantasy one susceptible to your imaginary charm."

"I'd use a weapon of some kind, a knife, a lead pipe, or a gun."

She couldn't wield a pipe with any efficiency, not against a man. A knife was too messy and again, a man would easily disarm her. Guns looked to be easy enough to handle. "Can you get me a gun? Something small to fit in my reticule if possible."

"Now you want a gun?" He gave her a long, pointed look.

She nodded. "A small one."

"I happen to have a Derringer I acquired on a job that I held off pawning." Addy waved away the barmaid who came with the beers he ordered. "Molly I've never wanted to know too much about what you're involved in but I'm concerned. Are you planning on killing someone? I'm not giving you a weapon if you are."

"No. Just scaring them into doing what I want."

"In that case, I'll loan the gun to you."

"Thank you."

We'll share a glass of wine Mr. Skinner. And when you think I've spared you by not shooting, that is when you'll truly begin to die.

Chapter Sixteen

Constable Flanders stormed over to Ruddy and Archie's desks. His laughing support team brought up the rear.

"Something troubling you, constable?" Ruddy asked although he could wager what the problem was.

"How much longer is this...?" Flanders made a sweeping two-handed gesture at the dress he wore. "This ridiculous nonsense going to go on? It's been five days and neither our team nor Young's have seen hide nor hair of the stocking thief. This is humiliating. It's not what I signed up for when I joined the police service and it's bloody damn hot in all these petticoats."

One of the team stepped forward and added, "He's angry because that drunk with the rheumy eyes at the White Hart pub squeezed his arse."

"Squeezed his arse and offered him sixpence for a storeroom shag," the other constable said, the team breaking into a laugh again.

Ruddy feigned a concerned frown. "Bad luck, Flanders. I take it you didn't have three pence for change." He couldn't keep a straight face. He, Archie, the support team and now Coopersmith and his partner, who'd been eavesdropping, all fell out laughing.

"Very funny, Bloodstone. But this isn't right, my having to bear the burden of wearing this foolishness. Why doesn't Archie's missus alter it to fit you and you parade around in it for a few days? After all, it's your case. I bet you wouldn't find it so funny then."

"I doubt she can alter it to fit me. Besides, even if she could, the disguise would be wasted on me. I am not as pretty as you, Flanders. I'd never be able to turn heads the way you do," Ruddy said.

"For the record, I hate you." Flanders turned to Archie. "What am I supposed to do about the furnace under these skirts? What does your wife do?"

"I haven't the foggiest. I can tell you she doesn't whinge the way you do. I'll ask her for suggestions."

"Since you're here, have you had any luck showing the suspect's picture?" Ruddy asked.

"Joking aside, the rheumy-eyed drunk said the suspect looked familiar. He thinks he's seen the fellow in there in the middle of the week around midday," Flanders said.

"We don't have to tell you, concentrate your patrol in that area," Archie told them.

Ruddy pulled a couple more drawings he'd made from his sketch pad and handed them to Flanders. "Give the barkeep at the White Hart a copy to hang in his backroom. If he sees the suspect, send for a copper right away. Ask if he's seen him at night. Leave the second copy with the closest pub to the White Hart. He likely drinks at it as well."

"Will do," Flanders said and the team left.

"What do you think?" Archie asked.

"I think our suspect is a day laborer who drinks when he's not on a job." Ruddy brought out the last drawings he had. He set them in a basket on his desktop so he'd remember to give them to the other team. He wanted the pub owners to hang them in their backrooms to really familiarize themselves with the suspect's face.

****

When his shift finished, Ruddy didn't bother going home to change. He went straight to Honeysuckle's hotel. This was her night off. He planned dinner at a nice restaurant first and from there they'd go to a fun music hall. No more ballets.

He didn't bring a large bouquet this time. Instead, he bought a nosegay of violets with a blue satin ribbon attached. The flower girl said the ribbon was so a lady could wear the flowers like a corsage on her wrist.

Ruddy knocked.

A hint of her rose-scented perfume wafted out when Honeysuckle opened the door. Unlike most ladies, she wore her dark hair down and pulled back on the sides with Mother of Pearl combs. He liked that she didn't wear it up like most women. Her dress was the color of burgundy wine. A thin deep red velvet choker with a pearl drop pendant drew his eyes to her delicate neck. He thought she looked like she should be on the cover of a fashion magazine—a fancy French one.

"You look lovely." He stepped inside and handed her the nosegay. "I'm afraid the violets clash with your dress."

"Any woman who complains of flowers given to

her by a handsome man clashing with her gown is a fool of a woman." She tugged matching wine colored evening gloves on. "The ribbon is too slippery. I need your help to tie this." She held her wrist out and he tied the ribbon in a bow with a double knot.

"Are you ready?"

Honeysuckle picked up her shawl from a chair by the door and laid it across her arm. "Ready."

After dinner Ruddy hailed a cab. "I thought we'd go to the Oxford Music Hall unless you preferred someplace else."

"The Oxford is fine with me. I know the Master of Ceremonies there. He's a multi-talented creature I tell you. Not a bad singer and dancer, he can fill in for a juggler when the need arises. If you keep the tricks simple, he can manage a bit of sleight of hand," Honeysuckle said. "His real talent and this is a talent, trust me, is generating excitement and lots of audience response to the acts."

"I take it you worked with him?" Ruddy asked, helping her into the carriage.

"I used to when I was new and still in the chorus."

"Why aren't you at the Oxford now?"

"The Odeon pays better and they agreed to everything I asked for in my contract."

It sounded like she conducted the negotiations without the help of an agent or solicitor. Ruddy didn't know much about the entertainment world but a woman in any profession entering into a business agreement without using a man as her advisor and representative? Unheard of. "You negotiated your own contract? You couldn't."

"I can and I did. Why not? I knew what the Oxford was willing to offer me for another year. I knew the Odeon wanted me. After all, they sought me out. Before I sat down with them, I told the owners I had a list of things I wanted. I said I would only consider moving if they were willing to negotiate."

Her reasoning was logical but it still didn't completely explain why she thought to go into the talks alone. "When you said that, did you intend at the time to try and transact a deal without a male agent?"

She leaned over and kissed him light and quick. She caught him by surprise, but he recovered quickly and bent to kiss her better. The carriage took a hard bounce on the cobblestones and he missed her lips and brushed her forehead instead. It wasn't what he was going for, but a kiss is a kiss.

"I wanted to kiss that shocked look off your face," she said, leaning back again. "In answer to your question, yes, I intended to conduct the negotiation by myself. I didn't and don't need a man to speak for me. I have a voice. I was and am perfectly capable of asking for what I want. I am quite adept at telling people yes or no when necessary."

"I believe you. But I have to say, I am flabbergasted at your willingness to take such a risk in spite of your confidence. In my line of work I see how easy it is for men to take advantage of women."

She laughed softly. "I'm sure you do, Rudyard. However, I don't see what I did as taking a big risk. As long as we're all speaking English, I knew I'd be fine. I understand words and their meaning."

Ruddy could only shake his head. He knew too well how some men wouldn't hesitate to take advantage of her gender's naturally more susceptible character. It took a special lady to keep them at bay.

The carriage stopped and Ruddy extended his hand to assist her to the sidewalk. "I'm still allowed to help you in and out of carriages and whatnot, right?" he teased. When she stepped on the bottom rung of the cab's ladder and her ear was level with his mouth, he whispered, as he lifted her the rest of the way to the sidewalk, "and do this too?"

Honeysuckle tipped her head a fraction and gave him a flirtatious smile. "I said I can speak for myself. I never said I can do everything for myself."

For a moment, the overwhelming temptation to load her back into the carriage and dash back to her hotel swept over him. But her boldness didn't mean she was less a lady than other women, so he slipped her arm through his.

Ruddy heard at the time it was built the Oxford's elegant façade, which was extraordinary for a music hall, had all of London abuzz. After seeing the building for himself, with its twin towers of carved stonework, rows of Palladian windows, and the mix of tall Ionic and Doric columns in between, he agreed it deserved every compliment.

The maître 'd' recognized Honeysuckle and showed them to box seats on the ground floor marked *reserved*. All the times he'd gone to music hall shows, Ruddy had never sat in the box seats. He'd been inside the Oxford before but always stood at the bar to watch the show. The Oxford's box seats were as elegant as the building's exterior. The chairs were covered in plush crimson velvet with an ebony table in between, while velvet curtains and mahogany folding doors shut out the noise of the crowd walking by in the hall. Brass railings topped the curved wall of each box and a similar railing ran along the bottom for guests to rest their feet.

Honeysuckle and Ruddy were discussing which champagne to order when a bottle arrived at the table compliments of the house. The waiter poured each a glass and replaced the bottle in a chilled bucket.

"Apparently, they miss you," Ruddy said. "As they should."

The Master of Ceremonies and the chorus opened the show with a toast to the Queen and then a rousing version of *If It Wasn't For the Houses in Between*. After he finished he introduced Honeysuckle and asked her to join them on stage for a song or two.

She stood when he'd introduced her but shook her head at the invite. "No thank you. I'm here with someone. We just want to enjoy the show."

"If you want to go up and sing, don't feel like you have to say no because of me. I'll be all right. It's good publicity for your show," Ruddy told her when she sat down.

"I don't need the publicity. I already play to packed houses or didn't you notice?"

"I've noticed quite a bit about you. I'm a detective—a trained observer you know." He winked.

"Fancy meeting you here."

Ruddy turned at the sound of the familiar voice of a man he despised. Napier was there with another man. "Good evening, Napier."

"Evening," he replied, his eyes fixed on Honeysuckle. "Aren't you going to introduce me, Bloody?"

Honeysuckle wrapped her right hand around Ruddy's arm gave his elbow a slight squeeze. "Bloody? What does he mean? Why did he call you that?"

Ruddy turned to her. "It's a ridiculous label he likes to call me."

"Since Bloody has neglected to it, I'll introduce myself." Napier reached in front of Ruddy and extended his hand. "Nathaniel Napier."

Ruddy laid his hand over her right. Honeysuckle made no effort to move her hand from under his, ignoring Napier's gesture. "Honeysuckle Flowers."

"I thought I recognized you." It was the man next to Napier. "You're the star at the Odeon Music Hall. I saw your show last spring. Names Ignatius Yarrow but everyone calls me Iggy."

Napier shot a weak smile toward Ruddy before smiling broadly at Honeysuckle. "A star at the Odeon, I'm impressed, I'll make it a point to see your act. I can't imagine how Bloody here managed to talk you into spending the evening with him. But I wish you both a lovely time. Nice meeting you." He and Iggy sat at a table across the room.

"You never said why that Napier fellow calls you Bloody," Honeysuckle said.

"He uses it to mock my military past."

"The two of you hate each other, that's obvious."

"Hate is a strong word. I find him a vile

bootlicker. I'd rather share a table with a wharf rat than with him, but I don't hate him."

Honeysuckle sat up higher and kissed his cheek. "Interesting distinction."

****

They stayed for one show and left. By London theatre goers' standards the evening was still young. At the hotel Ruddy walked Honeysuckle to her room. He hoped for a good kiss or two at the door. He'd ask to see her again, say goodnight, and then go home and read for a while.

He bent to kiss her but she pulled away and asked, "Would you like to come in?"

"I'd love to," he said taken by surprise. He had to work in the morning but he was one of those fortunate people who didn't require a lot of sleep.

Before they'd gone out, she'd left instructions with the front desk for the concierge to light the lamps in the main room of her suite. She didn't want to return to a dark chamber.

"It's nice they turned lights on for you. I wonder if they aren't concerned about the fire when a guest is out though," Ruddy said.

"They make periodic checks, I'm told." She poured him an Irish whiskey and herself a scotch and handed him his drink. "Hear that?"

Violin music drifted up from the street. The faint strains of a waltz filled the room. "It's coming from that busker we passed in front of the hotel."

The suite's French doors led to a small balcony. Honeysuckle opened them and stepped onto the two-person stone semi-circle. Ruddy joined her.

"Strauss," she said, swaying to the melody. "Do you dance?"

"I do." He took her by the hand and led her back inside. He set their glasses on a lamp table and they waltzed.

"Where did you learn to dance? The combination of coppers and dancing doesn't fit together in my head," she asked.

"I learned in Africa when I was in the army. When we weren't in the field, the younger men were requested to attend when balls were given by important officials. Men were in short supply and the ladies of the region needed dance partners. A local nurse taught me."

"Were you an officer?"

Ruddy chuckled. "I'm the son of a Welsh farrier. Our family had neither the influence nor the money to purchase commissions."

"Your brother has some rank."

"Sergeant-Major, yes. He's risen as far as he can."

The music stopped.

"Shall we sit?" Honeysuckle asked, retrieving their drinks.

They sat side by side on the sofa. "Why doesn't he retire and join the force? The two of you could work together."

"He wants to be a Yeoman Warder. To qualify for recommendation, he needs to have twenty-two years of military service. He has to stay four more."

"Yeoman Warder. Impressive. I hope he gets it.

What about you? Detective Inspector is impressive as well but later on do you want to be a Superintendent or Commissioner? What about Scotland Yard? Don't all detectives aspire to work there?"

"Many do. I don't. I like working Holborn Station. I've worked that part of London since I started with London Metro. I'm comfortable with the people and the area. It has a certain sensibility that I understand. As for being a Superintendent or higher, that's not me. I don't want to be that toffee-nosed fellow ordering lads about from on high. If something is afoot, I want to be in the mix."

"You're an interesting man, Rudyard, I like that." She set both their glasses on the butler's table and then scooted very close. "Want to canoodle? I—"

He kissed her before she could say another word. Her candor threw him. He'd never met a woman like her—but no worries, he could adjust.

She was the first to break off the kiss but continued to keep her lips a hairsbreadth from his. "I like the way you answer," she said, smiling up at him.

"I like your question."

Chapter Seventeen

The following morning Archie arrived at the station the same time as Ruddy. "Bore da, Arch, and a fine morning it is," Ruddy said and opened the door for his partner.

"Good morning to you too. You're grinning like a cat sitting in a bucket of mackerel. It's unusual for you to dip into your native tongue. Thank you by the way for using one of the easier Welsh phrases as they're not too many. I can only surmise you had a lovely evening with Miss Flowers."

"I did indeed. One of the best in memory."

Archie's brows nearly disappeared into his hairline with curiosity.

"You're desperate for details I know, which I'm not going to get into. Suffice it to say, we had a wonderful time together. I hope to see her again soon."

"Of course I'm curious. We've been partners a long time. We've shared a lot. I thought today would be no different. You haven't been this happy since Evangeline left. And no offense, but Miss Flowers being in the entertainment field and...well you know..."

Ruddy pulled Archie into a corner of the lobby out of earshot. "I don't like your inference. She's a lady who happens to be a talented singer and dancer."

Archie raised his hands in mock surrender. "Sorry, again, no offense meant."

He couldn't get too angry with Archie, actresses and female entertainers of any kind had unsavory reputations. Most were well deserved. He had made a conscious decision before asking her out that whatever past she had, was just that, the past. What mattered to him was the present.

"I'll not tolerate any ugly innuendo. Understood?"

"Understood."

Both detectives walked on but then stopped in the doorway of the detective bureau. Marsden was sitting by Ruddy's desk, puffing away on his pipe.

"Not the way I want to start the day," Archie said.

"What can he want this early?" Ruddy continued toward his desk where the reporter had dragged over a chair.

"Good morning, detectives," Marsden said and took a couple more puffs off his pipe. The smoke and acrid smell from cheap tobacco forming a haze around Ruddy and Archie's desks. "I'd love a cup of tea. I'd have gotten it myself but don't want to be pushy. Would one of you be kind enough?"

Ruddy waved the cloud of smoke from in front of his face. "You've feet. Get your own tea."

"I'm getting one for Ruddy and myself. You can shift for yourself," Archie said.

"Such shabby treatment even though I come with news that will help you," Marsden said.

"Fine, I'll bring you one as well," Archie said with disgust.

"What news, Marsden?" Ruddy asked.

"I've been at Kelly's Athletic Club daily. I really am going to do a story on the ring and the boxers there once this business for you is finished."

Ruddy expected Marsden to lose interest in spying for him. Or at the very least, offer little to no information of use.

"Go on," Ruddy said.

"Take no offense to what I'm going to say."

"That's the second time I've heard that this morning. I'm offended by the perceived need for the warning. Just tell me what you found out."

Archie returned. "Did I miss anything?"

Ruddy shook his head. "No."

Marsden took a sip of tea, then said, "What a scruffy, unwholesome lot who fight and gather there. I'd not like to meet any of them in an alley at night."

"Yes, they're a seedy group. Get to the meat of your purpose," Ruddy urged, cutting a circle in the air with his finger. Everyone and their mother knew the boxing crowd drew a hodge-podge of participants and followers. The majority of them were lowlifes from all over London.

Marsden moved his tea and rested both arms on Ruddy's desk. The times they were together he'd only seen Marsden in two different frock coats. The one he wore today bore the same frayed cuffs and collars as the other. Ruddy had a split-second's curiosity about the reporter's financial state. As he cared little for the man, his interest waned fast as it came.

Chris Karlsen

"I've never seen you fight," Marsden said, leaning in, speaking directly to Ruddy. "You never told me why exactly I was to act as a mole, but I'm not the total fool you take me for. I also overheard that London City detective, Napier, talking to another boxer about possibly fighting you."

Napier was bound to blab to all and sundry at his station. Ruddy had the slim hope news of any future fight would be kept between only the police agencies. Two coppers fighting, would have every ne'er-do-well and reprobate at Napier's athletic club would be chomping at the bit to witness that. No matter where it was held half the men from Kelly's would come and wager.

"Let's say that's true. How does you're not having seen me fight come into the situation?" Ruddy asked.

"I have to speak up for Ruddy here, Marsden," Archie interjected. "We had our share of fights with street toughs. When the fisticuffs start flying, you can't ask for a better man to have next to you. Don't underestimate him."

Ruddy started to speak but Marsden cut him off to respond to Archie, "Please, let me finish. What you say Holbrook speaks to my point. I've no doubt Bloodstone can hold his own with most any back alley ruffian. What Napier and those fellows in the club are doing is different." He turned from Archie to Ruddy. "A street fight has no rules. That boxing business is nothing but rules. I believe those rules, because they're alien to you, will trip you up. Napier has the advantage because he knows what's coming and you don't and what you're used to countering with won't work or be allowed."

"I know the rules are a problem. Why do you think we asked you to be a mole and take note of his weaknesses?" Ruddy asked, irritated with Marsden for saying what he didn't want to hear, irritated he couldn't tamp down the nagging worry he might lose.

"I've come up with an idea," Marsden said.

"I'm listening," Ruddy said.

"I noticed they use several older boxers as sparring partners for the younger men. The older fighters have all the moves." Marsden mimicked a boxer's left and right hook. "They have the footwork. They're just not as agile or fast anymore."

Ruddy didn't see the point. "What's that to do with me?"

"You could use a sparring partner who knows the moves and the rules."

"That's a good idea," Archie said in a surprised tone, looking over at Ruddy who nodded.

"Do you know one?" Ruddy asked. "I can't use one from there, obviously."

"I do. I scouted around and found a fellow at a Spitalfields athletic club. To describe the place as dodgy and dirty would be a kindness. I'd be hard put to name a place with a larger group of slippery rascals. That said, there's a man there, a former boxer about the same height as Napier, older so he's a tad thinner but close enough to Napier's girth. I figure you need to practice with someone similar to the man you'll be facing."

"Again, you're spot on, Marsden," Ruddy said.

"Did you ask him if he'd work with me?"

Marsden shook his head. "Thought I'd better talk to you first."

"Where is the club and who do I ask for?"

"A&E Athletic Club on Brick Lane, ask for Tony Critchlow." Marsden had it written down already on a card he handed to Ruddy.

From what Marsden said, it was possible the club owners were part of a criminal organization. Ruddy wondered if Napier had ever considered looking into the owner of Kelly's background. Ruddy didn't fancy getting associated with known criminals. Although as long as they didn't know who he worked for, if any unlawful activity was going on there, Napier could track it and build a case while working out. Just because Kelly's was hoity-toity compared to other athletic clubs didn't mean the owner wasn't involved in nefarious activity.

"What's the A & E stand for?" he asked.

"It's the initials of the owners of the building and the club. They're Jewish and don't want the people they associate with to know they own such a place."

"This is good. Thank you," Ruddy told Marsden. "I'm going there today."

"You can't miss Critchlow. He's the one that looks like he was running full speed and didn't stop in time for the wall," Marsden said.

Considering the damage that could happen to his face, Ruddy wondered why a preening peacock like Napier had taken up boxing.

Ruddy expected Marsden to leave but he stayed sipping the rest of his tea, which had to have grown cold. When he finished he said, "Let's not forget our agreement."

"Agreement?" Archie asked.

"I'm to have an exclusive on the stocking thief case. Is there anything new?"

"Sadly no," Ruddy told him.

Marsden gave him a skeptical look.

"Honestly. We have two teams working the area. So far nothing. We'll keep our bargain. If we get someone in custody, we'll send a runner to your office straightaway."

"I appreciate it. Let me know what Critchlow says. I'm sure he'll agree. I'd be surprised if he didn't need the money."

"I wonder how much he'll want," Archie said.

"From the look of him, I'd say he'd be happy with a jam butty, a pint, and a couple of crowns."

"We'll see," Ruddy said.

****

Marsden was right. Critchlow appeared every bit like a man who'd lost an encounter with a brick wall. With a head square as a shovel, a forehead broad as a man's palm, a nose which might've been hawkish once but now lay flat as possible while still allowing breath, Ruddy wouldn't attempt to guess how many beatings he'd taken. Critchlow's hair was a coarse black mass shot with grey that stuck out in all directions. The unkempt thatch did nothing to soften the man's rough appearance.

"Not to be unkind, but doesn't it look like a skunk has nested on his head?" Archie asked low.

"It does."

"He also looks a little touched in the head, if you ask me."

In Ruddy's experience, sometimes those folks turned out to be surprisingly gentle. Sometimes. "One way to find out."

He and Archie had taken the precaution of hiding their shields before entering the club. "Mr. Critchlow." Ruddy drew the boxer's attention as they approached. The fighter had been picking up equipment left strewn around.

Critchlow stopped tidying. "What?" He eyed Ruddy and Archie suspiciously. "I don't owe no money. So whatever you're here about, you've no quarrel with me."

"I have a possible business proposition and an associate recommended I speak to you regarding the matter," Ruddy said.

"Business? Me? I don't know anything about business. I'm just a fighter."

"It's regarding a boxing proposition." Ruddy stepped closer. "Is there a place we can talk in private?"

Critchlow nodded. "This way. I've a room here. The owner lets me stay in exchange for my cleaning up."

They were led past a three-tiered row of benches Ruddy assumed the owners reserved for spectators who bet the highest. Everyone else would crowd around the ring jostling each other for the best view. Kelly's tried to claim a better class of spectator and had installed two multi-tiered benches and chairs for the richer gamblers.

Critchlow lived in a tiny room in the back off the

alley entrance. The space consisted of a narrow bed covered with a shabby wool blanket, a pillow with no cotton cover, a scarred wooden table, one chair, one lamp, and a small two-drawer dresser. Except for the lamp and dresser, Ruddy thought his living quarters were comparable to a cell at Newgate Prison. Sad for a free man. Ruddy thought waking up to it day in and day out had to wear on a man's soul.

Out of the corner of his eye, he saw Archie take a deep breath through his mouth when Critchlow's back was to them. Ruddy had started breathing through his mouth when the boxer first opened the door. The room had the same eye-watering stench of a cell in Newgate: the odor of a resident who doesn't care anymore.

"Please sit," Critchlow indicated the bed.

"No thank you. We're fine standing," Ruddy said and forced a smile.

"I've a bit of tea if you'd like some."

"We're good. Let me get right to my purpose. I need coached in boxing, proper boxing, like in the ring. I've done my fair share of street fighting. I don't know how to fight within the rules of the ring. I'd like you to help me learn enough to hold my own. I'm willing to pay you," Ruddy explained.

"It's not easy. It's hard work. Lord knows I can use the dosh, but you can't learn enough to stay off the ropes with just a lesson or two. Plan on several weeks at least."

"All right."

This club, in this location, there was the outside chance Ruddy might run into someone who knew he was a detective. They might not be someone he arrested as this wasn't part of Holborn's district. But it might be someone who was in court when he testified or on another routine detail. Just in case, he'd rather not take a chance.

"I'd like to start tomorrow. Is there a time when no one else is here? I prefer to work in private."

"Early is best. Can you come at 7:00 a.m.?"

"Yes." That gave Ruddy time to work out with Critchlow, grab a cab home to cleanup, and be at his desk by 9:00. "You haven't asked how much I'm willing to pay."

"Don't matter. Whatever it is, it's more than I've got in my pocket now."

"We've a deal. I'll see you tomorrow." He dug into his waistcoat and retrieved a pound. "Here." He handed it to the boxer.

"What's this for? I haven't earned any money yet."

"It's a deposit. I want to make sure you remember."

Critchlow laughed. "I'll be here. I'm not going anywhere."

As they were leaving Ruddy noticed a shadowbox on the dresser with a medal inside. He picked it up for closer inspection. "This is a Kabul to Kandahar Star. You made that devil of a march?"

Critchlow nodded.

"When were you discharged?"

"I was cashiered out in 1882."

He'd been dishonorably discharged for some offense. "What did you do?"

"Struck an officer."

"What did he do?"

"He was a lieutenant and a self-righteous, full-of-himself prig."

Ruddy chuckled at what was common knowledge. "All lieutenants are full of themselves."

"He was a liar and a bully. One day I just tired of his nonsense and malicious lies so I knocked him on his arse."

Ruddy set the medal box down and dug out another pound. "Here."

"What's this one for?" Critchlow asked but quickly stuffed both pounds in his trouser pocket.

"From all of us who wanted to knock a lieutenant on their arse and didn't take the opportunity."

"You're a veteran?"

"24th Regiment South Wales Borderers."

"What I did felt good at the time. It came with high consequences."

"Most things that feel good *at the time* do."

"As I've discovered," Critchlow said in the tone of a man who's given up. He fingered the pound note and then looked up at Ruddy with weary eyes. "I should've checked my temper. Worst mistake I ever made, hitting the lieutenant. I liked the army. There was nothing for me in civilian life." He spread his hands out. "As you can see."

Ruddy had no words of consolation to offer him. As far as he could tell, the man was right. He'd made a major mistake and now paid a heavy price. Ruddy had no great fondness for army life and was happy to leave it behind. But for some men, the discipline, the routine is what they need. They need the sense of purpose the army gives them and the camaraderie.

"'Til tomorrow then," Ruddy said.

"Oh, I never got your name."

"Rudyard Bloodstone."

"Call me Tony."

"Call me Rudyard or Ruddy."

Tony shook his head. "Not while I'm in your employ. You're Mr. Bloodstone to me."

"Your choice."

As Ruddy stepped through the door Tony said, "I'll have an extra pint and a pie with real meat in it tonight on you, Mr. Bloodstone."

"Good. See you tomorrow."

Outside Archie said, "Two quid is more than that poor man has seen at one time in a year. He looks like the right person to teach you what you need to know though."

"I expect I'll find myself on my arse a whole lot in the coming weeks. Better it's from him than Napier."

"Napier is not going to expect you to know anything about Marquess of Queensberry Rules. He'll figure to run roughshod over you."

Ruddy smiled. "I'm counting on it."

****

After his lesson the next day, Ruddy spent the entire shift catching up on paperwork for his open case. The whole time he was trying and failing not to dwell on his miserable performance working out with Tony. He'd secretly believed he'd do better than he did in spite of being a beginner at the sport.

He ignored Archie's glances his way that went from curious to concerned as the first hour after morning roll call wore on. Ruddy hadn't finished his first cup of tea before Archie finally said, "You're very quiet. How did your lesson go?"

"I don't feel like talking about it."

Archie recoiled slightly like he'd been slapped. "We've always spoken freely with each other." He leaned in. "What happened? Tell me."

"Nothing terrible. I just don't want to discuss it right now."

"Ruddy, you..."

"Leave off the subject, Arch," Ruddy snapped, instantly regretting it.

Archie looked more worried than hurt. It was one of the qualities Ruddy appreciated the most about him. He'd put what a friend might be going through at a particular moment ahead of his personal injury.

"Sorry, Arch. The time's not right. Later maybe."

"Sure Ruddy."

Neither broached the subject the rest of the day. Ruddy and Archie kept their conversation to talk related to current cases. At the end of watch, Ruddy went straight home.

****

Ruddy hadn't even opened the boarding house front door when the aroma of Mrs. Goodge's evening meal washed over him. Whatever she was preparing it included sautéed onions. Onions being fried in butter, bread baking, and bacon cooking were three of the world's best smells. If you wanted to get him drooling like a junkyard dog, get those going on the stove.

He immediately headed for the kitchen. Mrs. Goodge would invite him to share the evening meal with the rest of the boarders. She always asked and meals came with his rent. But having grown up in a family of ten children and then spending nine years in the military eating with a company of men, he had no interest in sharing a table with large groups of people.

Besides the delicious smells from her kitchen drawing him like a lemming, he'd more than likely find Winky, the starving stray dog he adopted the year before in there. Mrs. Goodge watched the pup during the day while Ruddy worked. Winky was a regular sentinel in the kitchen at mealtimes, ready to snag any morsel that might fly from the skillet.

"Good evening, Mrs. Goodge." Ruddy perched over her cast iron fry pan, closed his eyes and inhaled. "Sautéed carrots and onions, they'll set a man's mouth-watering and stomach rumbling." He opened his eyes. "What are you making?"

"Good evening yourself, Mr. Bloodstone. It's shepherd's pie tonight. Does this mean you'll be staying and dining with us?"

"No, but thank you. I'm going to have a hot bath and then I am going out. Where's Winky?" he asked, looking around and not seeing him.

Just then the wire-haired bundle of canine energy raced in and leapt into Ruddy's arms as he did every night. Right behind was ten-year-old Luke, the son of a widow boarder of Mrs. Goodge's. All skinned elbows and knobby knees, Luke reminded Ruddy of himself at that age. The memory lightened the dour mood he'd been in all day.

"Luke, how would you like to earn sixpence?" Ruddy asked, knowing the boy never had sixpence to himself before. Sixpence to a ten-year-old was like six-hundred quid to a grown man.

Luke answered with a vigorous nod. "Yes, Mr. Bloodstone sir."

Ruddy gave each of Winky's ears a good scratch and then set him down. "Bring ten pails of hot water to my flat. I'll give you an extra tuppence if you can bring five additional ones. I've a mind to soak in a hot tub for a while. Can you handle that many pails up three flights?"

"No worries, sir."

In his flat, Ruddy shrugged out of his frock coat. Like always, he took time to brush off the city's dust before hanging it up in the armoire. All the frock coats and morning coats he owned were expensive, for a man of his modest means anyway. Suits and a decent set of shirts made of good material were a promise he made to himself years before when he was a young constable. He never doubted his ability and always believed he'd be promoted. Then he'd have the money he needed. As a child, he wore nothing but badly worn out cotton and linen hand-me-downs from his brothers. Serving her Majesty in the army he wore the roughest, itchiest, most godawful wool, and as a young Peeler the wool wasn't much better. It was that first year with London Metro he made himself the promise.

Ruddy left the door ajar so Luke could come and go. The last of the buckets of water filled the tub a little more than halfway. Ruddy was the only tenant with a private bathroom. He also had the entire top floor to himself, two rooms plus the bathroom. Mrs. Goodge liked having a policeman on the premises and rented the larger space to him for the same price as the smaller flats. He'd looked forward to a long hot bath all day. After his lesson, he'd cleaned up before going to the station, but that was a quick, cold bath. His sore muscles needed this soothing hot one.

"Did you catch any dangerous criminals today, murderers or masked highwaymen? Did you arrest anyone due for a hanging?" Luke asked, wiping away sweat from his forehead with his shirttail.

"Aren't you the bloodthirsty one? Sorry lad, not today." Ruddy had started removing his starched collar and shirt cuffs but stopped. He sat on the curved edge of the tub so he was closer in height to Luke. "Never wish to see a man hang, Luke. It's a terrible, terrible thing to witness, a sight that'll forever be a dark stain on your heart."

Ruddy stood and began unbuttoning his dress shirt.

"If you say so, sir." Luke dropped down onto the bathroom stool, clearly disappointed. When his mother came to live at the boarding house the year before, Luke's low opinion of Peelers was typical of boys his age. They heard the worst about cops from the broadsheets and many of the men in their lives who had run-ins with law enforcement. Luke's opinion began to change as he got to know Ruddy, who'd done his best to let him see the other side of the story. He also wanted the lad to have a more positive male influence in his life.

"Tell you what, we're working a case at the moment where the man we're hunting steals lady's stockings. When we find him, how about I bring you to the station and you can see him in lockup? It's not exciting as a highwayman. You'll not be allowed past the lockup door; but afterward, I'll take you around the rest of the station."

Luke popped up. "Oh would you? I'd like that very much."

"It's a promise."

Luke looked at him, clearly baffled. Ruddy thought you could almost see the gears and wheels of confusion grinding away in the lad's head. "What's the thief want with ladies stockings? Sounds like a silly thing to want."

Ruddy gave himself a mental kick. He should've anticipated a young boy's natural curiosity, having been one. He had to think fast. He certainly didn't want to discuss the thief's odd sexual proclivities with the lad. "He'll sell them on street corners to unsuspecting women. Now off with you. I need to undress and soak. I was hit by a locomotive called Tony today and am sore as the devil."

"Did you beat him back?"

"It wasn't that kind of fight. No, I spent a lot of time learning how not to be trounced. When I'm done, I'm going out. I'll give you a shout and you can come empty the tub."

Winky had lain patiently on the rug by the tub. He wagged his tail and watched with innocent eyes as Ruddy removed his boots. Ruddy wasn't fooled. Winky was an incorrigible sock thief. The moment Ruddy had his off, the chase would be on so he put his shoes and socks out of reach. The act resulted in a spurt of rebellious barking.

"This is why everyone says I'm a bad parent. These temper tantrums on your part," Ruddy admonished Winky. "At least you kept your crime to the gnawing of sock toes and heels." He gave Winky a pat on the head.

"Shall I walk Winky while you're out?" Luke still hadn't left but dawdled rearranging Ruddy's toiletries. Ruddy recognized the stall as a gamble for another pence or two. Ruddy was torn between pride and fear that he'd sparked a wicked mercenary streak in the lad.

"I'm taking him with me but thank you for the offer." Ruddy winced as he stripped down to his trousers. The left side of his ribcage hadn't discolored but was bruised enough to ache when his arm bumped the area. He didn't want to undress completely in front of Luke and told him, "Time to go. I want to soak before the water grows cold."

"What happened to your arm?" Luke pointed to the puckered skin of the burn scar on Ruddy's forearm.

"I was in a hospital fire many years ago."

"Did it hurt bad?"

"Yes."

"Does it still hurt?"

"Sometimes, when I sit too close to a fireplace with that side to the fire. Enough questions. Run along now."

Luke finally left and Ruddy hurried taking the rest of his clothes off. He moaned as the warm water soothed his aching muscles. The morning workout with Tony had left him drenched necessitating that fast cool bath before going to the station. He sank down into the hot water until it was up to his neck. The warmth felt like heaven to his battered body. His shoulders and arms had taken the brunt of exercise. They screamed in protest throughout the day whenever he moved wrong. He rested his head against the tub, closed his eyes and just relaxed, wiggling his toes and feet, the only parts of him that didn't ache.

Of course, Archie wanted to know how the session went. Ruddy wasn't ready to admit how embarrassed he was by his performance. He considered himself in good physical condition, far better than most. From the look of him, Tony had ten years on him. Ruddy figured a decade of hard living had to take a toll. Maybe it had but if so, then Tony was a force to be reckoned with in his younger years. Fast on his feet, quick with his hands, the jabs came at an insane pace. Ruddy hadn't taken a blow to the face. For pride's sake, he'd like to think it was due to an action he'd taken. He suspected that saving grace was more because of Tony not aiming for his face than any block Ruddy put up.

He stayed in the tub until the water turned lukewarm. After dressing, he went through his flat opening windows. On hot nights like tonight, most Londoners opened their windows in hopes the evening might bring a cool breeze from the river.

"Winky, come." Winky trotted over, tail wagging in anticipation of whatever adventure awaited them outside. A bundle of energy from the first day Ruddy had him, Winky loved exploring. Ruddy buckled the leash he made himself to a fine leather collar Archie and Margaret bought for the dog as a gift. On the way out of the boarding house Ruddy knocked on the widow's door. Luke answered.

"I'm done. Ask Mrs. Goodge for the key to my room. Empty the tub and when you're done, lock the door and give her the key back. Here's the six pence. If you don't do a proper job, I'll be getting my coin back from you," Ruddy warned.

"I'll go right now." Luke pushed past him and ran toward the landlady's room.

****

Ruddy's favorite table at the Boot and Bayonet was empty. It was one of Morris's smaller tables. Most of his customers didn't like sitting at it, as they had no room to play checkers or cards with more than two players. Ruddy wasn't big on either game so the table suited him. Winky sat at his feet gnawing on a marrow bone Ruddy brought with him to tide the dog over until dinner.

"Are you eating tonight?" June, Morris's granddaughter asked, setting a tankard of Ruddy's favorite beer down on the table.

"I am. Do you happen to have any shepherd's pie?"

"Not tonight. There's some left over from last night, if you'd like, we can reheat that for you."

"I'll take a big bowl for me and a small bowl for Winky." Ruddy stretched his legs out and leaned back to watch a game of darts with half-hearted interest.

Morris pulled a chair over from another table and joined Ruddy. "Is something wrong? You look like you just got assigned a month of latrine duty."

Ruddy shook his head, thinking there wasn't any point in discussing the problem. Morris couldn't help. Nobody could really help. "Nothing's wrong." Then he changed his mind. At least Morris offered an objective ear and would listen without prejudice. "That's not true. I have a potential problem at work."

June brought Morris a tankard without him asking. "You?" He looked genuinely surprised. "A problem at work? You're not on the fiddle, I know that. You've never been one to sneak about with another chap's wife, I can't see you as one of those sly boots Peelers who will lie about a man to justify an arrest. What's that leave?" Morris took a long pull from the tankard and eyed Ruddy over the rim while he pondered possibilities. He swallowed. Eyes wide, he set the tankard down and said, "Bloody hell, you beat someone good."

"No, but you're on the right trail."

Morris raised his tankard and took another swig while gesturing for Ruddy to go on.

"There's a good chance this bootlicker from the City agency is going to challenge me to a fight."

Morris shrugged. "So. You've been in dozens of fights. You haven't been trounced yet. What's the worry?" he asked and set his beer down.

"I haven't been in this type of fight. The bootlicker is the boxing champion of their agency."

"Boxing champ as in Marquess of Queensberry type of champ?"

Ruddy nodded.

"I don't know much about that style of fighting.

I've never been a fan. Is it that different than how you've fought?"

Different? Is lamb different than beef? "Yes. They're both meat but far from the same. Street fisticuffs and boxing are both fighting but they're more dissimilar than similar."

June brought the shepherd's pies. The bone cast aside Winky jumped up, his attention fixed on the bowl coming his way. Ruddy sprinkled salt on his pie without tasting first, a habit his mother chastised him for whenever he went home. Morris didn't notice or if he did, said nothing. After the salting, Ruddy dug into the delicious-smelling meal.

"You can take some lessons and learn the little differences, can't you?" Morris asked.

"Took my first lesson this morning. What a disaster. I stumbled around like a three-legged dog. I fell into the ropes more times than I care to count. Other times I floundered about completely unable to get my arms and legs to work together. A match is divided into rounds of three minutes each. For some inexplicable reason, I became obsessed with the time limitation. It kept preying on my mind that I had to get loads of hits in before the time ended. My foolish distraction was a horrible detriment which only added to my clumsiness."

"The bootlicker hasn't challenged you yet, right?"

"Right."

"He might not. All this worry could be for naught."

He gave Morris his best *you're smoking opium*

if you believe that look. "A confrontation between us has been brewing for a long time. Sadly, I stand a good chance of losing to the arrogant toady."

"So you lose," Morris said, shrugging the possibility off. "You've lost a few in the past. Life goes on."

"You don't understand. I'll never hear the end of it. I'll get an earful from him every time our paths cross. I don't doubt I'll get a ration of scurrilous nonsense even when I cross paths with his co-workers. I can hear them now: Bloodstone-you're the fellow Napier sent crashing to the floor. That will be followed by a jolly belly laugh." Ruddy drained his tankard and raised it high for June to see he needed a refill.

"You've a voice. Say no if he challenges you. There's nothing carved in stone that says you have to accept this Napier's challenge."

"Then I'd get labeled a coward."

"You've a bit of a pickle on your hands, my friend."

June brought another beer along with two shot glasses of rum. Ruddy had known Morris's granddaughter since she was a young girl. Morris and his wife, Bess, raised her after she'd lost both her parents to influenza when she was still small. She was a lovely young woman now. Ruddy had never seen her parents but June had inherited much of her looks from Morris and Bess. She had her grandmother's light brown hair and freckles and Morris's dark brown eyes and cleft chin. When she smiled, deep dimples framed the corners of her mouth. Neither grandparent had dimples. Ruddy assumed they came from her parents.

Both Morris and Bess were slight of build and so was June. For a tiny creature, she was strong as her one-armed grandfather. She carried trays of beer from the bar and food from the kitchen throughout the pub, no complaints.

"What's this for?" Ruddy asked with a nod to the rum.

"I know that sorrowful look, Budgie. Some things require a strong dose of rum. And there's no way I'd give you one without giving one to granddad as well," she said, patting Morris on the head.

Budgie. As a child, she called him Uncle Budgie. To her little ear, Ruddy sounded like Budgie. Over time the uncle dropped away but Budgie stayed. She was the only person who ever called him by anything that wasn't his name or a variation of it.

Ruddy threw back the shot of rum and quickly chased it with a swallow of beer. He turned and raised his empty shot glass. "June dear." When she looked over, he pointed and grinned broadly. "Better," he asked.

"Much. I take it you want another."

"Absolutely." Winky had finished, polishing the sides and bottom of the bowl until they shined, then he jumped up, two paws hitting Ruddy's sore ribs. Wincing, he made the dog sit. "Stay."

The pain reminded him of Tony's request, which he'd have forgotten with all the talk of Napier. Rubbing his ribs he said, "While we're on the subject of fighting, the man I'm taking lessons from is interested in finding a steady job outside of the boxing world. He seems a good sort. He's a veteran, fought in

Afghanistan."

"Afghanistan, nasty place."

Ruddy nodded. "Have we ever fought anyplace that wasn't?"

"Not very often and not in our time."

"Anyway, I can't blame him for wanting out of the seedy boxing world. He needs to make enough to pay for a steady room at night. If you hear of anything, let me know."

Morris nodded. "Have you decided what you'll do if you're challenged?"

"Accept. If I lose, then I lose. At least I'll get to thrash him some before he trounces me. I *will* get my pound of flesh first." Ruddy smiled over the rim of his beer.

Chapter Eighteen

"I've never seen a gun up close, let alone held one." Graciela stared down at the Derringer in her palm. "It's almost toylike, but it weighs more than I'd expect based on the size."

"What did you expect?" Addy asked.

"I don't know. Something lighter I guess." She didn't have a logical answer for him. She'd only seen drawings of guns. Those were in the paper and accompanied adverts for Buffalo Bill's Wild West show. The drawings showed Buffalo Bill with a much larger gun in his hand shooting at something in the distance. It didn't matter. In her mind, guns and cowboys all meshed together. She just pictured a weighty weapon in spite of the smaller size.

"Is it loaded?" she asked and pointed it at Addy.

He pushed the gun barrel to the side. "Careful where you point that, loaded or not and no, it's not."

"Sorry." Graciela tucked the gun inside her reticule. "I believe it is my turn to buy the drinks. Shall we?" Without waiting for him to answer, she headed for the rear entrance of the no name pub.

After they were served Graciela blurted, "Why do you continue to help me? You've worked off the five quid bail money I paid ages ago."

"Curiosity."

"What do you mean?"

"You're a runaway carriage with a brutal wreck the likely end. I should turn away but I can't. I've coached you, which means I've an investment in you to a certain extent. That compels me to want to see the outcome."

Addy had fatherly interest in her. Pleasantly surprised, she said, "I'm flattered. As your protégé, I won't fail you. You'll see."

"You're not my protégé. Far from it. I've given you some minor coaching specific to what your needs were. That's all. I told you, you're a wreck waiting to happen. What type of bad end you're bound to suffer is the mystery."

Anger surged at his ugly warning. What did he know? Nothing. The fool didn't realize she could kill him in the blink of an eye. In a matter of seconds, she could taint his beer with enough arsenic to drop him like a stone. Maybe she would just to teach him a lesson. She shook off the thought. She was not a murderer.

Addy called the barmaid over and ordered a kipper wrapped in newspaper. "Is there nothing that will dissuade you from this quest?" he asked after the barmaid left.

Graciela's surge of anger eased with the question. He'd always tried to talk her out of the nefarious plans she needed help with. "No."

The anger rushed through her again. Who was he to nag her so? He wasn't the one on the ground that day. He wasn't the one being held down. He wasn't the one that had his legs forced apart, undergarments ripped off as one after another man shoved himself into her tender body. He didn't know the feel of their heavy bodies pressing on her, or their panting loud in her ear, their calloused hands rough from rowing harsh on her skin. He didn't hear their horrible laughter as they stood smoothing their clothes and watching while the next one took her.

"What are you thinking?" Addy asked suddenly.

"Why?"

"Your face is beet red."

"A bad memory."

"The memory is the source of your quest?"

She nodded.

"I'll say one more bit of advice and then I'll drop the subject. To dwell on a dark memory is to dwell in a part of your world that essentially dead and gone. Let it go. Look to the future, to what your life can be."

The barmaid set the kipper down and Addy paid her. He slid it over to Graciela. "Here. I saw you eyeing that skinny cat that hangs around the back of the pub. Make the wee thing's day."

Addy rose. "Think about what I said. Careful how you use the Derringer," he warned and left.

****

Graciela spent an entire day off watching Skinner's office to see how he spent his time. The clerk didn't leave for lunch and neither did Skinner. The clerk arrived earlier in the morning but Skinner stayed later. That may or may not have been a regular occurrence, she couldn't be sure.

The following Monday, her day off, she packed her tapestry bag with the newsboy clothes and headed to Skinner's office. A block from the courthouse she snuck into the stable that housed the horses and carriages for the members of the court. She crept into an empty stall and changed into the newsboy outfit, tucking her hair up into the apple cap. Then, she made her way over to Skinner's office. In the alley behind his office, she secreted the tapestry bag, hiding it in the corner of a pallet with delivery boxes.

Graciela waited until Skinner left for the courthouse. She strolled by the front of the office and verified the clerk was at his desk. While he was busy, she quietly pushed the drapery to the side and quickly cut a piece of glass out of Skinner's window just large enough for her to fit her hand through to unlock it. As fast as she dared, she raised the window, crawled through, then shut it again. Addy had taught her well. The entire procedure had taken less than five minutes. She slipped Addy's glass cutting tool back into her pocket and removed the flask with the arsenic. She was tempted to pour herself a short glass of whatever the decanter contained to see what it was exactly and to steady her nerves. It smelled like claret but she'd like to know for sure. She ignored the temptation fearing the clerk might come in and instead poured the entire contents of the flask into the decanter. Finished, she climbed inside the large armoire where Skinner kept his black robes and frock coats. She'd seen it when she visited the first time and got a glimpse of his inner office.

The wardrobe had a double-door front. The

doors were narrow. She had to open both to climb inside. She tugged the first open without incident. She had the second open halfway when it let out the torturous and loud creaking of a hinge in bad need of oil.

No, no, no, Graciela hopped inside, silently swearing at the creaking armoire door. She immediately dropped into the far corner and made herself small as she could, knowing the clerk was bound to come and investigate the noise. He did. She heard him as he came to the desk area. He remained still there for a moment. She imagined he was looking under the desk in the foot well area. He moved toward the window. She cast a prayer heavenward that he wouldn't check behind the drapery and see where she'd cut the glass. He must not have since he came next to the armoire. She'd wrapped one of Skinner's spare black robes around herself.

The robe smelled musty and she feared the dank odor would make her sneeze. The toes of her boots stuck out. She couldn't pull her feet back any more than she already had. She put an extra pair of boots he had in the armoire in front of her feet and hoped that would work to disguise hers.

The clerk opened the armoire doors. She held her breath. She didn't dare sneak a peek but could hear him ruffling through frock coats and top coats and everything hanging in the closet. She pressed her back harder into the wood frame of the armoire when he came to her side.

The clerk sighed, stopped looking, and closed the armoire. She let her breath out, pinched her nose stifling a sneeze, as his footsteps grew fainter as he left the room.

Thank you, thank you, thank you. It struck her that there was something of a mortal sin aspect attached to thanking a deity for helping save her so she could murder a man.

"Stupid girl," she whispered as she sat huddled in the closet and the awkwardness of her plan became reality. In the plan she imagined, she'd step from the armoire, put the gun on Skinner, tell him to keep quiet and to sit and listen. She'd replay the rape for him so he knew why she sought revenge. She'd make him drink the arsenic, watch him die and sneak out the window. How smoothly it ran...in her imagination.

She burped up a small amount of bile, which she forced down again. "Ugh." Unanticipated miscalculations had her stomach in a queasy knot. No time to dwell on stupidity. How the deuce was she going to get out of the armoire without the squeaky door bringing the clerk back to investigate?

Outside the Fleet Street tram rolled to a stop, its steel wheels squealing along the tracks as it slowed. "Thank you, again," she whispered, "whoever is helping me, sinner or saint, don't care which. More like saint turned sinner, again, don't care." The tram was her salvation. She'd wait for the next and use the noise from it to climb out of the armoire.

Minutes later another tram stopped in front of the office. Graciela hurried and opened the squeaky door only as far as she needed to get out, uncertain of how long the tram would be loading passengers. She used the short noisy seconds as it pulled away to close the armoire door.

She'd hide behind the drapery and wait for Skinner. The velvet curtain hung to the floor and offered ample coverage. "Should've used it to begin with, ninny."

A velvet hotbox. A stifling, dust mote laden shroud that Graciela swore was alive with fleas. She'd begun to itch and sweat within minutes of hiding inside the heavy window cover. Perspiration trickled down from her hairline, stinging her eyes, and trickling down the back of her neck. She wiped the trails away as often as possible but still kept the action to a minimum. She feared moving too much and exposing some part of her without knowing.

It seemed like forever before Skinner finally returned. She heard the clerk greet him. After he did, Skinner immediately closed the door between his office and the reception area. He hung his robe in the armoire and as he was about to turn Graciela pushed the barrel of the Derringer into the base of his spine.

"Yell, say one word, scream, utter a sound and I'll kill you and your clerk. Nod if you understand."

He nodded.

"Turn around slowly. Go to the door and give your clerk some money and tell him to go to a café. Tea and biscuits are on you. If he starts to argue, convince him to leave. Insist you want to be alone. Remember it's his life at stake too."

She stood to the side of the door where the clerk couldn't see and held the gun inches from Skinner's right temple. "Mr. Button, come here. I had a good day in court. I thought why not share some of my good cheer with you. Here, take this." He reached into his pocket, pulled a pound from his money clip and handed it to the clerk. "You don't get out of the office enough. Go now and have a cup of tea on me."

From the surprised response on the clerk's part, Skinner didn't often buy the man refreshment, if ever. "Sir, I don't know what to say. This is very kind. Thank you."

"Go and enjoy your tea." The clerk was off in a matter of minutes.

Skinner closed the door. "Sit down," she ordered.

He did as she told him. "Who are you and what do you want?" he asked, taking his chair. He looked her up and down, his nostrils flaring as though she was stinking up his office.

"I didn't give you permission to speak. You don't get to talk. I do." She kept the gun pointed on him and set the poisoned decanter on the desk with her other hand and then a single glass. "Pour yourself a drink. Don't be stingy."

"See here—"

She raised the gun level with his eyes. A frisson of panic rifled through her at actually shooting someone. She tightened her grip afraid her hand might start to tremble. "Pour."

His eyes widened and he poured with a shaky hand, much to her relief.

"Drink it down."

He took a sip.

"All of it."

While he drank, she removed her apple hat and

shook her hair loose. "Recognize me? Just shake your head yes or no."

He shook his head.

"I didn't think you would. Sixteen years ago you and three of your Oxford friends raped a young village girl. She was alone walking by the side of the river and you three were drunk. Still don't remember?"

"That's an insane accusation."

"Let me give you a hand in remembering. The other three were Bartholomew Cross, Harlan Lloyd-Birch, and Nesbit Finch." She saw recognition light in his eyes. "Starting to come back to you now?"

Blue-green veins popped out at his temples. "What do you want? Money? Of course, you want money. You think to come here now and make something of an old story. You can't prove any of what you say. I won't be blackmailed." He looked her up and down again and waved a dismissive hand in her direction. "This threat won't go anywhere. Get out. If you pursue this, I'll file a crime report and all you get is jail time. I'll..." Skinner suddenly paled and rocked in his chair. "What...what was in the drink?"

"Arsenic. You see, money isn't what I want."

"What?" He laid his head in his hand. He straightened and pushed away from the desk and tried to stand.

Graciela hurried to his side and shoved him back down in the chair—hard. "Just stay where you are."

"Take my money." He reached for the money clip in his pocket.

She slapped his hand away. "I don't want *your*

money."

He looked momentarily baffled before puzzlement turned to a grimace of pain.

"Do you remember what you said to me that day? Of course not. You don't remember me."

He groaned and doubled over.

"Painful, isn't it? I'll tell you what else is painful—having tender virgin flesh torn and stretched by brute force—having that same tender bleeding, flesh bruised again and again by fellow attackers. Do you know what you were doing while I cried and begged for Cross and your friends to stop? You held me down. When they finished, you took your turn."

"You're here. You suffer no permanent injury. What do you want?"

"For you to die."

He looked at her and she didn't think eyes could grow that wide. "I don't deserve to die."

"I was only fourteen."

"So, I soiled you a bit."

"That little speech you made a few minutes ago about reporting me to the police, you said something similar then too. I curled into a ball on the ground, weeping as you stood and straightened your clothes. I threatened to tell the police the four of you raped me. You laughed. You waffled on and asked who do I think they'll believe, a little nothing of a village girl or you four? Oxford men. The sons and grandsons of Oxford men from influential families, or me?"

She spit in his face. "I knew in that moment, you were right. You're still right. They won't believe me now. Or, even if they do, too much time has passed.

They won't care. Justice is left to me." She pulled out the watch she'd pinned to the inside of the newsboy's knickers. "You've not much time left. Tell me where Finch lives."

"Go to hell."

"You're morally bankrupt Daniel. A rapist. Bravado from you is a hollow effort and we both know it. Tell me where Finch lives."

"Go to hell."

Graciela bounced on the balls of her feet. Anticipation coursing through her. Now he'd beg. Like she did. He might even cry. Like she did. "I wanted to avoid playing this nasty card but I see I must." That was a lie. This was her high card. Of course she planned all along on playing it. "I know where you live in Belgravia Square. I know the comings and goings of your lovely daughter. The man who gave me the gun has several friends with a criminal bent. I'm sure rape is among their talents. Tell me about Finch or I'll see your daughter ruined."

"No!" He tried to stand but collapsed on his knees to the floor.

"Yes, Daniel. What kind of life will she have when society learns she has been raped by four men? None of the young bloods of the Ton will have her. You might find a husband for her on the continent but no decent Englishman will want her. Whispers about the incident will follow her for the rest of her life. Is Finch worth more to you than her?"

How she was enjoying the moment. She desperately wanted to stretch the moment out, but had to hurry. The clerk would return soon.

"Haven't stayed in touch. Don't know where he lives. His club is Abercrombie's." Skinner crawled to where Graciela stood with the gun pointed on him. "Promise you'll leave my daughter alone."

Her promise would give him peace of mind.

"I promise you nothing."

He lay on his side, his legs thrashing as though climbing imaginary stairs. After what seemed forever, he flopped over onto his back, his eyes rolled into the back of his head and he died.

Two down, two to go.

Graciela put the gun in her reticule and then checked for a pulse. Satisfied he was dead, she left by the window so there'd be less chance of being seen. As she closed the window she heard the clerk return and call out to Skinner. She took off running. She ran to the end of that alley, grabbed her tapestry bag, and then ran down another and another before she stopped and hid behind a barrel. She wasn't even sure where she was when she finally stopped.

Light-headed, she'd almost been caught, she retched but didn't vomit. With trembling hands, she stuffed her hair under the apple cap, and then walked for blocks to work off the rush of emotions.

I have got to plan better. I cannot go through this with Finch.

Chapter Nineteen

Ruddy pulled the draperies in Skinner's office back to let in more light. "How long has this window been like this, Mr. Button?" he asked, looking at the cut out section under the lock.

Skinner's clerk turned his attention from talking to Archie to the damaged window. "Oh my! That had to have happened last night or this morning."

"Are you sure?"

"Positive. I was the last to leave yesterday evening. I closed the drapes myself. The window was intact then."

A clean and precise cut. Whoever made it used a tool specifically for that purpose. They also took care to make certain the glass didn't fall to the floor inside. The scene had all the appearances of a burglary occurring at some point between the time Button left and the time Skinner died. Yet Button said nothing was missing.

"You're sure you don't see anything missing?" Ruddy asked the clerk again.

"As far as I can tell, no."

"You didn't notice the window this morning because you didn't touch the draperies?" Archie asked.

"That's correct. Mr. Skinner prefers to do that himself."

"Everything was normal until midday, is that right?" Archie went on.

Button nodded. "A short time after he returned from court, he called me over and gave me money and sent me off to have tea and biscuits elsewhere." He lowered his voice as though he'd committed a crime. "I often have a nibble at my desk to tide me over until dinner. The point is he's never done that, just like he's never taken to drinking in the afternoon, as I told you already."

"Are we clear to take the body now?" a constable asked Ruddy, who told him to go ahead.

"I wonder if something happened at court to upset him?" Button asked as the constables covered Skinner with a blanket and carried the body out to the Medical Examiner's cart. "It's the only the way I can explain his odd behavior."

"You said he's not handling any contested probate cases. None of his clients are involved in family disputes over inheritances," Archie said.

"None."

"Could he have run into an angry relative from a previous matter?" Ruddy asked.

"Anything is possible," the clerk said, shrugging. "But no one like that comes to mind. Something was amiss with him though."

The more Button revealed, the more illogical the circumstances leading to Skinner's death seemed. Ruddy hated the uncertainty the absence of logic presented. Hoping for the missing piece that links all the other bits of information he asked Button, "Can you think of anything else, no matter how insignificant that was different about today?"

"Walk it out, do a step by step, if it helps," Archie suggested.

Button did. After going through the motions of his morning routine at his desk and making tea etcetera, he suddenly rose and went to the armoire.

"What's going on?" Ruddy asked. "What happened?"

"The door creaked." He opened the doors to the armoire to show Ruddy and Archie. The left door opened fine but halfway open the right one moaned in shrill protest. "I heard it at my desk and came to investigate. I shook all Mr. Skinner's coats and looked around the cupboard floor. I didn't see anything suspicious. I certainly didn't see anyone."

"Thank you." Ruddy looked inside for himself. A person, if they weren't terribly big, could possibly secrete themselves well enough for Button to miss seeing them. An intriguing possibility if the autopsy showed homicide.

Ruddy handed a third constable the decanters of wine and port and the glass Skinner drank from. "I want you to talk to the neighboring businesses. Ask if anyone saw anything out of the ordinary. But first, take these and ask the doctor to test them for poison."

Behind him the clerk gasped. "Who would murder Mr. Skinner?"

Ruddy instantly regretted speaking in front of the civilian.

"I didn't say he was murdered. We have to

consider many possibilities when a suspicious death is involved. You called us here because felt there was an extraordinary set of occurrences. You wanted us to investigate further and we are."

Ruddy walked away from the clerk. It was that or bring the man to tears saying what he really thought. *What were you thinking when you called the constable on this patch to the scene and told him Mr. Skinner was dead and you feared something was very wrong? That combination, dead body plus wrongdoing usually equals murder, goose brain. That's what Ruddy wanted to say but didn't dare.* His thoughts put to voice would come out sounding harsh to anyone other than another policeman.

Archie must've read Ruddy's patience thinning and told the clerk, "We won't need any more from you today. You should go home."

"What if a client comes in?"

Archie wrapped his hand around the clerk's elbow easing him from the room. "We'll take care of any clients. We need to finish our investigation here and your presence is slowing the process. Please go."

"Do you think he was murdered?" Archie asked when he returned. "I thought the same thing."

Ruddy nodded. If it had been simply a matter of the clerk finding his boss dead on the floor after he'd had a glass of wine, Ruddy might've been more inclined to consider Skinner had a heart attack. He'd have been peeved they were called. A man is entitled to break with routine and have a drink midday if he wishes. The clerk carried on so the responding constables had called him and Archie to the scene just to satisfy the man's insistence that police look deeper into matter.

"That cut window," Archie said.

"A burglar's cut just under the lock but nothing was taken. We have a dead victim with a goodly amount of cash on him and who's behaved strangely. The scene points to him having a drink. After finding Cross in similar circumstances, poison comes to mind right away."

"What if it is? What's the motivation?"

Good question. One Ruddy didn't have a ready answer for. "We still don't have one for Cross. Let's push for fast autopsy results and the lab work on the wine."

Outside a tram came and went. It occurred to Ruddy that someone may have broken in and what...made Skinner drink poison? How'd they do that? The tram reminded Ruddy how busy the street was with foot traffic. All Skinner had to do was yell out. Again, why break in and not rob the man? Why make the man drink poison? All he had were questions and no clues for answers. The idea that his two murder cases, if this turned out to be a murder, might be connected, drifted across his mind like faint smoke, floated there for several uncomfortable seconds, and then dissipated.

"I had a disturbing idea work its way into my brutally short list of theories," Archie said. "What if the Skinner and Cross murders are related?"

"I wish you hadn't said that," Ruddy said.

"You had the same thought."

"Sadly, yes. After the press mess last year with the Whitechapel murders, we do not need the additional attention of a string of influential men getting picked off." Ruddy searched Skinner's desk, stacking the calendars from the two previous years with the current one. They could contain a reference to Cross.

On the rethink, it might work out better for the investigation if they were connected. That should or could narrow the target field of potential suspects. It would be damned convenient if Cross and Skinner both availed themselves of the whore Violet's services. Or if they belonged to the same men's club, they might've offended the same person and thus have the same enemy.

Ruddy moved to the cut window. He stood, contemplating the significance. "Let's say for now, Skinner was murdered. Be the killer." Archie joined him. "You've chosen to kill Skinner here, at his office, rather than at home. Why?"

"Too many people at home. Too hard to get him alone."

"Makes sense."

"It's too hard to try and kill him en route between home and here. He has his driver and maybe a footman. I'd have to sneak into the stable, board the carriage and somehow secrete myself so Skinner doesn't see me when he gets aboard. Even if I succeeded, which I doubt, any struggle as I attacked Skinner would rock the carriage and draw both the driver and footman's attention. This is my best option," Archie said in a firm tone, reminiscent of the way the savviest of killers think.

"You come through the window to avoid being

seen. Is it because the clerk would recognize you or a different reason?"

"What other reason is there?"

"I don't know yet. It's just a thought I'm throwing out. Ready to go?"

Archie took one of the calendars and a black ledger book he found on a shelf. "Ready."

****

The autopsy report and test results on the contents of the decanters were returned by midmorning the next day. Skinner had died of arsenic poisoning. The claret in the decanter was the same as in his stomach and both contained arsenic. The port did not.

"What the deuce kind of maniac do we have on our hands now?" Archie lamented.

"A strange one indeed." And Ruddy meant it. "Shall we give Jameson the bad news?"

"Let's get it over with."

Jameson listened with a pained expression. The crease between his eyes deepened with each named similarity. When Ruddy finished, the Superintendent looked from Ruddy to Archie and back to Ruddy. "Is there no other way to look at these cases other than as connected?"

"We could. We can always take a different approach. Follow a different course of investigation but I think sooner or later we'd have to pursue this theory. If nothing else, to eliminate the possibility they're related," Ruddy said.

"I don't like it. I don't like it at all. The idea we may have a demented looney on the loose poisoning well-to-do businessmen curdles in me." He fixed hard eyes on Ruddy as he made his objection known.

Ruddy had a response sitting on the tip of his tongue. He'd love to tell the Superintendent the nature of the case didn't exactly set him doing a jig either.

"I'm beginning to think there's something about you Bloodstone, that attracts these cases involving influential people. Somehow, someway while investigating the case I just know you're going to overturn a rock and an ugly frog of information will pop out that has another influential person screaming like a banshee." Jameson pointed a finger in Ruddy's face. "I believe that. I truly do." He turned to Archie. "I can feel it. The two of you. Get out."

Back at their desks, Ruddy snatched his coat from the stand where he had carefully hung it. "I hope we do discover some toff involved up to his wealthy neck in these cases," he said without bothering to lower his voice. "I hope it turns into a carbuncle on Jameson's bum."

"Shh," Archie raised a finger to get Ruddy to quiet down. He'd drawn the attention of the other detectives who were listening with interest to the tirade.

"Let's talk to Cross's staff first. His residence is closest and on the way to Belgrave Square. If they don't recognize Skinner as a friend or associate, we'll move on and speak to Skinner's family," Ruddy said, changing the subject and putting on his coat.

"Good idea. I'm happy to get out of here for a while," Archie said with a quick glance toward Jameson's closed door.

****

Staff at the Cross residence confirmed they never heard Skinner mentioned by name nor did any of them recall a man by that name visiting. Skinner's family said the same about Cross.

Ruddy and Archie left for the financial district located in the City of London's jurisdiction. Cross was an investment advisor to a select group of private clients at the Bank of England. Hugh Smiley, the bank manager, led them to Cross's office, which had been locked up. Clients were notified of his death but formal reassignment of their portfolios hadn't occurred yet. "May I ask what you need in his office?"

"We'll need to read through the client base and document some of the pertinent information," Ruddy replied.

"You may not." Looking horrified, Smiley pulled the key from the lock. "Our client's privacy is of paramount importance. This bank will not allow you go mucking about into their affairs. How dare you even suggest such an invasion of their personal finances?" Smiley was a petite man, no taller than Ruddy's chin, sallow-faced with pale blue eyes, a weak chin, and a fuzzy grey ring for hair. He puffed himself up as he challenged the detectives with all the indignation of a man twice his size.

Under different circumstances Ruddy might've laughed. But it served no purpose to irritate Smiley more than necessary. The financial district fell under the City of London's police jurisdiction. The last thing he and Archie wanted to do was find themselves encountering Napier or Effingham.

"Mr. Smiley, we are investigating a double homicide, one of the victims is your former employee, Mr. Cross. Their brutal murders are far more important than the privacy of your clients. We believe the murders are connected. If so, the connection maybe be found in Mr. Cross's business relations," Archie explained.

As Archie reasoned with the banker, Ruddy gently but firmly wrenched the key ring from Smiley's hand and over the man's chirps of objections unlocked Cross's door.

"We are not interested in the private matters of your client's finances, not unless they pertain in some important way to how Mr. Cross handled them. If his advice impacted their financial performance in such a way that they might've been ruined and they sought vindication of some sort, then we'll have to take a hard look at that client," Ruddy explained further. "We'd see if that client spoke with or contacted our other victim. So you can see the need for our mucking about as you say."

"I do not. This is not over." With that Smiley spun and left.

"Lord only knows what mischief he'll get up to now," Archie said and began making two piles of ledgers, one for each of them to read through.

"He'll do the usual and write a long disparaging letter to Jameson declaring us smug Philistines. I'm sure we'll be held up as examples of that class of Englishman who have no appreciation for the world order, blah, blah, blah." Ruddy smirked, opened a ledger, and said, "He'd be right, almost, except I'm a

Welshman with no appreciation for the world order as he sees it."

An hour passed and neither detective found any client who seemed to fit the role of disgruntled party. No one had lost a fortune or seemed to have been put in dire straits in any way. They were on the last of the books when Archie looked up. "Bloody hell."

"What?" Ruddy asked. "Bloody hell," he repeated, looking up to see the tight-lipped, angry visage of Effingham and Napier striding toward them. "Bloody hell."

"What do you two think you're doing?" Effingham asked. "I thought I'd made it clear last year that any case involving one of our citizens needs to have Napier included."

"No," Ruddy said and clarified. "Napier's inclusion was specific to speaking to the Viscount Everhard. This is a different matter entirely and relates to two crimes committed in our jurisdiction."

Napier stepped around to see what they were reading. Archie slammed the ledger he was reading shut.

"Don't try and play fast and loose with technicalities. You should've known the rules apply across the board on all cases that now come into the City's boundaries. What are you after?" Napier asked.

"Since we didn't find what we were looking for, I don't see why you need to know," Ruddy said, shutting the ledger in front of him. "Our cases are ours. We don't require your permission to speak to anyone in an effort to solve them. If that's a problem, then please take it up with Jameson."

"I will do just that," Effingham said.

Ruddy shrugged. "Doesn't matter to us, we're finished here anyway. You are, aren't you?" He glanced at Archie.

"I am."

"Leave the ledgers. Napier and I will walk out with you." Effingham smirked and nodded at the bank manager who stood scowling a short distance away watching. Ruddy was certain Smiley labored under the misimpression Effingham and Napier had given them the boot. The Superintendent wanted to walk them out so it appeared they were escorting him and Archie out of the bank.

On the sidewalk, Effingham said, "Napier, you should tell Bloodstone about your new prize." Before Napier could respond, Effingham said, "Nathaniel's too modest. I'll tell you. He won the department's boxing championship this year again. That's four in a row." He leaned closer to Ruddy. "You'd better be on your toes if the day ever comes that our department challenges yours. More to the point, *he* challenges you."

"You needn't worry about me, Chief Superintendent."

Archie spoke low next to Napier, "One day Effingham will stop too quick and it'll take a squad of your men to pull your head from his arse. I just hope I'm there to see it."

Napier pivoted toward Archie, his cheeks brightly flushed with color. A vein in his neck stood out, reflecting every beat of his hear. A flash of surprise crossed his face when Archie didn't automatically step back but held his ground. "I am going to challenge your partner. Soon. I'm going to thrash and humiliate him. And I'm going to relish every minute of it."

Chapter Twenty

"Don't get too close to the forge. I worry the embers might catch your dress or the blanket," Ruddy warned Honeysuckle.

She backed up a few feet. "Is this far enough away?"

"Yes."

"What are you working on?" She set the picnic basket on the lawn, spread the blanket she brought on the ground and began unloading the hamper.

Ruddy stoked the fire in his forge. "The base for a table to match that bench I made last year for Mrs. Goodge. You're welcome to sit on the bench, you know. You don't have to sit on the ground."

"Don't be silly. What sort of picnic would it be if we ate sitting on the bench? Mrs. Goodge has a lovely garden. It's a beautiful sunny day. We shall have a city picnic. Now stop playing with your fire for a moment and come and kiss me."

Ruddy washed his hands in a bucket of fresh water he had on the side, splashed his face, grabbed a towel he kept handy and wiped his face. "I'm a dirty, sweaty mess. I hesitate to come within arm's distance, let alone kissing close. But since you asked, I shall oblige."

He bent and kissed her. She leaned into it and he rested his hands on her waist to draw her in tighter. Remembering his unclean condition he immediately raised his hands and hoped he hadn't soiled her dress already.

Honeysuckle broke the kiss first but lingered close enough for him to feel her body heat. "Sit for a moment and have a glass of wine with me. Then, I promise to be good and let you work for a while longer on your table."

She looked at him with absolute knowledge in her eyes that he would say yes. It occurred to Ruddy that his village priest was wrong. The devil did not come to men wearing horns and with goat-like hooves and a tail. He came to men in a woman's eyes. "Only one glass, then I have to finish this one table leg before I can stop for the afternoon."

"From the curly-cue pieces on the bench, I'm guessing this is a flower pattern. Is it a sunflower?" Honeysuckle asked, studying the bench.

"I'm not sure what kind of flower it is. I saw it in India when I went to visit Will once."

"Your ironwork is remarkable. Where did you learn it?"

"I learned the basics from my father who's a farrier. I learned how to shape hot iron working with horseshoes. I am self-taught with other types of ironwork, the more detailed kind like the wrought iron on fences and garden furniture. I draw what I intend to make first then use that as my pattern."

"I bet you're Mrs. Goodge's favorite boarder." Honeysuckle removed tea sandwiches from the basket, peaches, which she must've remembered him saying he loved, sweet biscuits, and a cut up pig's ear.

Ruddy kissed her on the cheek while she busied herself laying out the food.

"What was that for?"

"Do I need a reason?"

She kissed him back on the lips and said, "Never."

The food brought Winky dashing over. After initially greeting Honeysuckle by wagging and blocking her path until he'd received a proper belly rub, he'd returned to squirrel watch. Squirrel watch consisted of him trying to stay awake while sitting pouncing distance from Mrs. Goodge's walnut tree.

"Winky sit and behave," Ruddy ordered. "I take it that pig's ear is for him."

"It is. Oh look. He knows it too."

His idea of behaving was to roll over several times, stop and bark.

"Winky lay down," Ruddy said in a stern voice.

He did but with all the truculence of a human two-year-old ordered to stop misbehaving.

Ruddy pinched a piece off one of the sweet biscuits and popped it into his mouth. "Did you make these?" he asked, after finishing the little chunk he stole and reaching for the rest.

"Don't be silly."

Winky popped up and shot toward the house, barking.

"Hello Winky boo, don't you remember me?" a familiar female voice said behind them.

The barking stopped but Ruddy's heart shot to

his throat. He turned in time to see Mrs. Goodge hurriedly waddling after Evangeline.

"Winky, come here." The dog trotted back. "Evangeline, this is a surprise. I thought you were in New York," Ruddy said and stood to greet her.

"I was. But I earned holiday time. Since you wrote that you didn't care to see New York, I thought to come home for a visit."

"Mr. Bloodstone, I'm so sorry. She got by me before I could stop her," Mrs. Goodge said, breathing hard, having rushed from the front door to the garden.

"No worries, Mrs. Goodge. Everything is fine," Ruddy reassured her not feeling the sentiment all that much.

"Introduce us, Rudyard." It was Honeysuckle.

Mrs. Goodge's grimace at the request reflected his internal one. "Of course, sorry. Honeysuckle Flowers, this is Evangeline Bannister."

"How nice to meet you," Honeysuckle said with a pleasant smile. "You've come visiting all the way from America. I'd love to hear about New York. Won't you join us for a glass of wine?"

Ruddy shot a frown Honeysuckle's direction trying to convey his dislike of the idea. She didn't see. Was that a deliberate evasion, he wondered?

The brief surprise Evangeline showed at seeing Honeysuckle was quickly covered with a mild smile. "I can see this is a private picnic and I don't wish to interrupt. I just wanted to say hello and give this to you." She handed Ruddy a box the length of his hand with a ribbon around it. "It's from our men's department."

A tiny animal-like sound escaped Mrs. Goodge and she said, "I'm going inside now."

Ruddy desperately wanted to say, "Take me with you." Instead, he stared, frozen with the gift in his grasp unsure if he should accept. He certainly nothing to give Evangeline in return. Would it be rude? If he accepted, was it rude to open it in front of Honeysuckle? After a brief mental tug of war, he thought it best to decline. "Evangeline, how can I accept when I have nothing to offer you in return? I feel terrible."

"It's a gift, Rudyard. A person isn't supposed to give expecting something in return. How bourgeoisie. Open it," Evangeline ordered, tapping the ribbon.

"She's right," a wine sipping Honeysuckle chimed in. Her comment was followed by a traitorous bark from Winky.

He did as ordered. Inside was a pair of fine black leather men's gloves. Expensive gloves. His haberdasher carried similar ones. He removed them from the box.

"Try them on. They're from Italy," Evangeline said.

Ruddy tugged each on and had to admit to being pleased they fit. He really did want them. However, he ought to make one more half-hearted effort to not accept. "Are you sure you wish me to have these beautiful gloves? Is there not a family member you'd prefer to give them to?"

"I bought them for you. I'll hear no more talk of giving them back."

"Now you must join us," Honeysuckle said.

"Rudyard, we need another wine glass. Be a dear and get one from Mrs. Goodge."

"Be right back." He jogged into the house not wanting to leave the women alone to talk any longer than necessary.

Mrs. Goodge was in the kitchen goblet in hand, ready for him. "I heard," she said. "The window was open."

If it hadn't been open, she'd have cracked the door to listen. He knew better than to say as much. "Thank you," was all he said and jogged back with the glass.

"I never thought I'd leave London but the opportunity was too good to resist. Lord and Taylor is the nicest store in the city. The partner's families are modern thinkers when it comes to business. They were willing try women in management positions. There are three of us. I manage Ladies Accessories, the other two women manage Ladies Hats, and the Lingerie departments," Evangeline said as Honeysuckle poured her a glass of wine.

"Good for them and good for you. It took courage to leave home and everyone you know. You're very brave to start fresh in a different country and different job and in one with so much responsibility." Honeysuckle filled Ruddy's glass. "Don't you agree, Rudyard?"

"Yes."

"What sort of work do you do?" Evangeline asked Honeysuckle.

"I'm an actress."

"Like Sarah Bernhardt?"

"No. My career isn't so grand. I'm a music hall performer."

Evangeline shoulders stiffened so slightly, if Ruddy had blinked, he'd have missed the change. "Music hall, how interesting."

"She's the star attraction at the Odeon," Ruddy said.

Evangeline peered at Honeysuckle over the rim of her glass. When Honeysuckle wasn't looking, she eyed her in a judgmental way that set Ruddy's teeth on edge.

"Have you been the star there long? Rudyard and I went to the Odeon when we were courting. I don't recall seeing you," Evangeline asked.

Ruddy winced. Why'd she have to use the term courting? He'd explain to Honeysuckle after Evangeline left that courting was too strong a word for their relationship. He didn't have another word handy to describe the months they saw each other but it definitely wasn't courting. Not in his mind anyway. It hadn't evolved that far.

"I was probably still at the Oxford Music Hall. I started my career in London there," Honeysuckle told her.

"The Oxford, what a lovely building, such a fancy façade, one doesn't expect something so nice for a music hall."

"I was born in Bristol. My parents are theatre people. As a child, I traveled the length and breadth of the island touring with them. You'd be surprised how many elegant theatres there are."

"If you say so."

"Have you ever been to the Paris Opera House?" Honeysuckle asked Evangeline.

"No."

"It's one of the most beautiful buildings in that city."

The comment triggered an unnecessary eye roll from Evangeline. "Well, it's for opera performers. One expects elegance and beauty from their settings. They have grand stories to tell." She spread her arms stressing how much greater their needs.

Honeysuckle bristled. It looked like she grew two inches her back went so ramrod stiff.

Evangeline blithely continued, "A music hall is—no offense- a stage for song and dance performers, sleight-of-hand tricksters and the like. All their routines are fun. I'm not saying they're not but let's be honest, look how hard opera singers train."

No offense, indeed, Ruddy thought. Evangeline's glass was empty. Honeysuckle didn't offer her a refill. No surprise. Over the years, police work honed one's sense of timing. It was time to intercede. "I'd like to say something as a typical Londoner. I've never seen an opera. I've no interest. It's marvelous if you can hit the high notes of a great aria. But I'm always going to prefer a music hall. As the one in the audience listening, talent is talent, bringing joy to a jolly tune that brightens the day is just as great as putting tragedy in song. I can't do it and appreciate the ability of those who can. Both singers bring pleasure. One is not better than the other, each has different appeal."

"I'd like to add that the magicians or tricksters

as you call them work very hard at their craft," Honeysuckle snapped. "Nothing is learned overnight. And speaking for myself, my father started teaching me to dance when I was four."

Evangeline raised her hands in mock surrender. "Again, I meant no insult. It's a matter of taste, I suppose," she conceded. She drew a white enamel floral pocket watch on a gold chain from a waistband pocket. "I've stayed later than I planned. I must be on my way. Thank you for the wine and the lively discussion."

"It was nice meeting you as well," Honeysuckle said with a tight smile.

Ruddy stood when Evangeline did. "I'll see you to the door. Thank you again for the gloves."

"Perhaps one day before I leave we can meet for tea or an ice cream sundae at the parlor near the park," Evangeline said as they neared the kitchen door.

She hadn't spoken loud but Ruddy gave a fast glance over his shoulder to see if Honeysuckle heard. From her expression, she had.

"I don't think that's a good idea," he said, feeling stupid. He should've anticipated an invite of this kind when he accepted the gloves. "I must apologize. I've been remiss in not writing you back. I've no intention on visiting New York and I don't foresee us socializing while you're here."

Mrs. Goodge stopped chopping but kept her head down and her eyes on the cutting board as they passed through the kitchen.

"Why? You're not engaged, are you?" Evangeline asked.

"No."

"Are you promised to each other in some way?"

"No."

She stopped in the hallway and tugged on his arm so he'd stop. "Then why can't we have tea?"

"Two reasons. I'm not a smoothie, which is no shock to you, I'm sure. I'm not adept at juggling relationships with more than one woman at a time. Frankly, it's never been a skill I've ever aspired to. I'm currently in a relationship with Honeysuckle."

"What's the other reason? Is it anger at me for offending her?"

He shook his head. "No."

"I'm entitled to my opinion."

"True, although your harsh manner when you voiced it wasn't necessary."

Evangeline didn't respond. He'd never found a reason to criticize her in the past and wasn't sure how to interpret her reaction. He had an opinion as well and a right to express it.

"The other reason I'll decline tea is because I think Honeysuckle would be hurt by my socializing with a lady I had a former relationship with. I don't want to hurt her. I've no wish to hurt you either so I hope you understand why I'm saying no."

Evangeline turned from him and walked briskly to the door. A gust of wind blew over him as she yanked it open. "If you change your mind, I'm at my sisters for another three weeks. And no, I don't understand why friends can't have tea." She closed the door hard behind her.

As he cut through the kitchen to get to the garden, Mrs. Goodge blocked his path. "Never you mind about her," she said and patted him between the shoulder blades like his mum used to when he had a cough. "She was such a sweet thing the few times I saw her last year. America's turned her into quite the crosspatch. Pity. I suppose we'll see more of that attitude with the coming waves of American Dollar Princesses from there."

Dollar Princesses? He had no idea what Goodge was talking about.

Goodge chuckled. "Young American heiresses are landing here by the droves they say. Their families send them in hopes of arranging marriages with our impoverished young noblemen. The rich colonials are starved for titles. Our old families are starved for cash. It's all very mercenary now. I don't approve, not that anyone cares." She returned to her onion cutting.

Nothing really changed in those upper social classes since the beginning of time. It might be mercenary now. Before this, it was political. Sons and daughters have always been bargaining chips. He grinned at the snide term Dollar Princesses. Who thought it up, he wondered. Probably angry matrons of the Ton with unmarried daughters hoping for a marriage match in the same crowded field.

Out in the garden, Honeysuckle had removed a pillow from the bench seat and set it between her back and the bench leg. She sipped her wine and idly scratched Winky's ears. The dog lay next to her sound asleep.

"Sorry about the interruption," Ruddy said and sat next to her.

"No need to apologize."

Ruddy tipped her chin and kissed her lightly on the lips. "I'm not having tea with her," he said after breaking off the kiss.

"Rudyard, I wouldn't ask you not to. She's a friend to say the least. Clearly, you were important to her. We've no claim on each other's time or with whom it is spent."

"I don't like the way she spoke about your profession. I don't like the way she spoke *to* you at all."

"Let's neither of us pretend we don't know what is said about actresses, and in the main, it's true."

He thought it best not to answer. Their reputation for being more open-minded when it came to intimacy was well known. He'd be lying if he said it hadn't crossed his mind. He hoped at a point in the near future it proved true for him and Honeysuckle.

"I'm not having tea or anything else with her. Period. I'm ravenous. I am desperate to try one of your sandwiches." He took one of each, a watercress and butter, and a cucumber.

Activity involving food had roused Winky. Honeysuckle let him have the cut up ear, which he devoured. He plopped down in front of her again committed to a blink-less focus on her sandwich.

After taking a bite, Ruddy opened his cucumber sandwich up. "What is this smeared on the bread?"

"I don't know what they call it. It's a mix of egg, oil, salt, white pepper, and mustard. I think it's tasty and asked the teashop to use it on the cucumber sandwiches. What do you think?"

He nodded his approval. "I agree. I've only had buttered bread on my sandwiches. It's different but tasty." He finished and started on the watercress sandwich. Swallowing the bite he took, Ruddy brushed his cheeks with his fingers and asked, "Do I have food on my face? You're staring."

"No." Honeysuckle dipped her finger in her wine, ran it across his lower lip and then licked it off. "You know what else actresses have a reputation for?"

A rush of lusty thoughts filled his mind. Thoughts no gentleman would repeat, unless he was sure the lady wished to hear them. Ruddy opened his mouth to test the territory, so to speak.

"Shh," Honeysuckle said, touching her wet finger to his mouth, then she dipped her finger in the wine and ran it over his lip again. She kissed him. "They're known for boldly speaking their mind. I think we should have dinner in my hotel tonight and that you should stay past midnight."

Words failed him. Women had flirted with him but he'd never been propositioned by a woman. He'd never been propositioned by anyone.

"Rudyard, you should see your face. I take it from your expression and silence, that you're shocked by my forwardness."

He searched for a better word than shocked. "It was definitely unexpected."

"That doesn't tell me how you feel about the suggestion."

"Unexpected is not unwelcome. I'm delighted. Please be as bold as you wish as often as you wish."

Chapter Twenty-One

Ruddy lay like a damp rag on the bench outside the boxing ring. Every part of him ached with the possible exception of the bottoms of his feet and his butt. "Is there a point where I stop hurting?" he groaned out loud.

"Eventually. You're getting better, stronger every time we meet. I can see you're coming along well." Tony sat next to him wiping his sweat-drenched face. The perspiration barely disappeared before rivulets reappeared and ran from his scalp down his cheeks to his chin.

Ruddy rubbed his towel across his wet chest and down his arms. He brought a towel from home with him whenever they met for sparring. Tony swore the towels at the athletic club were washed after each use but Ruddy had his doubts. Grey and dingy as they were, he questioned if they were laundered regularly, what they used for soap, and what was left behind.

"I visited Kelly's Athletic Club," Tony said.

Intrigued, Ruddy sat up and hung the towel over his neck. "When?"

"More than once, actually. You said early on that the fellow you'd face worked out there. I thought

I'd go and see if I might observe him."

Ruddy racked his brain and couldn't recall ever telling him Tony Napier's name. "I don't remember mentioning his name."

"You were discussing the fact that the fellow was a local champion. You were putting your gloves on and the name Napier came out at the time. I could sit in on sparring sessions there without drawing attention. No one in a hoity-toity club like Kelly's would know me. I asked a few discreet questions and found out when Napier usually came and slid in to watch."

"What did you think? Do I stand any chance of beating him?"

Tony clasped Ruddy on the shoulder. It didn't take a genius to recognize the universal man-to-man shoulder clasp preceded the worst possible answer. "There's always a chance, my friend."

"So, no."

"Not a full blown no, like I said, there's a chance. Napier is skilled. His years of practice reflect that but he's not without faults, faults that can be taken advantage of. Our next session, we're going to concentrate on those."

Finally a ray of light. He might walk away from the fight with his pride and his arse intact. "Tell me there are a lot," Ruddy said. Sweat had gathered at his temples as he talked and ran down his cheeks and dripped from his jaw. He grabbed a club towel from the stack and wiped his face, forgetting his hung around his neck and how disgusting the club towels were.

"Sorry to say, but no, he's not a sloppy fighter. He hasn't many flaws but he has a couple, which may get you a razor thin win."

"I'll take it."

"Your ability to take advantage will depend on how observant you are. Napier is right-hand dominant by nature. However, he's a fooler in the ring. His power punch is in his left. He signals when it is coming though. It's subtle but it's there if you're observant." Tony crawled between the ropes and back into the ring. "Come back in for a minute and I'll show you."

Ruddy did as he asked.

"Take your ready stance, fists up, feet positioned like they'd be at the start of the round. Don't bother trying to counter strike, just block me." Tony threw a slow-motion punch with his right, which Ruddy blocked. Tony drew his right hand back and threw another slow-motion punch and Ruddy blocked it. "Now watch close," Tony said.

Ruddy expected the left and had his right arm ready to block. Tony threw the punch faster than the two from the right. Ruddy only managed to partially block the hit and Tony made contact with the side of Ruddy's jaw.

"That left of Napier's is going to come at you fast and furious. He'll go for your face or chin, hoping to either break your nose or knock you out with a good hard shot to the jaw."

"What did I miss?" Ruddy pressed his fingers to the spot on his jaw where Tony's left connected. It'd be sore later but probably not bruised enough to discolor. He didn't want to discuss his workouts with the other detectives. Only Archie knew. If the others knew he was trying to train, they'd be naturally curious about his progress. He'd rather not answer a bunch of questions. "Show me what he does."

"I said he's subtle. First, he'll lean his right shoulder in but not too far." Tony took Ruddy's hand and placed it on his shoulder. "Feel the movement?" Ruddy nodded. "Just that far. At the same time, he'll tip his head to the right and rise up on the ball of his left foot. He's readying to push off and give that left hook of his impetus, put extra force behind. But that's also when he's most vulnerable because for a fraction of a second, he's off balance."

Ruddy jerked back as Tony lunged coming inches from Ruddy while simultaneously hitting his own left palm with his right fist. "That's when you hit him and hit him hard," Tony stressed.

"I've a bit of time until I need to leave. Let's practice that move of his and my attack."

Tony smiled his usual tight-lipped way. He was missing several teeth. Ruddy thought he was probably self-conscious about it.

"Get ready," Tony said.

Ruddy got into position. They worked out the moves several more times before he finally had to leave.

****

Ruddy and Archie left the last of Skinner's neighboring businesses. They'd re-interviewed the employees and tenants previously questioned by a constable who had been at the murder scene.

"Strange, an alley open to a busy street and lined with busy offices yet no one saw someone breaking into Skinner's office," Archie said.

"The more I think about it, the more I believe, with all the foot and court traffic, dozens had to see him. They just don't know it. A person stood at the window long enough to cut a hole that they could fit their hand through and undo the lock. I believe that person is someone we see but don't notice, someone common to our everyday life," Ruddy said and worked his sore jaw side to side a couple of times.

"What's wrong with your jaw?"

"This morning Tony was demonstrating a left hook. I didn't block in time."

They'd left the last business by the rear door and walked back to Skinner's, stopping in front of the damaged window.

"How are your lessons coming?" Archie asked. "You're moving better this week."

"I'm doing all right, not terrible. Walk part way down the alley," he told Archie. Archie did. "You're passing by and look at me standing here doing something to the window. No one called us so even if you can't make out what I'm doing you're not alarmed. Who am I?" Ruddy turned to Archie. "Who holds no interest for you?"

Archie paced, eyeing Ruddy. "Window cleaner, rag man, janitor, he had to be dressed like a workman. He couldn't look like a ruffian who'd been a defendant at the courthouse."

"They dressed to blend into the background, brought a glass cutting tool, toiled away without consequence, and managed to have Skinner get rid of Button. The audacity to even attempt this in an active location during the day astounds me. We've yet to find the hint of anyone who hates him this much to risk this."

"It's as baffling as Cross's murder in that regard. Who in their right mind cared nothing of risk and entered his home while it was fully staffed? Who hated him that much?"

"Nothing makes sense," Ruddy said. "Shall we start for the station? I'm peckish and would like to buy a bite of something to eat at my desk."

"I can eat."

As they were about to step inside the teashop, a woman screamed from up ahead. Her scream was followed by the rapid calls of police whistles. Ruddy and Archie broke into a run. Somewhere a copper needed help. When they crossed into the next block a man carrying a knife shot out from a side street. Running close behind him was an exceptionally fast woman holding her skirts high out of the way and two men flanking her. Ruddy recognized the three as Flanders and his stocking thief decoy team.

Flanders reached the thief first and tackled him to the ground, struggling to disarm him. Ruddy and Archie caught up to the team. The five of them wrestled with the suspect who fought like a rabid dog, slicing at the officers with the knife.

The suspect booted one of the team in the face. Blood spurted from his nose but he managed to hold onto the offending foot and twist, eliciting a screech from the suspect. The other officer grabbed the suspect's other leg. Flanders was still fighting, fending off blows from the thief's free hand. Archie pummeled the thief as Ruddy bent the knife wielding arm backwards and stepped on the suspect's elbow. The thief cried out.

"Let go of the knife." Ruddy applied more weight and twisted the wrist of his knife wielding hand. "Let go or I'll break your arm."

The suspect screamed and Ruddy wrenched the knife from him.

A woman in the crowd that gathered fainted. Several other ladies near her stood wide-eyed. The rest of the crowd who'd grown around the battling men appeared disappointed at the donnybrook's end. A ripple of laughter and whispers passed through the group when the police stood the suspect up and Flanders was revealed as the tough woman in the dress.

"Here," Archie handed the officer with the bleeding nose his handkerchief. "We'll meet you at the station. Get yourself to a doctor first and then ask him to come to the jail. I think the suspect will need his arm looked at."

The suspect whimpered and cradled his elbow in the palm of his other hand. "I think you broke my arm," he moaned. Ruddy shrugged. "You shouldn't try to stab Peelers."

The suspect yelled when Flanders pulled his arms back to cuff him. "Stop squealing like a woman," Archie told him. "You're embarrassing yourself."

Ruddy patted Flanders on the back. "Good work. Let's get this knapper to the station," he ordered, relieved they had this case solved. After the disappointment and lack of leads on their double homicides, this was a great opportunity to please Jameson.

"I'll sneak Northam in to get a photograph of Flanders in the dress before he can change," Ruddy said low to Archie.

"I'll make sure to delay him until Northam is set up," said Archie, grinning.

Chapter Twenty-Two

"Drat, Me-Too, I have to do more research at the British Museum Library again," Graciela said as she removed her bonnet. "The Chief Librarian there is so snippy. He was so condescending to me last time, I wanted to give him a swift kick in the shins."

The cat sat up, her light eyes following Graciela as she walked around the bedroom, her pinkish feline brows furrowing at the mention of the Chief Librarian.

Graciela noticed and plopped on the bed next to Me-Too. "It can't be avoided. I did some reconnaissance at Finch's townhome. He lives in Mayfair, not far from the park. I could easily walk there from here and return in a decent amount of time. But I have the same problem as I had with Skinner; his family. I can't guarantee that only he will drink the arsenic."

Me-Too dug her nails into Graciela's thigh. "Ow. I've no choice but to search the society pages of the newspaper archives. I need to find out where Finch works." The cat dug the nails of both front paws into her thigh. "Stop it." Graciela pushed the cat away. "No, I won't give up. Two down, two to go."

The cat jumped off the bed and onto the sill of

the window, turning her back to Graciela.
****

"Weren't you here several weeks ago?" the Chief Librarian asked. "Don't bother answering. I know you were. I told you then, this is a serious place. Again, I repeat myself and tell you there's nothing of foolish womanly interest here. You had need of one book we possessed last time, but I find it difficult to believe you have need of any of our resources a second time." He sat back wearing that same thin-lipped arrogant expression he wore last time.

Graciela didn't say, "Listen you parrot-faced little worm fobbing himself off as a man, let me in or else." Although those words hovered on the tip of her tongue, she said, "I need an entrance ticket. I wouldn't have come except it is important to my employer, Lady Zachary. I must search some newspaper archives for her. As soon as I have the information she requires, I will be gone from here." Mrs. Zachary's husband was a man of influence in his time and her name still carried some authority.

Upon hearing it, the Chief Librarian mumbled his displeasure but issued an entrance ticket. "Do hurry and sit in the back so as to not disturb the men who are conducting important work."

Behind him, the Chief Librarian had a tea tray with a pot, a small tub of sugar and pitcher of cream. His half-filled cup of tea sat at his elbow on the desk. Graciela eyed the teapot on the tray as he wrote out the ticket. *If I had my flask of arsenic, I could make you sorry you gave me or any other woman who came here stick.*

"What are you staring at?" the librarian asked and looked over his shoulder.

"Nothing. I was just thinking."

"Here's your entrance ticket. Again, don't be long." He held the ticket out.

She found the information she sought in the Illustrated London News. The paper carried a story of the banns and description of the wedding of Finch's daughter. In the banns, Finch was described as a renowned Harley Street doctor.

A doctor, Graciela thought, could work to her advantage, much more so than trying to find a way into Skinner's office. She could always fake an illness. A shadow appeared in her peripheral vision. She covered the card she'd written Finch's information on with her hand and looked over. It was the librarian.

"Are you almost done?" he asked, eyeing her hand covering the card.

Momentary worry crossed her mind as to what he might've seen. But even if he did see the information it was just a woman writing the name of a well-known doctor down. Nothing suspicious in that. "Soon."

"Good." The librarian left.

On her way out, she dropped the ticket on the librarian's desk. He wasn't there. She glanced over at the tea tray where the pot sat unattended. *You're lucky I'm not a murderer, Mr. Librarian.*

****

She'd chosen headaches as her particular medical problem. The directory of doctors included short commentaries from many regarding some of the various illnesses they routinely treated. Finch was among those who treated ladies who suffered headaches. All the doctors who mentioned treatment for those women said it was the result of an inherited gender flaw not found in men. According to those same doctors, men who suffered headaches always had medical problems as the root cause. Women, by virtue of their sex were given to hysteria; headaches were a natural byproduct.

"Balderdash," Graciela whispered reading their arrogant assumptions and male crowings about so-called feminine defects. She'd nearly gone mad with crushing headaches for months following the rape. Headaches never troubled her prior to the incident. Eventually, they subsided. One thing she knew and didn't need a medical degree to tell her, the painful episodes had nothing to do with her gender or hysteria.

On occasion, she battled other weaknesses. All her life she had loved swans. She loved to sit by the river and watch them swim by in pairs. Such elegant birds, such a sense of peace surrounded them. She'd been riverside gathering wildflowers and watching the swans that day when Finch and his buddies caught her. After that day and ever since, the sight of swans was no longer a thing of beauty to her but a sight that made her heart race and shortened her breath. When she and Zachary visited places where swans were present, she'd been fortunate and hidden the problem from Zachary by focusing attention elsewhere. She wondered sometimes if other rape victims had similar reactions. There was no way to know of course, no woman in her right mind admitted to rape.

Graciela had to take three trams to Harley

Street. She'd been to Harley Street before when accompanying Mrs. Zachary to the doctor and the one solo trip. Those times they came by carriage, which was far more comfortable. This wasn't the first time on public transportation. She'd taken streetcars visiting places on her days off but earlier in the day before the afternoon rush. Today the overcrowding on two of the trams and press of strangers on all sides of her as the cars lurched along, stopping and starting set her teeth on edge. She had enough on her mind thinking about fooling Finch without the additional irritating distraction the crowds caused.

She wanted to at least get a look at the building where Finch had his office. If possible, she'd like to take a peek inside. If he was as successful as Cross and Skinner, and in all likelihood he probably was, he'd have an assistant. She'd have to find a way of getting the assistant off the premises when the time came. *Wouldn't it be lovely if the ruse of a midday meal worked again, as it did with Skinner's clerk?*

Finch's office was in a two-story brick building midblock from the tram stop. Finch was listed on a brass plaque by the entry door along with several other doctors. Graciela went inside where another directory in the vestibule listed Finch and indicated his office was on the second floor. *Hmm, there'll be no cutting of windows and breaking into his place.*

She stood outside his door for several minutes debating whether to go in today or come back on her next day off. There was no reason to put off going in today and making an appointment. She grasped the doorknob but couldn't bring herself to turn it and go in.

A horrible sense of foreboding bore down on her and she jumped away from the door.

"Stop it, Graciela. What's wrong with you? You're just going into a doctor's office. You've done that a dozen times."

She stepped up and grasped the knob again. Again, she backed away as the press of a warning shadow filled her with an inexplicable fear. She leaned against the opposite wall and closed her eyes, trying to gather courage.

She pictured the attack in her mind. She went over the details step by step, remembering who did what, remembering the horror of how each pig felt pushing into her. She let the memory and her hate sustain her and give her what she needed. With hate buoying her, she entered his office.

An overhead bell jingled as she stepped across the threshold into the well-appointed room. Two chairs with a table between them were arranged along the walls to her left and right. Elegant and beautiful Meissen and Sevres porcelain plates sat on the tables. Directly ahead was a large walnut desk with a brass and green glass gas lamp. Wall sconces kept the room nicely lit. Behind the desk on one side was a tea tray and on the other a file cabinet.

The waiting room had a more welcoming feel than Mrs. Zachary's doctor's. He had only two chairs and they were uncomfortable ladder back wooden ones with hard seats. The chairs here had leather padded arms and seats. The lighting in Mrs. Zachary's doctor's office was dim and dreary. No wall sconces, just a gas lamp on the nurse's desk. This room was papered in a soft green moiré with paintings of different native English trees. The wallpaper in Zachary's doctor's office was shades of grey stripes. Sitting there was akin to sitting in a rain cloud.

A nurse in her late twenties came out from the inner office. How crisp and professional she appeared. Her light blue gown looked fresh pressed with hardly a wrinkle. Her white apron hadn't a speck of blood or smudge on it. Her hair was neatly tucked under her headdress and her gold wire-frame glasses added an additional air of seriousness.

She gave Graciela pause and an idea for her future. Mrs. Zachary wouldn't live forever. Graciela thought nursing offered a good switch of professions. To move from lady's companion into a profession where her livelihood didn't depend on the whims of an old woman made a lot of sense. She wondered how long she'd have to train. How much would she have to save to afford nursing school?

"May I help you?" the nurse asked Graciela, interrupting her thoughts.

They were alone in the waiting room, so Graciela spoke in a normal tone. "I would like to make an appointment. I've been suffering headaches."

"You're not one of Dr. Finch's regular patients. Do you have the name of one of our patients as a referral?"

A referral. Graciela hadn't counted on that request. Of course, it never came up before. Whenever she had need of a doctor now, she used Zachary's. She had an automatic referral with her employer. She did a mental scramble of ways to get around the referral

240

issue and came up with little to nothing to offer the nurse.

"I am currently Dr. Fitzhugh's patient. I am Mrs. Esther Zachary's companion and Dr. Fitzhugh is her doctor."

The nurse sat in the desk chair and folded her hands in front of her on top of a leather bound diary. The book the doctor kept his appointments recorded in, no doubt. "Then why come to Dr. Finch? We are familiar with Dr. Fitzhugh. He has a fine reputation."

The nurse's somber manner, her stiff posture, and the way her mouth tightened after asking the question brought memories of Graciela's old headmistress to mind. The way the nurse's pale, untidy brows and intense blue eyes focused on Graciela reminded her even more of the headmistress. A foolish temptation to confess what her true intent was darted in and out of her mind along with a sense of guilt she hadn't experienced in years.

"I hope anything I say is held in the strictest confidence," she said, shaking off the uncomfortable feeling.

The nurse nodded.

Graciela approached the desk and hung her head for five seconds. She stared at the floor and counted to five before raising her eyes to the nurse. Hopefully the delay lent an element of genuine dismay. "I find the man has a less than caring attitude. That may not be true but it's how I feel. I'm suffering headaches. When I discuss the matter with Dr. Fitzhugh, he's been rather cavalier about my pain."

Doctors didn't like to poach from other doctors,

especially ones they were acquainted with. Graciela chewed her lower lip and hung her head again, hoping to convey discomfort at disloyalty to Dr. Fitzhugh. She took a deep breath, looked up and said, "I just want them to end. But I need a doctor who truly wants to help me."

"I don't know if the doctor will accept you as a patient without a referral. Nor can I say without consulting him if he is willing to take on a patient from Dr. Fitzhugh. He's not good friends with Fitzhugh, but even so, it's not good form to purloin another's patients."

"He's not really purloining if I've come to him on my own. I voluntarily left Fitzhugh."

The nurse spread her hands in temporary peace. "Semantics. It's in the perception. You were his and then you weren't."

This was the only means Graciela knew to gain access to Finch. She had to convince him to take her on as a patient. "Please...I'm sorry, I don't know your name."

"Miss Keating."

"Please speak to him, Miss Keating. I beg you. I need help. I'll wait here until he is free of his current patient and you can talk to him."

"I'll do what I can. No promises."

When she slipped inside the exam room, Graciela got a fast glimpse of a dark-haired man standing in front of a worried looking woman. He was holding her hands in his. His head was bent as he talked to her. He didn't turn his attention from the woman when Keating entered.

Graciela sat under a painting of an ancient oak. Outside the bell tower on a nearby church rang eleven. She'd only been on Harley Street when she or Mrs. Zachary went to Dr. Fitzhugh. They came by carriage and left immediately. After she left today, she'd stroll down the street. Maybe there was a tearoom in walking distance. She could do with a scone and a cup.

She found she couldn't bear to sit while awaiting his decision. She began to pace, circling the room from the desk to the front door and back. To her dismay, no decanter of wine or brandy was displayed in the room, nor a tea service. She could only hope Finch kept one or the other in the exam room. If he didn't, she had no idea how to proceed with administering the arsenic.

After what seemed like forever, the female patient came out of the exam room. A few more minutes passed then Nurse Keating stepped out and told Graciela to come inside.

The exam room was almost identical to Dr. Fitzhugh's. The room had a long table covered with a white linen sheet, a tri-fold screen for patients to undress behind, a stand with a basin, pitcher and stack of towels, and on the other side of the door was a steel multi-shelf stand against the wall. On the top of the stand were several common instruments used by doctors in routine exams. Grim looking tools in Graciela's opinion. Angled in the corner was a desk with the usual desk materials, a lamp, inkwell, and a wooden tray. Unfortunately, Graciela didn't see any display of teacups or decanters near this desk either. *Not good.*

Finch was standing by the desk when she entered. He wore a tweed frock coat with black trousers and waistcoat and a diamond pattern ascot. She needn't feel the cloth to know the wool was of the finest weave. Of course he was successful. She expected nothing less.

"Good morning. You made no appointment but no matter, I'll still speak with you. Before we begin, let me introduce myself. I'm Dr. Finch, and you are?" He remained where he was and kept one hand in the pocket of his trousers and the other resting on his middle. Graciela had the sense that he waited for the first opportunity to politely send her on her way.

She searched his eyes for the slightest sign of recognition of her on his part but saw none. "Graciela Robson."

Of the three rapists she'd now seen again, Finch aged the best. He still had a fine head of dark hair with grey touching lightly at the temples alone. His facial muscles were still firm. He was clean shaven then. Now he wore a neatly trimmed beard but it was easy to see his jawline stayed strong without the early wattle men his age begin to develop. His eyes were a deep, warm brown. How strange to stand in front of him and stare into them so hard. The day of the attack he insisted she close her eyes and not look at him while he raped her.

No, not now. An involuntary whimper slipped out. The emotions of the attack suddenly gripped her, the rush of terror, the horror that engulfed her as she was overpowered. The acute sting of the first penetration and the pain of them pushing, prodding, stretching her. Light-headed and afraid she'd faint,

Graciela grabbed the edge of the exam table and tried to force even breaths.

"Miss Robson, please sit. Tell me what's wrong. Are you in pain?" Finch wrapped his arm around her waist and led her to the chair in front of his desk.

She'd flinched at his touch. In her plans, she had focused on the logistics of getting him alone, not on the emotional effect his touch would have on her. Nor had she considered what she'd feel having a true conversation with one of her rapists. She'd only pictured talking to them after they drank the poison. With Cross and Skinner that was all that had transpired. Facing Finch now, forcing herself to keep a tight grip on her emotions, on her memories while speaking to him, as though they had no past, as though she had no prior loathing of his touch.

Without asking, he removed Graciela's bonnet, then unbuttoned and loosened the collar on her dress. "Miss Keating, bring me a cool wet cloth, a cup of water, and my stethoscope.

"I'm not in pain. I was just overtaken with dizziness for a moment."

"Is your stomach upset? Do you feel like you might vomit?"

Graciela shook her head. "No."

Keating returned with the cloth and cup and Finch pressed the cool compress to Graciela's forehead. "Hold this against your head. You'll be fine in a moment. Try to breath normally. When you feel you are able, take a sip of water. It will help refresh you. I'd like to listen to your heart as a matter of routine."

He stroked her back along her spine as he

spoke. The action relaxed her and her breathing returned to normal quickly. He pressed the stethoscope to her chest in three different places. "Your heart is beating faster than normal but not at a worrying rate."

"Thank you." She finished the cup of water and Finch handed Keating the compress. "Are you up to discussing your headache situation?" he asked.

"I am."

"Miss Keating explained your situation to me. She also explained to you it is not my habit to acquire another doctor's patients without his awareness or agreement."

At the mention of her name, Keating wet the tip of her little finger and ran it over her untidy brows. That's interesting, Graciela thought.

"As I explained to Nurse Keating, I'm not satisfied with Dr. Fitzhugh's handling of my headaches. He's not helping me. I must beg your willingness to not discuss the matter with him. It could cost me my position. If he feels I've insulted him or insinuated his skill as a doctor is not up to par, he will tell Mrs. Zachary. She thinks highly of him, and if he asks her to dismiss me, she might."

Finch stood next to her chair. The fact she was sitting and he standing emphasized his height. A grim reminder he'd been the tallest of her attackers. If she turned her head to the right, she was eye-level with the buttons on his trousers, which she couldn't bear. She kept her eyes raised to his when she spoke and otherwise looked straight ahead.

He reached over and took a ledger of some kind from the tray on his desk. As he moved, his trousers brushed the sleeve of her dress and she involuntarily flinched. She glanced over at Keating, hoping the nurse didn't notice but Keating's eyes were on Finch. The observation provided a nice distraction. Graciela recognized the desire in her eyes and was curious if Finch saw it too and acted on it. That could be a problem. If they had an on-going affaire de coeur, it might make getting Finch alone much more difficult.

"I'll want to conduct a complete examination before seeing to your headaches," Finch said. "I have an opening this Thursday afternoon."

"My day off is Monday. I'd like to come then."

"Sorry, I am not in the office on Mondays."

"Can't you make an exception?" Doctors set their own hours. Graciela thought a refusal to make an exception on his part would be wanton stubbornness.

"No. I do rounds at Our Lady of Mercy Charity Hospital on Mondays."

Mrs. Zachary always took a nap in the afternoons. Graciela did a fast calculation of time in her head. It would be tight but she might be able to see Finch and return home while Zachary napped. "What time is the Thursday opening?"

"Two o'clock."

"I'll take that appointment."

He wrote her name in his ledger. "Nurse Keating, please have Miss Robson fill out the patient form." He removed the stethoscope from his neck. "And please put these back."

"Certainly." The back of her hand brushed his as she took the instrument and they shared a brief but intimate glance.

Definitely something going on between these two. Ugh, another problem I didn't need or anticipate. I wonder if she's the type who wouldn't want to live without the man she loves?

Chapter Twenty-Three

Morris joined Ruddy and Winky at Ruddy's favorite table at the Boot and Bayonet. June was right behind Morris with their beers and a plate of meat scraps for Winky.

"No banger scraps in there, I hope," Ruddy said. "Winky loves them, but they play havoc with his digestion, which I pay a price for if I dare breathe through my nose."

"No, no banger bits. I remember you didn't want him to have those. Just some lamb, chicken, and beef fat." June laid the plate on the floor. Winky jumped down and began devouring the treat. "Will you be eating tonight, Budgie?" June asked.

"What's the special?"

"Haddock fish pie." June wiggled her brows. "Grandma made her tasty sticky toffee pudding if you're in a mind for dessert after."

Ruddy wasn't overly fond of desserts, but Morris's wife made the best sticky toffee pudding he'd ever had, better than his mum's. He'd never tell his mum that, of course. "Yes to both."

"Are you still taking boxing lessons?" Morris asked and took a pull from his tankard of beer.

"I am."

"How are they going? You weren't happy with your slow progress the last time we talked."

"Better. I'm not spending as much time flopping about in the ropes like a wounded fish anymore." Ruddy smiled over the rim of his tankard before taking several refreshing swallows. The day had been hot and the beer, although warm, still tasted sweet and refreshing washing its way down his throat.

"Think there's a chance you can beat this Napier fellow?"

Ruddy raised his hands in a universal who knows gesture.

"Your lessons are still with that Afghanistan veteran?"

Ruddy nodded.

"You still interested in finding him another job?"

Ruddy put his tankard down. "Yes, do you know of one?"

"I need a man to help here. My man Tom is going home to Herefordshire back to his family's sheep farm. I can't do it all myself, not one-armed."

"Morris, he'd love to work here. This would be a good change for him. If I recall right, Tom has a room here above the storeroom. Is it possible Tony could have the same arrangement?"

"Yes, but with rules. He must keep his area clean. *He* must be clean. I won't put up with slovenliness. He must be a gentleman and no rough talk around my Bess or our June. How he is with this lot..." Morris glanced around the pub. "Is a different story. I'm sure his fighting skills will come in handy on occasion."

"I'll tell him. Thank you. I appreciate you giving him this chance." Ruddy polished off his beer faster than usual, excited by the idea of delivering the news to Tony Critchlow. Ruddy hadn't told him he'd looked into the possibilities of Tony working somewhere other than the athletic club. He didn't want to get his hopes up.

"Are you working any new interesting cases?" Morris asked.

"As a matter of fact, I'm working on a couple of interesting poisoning cases."

A young corporal sitting with his buddies at another table tossed a half-eaten banger on the floor in front of Winky, who wolfed it down. He followed that by quickly lapping up a splash of spilled beer.

Ruddy groaned and called to the table of soldiers, "no more bangers please, lads." He waved to June who came over. "Bring a round of beers to that table," he indicated the corporal and his friends. "Charge my bill for the drinks."

"You don't have to do that, Ruddy. I'll put the drinks on the house," Morris said. "As for your case, is that interesting in a good way or messy way?"

"In a baffling way, which walks a fine line with messy way."

"One advantage to owning a pub is I'm never baffled."

They sat quietly drinking and watching a game of darts between two talented teams. "You used to play darts when you first started coming here, but I haven't seen you play for quite some time," Morris said.

"I enjoy darts better than cards or dice. Your boards are generally busy by the time I arrive. I don't want to put my name on a wait list. I'm fine watching and drinking."

June brought Ruddy's fish pie and fresh beers for him and Morris along with the beers for the corporal's table. How the petite young woman managed the heavy tray impressed Ruddy. She carried it shoulder height without a grimace of pain or struggle.

He'd just dipped his fork into the pie when the corporal came to the table. "Thank you. Very kind of you sir."

"You're welcome, but Morris here deserves the thank you more than I. The Boot and Bayonet bought your drinks." Ruddy smiled and returned to his dinner expecting the soldier to leave. The young man hovered in his peripheral vision. Turning back to him, Ruddy asked, "Is there something you want to say?"

"One of the lads at our table heard a rumor that you've a V.C.? Is that true?"

Ruddy sighed. "Yes."

The soldier snapped to attention, clicking his heels together and saluting.

"At ease." Ruddy gestured for the young man to relax. "Where's your regiment deployed?"

"Gibraltar, sir."

"Don't call me sir. I never got past your rank. As for Gibraltar, that's not a bad posting. Well done you," Ruddy gave him a congratulatory smile touched with faint nostalgic envy. In his army days, he'd have welcomed Gibraltar with her sea breezes and temperate climate, unlike the insect-infested and hotter-than-the-devil's-boudoir Africa. "I hope you find your time with the military fulfilling. Take care of yourself, soldier."

The corporal continued to hover at Ruddy's elbow. He didn't want to get into a deep conversation with the milk-bearded soldier but he'd had similar situations with the young ones. The medal was a source of fascination for them. The glory of battle they imagined. "Is there something you want to ask me?"

The corporal nodded. "We were wondering. What battle was it?"

"Rorke's Drift."

The young man twisted around and told the friends at his table, "Rorke's Drift."

Their eyes widened, no doubt having heard of the incredible forces the British contingent overcame.

"What was it like, fighting such a fierce battle? We don't get much by way of excitement on the Rock," the corporal said, using the soldier's slang for the colony.

"Bloody and brutal."

"Let the man eat his meal, lad," Morris told the corporal. "Get on back to your mates now."

"Sorry sir, just never met anyone with a V.C. before," the soldier said with a quick nod to Ruddy.

Ruddy dived into his fish pie as the soldier turned and left. He finished the bite he took. "It makes me feel old as my dad when the young ones call me sir like that. There are a couple at the station who do it as well. Very annoying." He had at least a decade on the corporal, but he wasn't in the sage old man age bracket either. "My pie is cold."

"Want another?"

Ruddy shook his head.

"You were saying you're baffled by these poisoning cases. What happens if you can't solve your murders?" Morris asked. "This wouldn't be the first time a case or two has gone unsolved."

"No. But with these two, any follow-up action by the department depends on the families. Cross only has a sister who lives in the country. We haven't heard much from her. I don't believe they were close. Skinner is a different story. His family has some political influence. How much, I'm not certain. They could request the cases be turned over to Scotland Yard." The pie's gravy softened the bottom crust into a tasty sludge. Ruddy broke down the sides of the crust and mushed them into the gravy, turning them into similar sludge. "That would certainly be an embarrassing blow to my pride."

"If you can't solve the murders, there's no guarantee the Yard can."

"Not the point. The point is—I've never had a case reassigned due to a failure of action or inability on my part. It's..." Ruddy considered how to best describe how he'd feel. "It'd be an awful blow. I'd be beyond embarrassed."

"Then you'd better find your killer," Morris said in a dry tone. Someone who didn't know Morris might've taken the comment as acerbic and unkind. Ruddy knew better. This was his friend's way of telling him steady on, he'd get it figured out.

****

Ruddy told Tony about Morris's job offer and

had arranged to meet Tony after his shift at the station. For Tony, this was the light at the end of the tunnel he never thought he'd see, an escape from the dismal work and living conditions at the athletic club.

"We'll go to the public bathhouse first and get you cleaned up before you meet Morris. He'll want to talk to you and make sure you'll fit in working with the family. Let me see what decent clean clothes you have," Ruddy said.

Tony looked sheepish. "I don't have much." He opened a drawer and pulled out a shirt that had been white and now had a yellow tint. Sweat rings marked the underarms and some buttons were broken. His trousers hung on a hook on the back of the door. Tony took those down and laid them on the bed for Ruddy to examine. The trousers were coarse black wool worn so long a light sheen had formed over the knees and thighs.

"These clothes won't do. You don't have anything else?" Ruddy immediately regretted the question. The man lived in a squalid room, in a seedy neighborhood, and was poor as a church mouse. What need did he have for decent clothes? He probably thought himself lucky if he had a winter coat that wasn't too tattered to wear.

"No. Sorry, Mr. Bloodstone."

Ruddy thought for a moment. "Tell you what. Put your good trousers and shirt on. I'll leave you at the bathhouse. While you're there, I'll get an old shirt and trousers of mine and bring those to you. You'll have to roll up the sleeves and the hem of the trousers as they'll both be too long but they should fit well enough otherwise."

Tony dropped onto the edge of his cot. His elbows resting on his thighs, he dropped his head into his hands.

"Tony, if I've insulted you, it wasn't my intent. I'm just trying to help. A moment ago you were glad for the opportunity to work at the pub. I'm not sure what has changed."

"No one's ever done something like this for me," Tony said, finally looking up. "No one has ever helped me." A tear rolled down Tony's cheek.

Seeing the strong boxer cry threw Ruddy for six. God, but it was worse than when a woman cried. "No need for tears. This is just one veteran helping another. Get dressed so we can go to Morris's."

Tony wiped the wet streak away, rose, and crushed Ruddy in a bear hug that left his spine feeling good, after the shock of the initial crack.

After Tony had finished dressing, Ruddy handed him a five pound note. "Here. Tomorrow buy yourself another shirt and trousers and make certain you have a good pair of boots. You'll be on your feet a lot."

"I will. When I do, I'll be sure to have the clothes you loan me washed and return them to you straight away."

"Don't. They're yours to keep. I can spare them."

"In all the excitement of the job news I forgot to tell you what I discovered about that Napier fellow."

"Does it pertain to me?"

Tony shrugged a shoulder. "Might. He's started

working out twice a day. He goes early in the morning right after sunrise and again late in the afternoon."

"Don't you have any boxers here who work out twice a day?"

"Yes, when they have important fights coming up. There's something else. I heard the name Bloody Ruddy mentioned when he was talking about the new routines. Bloody Ruddy is you, isn't it?"

"That's me all right."

"Want to start doubling up on your sessions?"

"I think it best."

Chapter Twenty-Four

Graciela watched with increasing unease out the carriage window at the change in the neighborhoods. The cabbie hadn't passed a park or well-tended building for many blocks. More and more buildings had windows that still remained boarded from the days before the repeal of the window tax. Lace curtains and velvet draperies were everywhere in Belgrave Square but her destination was a different London from the one she knew.

"Do you wish me to wait, Miss?" the driver asked as she stepped onto the sidewalk in front of the hospital.

The eyes of a cluster of men loitering outside a pub fixed on her. Graciela quickly looked away. A horse tied by a slaughterhouse up the street squealed. She shuddered at the animal's panicked cry. In all the years she'd lived in London, she'd never been on this side of the city. She'd only read about the East End in the broadsheets. What a shocking sight to see in person. An abomination to beauty and human decency.

"It would be best if I do, Miss. There aren't many reliable cabbies who work this area if you take my meaning," the cabbie said.

"Yes, please wait. I won't be terribly long." She had opted to take a cab rather than trams from Mrs. Zachary's to Our Lady of Mercy Hospital. With the hospital being across town, she'd never make it there and back before Mrs. Zachary awoke from her nap.

Instead of moving toward the hospital entry, she turned and placed a foot on the step of the carriage.

"Do you wish to leave? A wise choice, Miss. This is no place for a gentle lady like yourself." The cabbie took her other hand in his to help her up the rest of the carriage steps.

Stricken, she couldn't decide which way to go. Part of her was desperate to talk to some of the patients at the hospital. Curiosity over the possibility of Finch having become a reformed man from the young buck rapist drove her decision to go to the hospital. Zachary believed every man no matter how wicked, with the right provocation, had in them the capacity for redemption. Graciela never challenged her employer but actually believed the opposite. She believed every good man with the right provocation could be turned to wickedness.

Finch would be a good test to see who was right. Now that she was here she wasn't certain she wanted to proceed. This place, the filth, the hopeless faces of the people on the street and those huddled in doorways, there was nowhere her eyes landed that offered relief.

"Miss, shall we go then?" The cabbie gave her hand a little tug.

I need to know. You brutalized a young woman, doctor. Because you volunteer your services and treat these poverty stricken women and children, am I now to believe the darkness in you has supposedly gone? I would know for sure.

Her curiosity prevailed. Graciela stepped down onto the sidewalk again and turned back toward the hospital entry. "No. I have information to gather here. I will stay. But don't you go anywhere. Wait for me," she added in a rush.

"No worries, Miss."

She'd never been in a hospital. As soon as she was inside the smell blanketed her like a thick fog. It was a stomach-churning combination of camphor, vinegar, and sick.

"May I help you?" a nurse in a dark uniform with long white apron and crisp white headdress asked. She set the tray of medicine bottles she carried onto a wheeled cart.

Graciela hadn't seen or heard her until the woman spoke. "Where did you come from?"

"Here," she tipped her head toward a door. "One of our supply rooms, not that it's anyone's business. Back to my question, how can I help you? You don't appear sick or poverty stricken."

Graciela anticipated the question and had an answer ready. "I've been considering volunteering. Before I made a commitment I thought it best to visit. I want to make an informed decision."

"Lord knows we can always use an extra pair of hands." The nurse busied herself with switching out bottles. "You're not the first to come here with a notion of doing something altruistic for the desperate East Enders. If after today you return, I'll be surprised. Your kind rarely does. It's much easier to leave a few shillings in our poor basket and scurry away." The nurse looked up from her work. "What you'll see is nothing you've ever been exposed to and will wish you hadn't seen."

The nurse pressed her fists into her lower back, closed her eyes, and rolled her head around on her shoulders one turn in each direction. When she finished, she straightened and pulled the cart out. "I'm afraid none of us nurses have the time to show you around at the moment. You're free to walk through the wards and speak to some of the patients. I would ask that you use discretion regarding whom you speak with. Please leave the painfully weak children and women alone to rest and don't pester any patients you talk to with too many questions."

"I won't."

"There are nurse's stations at the end of every ward if you have questions."

The first ward she entered was all children. They appeared to be of various ages ranging from toddlers to ten years of age. Some were curled up asleep, some sat up in their beds. As she walked down the center aisle, the state of their small bodies horrified her. All were reed thin, their coloring either an unnatural grey or lily white. One or two had a jaundiced cast to their skin. A streak of panic hit her and she wondered if they didn't have a contagious disease. Only a few bothered to note Graciela as she passed by.

Why did so many have racking coughs? Wasn't the purpose of admitting them to the hospital to rid the children of such problems? Didn't they receive cough medicine? One toddler began brutal fits of coughing. In the brief seconds between fits the child struggled for breath, wheezing loudly with halting starts. Graciela ventured over. She had no idea how to help other than to hold the child. But no nurse was in sight and she couldn't stand by and do nothing while the child suffered. The toddler was curled up under a cheap blanket. Graciela sat on the edge of the cot and drew the blanket back.

"Dear Lord." Her heart broke seeing the child. The little girl was about two, pale as chalk with blue eyes set deep into the dark hollows of illness. A haunting sight in one so young and small. She lifted the child and set her down on her lap. "Shh, little one." She began to rock the child. When the toddler was struck with another coughing fit, Graciela held her tight to her chest and stroked her back.

"That's my sister, Siobhan." It was the boy in the next bed.

"How long has she been sick?"

"I'm not sure. I lost count of the days we've been here."

"Is your mother sick too?"

"Don't know. I haven't seen her. She never came back after dropping us off. This is the orphan ward."

What the devil kind of mother does that? "Where's your father?"

"Dead. He fell from a roof last year and broke his neck." The boy bent double, coughing.

She waited for the boy's bout to end. "What's your name?"

"Danny."

"Does a doctor named Finch ever treat you?"

Both Danny and Siobhan broke into more fits. Graciela's eyes filled with tears as the girl's face turned bright red with her fight. Her sunken chest heaved in a staccato pattern at her continued battle for air between the hacking bouts.

"Yes, Doctor Finch comes every Monday to the ward, sometimes alone, sometimes with his lady nurse. He doesn't always see both of us. Not anymore."

"What do you mean?"

Danny shrugged. "I heard him talking to his lady nurse. He said Siobhan is hopeless. He only treats me now."

"Does he help you?"

"Yes, but I don't want to get better."

"Why?"

"Then I have to leave. I don't want to leave Siobhan alone. She shouldn't be alone when she..." Danny hung his head. "When she, you know..."

Graciela wanted to tell him perhaps death would be a mercy, considering her suffering, but she wasn't certain Danny was ready to see it that way. "I understand." Siobhan had finally quieted and Graciela laid her down and covered her up. "You're a good brother, Danny."

The greater test of Finch's possible redemption would be found among the women. Graciela stood. "Which way is the ward where the sick women are?"

"That way." Danny pointed to the left.

She passed a different nurse than the first. This one looked up from putting linens in a cupboard. She was much older than the other nurse. Wrinkles creased every inch of her face and brown age spots dotted the backs of her hands. "We were told a possible volunteer was walking around the wards. Do you have any questions?"

"Not yet." Graciela smiled and continued on for a few steps then stopped and turned. "Actually, I do have a question about the women who are treated here. What sorts of diseases are most common? Are your women patients poxy ladies of the night?" She assumed they were. If Finch didn't press them for sexual favors, that might be why, which would affect her test.

"No. The syphilitic ones receive initial treatment here but they are transported to other hospitals as soon as possible." Her lips pursed in moral superiority. "As a charity we welcome any and all sick and destitute women and children, except those who are suffering results from the wages of sin." She eyed Graciela suspiciously. "Why do you ask?"

Graciela pulled the necklace she wore with the tiny gold cross out from under her collar. The nurse eyed it and she looked a tad less sour. "I was curious. One reads about the rampant crime and loose morals of the East End. I hoped it hadn't corrupted hospital life. I wouldn't want to volunteer in such a place."

"Of course not. I couldn't blame you. Worry not."

"If you'll excuse me, I'd like to see the women's ward now."

"Straight ahead," the nurse said with a smile.

Graciela didn't waste time speaking to the very old or very homely. If Finch were to trouble any women, he'd surely approach the younger, prettier ones.

She talked to the three prettiest she saw. All spoke well of Finch. He'd treated each and all were on the mend. When asked, they expressed their gratitude for the chance of having a doctor of his reputation helping them.

It appeared Mrs. Zachary was right. A wicked man can change. He helped the children and the women. How could she kill him and deprive them of that?

Graciela thanked each woman and was headed toward the door when a hand grabbed her sleeve. Startled, she turned to see a young red-haired woman in a hospital gown hiding behind a privacy screen. The woman's cheeks and nose were covered in freckles but they did nothing to detract from her lovely face and bright green eyes.

Unsure of the woman's mental state, Graciela warily asked, "What is it you want?"

"Come closer." She gestured for Graciela to step behind the screen. Graciela hesitated but stepped just far enough to be out of sight of the other yet still be arm's length from the woman. "Follow me." The woman quietly opened a door and went through.

Graciela paused in the doorway before going further. The room the woman entered was for surgery. No one other than the redhead was there. Graciela went inside, but she palmed a scalpel from a nearby table just in case.

"Close the door," the patient told her and Graciela did but not all the way.

"Why am I here?" Graciela asked.

"The others won't tell you the truth," the patient said.

"Truth about what?"

"Doctor Finch. They're afraid he'll stop coming if they do."

Curiosity piqued, Graciela asked, "What truth?"

"He makes us have sex with him. Not all of us but me and the ones you talked to. He takes us into the storage closet and makes us do things to him."

"Do you tell him you don't want to?"

She looked away and sighed. "I tried, once. He shrugged and walked away without treating me. I called after him and told him I changed my mind." She turned back to Graciela. "After all, he's just one more," she said in a bitter tone.

"Are you a prostitute? The nurse indicated they don't accept them here."

"Most of us try to find jobs at the workhouse. Sometimes failing that, you do what you must to eat."

"I understand. Someone should tell the nurses what he's about."

"Goodness, you are a thick one. Of course they know. They'll never speak against him. That'd be daft. They'd never get another Harley Street doctor to come here on his own."

"Why are you telling me this?"

She was quiet for a long moment as if searching for the right words to explain. At last she said, "I'm tired of people taking things from me I don't wish to give. I don't have much but there's always someone who wants to take that little bit."

"Who knows, maybe the doctor will get his just

deserts."

"No he won't. Men like him never do. I just wanted someone to know I'm angry. Nothing I can do about it, but I'm angry."

"We'll see." Graciela left the hospital. Inside the cab she smiled knowing she'd been right and Zachary wrong.

Wickedness is a stain on a man's soul and no amount of false altruism can wash it out. You're still a rapist. The only thing that's changed is the type of force you exert.

Bastard.

Chapter Twenty-Five

Soft, feminine hands clasped over Ruddy's eyes. "Guess who?"

"I'd be in trouble if I didn't recognize that lovely voice, Miss Flowers."

She lowered her hands and came around in front of him and Tony. Both men removed their hats and Ruddy introduced her. "Honeysuckle this is a friend of mine, Tony Critchlow. Tony, this is the delightful Honeysuckle Flowers."

She extended a gloved hand that Tony bent and gave an awkward kiss to and then said, "Nice to meet you."

"So this is the Boot and Bayonet I've heard you speak of," Honeysuckle said. Ruddy and Tony had just left when they ran into her. "My modiste is down the street. I've passed it numerous times but never paid attention."

"Mr. Bloodstone was kind enough to get me a job here. It's a kindness I never expected when we started our boxing lessons," Tony told her.

Ruddy had been standing to the side and slightly behind her. He shook his head, willing Tony to glance over and see him signaling not to talk about the lessons.

To Ruddy's chagrin, Tony didn't notice and babbled away. "Mr. Bloodstone's a quick learner. He's fast on his feet."

Honeysuckle turned. "Rudyard, you never mentioned boxing lessons. What are they for?"

Ruddy shot Tony a deadly glance defying him to contradict his explanation. "No special reason. I thought it good to know some moves. I have the occasional arrestee who resists."

"Rudyard Bloodstone, you're a terrible liar. I believe I told you so when we first went out, that you shouldn't play cards. You've a face that can't keep a secret."

"I don't know what you mean."

"I saw the look you gave Tony. I know a keep-your-mouth-shut look when I see one. Something is going on and you don't want to tell me. You might as well fess up, Rudyard. I'll find out. I have ways."

He was an awful liar, always had been, even as a child. But, no matter. Since she couldn't prove different, he'd deny any secret intent. "Nothing is going on. Tony, I'll bid you good evening and see you tomorrow at the appointed time," Ruddy said.

"Nice meeting you, Miss Flowers." Tony put his hat on and mouthed sorry to Ruddy, before he left.

"Have you eaten?" Ruddy asked Honeysuckle.

"No, I'm famished. What about you?"

"I could eat."

"Want to eat in my room at the hotel?"

"Can I bring Winky?"

"Of course." She looped her arm through his.

"You might want to bring a change of clothes, too." She tipped her head and looked up at him and batted her dark lashes in a slow, carnal way. The woman could mesmerize a cobra.

"The detective in me suspects that your invitation will include a ruse using your feminine wiles to discover more about my boxing lessons."

Honeysuckle smiled. "A lady must use what weapons she has to get what she wants. Men have the advantage of strength. We must rely on our wiles."

"I'm very fond of your wiles. Feel free to apply as many as you wish upon me."

****

Ruddy and Honeysuckle passed a wonderful evening without one question regarding his boxing. The next morning after the room service waiter had gone, Ruddy poured coffee for the two of them while she tidied up in the bathroom. A complimentary copy of the London Times came with their breakfast. He read an article on the passage of the Children's Charter. The new law established criminal penalties to deter child abuse. About time, Ruddy thought.

The article offered a temporary distraction. His main thoughts were on the lovely Honeysuckle. When she finished her morning ablutions the questions were bound to start. Her interest in his boxing wouldn't go unaddressed and he wondered how she'd broach the topic.

Honeysuckle came out in a light blue day dress. The only adornments on the gown were an embroidered collar and cuffs. Fashionable and uncomplicated. She hadn't bothered to pin her hair up.

Instead, she'd simply pulled it back and used combs to hold it in place.

With the waiter's help, Ruddy had moved the table set for breakfast closer to the French doors leading to the suite's balcony. He opened the balcony doors so the morning sun shone on the table and bathed the room in light. Honeysuckle hadn't bothered to powder her face or use any rouge when she joined him. In the sunlight, when she tipped her head to butter her toast, her cheeks and nose had a faint youthful glow.

"Why won't you tell me?" she blurted out as she swirled a strip of toast in runny egg yolk.

"Tell you what?" It was a weak stall that would do little to nothing to put her off.

Seeing Ruddy slather his toast with jam, Honeysuckle slid her small jam pot over to him. He greedily accepted hers and finished it off layering it thick on another slice. Jam was a precious treat in his home growing up. His mother made a couple dozen jars every summer. But with ten children, by spring the lot was gone.

The hotel had provided both strawberry and raspberry jams. The thought of his mum's jam brought a smile and pleasant summer memories.

"You're smiling at your toast," Honeysuckle said.

"I was reminiscing over family memories when some of us set out on berry picking forays. When the different berries came into season, my sisters and the youngest boys in the family, which happened to be Will and I, had the job of berry picking. Since all but one sister was older than Will and I, we were assigned the nasty task of gathering the blackberries from their thorny bushes.

"My mum makes the best bramble jelly and fruit tarts in all of Wales, maybe the whole of the Empire." He bit off a corner of the toast, chewed fast and swallowed. "I see doubt in your eyes. I know everyone says their mum's cooking is the best but my mum's truly is. Was your mother a good cook?"

Honeysuckle said with a light laugh, "No. Not at all. I didn't grow up in the country like you. We lived in boarding houses and inns close to the theatres where my parents were performing at the time. My mum never had a kitchen of her own. She was a remarkable seamstress though. When she wasn't performing she was usually backstage working on costumes."

Ruddy polished off his bacon rashers and the extras the kitchen sent.

"When was the last time you saw your family?" Honeysuckle asked.

"Five years ago when I was promoted to detective."

"You should visit them again soon, maybe at Christmas."

"Will you come with me? I'd like you to meet them."

Honeysuckle's face flushed pink. She didn't answer. Instead she took a long sip of tea while avoiding eye contact. She lowered her teacup and showed renewed interest in her eggs, swirling the sautéed mushrooms into the yolks.

"Honeysuckle, will you come with me?"

She looked up. The youthful glow that the sunlight had given her freshly washed face was overshadowed now by trenchant worldliness in her eyes. "I don't think you've really thought about the invitation."

Ruddy had no idea what to make of the cryptic comment. What was this about? "I don't have to think on it. I'd like you to come with me and meet my family. They're not terrible people. I think you'd like them. You like Will."

"This isn't about them, Rudyard. Don't you understand?"

There was crisp irritation in her tone. Again, he'd no idea what caused her sudden upset. It couldn't be the invitation. People invite those they care about to share the holidays the world over. What else troubled her? "No, I don't understand," Ruddy said, honestly confused.

She stared at her plate again but made no effort to eat or play with it like before. "Why must you be so obtuse?"

"It's not deliberate."

"Most men don't invite *actresses* to meet their families. It's just not done." Tension continued to color her tone.

The penny dropped. The reputation issue. She feared his family would disapprove of her. Ruddy reached over and gently lifted her chin so they were eye-to-eye again. "I'm not most men."

She gave him a you're-being-daft-look and pushed his hand away. "Let's see how you feel in December."

"I'll feel the same but you won't believe me until then."

"Onto a different topic," Honeysuckle said. "You're going to engage someone in fisticuffs. I'd like to know with whom and when? The lessons aren't to help with street ruffians. You've been managing them for years and years."

"Just years, not years and years. You make me sound like a coot."

"Don't deflect."

"Fine. Nobody and nowhere, yet. That's the truth. I have reason to believe a person I dislike intensely and who feels the same toward me might challenge me. Notice I said *might*."

"That doesn't explain the lessons. If it comes to a punch-up, you don't need lessons. He takes a swing then you swing back. One or both of you connect and keep on until one or both of you have had enough."

She leaned in to rub a speck of jam from the corner of his mouth. Ruddy grabbed her finger and clamped his lips around the jammy tip, licked the end and let her finger go. "Under normal conditions, the fight would go like that. The other fellow is a champion boxer for the City of London's Police Department. If we're to face each other, the only way I stand a chance of not having him tear a piece of my hide off is to develop some of the same skills."

"If he does challenge you, I'd like to be there. I can sit with Archie and the other officers from Holborn. I assume they'll come. How could they resist?"

"They'll be there. Men from both agencies will fill the club. Wagers will fly. But you can't come."

Honeysuckle had been sipping her tea, nibbling her toast, and taking the occasional bite of egg. Suddenly, the cup clanked against the saucer. The toast was unceremoniously dropped onto her plate and her soft, sweet sunlit face turned to granite.

"What?" Ruddy asked.

"What do you mean, I can't come? Why not? Do not confuse intimacy with ownership, Rudyard. I won't be ordered about. I can do whatever I wish."

Why must women take the smallest direction so personal? He'd never understand what ticklish trigger they all had within them that resulted in feisty overreaction. "I know I don't own you. My mild direction is not meant to be interpreted that way. You're overreacting—"

"No, I'm not."

It served no purpose to belabor the point. Better to clarify. "I didn't tell you not to come in an effort to boss you around because I thought I could. I did it to spare you exposure to the rough trade that frequents the club. The men there will watch sparring demonstrations in their undershirts or shirtless sometimes. They scratch their man parts, spit, curse, and do all manner of mannish things a lady shouldn't see or hear. I was trying to be chivalrous."

The reason was half true. He also didn't want her to witness his defeat if Napier trounced him. She was the last person he wanted there.

"Rudyard, I see men backstage in undershirts or shirtless while changing costumes. I am quite capable of withstanding the sight without falling into a faint. As for the rest, actors scratch and curse and do all that you mention as well. I really don't see your reasons as a cause for me not to go."

They'd had such a lovely time together why did she have to press him on this issue? Why couldn't she leave things well enough alone? He didn't want her there. Period.

He tossed his napkin onto his plate. "Can you just not do something because I asked you not to?" he snapped back, angrier than he meant to. He stood and put Winky's leash on and grabbed his satchel with his clothes from the previous evening. "I have to leave for the station."

Honeysuckle came over and laid her hands on his chest and kissed him. "I'm sorry I angered you. I didn't realize you were being a dear knight and not trying to bully me." She kissed him again. "Forgive me?"

"Not quite. Kissing is a good start. I shall call on you tomorrow after your show, if you're available."

"For you, I am."

****

Ruddy hung up his jacket and hat and was about to sit at his desk when Jameson came hurrying over. "Where's Archie?"

"He's coming through the door right now," Ruddy said, pointing.

"Good. No time to sit. The two of you need to get to a Dr. Finch's on Harley Street. The desk sergeant has the address. There's been a murder at the doctor's."

"On our way."

Ruddy asked the desk sergeant to send Northam to the scene with his camera. The young constable was in the field and Ruddy didn't want to wait for him. The desk sergeant only had the sketchiest of details but from what he was told by the responding constables, Finch's nurse was the victim. That fact conjured a variety of possibilities in Ruddy's mind. Did the doctor kill the nurse? Maybe a patient? Compared to the randomness of the last two murders, a nurse's untimely demise at a doctor's office had limited suspect choices. He liked that. Nice change.

****

As doctor's offices went, Ruddy thought Finch's the most pleasant he'd been in, but he'd only been in a handful and those on police business. He didn't have a personal doctor. He was lucky and never needed one. Other than the occasional cold, the only physical issues that troubled him were his war wounds. The spear scar on his throat had often been rubbed raw when his collars were over starched. He'd gone to the doctor the department used for autopsies. The doctor recommended a salve Ruddy could purchase at any chemist shop. His burn scar hurt if he sat with that side too close to a fireplace. Nothing for the doctor to do about that. Every once in a while it wept a clear fluid. On those occasions, Ruddy kept a light wrap over it until the weeping stopped.

Flanders and Young had been the first constables on the scene. Flanders met Ruddy and Archie in the reception area while Young stayed with Finch in the examination room. Obviously Finch could've tampered with evidence at any time prior to contacting the police. But as a precaution, once they arrived, they'd not leave him alone in case he might tamper further or even accidentally destroy valuable evidence, if this turned out to be a crime.

"Finch said he arrived at his usual time, half nine. When he entered he discovered Nurse Keating as you see her, lying face down. He checked for vital signs and found none," Flanders told them.

"Did you examine the body for wounds or marks?"

"First thing I checked. I couldn't find anything to indicate foul play."

"Any sign of forced entry?" Archie asked.

"No. I checked for that as well. I noticed the bottle of port and the glass sitting on the desk. From what you can see, there's only a glass missing from the bottle but I wondered if she hadn't drunk herself into the afterlife. I thought maybe she had a secret store she tippled from when Finch wasn't here. The doctor said he's never seen that bottle before and that Keating wasn't a souse. Took umbrage to the fact I even asked about her drinking habits."

"Let's bring Finch out here," Ruddy said. While Flanders went to get the doctor and Young, he knelt over the body and checked if there were any visible marks on her. She was cold. Rigor and lividity had set in but he didn't find any defensive wounds or unusual marks.

Young brought the doctor into the room. Archie instructed Young and Flanders to contact the other office residents in the building and ask if they'd seen anyone or any odd activity in or around Finch's.

Ruddy stood and sniffed the glass on the desk. A small amount of liquid remained in the bottom that smelled like port. "When did you last see Nurse Keating?" he asked Finch.

"Last evening. I left at half five to go home and have dinner with my wife."

"She could've died any time between then and now?" Archie asked.

Finch shook his head. "No. See that blood smear on her apron? That happened yesterday afternoon. She'd never wear a dirty apron to work. She was murdered sometime last night."

"Why do you think she was murdered?" Ruddy asked. "Isn't it possible she simply had a heart attack?"

Finch gestured toward the nurse as though Ruddy and Archie were morons. "Look at her. She's a young healthy woman."

"Doctor, young healthy people do die, every day. It might be uncommon but it is not impossible," Archie interjected.

Finch shot a withering glance Archie's way and then turned back to Ruddy. "I've examined her myself. She's never been sick a day since I've known her. She's not one to overindulge in a sinner's ways in private. She might've enjoyed a nip of port or sherry now and then, who doesn't? But Miss Keating was not one to lead a lifestyle that would result in an early death. I don't have to be a detective to know that wine is tainted."

The mere suggestion pricked the hairs on Ruddy's neck. There are times you want to beat your head against the nearest wall. Eyeing the sight before him, Ruddy considered the option. Dead body and a bottle of port drank from, and on the surface some ugly similarities to his other two cases. Fortunately, if this did turn out to be a poisoning, those looked to be the only similarities. If he was lucky, those two things would turn out to be a weird coincidence. The hope brought a small measure of relief.

Ruddy searched through the paperwork on the desk in hopes there might be a card that came with the port. Everything he found was related to the office or a patient's history.

"Constable Flanders said you told him you've never seen this bottle of port." Ruddy looked for but couldn't find any tag on the bottle to indicate what shop it was purchased from. "Do you have any idea who or where it might have come from?"

"No. I've never been given this type of gift before. I rarely receive gifts from patients or other doctors. The few that the patients have sent were from women whose babies I delivered. They were a knitted scarf or a monogramed handkerchief." Finch began to pace. "Why would other physicians send me gifts?" His voice rose with the question and he stopped pacing. "They wouldn't," he said, flapping his arms.

"We have to ask," Archie said in a calm voice. He laid a hand on the doctor's arm.

The doctor spun, pressed in close to Archie, and stuck his chin out. "See here—"

Even Archie's affable nature had its limits. He put his hand on the doctor's chest. "You're too close."

Finch pivoted and moved to less than arm's distance to Ruddy. "Just what sort of idiocy test do you have to fail to get this job, detective?" he asked, his breath warm in Ruddy's face. "No wonder the public hates your lot."

The doctor had no idea how tempted Ruddy was to lift him by his silk cravat until the toes of his polished boots barely skimmed the floor and shake him till he squealed like a chased piglet. But Ruddy liked his job and preferred to keep it, so there'd be no shaking of the pompous jackass. Tamping his temper down, Ruddy told him, "Step back."

Finch hesitated for a fraction of a second, then retreated several steps.

"Doctor, we realize you cared for Miss Keating. We're not disregarding your thoughts on her death. But speculation and investigation are two different things. We will consider all the evidence, of course. But we're trying to get you to see that no matter how exemplary a life a person lives, sometimes it is their destiny to die early." Ruddy still wasn't ready to believe murder was afoot, not without additional evidence.

"Yes, there are those people but you will see when you have the autopsy, Miss Keating is not one of those people."

Northam arrived and Ruddy told him to take a minimum of pictures. "I'll only need a few of the body's position. Take a few of the glass and bottle and the lock on the door showing it intact," Ruddy said.

Flanders and Young returned. "Sir, a word." Flanders jerked his head indicating he wanted to speak to Ruddy out of earshot of Finch. Both Ruddy and Archie came to where Flanders stood at the other end of the room.

"Interesting bit of information from the accountant's office across the hall," Flanders said in a low voice.

Ruddy already didn't care for the information. "Yes..." he dragged the word out, dreading what Flanders would say.

"The accountant heard a knock, a knock loud enough that the man thought it was at his door. He came out and saw the bottle outside Finch's door. Just then the nurse opened the door, looked curiously at the bottle as though she was surprised to see it. She was turning the bottle like she was trying to find a card as she brought the port inside."

"He didn't see the delivery person?" Archie asked.

"No."

"Bloody hell," Ruddy whispered. This was a twist they didn't need. "Thank you, Flanders. Write up a report of the interview and put it on our desks." Ruddy turned to Archie. "I guess we'll see what we have after the autopsy."

"Flanders, you and Young stay until the Medical Examiner's wagon arrives. The M.E. can reschedule any appointments he has today. He's to handle the autopsy as a priority," Ruddy said. "Once the body is removed, you may clear the scene. Take the port bottle and glass to the M.E.'s office and have him test for poison."

Ruddy and Archie joined Finch. "Doctor, I'm sure you realize you'll have to reschedule your appointments for today. We can't have any patients enter until the scene is cleared. If you wish to leave, our officers can post a note on the door. They can instruct patients to return tomorrow for new appointments or you may want to wait out the M.E.'s arrival. I'll let that decision rest with you."

Ruddy handed Finch his business card and Archie handed him one of his. If you have any questions or wish to add any information, please feel free to contact us."

"I'd like you to do one thing for me, *detective*." Finch stressed Ruddy's title, an indicator Ruddy expected meant an insult hovered on the tip of Finch's tongue.

"I'll do what I can."

"If that wine is tainted, if this is murder, I want you to tell me, in person, I was right and you were wrong."

Arrogant bugger. The doctor's wish wasn't going to occur anytime soon, whether the wine was poisoned or not. "If it is poisoned, I'll have a constable deliver a message to you."

"I want *you* to deliver the message."

Ruddy gave the brim of his bowler a quick tug and smiled. "Want what you will but that won't be happening. I don't answer to you, Doctor Finch. And I'm not your messenger boy."

****

No other useful information came in the rest of the day regarding the Keating murder. Ruddy and Archie had interviewed her landlady and the few other tenants in her boarding house who were available. It was a boarding house that catered to women only. Men weren't allowed past the vestibule. No alcohol was allowed on the premises and doors were locked at 10 p.m. sharp. The landlady and other women they'd interviewed all said Keating was quiet and kept to herself. She ate with the tenants on most mornings and evenings. She showed interest in their lives and what news they brought to the table, but rarely spoke of her personal or business life. No one knew if she had any family to notify.

Her financial situation was comfortable to the point that she was one of the few tenants who had a room to herself. Ruddy and Archie searched it but found nothing to help them regarding a possible suspect or family to claim the body.

"Sad isn't it?" Archie said, looking at a postcard of Brighton Beach.

"What?" Ruddy shook the last of her books hard. Sometimes personal notes and letters were stuck in books. When nothing fell out, he set it back onto her nightstand.

"This postcard is blank. I'd begun to hope a friend had sent it to her or she'd written something personal on it after having gone on holiday there."

Morris spoke highly of the nurses he met during the Crimean War. Florence Nightingale had brought a contingent of nurses to the military hospital at Scutari, Turkey to treat the British wounded. He'd been taken there for the surgery to have his arm amputated. Morris had said, "Miss Nightingale often came late at night to visit the worst wounded of us. She'd come with her flickering light and move from bed to bed to speak with us. We called her the Lady with the lamp. What fine ladies her nurses were and what stern stuff they were made of."

Remembering Morris's comments, Ruddy thought perhaps Keating was cut from the same cloth.

"She does seem to have led a solitary life. Maybe she derived all the satisfaction she needed from her work. I hear many women who go into nursing do."

"Maybe, but it hurts to think there won't be anyone to see to her funeral, to shed a tear, or sprinkle a handful of dirt on her coffin and see her on another journey."

One of the qualities Ruddy appreciated most about Archie was his ability to commiserate in sorrow with strangers. In spite of the fact Ruddy hardly ever shared the quality, he could appreciate it. "I imagine if another journey does await us, she'll be well on her way before going into the ground."

"Still..."

"Time to ask Finch if he knows of any family to notify, or has an idea who can claim the body."

"I dread talking to the man again."

"Me too. We'll send a constable."

As they left the building, Flanders and his partner were waiting for them. "Sir, the desk sergeant said we'd find you here. We were about to join you. He has the M.E.s report on Keating and said you should come back right away."

"That sounds ominous," Archie said.

"Sadly, it does," Ruddy agreed. "Flanders, you and your partner go to Finch's and ask if Keating has any family he knows about and if so, how to contact them. If not, does he have any thoughts on who might arrange her funeral? Otherwise, if she has the funds, the department will see to a basic burial in a local parish cemetery with no service."

"Will do." Flanders and his partner hurried off.

"What do you think the news is?" Archie asked.

"I don't know. I only know what I don't want it to be."

One look at the desk sergeant said it all. The news wasn't good. "You have the results?" Ruddy asked.

"Not anymore," the sergeant told him. "Jameson has them now. He wants to see you both straight away. Today, I'm happy to be on the desk and not a detective."

Ruddy knocked and cracked Jameson's door. "You wanted to see us, Superintendent?"

"Yes, come in and sit." Jameson waited for them to be seated and then handed the reports to Ruddy.

Ruddy handed the report on the port's contents to Archie. While Archie gave his paper a cursory read, Ruddy skipped to the final analysis on cause of death.

They looked up from their reading at the same time and said in unison, "Arsenic poisoning."

"Indeed and again," Jameson said. "I realize this murder is extraordinary due to having a female victim. However, I don't see how we can discount the possibility it is the same killer, considering we're looking at the same method and same delivery system. That said, give me some ideas, some thoughts, some theories we can work from."

Archie said to Ruddy, "I was going to discuss this with you first but since the topic has now been broached, I'll say it here." He turned from Ruddy to Jameson. "I wonder if our latest victim truly led the unsullied life we were led to believe. Perhaps she's the thread tying all the murders together. I just don't know how."

Ruddy did, or thought he might know. "Let's say she was at some point a lover to Cross and Skinner. Our killer is a recent lover she's jilted or someone she's shunned. He's eliminated current or former lovers or anyone he perceives as competition."

"But that wasn't enough for him," an excited Jameson jumped in with.

"So, it morphed into a classic case of—if I can't love you, then nobody else can," Archie said. "The only way to ensure that is to kill her."

"It's a viable theory," Jameson said, his excitement waning a bit. "Keep me apprised of any new developments."

"Let's get a copy of the best facial picture Northam has of Keating. We'll show it around to Cross and Skinner's club members and staff. See if anything turns up," Ruddy said as they left Jameson's office. "Let's leave Finch for last. I want to thoroughly read the autopsy. Maybe there's something to poke him with."

Ruddy sat at his desk, pulled out the bottom drawer, and propped his feet up, then read the entire report. Archie went in search of Northam. When he returned with two pictures of Keating, Ruddy told him, "I think I found something that might be useful against Finch." Archie's brows notched up. "She'd had sex, very recently too, the night she died. Interesting."

Archie's brows notched up a fraction. "Interesting indeed. Where to first?" he asked.

"Let's show Keating's picture to Cross's staff. They already said he never brought a woman to the house. But just to be thorough, let's show them her picture anyway. Next we'll stop at Skinner's office and show Mr. Button her picture. I can't imagine Skinner bringing a mistress to his home, but the office is another story."

"You think Button would tell us if Skinner had an affair with Keating?"

"He might be reluctant at first. I think he'll cooperate once he realizes the information might lead to finding his boss's killer."

"True. This means we have to speak to Finch again but we'll do him last. I have to think he's the one she was intimate with the day she died. I have a feeling he is not going to admit to it, no matter what."

Ruddy had to agree. What could he and Archie use to force the truth out of him, confirm if the doctor was her lover? Ruddy sat at his desk staring out the window trying to come up with a means to achieve that. Two women passed by engaged in animated conversation. The woman closest to the building had linked one arm with the other lady and in her other hand carried a book.

A book.

"Ready?" Archie asked.

"Almost. I need to stop at the evidence room."

In the evidence room, Ruddy found the box from the Everhard murders. The year before the Viscount Everhard had killed several lovers and conveniently kept a journal discussing the murders. Ruddy pulled the journal from the box and tucked it into the inside pocket of his coat.

"What do you want with that journal?" Archie asked.

"We might not need it, but if I suspect the doctor of lying, it might serve as a...for lack of a better term, inspirational tool."

Archie looked more baffled than convinced. "If you say so."

****

To Ruddy and Archie's disappointment, the Cross staff said they'd never seen Keating at the house, never heard her name spoken by Mr. Cross. Adding to their disappointment, Mr. Button said he'd never seen Keating, nor heard her name mentioned by Skinner. He also told the detectives that in the twelve years he worked for the solicitor, Skinner never made a reference or comment about having a mistress or seeking one. Button said the only women he spoke of were family members or clients. The family he talked of in general terms and the clients he only discussed in the most professional manner.

Finch opened the door and groaned. "Constable Flanders and his partner just left. I told them I don't know of anyone who can take care of the funeral arrangements." He started to shut the door in their faces. Ruddy was faster and got his hand up to push the door open. Finch stumbled back, barely keeping his balance.

"Get out. Now." The ropey vein Ruddy noticed the first time they interviewed Finch popped out on the doctor's forehead again, more prominently this time. Ruddy dispassionately thought Finch might be on the verge of apoplexy.

"Can't do that, doctor. We have questions that need answers. You can sit or stand. We don't care which but you will answer," Ruddy told him.

"I don't have to answer any of your questions."
The vein pulsed with his heartbeat. He rocked ever so
slightly on his feet.

Ruddy shoved his hands in his trouser pockets
in case the irritating fool started to fall over. He'd make
no effort to catch him.

"The quicker you tell us what we need to know,
the quicker we can leave," Archie interjected.

Finch turned his attention to Archie. "Fine. Ask
your questions."

"Nurse Keating had sexual congress the
afternoon she was killed."

The color drained from Finch's face.

"The autopsy showed semen traces and vaginal
swelling. The activity was definitely recent," Archie
said.

Finch screwed himself up. His shoulders rising,
narrow chest puffing. He began to stammer, "How dare
you." He pointed an accusing finger inches from
Archie's nose.

Archie batted his finger away. "Get that out of
my face."

Finch flinched and retreated behind the lobby
desk. He stuck his finger out from the new safe
distance. "If you're suggesting she and I had a tryst,
this conversation is over. I don't have to put up with
your insulting insinuations."

"We're not suggesting anything at the moment.
We're trying to document Keating's activities the day of
her death. Who she might've seen," Archie said. "She
was intimate with someone."

Finch brought his hand down. His gaze shifted from Archie to Ruddy then back to Archie. "It must've happened after I left. I have a witness to confirm I left at half five. I bought a packet of sweets from the costermonger at the corner to eat on the carriage ride home."

Ruddy fingered the journal in his coat pocket. "That doesn't mean you weren't the one she had relations with."

"Are you calling me a liar?" Finch asked Ruddy.

"It might save your life. We believe a former jealous lover could be her killer. If so, there's a chance your life is at risk. It's important we know the truth."

"I don't believe you."

Ruddy had enough of the pompous doctor. Nor did he believe the doctor's denial of having an intimate relationship with Keating. Time to bring out the journal. "She kept a journal." He waggled it, then opened and closed it quickly just to show the written pages. "Your name is mentioned several times and not solely as her employer. Do you wish to stay with your version of what occurred that afternoon?"

There it was-the brief guilty widening of his eyes like a stomped-on toad. Finch sank down into the desk chair and buried his face in his hands. After a long moment, he lifted his head. "This cannot get back to my wife and children or be made public. My female patients wouldn't understand."

"What you say will remain confidential," Ruddy assured him.

"Then yes, she and I had several trysts over the past year but none prior to that. As for other lovers, she never talked of any to me. But then, she wouldn't. It'd be most improper."

Ruddy and Archie exchanged an amused look. Both keying on the fact Finch didn't see the irony of her relationship with him as far more improper than her discussing other lovers with him.

Ruddy tucked the journal back in his jacket pocket. Finch watched, suspicion creeping into his expression. "Detective Bloodstone is it?" Ruddy nodded. "If she kept a journal, wouldn't she have mentioned other men in it? It strikes me as odd she only talked of our relationship."

Good question. Ruddy hadn't thought that far ahead when he grabbed the journal. He scrambled for a logical answer. "She's only been keeping it since the start of the year. If she had another diary, we didn't find it when searching her room."

"Oh." Looking concerned he asked, "Will that be all?"

"For now," Archie said. Ruddy was already at the door hoping to escape before Finch asked to see the journal.

Outside Archie waved down a cab. "That was a close call with the journal," he said as they climbed into the cab. "I was afraid he might ask to see what she wrote."

"Me too. He asked that question about the mention of others and the first thing that popped into my head was: Ruddy, you're an idiot."

Chapter Twenty-Six

"Mercy me, this is awful," Mrs. Zachary said, holding her teacup midair as she read something in the morning paper.

"What?" Graciela asked, forcing interest she didn't feel into her voice. Depression over the lack of news about Finch's death still clouded her mood. She'd eagerly read every page of yesterday's paper searching for any blurb about it. Nothing. How could that be, she wondered. She thought a man like him would at least have one glass of an expensive port he'd received as a surprise gift.

"A Harley Street nurse has been murdered. She worked for a Nesbit Finch." Mrs. Zachary looked up from the paper and took a swallow of her tea. She put the cup down and the footman poured another without her asking. "Dr. Finch's office isn't far from Dr. Fitzhugh's. Can you imagine? A murder, right there on Harley Street. We'll have to have an escort the next time I go to Fitzhugh's."

Graciela's mouthful of tea went down hard almost choking her. *Had the nurse gotten into the poisoned port? Would she dared have opened wine meant for Finch? No. Her murder had to be unrelated. How bizarre.* She had turned a deaf ear to the rest of

Mrs. Zachary's timeworn rant about the decline of civilization and society.

"Graciela, are you listening?"

"Of course, Mrs. Zachary."

"I was saying boorish manners and practices of the lower classes are becoming acceptable. Too easily people are forgetting their place. It's a slippery slope." She shook her head in disgust. Fixing on Graciela and clearly expecting her to agree, she repeated, "A slippery slope."

"That it is. By any chance does the paper say how the nurse died?" Still quasi-panicked about the coincidence of the nurse's murder, Graciela sent a silent prayer to the heavens that it wasn't by her poison. Maybe the woman was attacked by a street ruffian as she left the office. Graciela hoped so anyway.

"No, the police aren't releasing too much information yet according to the article. They're still trying to locate family. They also say there are unusual circumstances and they don't want to jeopardize that end of the investigation."

"May I go to my chamber?"

"Yes, I won't need you until midday."

Graciela snatched Me-Too from her basket on her chamber windowsill and cradled the cat in the crook of her arm as she paced. "What do I do now? That fool of a nurse probably drank my port. The police didn't say for sure, but I'll wager that is what happened to her. Now I have to think of another way to kill Finch. Ugh. This is so annoying. Stupid, stupid nurse."

She stared out the window at the people and traffic passing on the street below. She'd never meant to kill an innocent person. There was the off chance the nurse died by another's hand but Graciela couldn't dismiss the feeling in the pit of her stomach that she was the guilty party.

"But you know, Me-Too, Finch's nurse wasn't the most innocent of innocents. She had to have had an inkling, if not full knowledge what he got up to with those poor female patients at the hospital. So, if it was my poison, her actions neutralize my actions."

Graciela considered several different means of disposing of Finch. Most she discarded. Stabbing she disliked as too messy and she had to get too close to him to be successful. There was too much risk involved. He could overpower her and stab her or call the police or both. She didn't think poison would work. If it was the port that killed the nurse, Finch wasn't going to drink anything sent to the office. His office was on the third floor. She could push him out the window. Maybe. Maybe not. Again, she'd have to get close, not get overpowered, and the window would have to be open. Not to mention he might survive the fall and tell the police who tried to kill him. That left shooting him. She still had Addy's derringer. He had warned her if she shot someone, he'd disavow her and never be in contact with her again. She hated to lose him as a resource. But, Finch had to die and shooting was the best option. The cleanest.

She put the cat down. She had to think about making this work with no mistakes.

I need to practice somewhere so when I kill him there's very little noise, no blood-at least on me, and no mistakes this time.

Chapter Twenty-Seven

Ruddy hadn't gotten much sleep the night before. Mrs. Goodge put together a tray for him and a bowl of food for Winky, which Luke brought up.

Ever since Ruddy had taken Luke to the station and shown him the stocking thief, as promised, Luke was obsessed with crime fighting. The boy had overheard Mrs. Goodge and the maid talking in the kitchen about the Harley Street murder. Luke now wished to discuss the crime with Ruddy, talk theories and "whatnot." Ruddy didn't have the heart to say no. Tired as he was and wanting only to eat, soak in the tub and go to bed, he chatted with Luke until it was the lad's bedtime. By then Ruddy had his second wind kick in and was wide awake.

"Come on, Winky. Let's go for a walk." Ruddy walked to the British Museum gardens before he finally stopped. No one was around that late at night so he let Winky off his leash.

Ruddy had come to the gardens late one night last year when he'd hit a wall on a tough murder case. He didn't receive any brilliant strokes of genius on that case then and he didn't expect to now. But the setting was pretty at night and the roses and flowers in the different garden beds smelled nice.

"What is motivating this killer, Winky?"

The dog lifted his leg in response to mark yet another bush. Ruddy was sure at this point Winky was out of marking solution and just going through the motions or kidding himself.

"It's not political. No one kills a nurse for political reasons, the banker or the solicitor, maybe, but not a nurse. It's not a religious statement. All the victims were Church of England. With the exception of her affair with Finch and based on what both he and her landlady said about her modest lifestyle, it was doubtful a jealous lover killed her." Winky was sitting in front of him now, licking his privates. "Don't do that when I'm talking to you."

Winky stopped.

"You're no help. Let's go home." Ruddy hooked up his leash and they headed back. As they neared the edge of the gardens, Winky stopped to pee on a statue of a young woman holding a basket of flowers.

****

The next day, Ruddy left work early. He and Honeysuckle had plans for a late supper after her show, and he wanted to squeeze in a nap. He'd rather not go face down from exhaustion into his dinner entrée. After a quick bath, he slept like a dead man for a couple of hours.

Whistling the cheery tune *The Ratcatcher's Daughter*, Ruddy waved as he passed Sergei, the wall-eyed Russian who manned the back door of the Odeon. Sergei wasn't really Russian. He was from a place no one ever heard of at the far end of Russia but he sounded like a Russki so that's what everyone called him. His main function was to make sure no one snuck into the music hall.

His face was pointed Ruddy's direction when he said, "Good evening, Mr. Bloodstone," but Ruddy couldn't be sure what he was looking at. The Master of Ceremonies once told Ruddy Sergei wound up in England by accident. Supposedly, he left his homeland headed for Spain but being wall-eyed, couldn't see straight and turned the wrong way.

"Good evening to you, too, Sergei."

"Miss Honeysuckle's popular with your lot tonight," Sergei said as Ruddy started to walk on.

Ruddy stopped. "What do you mean?"

"Another Peeler came back asking where her dressing room was a short time ago."

"You're sure it was a copper?"

Sergei snorted. "I may not see well, but I see well enough to know a badge flashed in my face."

"Huh." No surprise someone wanted to see her. She was the Odeon's star attraction. Ruddy was curious to see if it was a copper he knew.

"I must ask you to leave," Honeysuckle told someone. The order came from her dressing room.

Ruddy took off in that direction. As he approached Honeysuckle's dressing room, he heard her add, "It's always nice to hear from fans of the show and of course, I'm terribly flattered by your invitation but I must decline."

"Miss Flowers, you can't mean to break my heart without giving me a fair chance. You must have dinner with me. They're holding a table at the

Criterion."

Napier. He could see the man's reflection in the large, glass-framed posters that hung directly across from Honeysuckle's door. Ruddy thought he looked like a dandified monkey in the tuxedo he wore, which was an unkindness to simians.

"But, Miss Flowers—"

"The lady asked you to leave. Get out." Ruddy stepped between the dressing table where Honeysuckle sat and Napier.

"This is none of your business, Bloodstone. This is a private conversation between the lady and me. If anyone should leave, it should be you," Napier said.

"It became my business when the lady asked you to go and you didn't. Now get out."

"Who do you think you are talking to? I'm not some mealy-mouthed whelp like Northam or one of those others who yes sir and no sir you." As he argued, Napier moved in close to Ruddy. He brought his hand up fast toward Ruddy's chest. A faster Ruddy anticipated a shove or blow and clamped his hand around Napier's wrist.

Ruddy twisted Napier's wrist and gave him a firm shove. "Try to touch me again and you'll be on your arse looking up."

Honeysuckle stood and laid a hand on each man's arm. "Gentlemen, please don't fight over me." Both ignored her.

Napier smirked. "I love a challenge." He immediately raised a hand and made to push the issue.

Ruddy didn't wait for the touch. He punched Napier in the mouth. Napier stumbled back, nearly knocking over Honeysuckle's chair. "It's time, Napier. I'm tired of dancing around this issue of a challenge. You and I. Pick a day and it has to be a neutral spot."

Napier pulled a handkerchief from his inside coat pocket and dabbed his bloody lip. "For once, I agree with you. I'll ask Chief Superintendent Effingham and Kelly from my club to find a good location."

"Oh no. He's not going with your boy Kelly. I want Archie to go with them. You're not stacking the deck against me by choosing a club where Kelly's in league with the referees."

"You don't trust Chief Effingham?"

Ruddy would love nothing more than to give an honest answer. Speaking ill of a man of Effingham's rank could land him neck deep in an intradepartmental political manure pile. "I'm saying I want Archie to go along."

Napier bent and quickly checked the damage to his mouth in the dressing table mirror. Finished, he turned to Honeysuckle. "I take it Bloodstone here is the reason you're not going to dinner with me."

"Mr. Napier, I try to avoid being rude or mean spirited. That means I don't always tell the whole truth, but in your case I'm making an exception. Yes, I do have plans with Rudyard this evening." Honeysuckle flipped the silky skirt of her gown back and straightened to a stiff-backed regal position. "And even if I didn't, I wouldn't go to dinner with you. I don't like you. You wouldn't accept no when I declined your invitation and you're arrogant. Too arrogant to believe I know my own mind. I sir, am one woman who always knows her own mind." Finger out, she pointed toward the door. "Go."

"Like many women who have a limited view of the world, you mistake confidence for arrogance. How unfortunate for you." Napier tipped his head.

"Snap to and get out, Napier. Your organ grinder master is waiting," Ruddy said.

Napier whipped his top hat from the chair where he'd laid it and said, "You and me, Bloodstone, been a long time coming."

"Looking forward to it."

Napier's heavy footsteps echoed off the corridor walls all the way to the back door.

"His organ grinder master? Really Rudyard." Honeysuckle came over and slipped her arms around Ruddy's neck.

"Tell me *Pop Goes the Weasel* didn't jump into your head when you saw him done up that way."

She kissed him. "It didn't. I think you'd be very handsome in a tuxedo, nothing like an organ grinder's monkey. Maybe one day we'll go somewhere formal. I'd love to see you in that kind of elegant garb."

"We'll see."

Chapter Twenty-Eight

"It's not far across the river on Blackfriar's Road," Archie said. "Nice club, clean like Kelly's."

"You say Jameson went with you," Ruddy repeated what Archie had told him, surprised by his Superintendent's decision to go along.

"He did. He took me aside and on the sly said he wouldn't put it past Effingham to use his rank to exert undue influence on me so I'd agree to wherever he and Kelly chose."

Ruddy couldn't argue with Jameson's assumption. Effingham had shown himself to be a haughty sly boots more than once. Napier was his official bootlicker.

"What about referees?" Ruddy asked.

"Turns out Jameson is a bigger boxing fan than we thought. He knows some of the successful current boxers. He took our group to visit them and we had a nice list of fair and trusted men. Once you agree to a day, we'll approach the men on the list and see who is available." Archie pulled a piece of paper from his coat pocket. "These are the days that Napier liked."

Ruddy thought the sooner they got this over, the better. With less time for word to get around the different station houses, there'd be fewer men to witness the event since the outcome was uncertain.

"Next Saturday is fine."

****

The fight was scheduled for midday Saturday. Tony accompanied Ruddy to the Blackfriar's Athletic Club. Archie and Jameson greeted them as they came through the door.

"Looks like most of our constables are here," Ruddy said, scanning the rows of benches."

"Most everyone who has the day off," Jameson said. "Coopersmith and Northam are manning the wagering table, just there." He pointed. "The other two at the table are Effingham's lads. He gestured to a dignified man about his same age standing at his side. "Bloodstone, Holbrook, I'd like to introduce you to a friend of mine from my club, John Daley. He's a boxing fan."

"Nice meeting you." Ruddy shook Daley's hand.

"Sir." Holbrook did the same.

Ruddy introduced Tony to Jameson whose interest was immediately sparked by the boxer's background as a fighter. While Jameson was distracted talking to Tony, Ruddy whispered to Archie, "How's the betting look?"

"Our fellows are putting a decent amount of coin down on you."

"More than on Napier?"

"I take it Tony will be your corner man?" Archie replied, changing the subject.

The evasive answer told Ruddy what he needed to know. He couldn't blame the Holborn men for not wanting to lose money. The safe wager was on Napier.

"What are the odds?" Ruddy asked.

"4-1 for Napier."

Ruddy took offense. Who wouldn't? At worse, he thought the odds might be 2-1. "Really, I'd have thought they had more faith in me than that. I am a good street fighter after all. They've seen me in enough donnybrooks."

"It's not a donnybrook where anything goes. I think they're nervous about Marquess of Queensberry rules holding your feet to the fire."

"How'd you bet?"

"On you, of course. We're partners aren't we?"

"How much did you bet?"

"Five quid." The words were barely out when Northam came over and handed two betting slips to Archie.

"Here you go, Arch. A fiver note on Bloodstone and a two quid note on Napier."

Archie had the decency to look sheepish.

"You covered part of your bet on me with one on Napier? You wound me, Arch," Ruddy said and shook his head, hoping to shame his partner more. "What about you, Northam? Did you cover your bet on me?"

The young constable flushed deep red. "Ah...ah..."

"I see. Et tu, Northam?"

"Pardon?"

"It's a Shakespearean reference, Northam," Jameson said. "Run back to the wagering table before he starts quoting Milton." Northam dashed off.

"Before we take our seats, I just want to

reassure you Bloodstone that I have wagered only on you." Jameson shot a pointed glance at Archie.

"I hope you'll excuse me if I decline to reveal who I've wagered on," Daley said.

"No worries," Ruddy said.

Tony came from the back of the club and joined them. "Ready to get changed?"

Archie flashed two thumbs up as Ruddy turned to follow Tony.

Ruddy and Napier would fight shirtless wearing close fitting bottoms similar to long underwear, leather flat-soled boots that laced up past the ankles along with boxing gloves.

"Remember what I told you," Tony said as he tied Ruddy's boots. "He'll come at you hard and fast. From what I observed in his sparring routines, he'll go for the jaw. I think he hopes to knock you out early with an especially hard strike to the chin. So keep your hands up."

"I will."

"And?"

"Watch for the signs of his split second of weakness."

Ruddy nearly bumped into Napier as he left the section of the changing room that he'd been assigned. Napier was alone. "I sent my corner man ahead. You might want to do the same. I've something you might want to see."

Ruddy thought it an odd comment, especially under the circumstances. "Go on, Tony. I'll join you in a moment." Once Tony was out of earshot, he asked, "You wanted to show me something?"

Napier gestured for him to follow. They re-entered the changing area and Napier pulled a letter sized portfolio from a leather bag. "I collect erotica from the continent." He gave a short snort. "From the look on your face, you disapprove. As if I'd believe you haven't enjoyed fingering through it when it has crossed your desk."

"You mistake my disinterest for disapproval. I couldn't care less about your personal penchants. What's this to do with me?"

Napier removed a photograph from the portfolio and held it up for Ruddy.

Ruddy immediately recognized the woman in the sepia-toned picture as a young Honeysuckle, perhaps as young as fifteen. Her chin and cheeks were still chubby with baby fat. She lay on her side on a sofa. Rose petals were scattered over the sofa and on the floor. She held a bouquet of roses beneath her breasts and peered up coquettishly at the camera. A sheer panel had been draped over her hips but the dark thatch between her thighs was still visible.

Notre Dame Cathedral could be seen through the window behind her. Ruddy briefly wondered if she'd posed for money, or had the photographer dazzled her with talk of Paris and then talked her into posing nude? It didn't matter.

Ruddy tried to take the picture from Napier but Napier immediately jerked the photo out of his reach. "No you don't. I'm not giving you a chance to tear it to pieces."

"Why did you want me to see this?" Ruddy had a guess but he'd hear it from Napier's lips.

"Side wager, I thought to make the fight more interesting for you and me. If you win, I give you the picture. If I win, I keep it."

Ruddy checked his feelings. Of course he was disturbed by the idea of Napier having the intimate photograph of Honeysuckle. But dwelling too deeply on the private activities pursued by men with these collections was a distraction for another time. To offer the photograph as a prize, Napier had to have other plans. "Say I lose, what purpose do you have for it, other than the usual leering?"

"None for now. But you never know. Perhaps, if the mood is right, I'll sell it. I'm sure one of the broadsheets would love to publish it with a headline about the star of the Odeon's scandalous past."

A nude picture like this was scandalous, even for an actress. "Doing that would destroy her career. Why do that to her? Is this because she turned you down for dinner?"

Napier shook his head and said, "Don't be ridiculous." He licked the length of Honeysuckle's nude form, smirked, and then tucked the photograph back into the portfolio. "I've no trouble finding dinner companions. I don't give a whit about what happens to her or her career but you do. I think it matters a great deal to you that I possess this."

"Bastard." Ruddy lunged, knocking Napier into the wall. The two wrestled for possession of the portfolio.

"What the deuce is going on here?" The referee separated them. Napier used the interruption to yank the portfolio from Ruddy.

"Save the fisticuffs for the ring. Get a move on, you two. The crowd is getting restless." The referee left and Napier replaced the portfolio into his bag.

"All right, you bloody bastard. Let me make sure I have the right of it," Ruddy said. "The crux of this wager is: I win, and I keep the picture. Lose, and you threaten to hurt her, or I assume there's something you want from me to keep that from happening.

"I haven't decided but yes, there may come a day when I want a favor from you. The picture is my insurance you cooperate."

"Fine. I accept your wager. Is this the only photograph of her?"

"It's the only one I have. That said; I doubt a photographer with a lovely, nubile model like the young Miss Flowers only took one."

Sadly, Napier was probably right.

"Shall we? The crowd awaits," Napier said, and the two of them left.

When Ruddy entered he joined Tony in the corner of the ring. "What did that Napier want?" Tony asked.

"I don't want to talk about it right now." He glanced over at Napier in his corner who was bouncing on alternating feet, throwing punches in the air.

Napier nodded his way, giving him a wide, smug smirk then making a comment over his shoulder to his admirers that had them laughing.

Jameson and Daley sat with the Holborn men. Ruddy half expected Jameson to sit with Effingham, high-ranking officer with high-ranking officer. Jameson shocked him by leading the Holborn group in a cheer when Ruddy came to the center of the ring in a face-to-face with Napier and to hear the rules gone over by the referee.

"Gentlemen, return to your corners and at the sound of the bell, come out fighting," the referee said.

The bell rang. Napier came at Ruddy exactly as Tony predicted, hard and fast. Ruddy ducked and weaved. Napier missed the first few shots, then he adjusted and some connected. Ruddy reeled from a sharp blow to the side of his jaw but he immediately countered and caught Napier on the chin with a hard right cross.

Anyone who believes three minutes goes by in the blink of an eye never faced a man with fists like bricks in a boxing ring.

Finally, the bell to end the round sounded. Tony wiped Ruddy down with a cool wet towel and gave him a sip of water.

"Don't drink too much. You'll vomit," Tony warned.

Ruddy's mouth was dry as the Sahara and if he could, he'd drink the bucket of water at his feet.

The round two bell rang.

Within seconds salty sweat rolled into one of Ruddy's eyes, blurring his vision. He saw the fist coming at him, tried to pivot and block but took the brunt of the blow on his brow bone. His eye involuntarily closed and filled with fluid. Ruddy couldn't tell if it was sweat or blood or both. Napier delivered a set of rough body blows to Ruddy's ribs, knocking him several steps back into the ropes. Ruddy lost his balance but didn't go down. Instead, he rallied and even with limited sight went after Napier with two right crosses and then a left.

Napier moved in close for a jab to Ruddy's face, too close. He couldn't get a power hit in but neither could Ruddy initially. Ruddy was the first to correct his position. When Napier realized his mistake, he broke the rules by wrapping Ruddy in a bear hug to keep his arms contained. The referee broke them up just as the bell ending the round came.

Fluid continued to flood Ruddy's one eye. "Is it blood?" he asked Tony? "Or sweat?"

"Blood. You've a nasty cut. I can get it stopped and maybe, just maybe fix it so you can see a bit out of it again. It hurts. Try not to let your opponent see you flinch too much."

"Do what you have to."

Tony wiped Ruddy's face with the cold wet towel and used the corner of a fresh towel to clean the cut eye. He held the cloth there long as he dared with the time limitations. Ruddy couldn't see what he poured onto a wad of gauze. Tony quickly had the treated gauze onto the cut.

"Bloody hell." Ruddy jerked back. Forget Tony's warning. Whatever Tony used it felt like he'd seared Ruddy with a red hot poker. "What the devil is that stuff?"

"Cayenne pepper."

"There was nothing else you could use?"

"This works fastest. Try to open your eye."

Opening his eye fully wasn't an option. He was able to blink, which allowed him to see a fraction better.

The bell rang.

In the middle of the round Napier made the move Tony told Ruddy to watch for. Napier tipped his head to the right and rose up on the ball of his left foot. He was readying to push off to add impetus to his left hook. That split second he was off balance Ruddy struck, hitting him hard again with his right followed by a left and then a body blow as Napier reeled. Napier staggered but didn't go down. Both men bobbed and weaved around each other for a long moment, exhaustion starting to take a toll on both.

Ruddy glanced Tony's way and as he did he caught a glimpse of a young man in the audience who he swore could be Honeysuckle's twin brother. The distraction proved painful. Napier hit him with a left that carried everything he had square on the bridge of Ruddy's nose.

His head immediately dropped and Ruddy covered his broken nose with his hands. Blood spurt through his fingers. *Lord have mercy it hurt.* Furious, he shook off the pain and went after Napier using every move, every tactic, and every power maneuver Tony taught him. He and Napier battled along the ropes, bleeding and staggering, but neither falling. Ruddy couldn't find the space he needed to land a winning punch and his arms ached as though stone weights pulled at them.

Napier came at him again, a stumbling step but with fire in his eyes. Ruddy didn't bother to wipe the blood away that dripped from his nose. Napier had drawn back with his right and opened himself up for a brief moment. Ruddy hit him with a hard body blow.

The punch knocked Napier backward into the ropes, where he lost his footing, and fell onto his knees, his breathing labored. Blood and sweat dripped onto the ring under him.

Ruddy stood over him. He wiped the blood running from his nose on his arm, his chest heaving as he spoke, "Get up and I swear I'll beat you into a coma. I'll have that photograph."

Napier turned to look at Ruddy with defiant eyes. He tried twice to rise and collapsed both times. The referee began the count. At ten, Napier remained down and the referee declared Ruddy the winner.

Napier made a brief but weak protest before allowing his corner man to lead him away. Tony had Ruddy sit while he washed the blood from his face and hands.

"My nose is broken, isn't it?" Ruddy asked.

Tony nodded. "It's a clean break. You'll have a bump but that's all, if it is set soon. Want me to set the break?"

"Have you done it before?" He did like the idea of only a bump and nothing worse.

"Yes. It will hurt but it's over quick."

Ruddy didn't have to think too long. Setting broken noses always hurts. Setting any broken bone hurts. He took a deep breath. "Go ahead. Just hurry."

Tony pressed a thumb to one side of Ruddy's nose and used his other thumb to press the bone back in place. Sharp pain shot from his nose to his brain and back. Ruddy reeled. His eyes instantly watered. "Oh sweet heaven. Do you need to bandage it or anything?"

"Best to leave it alone now. Be careful not to

bump it while you're shaving and washing. You'll lose your sense of smell and taste for a short time."

"That maybe but I haven't lost my desire for a beer or two or three. Let me get cleaned up and changed. We're to meet the Holborn lads on our side of the river at the Hare and Hound pub."

Tony gave him a hand to help him up. "You did real well in the ring, Mr. Bloodstone. I am proud to say I trained you. You should be right proud. You fought their champion and it ended in a victory. That's bloody damn good."

Jameson had waited for Ruddy in the arena room. "Good show, Bloodstone. You did Holborn proud."

"Thank you, sir."

Jameson handed Ruddy three sovereigns. "I assume you're going to the Hare and Hound." Ruddy nodded. "Buy the Holborn men a round of drinks on me." He turned to Tony and extended his hand. "Mr. Critchlow, I understand from Archie you trained Rudyard."

"I did," Tony shook Jameson's hand.

"Well done. You kept him on his feet." Jameson turned back to Ruddy, smiled and added, "I wasn't certain you'd stay standing."

"I wasn't certain either, sir," Ruddy said.

"John and I are going onto our club. But before we do John was telling me something about the history of your murder victims that might be useful to your investigation. John, please tell Bloodstone what you told me."

"I attended Oxford at the same time as Cross

and Skinner. They were on the university's rowing crew. In fact, they were the championship team three years running. When I read they'd both been murdered I thought it oddly coincidental, but not so much so as to mention it to Henry here," Daley said, indicating Jameson.

The small fact about the men attending university together, let alone being on the rowing crew together was worth the broken nose. He and Archie were desperate for any scrap of a lead to follow. "Go on sir, please."

"Then when I read about Dr. Finch's nurse being murdered, I thought this was too peculiar not to mention to Henry. I knew I'd be seeing him today, which is why I didn't contact you sooner. You see, Finch was part of the crew as well. There were four on the team who were thick as thieves. Four of the most annoying jackanapes and braggarts you'll ever meet. Cross was their leader, the worst of them. They followed along with whatever he wanted to do."

"You say there were four. Do you recall who the fourth fellow was?" Ruddy asked.

"Harlan Lloyd-Birch."

"Do you happen to know where he works or lives in the city?"

"He doesn't. I was never friends with any of them but I heard through social contacts that Harlan's lungs are in bad condition. His health won't tolerate the city air. He stays at his country estate outside Guildford, Surrey. He conducts his family's business from there. That's as much as I can tell you. I hope it helps."

"Oh, it does. Thank you. Enjoy your evening," Ruddy said. "We'll be off to the pub ourselves shortly."

Napier's corner man came over and handed Ruddy the leather portfolio. "Nathaniel said to give this to you."

"Don't go anywhere yet." Ruddy stepped to the side and pulled the picture out just far enough to verify it was the one of Honeysuckle. Ruddy closed the portfolio and moved back to where Tony and Napier's man waited. "Everything is fine," he told the corner man who turned and left.

Archie and Northam joined them just as Jameson and Daley left the building. "We might finally have a decent lead in our murder cases," Ruddy told Archie.

"Do tell."

"For a start, it looks like Keating might not have been the intended victim. We may be looking for someone with a grudge against the good doctor."

"And the others?"

"The same. They're friends of his from Oxford." Ruddy gingerly felt the bridge of his nose.

If thoughts had sound, a dull thud would come from Archie as previous theories for the murders got pushed aside. "If we're talking someone who hates them from Oxford days, then we're talking almost twenty years of hate. Merciful heavens. That's a lot of hate."

"Isn't it though? The connection makes for an unusual lead but I'm happy for any lead."

Archie removed his handkerchief from his coat pocket and gave it to Ruddy. "You shouldn't fiddle with your nose. You've got trickle of blood coming out now."

"Are my eyes going black yet?"

Archie and Northam both nodded. "Getting there," Archie said.

****

Ruddy and his friends celebrated his victory at the Hare and Hound. They enjoyed themselves mocking Napier's supporters and rehashing when Ruddy delivered his best blows. Typical for a gathering of coppers, the conversation moved from the highlights of the boxing match to the best rough and tumble fights with street ruffians the different men had. Those stories always have a way of morphing into the comical calls they've had. Ruddy wasn't sure how well Tony would fit in a group of Peelers. He needn't have worried. This was the jolliest he'd ever seen his sparring partner. Tony shared equally funny stories from his army days that had everyone laughing.

By the time the party ended and Ruddy was home, all he wanted was a soak in a hot bath. Every muscle in his body ached and reminded him how sore he'd be in the morning. To his pleasant surprise, Luke's mother and Mrs. Goodge were still awake playing whist in the parlor, while Luke sat nearby playing marbles.

"Luke, want to earn a shilling?" Ruddy asked, stopping in the doorway.

Luke jumped up and dashed over to Ruddy. "A shilling? For a shilling, I'll run to the Thames itself to fetch the water, sir."

Ruddy grimaced at the disgusting thought of bathing in the river's filthy water. "While I appreciate your enthusiasm, Luke, the only thing I can think of worse to bathe in is donkey urine."

"Mr. Bloodstone, such talk."

"Sorry Mrs. Goodge, I forgot myself. I've been drinking with some raucous friends the last couple hours and my language has suffered. I'm desperate for a hot bath. Would you mind interrupting your game to heat water for me?"

"You don't mind, do you?" Goodge asked Luke's mother who shook her head.

"I'll get the large pot on straight away." Goodge set her hand on the table and headed for the kitchen.

Ruddy ruffled Luke's hair. "Let's pass on the Thames. Ten pails of Mrs. Goodge's water will do."

"Yes, sir.

****

Ruddy had stayed in the tub until the water cooled. He'd told Luke not to bother returning to empty the tub. He could do that tomorrow while Ruddy was at work.

He warmed a kettle of water in the small fireplace in his parlor and made tea. On the side table next to the overstuffed chair in the room, Ruddy laid his drawing pencils. He settled back into the chair and with the photograph of Honeysuckle on his knees, he began to sketch his version of the picture. Fatigue blanketed him before he got more than the outline of her form finished and minor features of her face.

He closed his sketch pad and put it up on the top shelf of his armoire, lest Luke get nosy. He was at that curious age and might be tempted to look through it when he came to empty the tub. Ruddy placed the photograph in his dresser drawer alongside his Victoria

Cross. As he did, he wondered if Honeysuckle would pose in the nude for him one day.

"Wouldn't that be lovely?"

Chapter Twenty-Nine

Ruddy and Archie took the first train out from London to Guildford. They'd decided to interview Lloyd-Birch first rather than Finch. They hoped to learn something useful from him before they approached Finch again.

"Such lovely countryside in Surrey," Archie said. "I should bring Meg and the girls here one Sunday for a picnic."

"You should. What a world of difference considering how close the shire is to the city," Ruddy said.

They took a carriage for the short ride from the train station to the Lloyd-Birch estate. A combination of Tudor and Georgian architecture the windows were done in the Tudor fashion both paned and leaded and framed out in black wood. The rest of the exterior was red brick, too staid and boxy for Ruddy's taste. They had the carriage wait.

The butler led them out to the rear of the house and the area adjacent to the formal gardens where Harlan Lloyd-Birch was having tea with his daughter.

"Detectives Bloodstone and Holbrook," the butler gestured to each as he said their names.

"Good day, detectives," a man sitting in a

319

wheelchair greeted them. The loud wheeze that trailed the greeting softened after a brief moment. In spite of the warm weather, a plaid blanket covered his legs. He appeared about forty years of age, which was the same as the other victims. He had a thick mane of bright ginger hair that was in stark contrast to his pale complexion.

"Good day, Mr. Lloyd-Birch," Ruddy returned.

"This is my daughter, Frances." Lloyd-Birch indicated a young woman in her early teens with equally fiery hair. "Frances, pour tea for us and then go on about your business while we talk."

After she left, Lloyd-Birch said, "Your message mentioned that you wanted to speak to me about my university days and the rowing crew. We were young men with a penchant for wildness that is common to youth. I didn't care to discuss any indiscretions in front of Frances, in case they came up."

Archie explained they were considering the possibility that someone from their university past, someone with a grudge was executing his group of friends from the rowing team.

"Can you think of anyone who disliked the four of you enough to carry a grudge this long?" Ruddy asked. "Someone on the team perhaps, someone incredibly jealous of the attention you and your friends received. You say you four were the best on the team and the most admired."

A faint smile touched his lips. "You wouldn't know it to look at me now, but I was once one of the strongest rowers on the crew." He sighed and went on, "Honestly, I can't think of anyone who hated us with such venom. We were resented because we were fawned over. But hated enough to kill us? I don't see it." He finished his tea and offered to refresh the detective's before he poured more for himself. "What mystifies me is the timeframe. You're pursuing this avenue about the rowing crew and we're speaking of sixteen years ago. Who, if someone hated us that much, would wait that long to murder us?"

Ruddy and Archie had the same question. Neither had an answer that made sense.

"We appreciate you taking the time to speak with us, Mr. Lloyd-Birch. I'd advise to you to take extra care in the next weeks. Perhaps hire additional security for your home and to accompany you if you go anywhere. Use caution with strangers who might approach you. Your former associates were poisoned. Be especially cautious about any food or drink brought into your home. It may come in the form of a gift."

"I will, Detective Bloodstone."

"Also, if you can think of any incident that might've been the root cause of someone wanting to take serious revenge, send us a message. Or if you think of anyone who menaced you or your friends at the time, we will investigate further." Ruddy handed him his card. Archie did the same. "You have such beautiful formal gardens. I can't help but to admire your gate into them. Would you mind if I take a closer look?"

"No, walk around as much as you like."

"I'm surprised you want to see his gardens," Archie commented to Ruddy when they were out of earshot of Lloyd-Birch. "We've been to fine homes with elegant gardens and you've never shown interest before."

"I'm not as much interested in the gardens as the iron gates. I couldn't help noticing them as we were talking. Those on the border that I could see had incredible ironwork. I wanted a closer look."

As they strolled through the gardens, Ruddy stopped at every gate, wishing he had his sketch book. Each one had an individual design, most with elaborate floral patterns.

"This is so striking," he said of the one he liked the best, a series of cabbage roses on a vine. "I'm going to try and replicate this the next time I'm commissioned to do a gate for a client with a garden of this quality."

Archie stopped and took a deep breath. "Poor health aside, it's understandable why a man would choose to live here instead of the city. The air is so sweet and fresh."

"It is," Ruddy said, thinking that living in the city you forget how pleasant something as simple as the air is elsewhere. "It reminds me of home." The valley where he grew up was lush and green and awash with waterfalls and streams. Honeysuckle was right. He missed Wales more than he realized and should go home for the holidays.

Archie pulled his watch from his vest. "We should head for the station. The next train to London is in forty-five minutes."

"I'm ready to go."

From the train station in London, Ruddy and Archie went straight to Finch's office. They asked him the same questions and received the same response.

Finch couldn't think of any enemy who'd resort to murder.

****

At the end of his shift Ruddy picked up Winky and went to Honeysuckle's hotel. She was working, but she'd made arrangements for him to wait in her room. All the front desk staff knew him by now. When he came with Winky a staff member sent word to the kitchen for scraps to be sent to the room.

Ruddy and Honeysuckle shared a late dinner in her room that night. He told her about the disappointing interviews with Lloyd-Birch and Finch. He trusted her discretion and discussed the hope he and Arch had that something might come of the rowing team lead, however slim it might be considering the time delay.

Honeysuckle relaxed back on the velvet sofa and propped stocking feet on the butler's table. She'd removed her corset and wore a loose-fitting satin gown and deep blue silk robe with Chinese dragons embroidered on the front.

"Is it possible one or more of your four men is or was a man who enjoyed the favors of both sexes?" she asked, sipping Moet champagne, her favorite.

He and Archie had touched on the possibility of a jealous lover with Cross and Nurse Keating. They hadn't explored the idea of a homosexual involvement.

"Three of the men are married. I'd tend to exclude the fourth, Cross, who's a bachelor. He frequented a local whore house and favored a young female prostitute there." Ruddy figured if Cross had other leanings it would've come out when they were there.

He wanted a moment to think on the other three so poured a tankard of beer and then joined Honeysuckle on the sofa. "The married men can be leading double lives, of course. It's not that difficult especially for a wealthy man. I'd eliminate Lloyd-Birch mainly due to his health. He can't handle the coal smoke air of the city. He also needs a wheelchair to get around."

"I never met Skinner. Nothing his family or his clerk said indicated any kind of relationship outside of his marriage. But that doesn't mean he wasn't an expert at leading a double life." Then there was Finch, who had something of a double life, if you count his affair with Keating.

He took a large swallow of beer. "What made you think one of them might be having a, shall we say, forbidden relationship?"

"The means the killer is using to murder the men. Poison is a feminine weapon."

Ruddy bent and gave her a kiss. "Now you're thinking like a detective. Go on. I want to hear your thought process."

"If I were going to kill someone, I'd use poison. Guns are loud and you need to know how to handle them or you just wound your quarry. At least that's what I'd be afraid of doing. Stabbing is bloody and messy. You have to get in too close and it's too easy to be overcome and wind up on the wrong end of the knife." Honeysuckle sipped more champagne and said, "Poison is simple and clean. Very ladylike."

"You've thought this out quite thoroughly.

Should I worry that you've given murder such detailed analysis?"

"Not yet." She smiled that-the-Devil-is-a-woman-smile up at him.

"If it is an intimate relationship we didn't consider, I still haven't an explanation for the time lapse. The victims haven't socialized with each other since leaving university. There's no reasonable cause for jealousy now. What is motivating these sudden attacks?"

"Hmm, that's a poser."

They sat silently drinking, trying to figure out how the time piece aberration fit the murder puzzle.

Honeysuckle perked up. "Maybe it's the sibling of a person they hurt in some way. A fellow student they relentlessly taunted. A sensitive soul who committed suicide or suffered cruelly while they were students together."

"And the sibling is getting revenge now? It's been a decade and a half."

"The sibling might've been too young to do anything when the incidents occurred. I'm leaning towards them getting revenge for a brother committing suicide."

Both theories, the homosexual one and the cruelty one, had merit. Ruddy couldn't offer a better one. Oxford was loaded with randy young men. It wouldn't be unusual for many to find lusty satisfaction with those close at hand. The universities were also breeding grounds of snobbery. A poor soul attending on a scholarship or living on limited funds would be at the mercy of razor-tongued fellow students. He and

Archie needed to interview Finch and Lloyd-Birch again. How interesting if it turned out to be a long held hatred that just wanted the right moment to surface.

****

"No, none of us had any sodomite leanings," Lloyd-Birch said. "You know the four of us went to Eton together."

"No, I didn't know," Ruddy told him. "Does that make a difference?"

"Only in passing. As you might imagine, we were just coming into our teens at Eton, there might have been some interaction. Touching, kissing, perhaps a bit more. You're naturally curious at that age. But nothing that carried over into the university time."

"If one of the others did engage in a relationship of that kind, would they have told the other three in your group?" Archie asked.

Lloyd-Birch thought before answering. "I'm not sure. That said, I don't think it is something you can hide, not from friends as close as we were. I'm afraid I haven't been much help again."

"Actually you have, eliminating theories is as important as proving them," Ruddy said. He and Archie stood to leave. "If you think of any person you had a serious negative encounter with at the time, you have our cards, get a message to us."

"Of course. The butler will show you out."

"At least he was more honest than Finch about their possible sexual experimenting," Archie said after they were settled into the carriage.

"I never expected much from Finch. He'll have to get truly scared before he really cooperates."

"I don't know about your school, but at my school in Yorkshire, the lads kept their curiosity to themselves," Archie said. "What about yours?"

"Please, Brecon is a small village. We only had two rooms to our school. Lads did not secretly go about touching other lads just to see what it felt like. You'd get a not so secret punch in the nose.

Ruddy had preferred the vengeful sibling theory. It solved the more daunting problems in the case. He had it in his head that a waiter in one of their clubs recognized one of them. Hurtful memories were triggered and were acted upon. It was perfect motivation or would've been. "I wish he or Finch remembered someone they'd bullied."

"I wonder if they did bully someone but because they were toffs, they didn't see their actions for what they were. I mean, consider Finch. He truly believes himself superior. I don't doubt he's always believed it's his right to treat people he thinks lesser beings anyway he wishes."

The waiter idea hung in the back of Ruddy's mind on the ride to the station. Maybe his frustration with their lack of progress kept him circling back to the revenge theory, frustration with a healthy dose of desperation and a stubborn unwillingness not to follow every possible lead.

"Let's go along with the revenge theory. I don't care that Finch and Lloyd-Birch claim they're innocent of ugly behavior. What do you think of the idea that our killer is a service person of some sort, a waiter or doorman at one of the clubs the men belong to, someone in that capacity? He works somewhere and saw one of the men."

"Has merit. The question is did the killer make contact in some unremarkable way prior to the murders, some way the victims didn't find suspicious?"

"I believe he had to since he accessed Cross's brandy, he knew the layout of Skinner's office and knew where to find Finch. Tomorrow let's see if Skinner, Finch, and Cross had a new client, the same new client."

"Yes," Archie said with sudden optimism. "Wouldn't it be funny if we missed a clue so obvious?"

"Funny, a little embarrassing, but I'd be mighty grateful nonetheless."

****

Ruddy and Archie went to Skinner's office first.

"No, Mr. Skinner hadn't acquired any new clients, not for the past several months," Mr. Button told them.

Not the news the detectives hoped to hear. Ruddy didn't see much point in checking with Cross's associates. Cross handled commercial accounts and the detectives doubted their possible revenge suspect fell into the same financial category as the rest of Cross's clients. But if nothing turned up at Finch's, they'd go to the bank just out of thoroughness.

"We have another party to interview. Should some additional information come from that and we need to speak with you again, will you still be here? I'm surprised to find the office open today," Ruddy said to Button.

"The office isn't technically open. I'm here tidying up the unresolved cases of Mr. Skinner's and referring them to other solicitors. In answer to your question, I will be here all day and for the rest of the week," Button said. "Best of luck detectives. I hope you do discover more information. Mr. Skinner deserves justice."

They took a carriage to Finch's rather than the tram, which made too many stops. Both Ruddy and Archie were anxious to either uncover something worthwhile.

Finch was civil to them, for once. "Although I treat both men and women, the only new patient I have acquired recently was a woman."

Honeysuckle's words from the other night struck Ruddy like Napier's left hook. *Poison is simple and clean. Very ladylike.* Could their killer be a woman?

Archie poked Ruddy in the ribs with his elbow. "Ruddy, you're staring."

"What if it's a woman?"

"Never crossed my mind," Archie said, shaking his head. "Interesting and possible now that you mention it."

"When did you acquire this new patient?" Ruddy asked Finch.

"A week before Nurse Keating's murder. Are you suggesting my patient might've murdered Nurse Keating?"

"We don't know. Maybe. She's someone of interest to us, most certainly. We'd like all the information you have on her," Ruddy said.

Finch pulled a ledger from the lobby desk drawer. "Here. She is the companion to Esther Zachary of Belgrave Square. This is her house number. Mrs. Zachary is a patient of an associate of mine, Dr. Fitzhugh. The woman goes by the name of Graciela Robson. I'm not sure what else you wish to know. She came to me suffering headaches."

"Have you seen her since Nurse Keating's death?" Archie asked as he wrote down her information.

"Now that you ask, no I haven't."

"Describe her for us, please," Ruddy said and took out his notebook and a pencil. He began to sketch on the small pad as Finch described Robson. Every so often he stopped to show the drawing to Finch to verify he had her features right.

Finch finished. "What happens now?"

Ruddy tucked the notebook back into his coat pocket. "We will show this picture to another possible witness. Whether he says he's seen her or not, we're going to interview her."

They went from Finch's straight back to Skinner's office and showed the drawing to Button.

"Goodness me, I know that woman." Button looked from Ruddy to Archie and back. "She came in with a story about a dithery aunt. She asked a few questions about Mr. Skinner's practice. She never filled out our forms. She said she'd bring them back but never did."

"When was this?" Ruddy asked.

Button recoiled, eyes wide. "Just before Mr. Skinner's death. Why? Do you think she's involved? A woman?"

"We're not ruling anyone out," Archie reassured

him.

"Good luck detectives."

Archie stepped off the curb and hailed a cab. "Zachary's next?"

"Yes, let's talk to Mrs. Zachary first, get some background on Robson before we interview her."

"We've never had a female murderer," Archie commented as they settled into their seats in the cab. "If she did it, that is."

"She's our killer. It'll be interesting to find out why," Ruddy said, genuinely curious.

****

Esther Zachary's butler showed Ruddy and Archie to the parlor. Ruddy immediately noticed the room wasn't private. The entry was an archway open to the main corridor of the townhome.

"Is there a room we can speak to Mrs. Zachary that is private? One with a door we can close?" Ruddy asked the butler.

"The library, although Mrs. Zachary rarely uses the room these days. Her eyesight has grown too weak for her to read with ease. She prefers to greet visitors in the parlor."

"I understand but we're not the usual visitors. What we wish to discuss is confidential. We'd appreciate it if you'd explain that to her. Please, we'd like to go to the library."

"Certainly." He led them to a smaller room than the parlor. Stuffy and far hotter, Ruddy suspected the windows hadn't been opened in ages. He also suspected Zachary wasn't the only one who ignored the room. The maid did as well. A fine layer of dust covered the book shelves and the table separating two chairs at one end of the room. At the other end was a rolled-up carpet of a different pattern from the threadbare one on the floor.

A few minutes later the butler entered with a petite, grey-haired woman about sixty years old, carrying their business cards. She wore gold-framed wire spectacles but her blue eyes were cloudy and she blinked rapidly when the butler opened the drapes to let sunlight in. She wore a lavender high-collared dress. There was a translucent quality to her skin and her complexion took on a faint lavender color too.

"Can I get you anything, Mrs. Zachary?" the butler asked and helped her into one of the chairs. She didn't offer the other chair to either detective.

"No, I'm fine for the moment, Sternbaugh. You may go. Please close the door behind you." She waited for the butler to leave and then said, "How awful you look, detective. Did you lose an encounter with a hooligan?"

"I didn't lose." Ruddy thought it easier to let her think his nose was broken that way than tell her the truth.

She sighed and sat very straight in the closest chair. She didn't offer a seat to them. "Our civilization is falling apart. I mourn for its loss." She looked to Ruddy. "You are?"

"Detective Bloodstone and this is Detective Holbrook."

"I've never talked with detectives before. I'm intrigued. Sternbaugh tells me you wish to discuss a mysterious matter involving my household."

"We have some questions regarding your lady's companion, Graciela Robson," Ruddy said.

"What would you like to know?"

Archie took out his notebook and a pen. "Her history with you to start. Where did you find her? How long has she been with you?"

"She had placed an advertisement in Myra's Journal of Dress and Fashion offering her services as a lady's maid. I didn't need a lady's maid but I was newly widowed and in need of a companion. I interviewed her and found Graciela sweet. She was also well spoken in spite of the fact her father was only a simple cobbler. That was ten years ago. At the time, she was living in the Oxford area and she came to London to meet with me."

At the mention of Oxford, Archie and Ruddy exchanged a subtle look but kept their expressions neutral in front of Zachary.

"You're certain she lived in the Oxford area?" Ruddy wanted confirmation.

"I've lost my youth Detective Bloodstone, not my wits."

"No offense meant. It's important we're certain of our facts." She looked unmoved by the explanation.

"Do you know if she has an elderly aunt?" Archie asked.

"She's never mentioned one. To my knowledge she only has an older brother who lives in Oxfordshire somewhere. I don't believe they keep in contact. Her mother had been dead for ages when we met and her father passed away a year ago."

"Does she have a day off?" Ruddy asked, hoping

it was Monday.

Zachary nodded. "Monday."

"Do you ever give her time off in addition to Mondays?"

"On occasion she'll run personal errands on afternoons when I don't need her or if I am napping. What exactly are you looking to know about Graciela?"

"We can't really say at this time, Mrs. Zachary, only that it is related to a case we're investigating," Archie said.

"Has she ever talked about any of the men in her life?" Ruddy asked.

Zachary removed her glasses. Ruddy figured she did so to emphasize her scowl and disapproval of the notion. "She wouldn't dare. I have a strict rule about flirtations. Graciela knew when I hired her that I did not approve of male visitors nor did I wish a companion seeking marriage. I've nothing against marriage. But I don't have the patience to constantly search out new companions and train them because the previous one has fallen in love."

Ruddy pressed to know if one of the four men's names were mentioned as part of her past. "Did she ever talk about having been smitten with a young man from the university when she lived in Oxford?"

Zachary shook her head. "I'd really like to know what this is about. After all, she is part of my household and if there's a criminal matter at hand, I believe I deserve to know."

"We will tell you as soon as we are at liberty to do so. At this time, we can't without jeopardizing our investigation," Ruddy explained again.

"In that case, are we done?" Zachary reached for the butler's bell cord.

"We will need to speak to Miss Robson. Is she here?" Archie asked.

"She is. I'll have Sternbaugh bring her to the library."

There was a knock at Graciela's bedroom door. "Miss Robson."

Sternbaugh

She opened the door expecting he'd tell her Mrs. Zachary wanted to go somewhere and for Graciela to join her.

"There are two detectives in the library who wish to speak with you," Sternbaugh said.

Her heart stopped at his words. "Detectives? What do they want to speak to me about?"

"They spoke to Mrs. Zachary in private but Millie listened at the door. She heard them asking a lot of questions about you. They even inquired if you had headaches. Odd, I know. You best come now and not keep them waiting." Sternbaugh stepped aside for her to pass.

Graciela never liked Millie. The maid was the house busybody and gossip. For once her nosiness came in useful. If the detectives were asking about the headaches, they'd found a way to associate her with Dr. Finch. *What else did they know or suspect?*

"Sternbaugh, please tell them I'll be right down. I have a personal moment to attend to first."

"As you wish."

Graciela shut the door. The time had come to

take care of Finch. She'd likely never get the chance to take revenge on Lloyd-Birch but Finch was within her grasp.

She dropped Addy's Derringer into her reticule. She'd have to shoot him. Poison took too long to take hold. She couldn't risk the time. Graciela foresaw two possible endings. In the perfect one, she'll kill Finch and get away. She'd need every cent she had to start over, perhaps in Canada or America. She reached into the back of her dresser drawer and retrieved a small satin bag with all the money she had on hand.

In the second ending, the terrible one, she'd still kill Finch but get caught by the police. She thought the chance remote since the detectives only said they wanted to question her. They didn't indicate they were there to arrest her, which she was sure they've have said if that were the case. But Peelers were a slippery lot. She lumped them into two groups, haughty bully-boys or sly and cunning. She put Bloodstone and his partner in the last. How else did they get to be detectives unless they were cunning?

Once the detectives heard she evaded them, they might anticipate where she was headed. Even if the chance was slim, she had to consider the end result. "I don't have the courage to put a gun to my head, Me-Too. I definitely don't want the horror of the hangman's rope." She pulled the flask of arsenic from her dresser. "Live by the sword, die by the sword. Isn't that how the expression goes, sweet kitty?"

She squeezed the cat to her chest tight and kissed the top of her head. "I shall miss you dearly, little one."

With Me-Too in the crook of her arm, fast as she could while trying to keep her footsteps quiet, Graciela hurried down to the kitchen.

Sternbaugh, Millie, and Tess the cook were at the table drinking tea. Graciela shoved Me-Too into Tess's arms. "If something happens to me, promise you'll take care of Me-Too. Promise."

"What do you think is going to happen?" Tess cradled the wriggling cat to her ample bosom.

"I don't have time to explain. Just promise you'll take care of her."

"Of course. We all love her."

Sternbaugh stood and said in a stern voice. "You can't leave. The detectives are waiting."

Graciela didn't bother to answer. She dashed out the back door and ran down the alley. At the corner, out of sight of the house, she waved down a cab.

The butler rushed into the library. "She's gone," he said in a burst to the detectives. "If you hurry, you might still catch her. She left by the kitchen door."

"Robson?" Archie asked.

"Yes."

"Take us through to the back, hurry," Ruddy ordered as he and Archie fell in behind the butler.

A woman in maid's garb stood at the kitchen door but quickly moved as the detectives came into the room. "She went to the right."

Ruddy and Archie ran to the end of the alley. She was nowhere in sight.

"Where do you think she's headed?" Archie asked. "My guess would be out of the country."

"Good guess. We can't watch all the train stations or the ports. I wonder how much money she has on her? The clever move is to get out of London, then head for Southampton or Liverpool and onto a boat across the Atlantic. Go somewhere no one knows her. She can sail fairly cheap in steerage," Ruddy said. "First, let's warn Finch and then Lloyd-Birch, just in case she makes a final attempt on one of their lives."

Ruddy and Archie entered the doctor's empty waiting room. He hadn't replaced Nurse Keating yet. As Ruddy raised his hand to knock on the exam room door, Finch's excited voice could be heard pleading, "Don't please. Why are you doing this?"

Ruddy turned the handle. The door was locked. He took a few steps back and gave the lock a hard kick. The door banged open, bouncing against the wall and part way back.

A mildly attractive brunette woman about thirty years of age stood over Finch with a Derringer pointed at his head.

"Help me," a saucer-eyed Finch, begged the detectives, his shaking hands partially up in surrender. "She's insane."

"Take one step closer and I'll shoot," the woman warned.

Ruddy stopped a couple strides from where she stood but offset to the right so the desk didn't block him. "Graciela Robson?"

"Yes, not that my name is important."

Ruddy did a fast analysis of the situation. Robson didn't murder out of blood lust. She wasn't a two-legged rabid dog style killer. She killed with a purpose. Her victims were connected. Murderers like that have a story to tell. If he could get her talking, she'd likely grow distracted enough to pay less attention to Finch. A small distraction was all he needed.

Archie fanned out to Ruddy's left. They'd been in similar situations before where a suspect had a weapon on a victim. The plan was for Ruddy to rush the suspect and Archie to wrap up the victim and pull them out of harm's way.

"I like to know who I'm talking to and the doctor should know who holds his life in her hands. My partner here is Detective Holbrook and I'm—"

"I know who you are, Detective Bloodstone. I've been in Holborn Station and heard other detectives refer to you. I remember reading about you last year and that Viscount killer."

"Speaking of killing, did you murder Bartholomew Cross and Daniel Skinner?" One corner of her mouth tipped up in an awkward ghost of a smile and for a brief second her gaze dropped to the floor. Ruddy crept forward a fraction.

Robson raised her eyes to Ruddy. "I did and now it's this one's turn." She pressed the barrel of the gun into Finch's temple.

Finch chirped like a wounded bird.

"Why?" Ruddy asked.

"He deserves to die. He and his three friends raped me. There was no justice for me then, but I'm taking it now."

"I barely remember the incident." A baffled

looking Finch turned from Ruddy to the woman. "It was nothing worth dying for. You weren't hurt. We had a bit of fun with you." He shifted his attention back to the detectives. "We had a bit of fun is all. She was just some village girl we used to see walking along the riverside."

She struck Finch on the temple with the gun butt. "I was only fourteen." The gun left a red streak mark but didn't draw blood. The gun was too small and her strike too weak.

Finch squealed like she'd struck him with a rifle butt.

As victims went, the doctor offended Ruddy to the core. *You really are a disgusting weasel, sniveling with fear. You and your wealthy young male friends rape a girl because you can, and now whimper when she hits you. Someone should knock you in the head with a real gun and not that lady-ish thing she's carrying.*

"Did you report the crime when it occurred?" Ruddy asked.

"No. What good would it have done? They were rich boys from the university. Who were the Peelers going to believe, me or them? A poor cobbler's daughter or the sons of wealthy influential businessmen?"

"Since you never gave the police a chance, we'll never know," Ruddy said.

She pulled a flask from the pocket of her skirt, uncorked it with her teeth and tossed back the contents.

Ruddy rushed her as Archie dived for Finch.

Robson managed to fire a round before Ruddy tackled her to the floor. The shot missed Finch but grazed Archie's upper arm.

"Arch, are you all right? Are you hit?" Ruddy asked as Archie and Finch scrambled up from the floor.

Archie stuck his hand inside his coat and felt around. "My coat's ruined but it doesn't feel like any other harm's been done. I wonder if the department will pay for a new jacket?"

"That was the last of my arsenic," Robson told Ruddy as he brought her up and forced into the chair the doctor had occupied. "I won't go to the gallows for those bastards. I'll die on my own terms."

"What's the antidote for arsenic poisoning?" Ruddy asked Finch, setting the Derringer on top a high cabinet out of her reach.

"Why should I help her? She was going to kill me."

"Because I asked. Is there a treatment?"

"Was it pure arsenic in the flask?" Finch asked Robson.

"Yes."

"She'll die. There's no miracle medicine," he told Ruddy.

Robson eyed Finch with palpable hatred. "I'm glad I did what I did. I only regret not completing the job."

Ruddy shook his head. "Why after sixteen years did you go after them?" He was genuinely curious. "You had a decent life working for Mrs. Zachary."

"My life with Mrs. Zachary was pleasant enough. She took me places I wouldn't have seen otherwise. To be honest, I thought I'd shoved the memory of what they'd done to the deepest recesses of my mind." Robson paled and put her head down on her arms. "Give me a moment. I'm queasy."

Ruddy knew her loss of color and the nausea were signs the poison was taking hold. But he hadn't witnessed the effects of arsenic poisoning as it worked its effect on a living body. The speed it worked surprised him.

She continued but kept her head down. "Mrs. Zachary and I were having tea at the Kew Gardens café when I saw Bartholomew Cross there. He'd come in with a couple. He looked right at me, walked by me, and I could tell he had no idea who I was. I was nothing to him then and nothing now. All the memories of that horrible afternoon came flooding back." Robson raised her head. Tears ran down her cheeks. "Do you have any idea what it feels like to be nothing? To mean nothing to people like him? The man who lights the streetlamp outside his townhome is more noticeable to him."

She wiped at her tears with the back of her hand.

Finch dabbed at the red mark where she'd struck him with the butt of the gun. Archie snatched the handkerchief from his hand and gave it to her.

"I've got this," Ruddy told Archie. "Why don't you go to the station and tell Jameson what's happened and order the Medical Examiner to respond."

Archie nodded and left.

Robson retched but nothing came out. "They laughed at me when I begged for them to leave me alone. They mocked me when I said I'd report them. I knew I was being foolish. Rich men write the laws. Rich men choose which to break, which laws other men like them will turn a blind eye to." She clamped her arms over her stomach and doubled over, groaning.

Ruddy helped her from the chair over to the exam table. "Lie down on your side and bring your knees up to your stomach. It might ease the pain."

Finch stood at the foot of the table and pointed to Robson. "Get her off there. I don't appreciate that filthy criminal using my exam table."

"I'm sure she didn't appreciate getting raped. So sit down and hold your tongue." Ruddy ordered when Finch didn't obey immediately.

"Where...where..." Robson's breathing was growing jagged. She struggled to draw in a deep breath. "Where did you learn about lying on your side with your legs up?"

"The army. Dysentery is a common problem. It causes severe cramps. The company doctors often recommend doing this. Has it helped?"

"A bit." She closed her eyes and gripped her stomach tighter, whimpering as she did. After a moment she said, "You're naïve and blind too, detective, in your own way." She opened her eyes. "You believe by enforcing the law you're pursuing justice."

"Not naïve and certainly not blind. The law isn't always fair. There are those justice fails to serve. But for all its failings, the law is the difference between order and chaos. For that alone, I won't abandon her," Ruddy argued.

"My way had sure results."

"No. Your way was only half effective for which

you're paying a mighty price now."

She gave a faint cry and then stilled.

Ruddy covered her with a linen cloth that had been hanging over the privacy screen. "Be at peace now."

****

Two days later

Ruddy had just put on his coat ready to leave for the night when the desk sergeant approached.

"There's a constable from the Whitechapel Station at the desk asking to speak with you. Want me to tell him you've gone for the night?" the sergeant asked.

"Why don't you go on and leave. I know you have plans with Honeysuckle. I can take care of whatever the fellow wants," Archie offered.

Whitechapel. Ruddy couldn't think why someone from their district had a reason to specifically speak with him. Strange. "No. I'm in no rush. I'll talk with the fellow. I'm curious what this about. Let's both talk to him."

The sergeant didn't need to point out the Whitechapel officer. His was the only new police face hovering around the lobby desk.

"I'm Detective Bloodstone. The sergeant said you asked for me in particular."

"I did." A boyish looking, lanky constable with a faint blonde mustache stepped forward. "Our detectives sent me over. They're handling a homicide at Our Lady of Mercy hospital, a Dr. Finch is the victim. He had your business card on him. I was told to ask if you had time to come by and give the detectives what

344

information you have on Finch."

The minute the constable said the murder occurred at Our Lady of Mercy, Ruddy knew all he needed to know about the motive. "That's a hospital for indigent women and children, isn't it?" he asked, just to verify.

"It is. Will you come?"

"Yes."

"I'll come too," Archie said.

The three hired a carriage to take them back. At that hour, the trams would be packed with workers whose shifts recently ended. A carriage was also the fastest means through traffic.

At the hospital the Whitechapel constable led Ruddy and Archie through a small ward where another constable kept watch over a handful of female patients in hospital issue gowns. The presence of the officer indicated the women were likely witnesses.

The crime scene was in the next ward. Finch lay on the floor with a butcher's knife sticking out of his chest. Considering the type of wound and the weapon, the scene was relatively clean. Finch's shirt and waistcoat absorbed most of the external blood. An autopsy would show how much he'd bled internally.

The constable led them to a bespectacled detective in his forties with a well-trimmed beard in civilian clothes. The detective finished giving orders to another officer and turned to greet Ruddy and Archie.

"Detective Echols, this is Detective Bloodstone and his partner, Detective Holbrook," the constable who escorted them said.

"Thank you for coming," Echols said. "This is an

unusual murder. Our killer is that sickly looking creature sitting on the bed there."

The woman was in her mid-twenties with dull straw colored hair, skin pale as milk, and thin as a candle wick. Ruddy thought manacles a waste on her bony wrists. She could slip them off with no effort if she were so inclined. Finch had been stabbed in the heart with fierce determination. It took strength to power through muscle and bone.

And it took hate.

"Has she confessed?" Ruddy asked.

"Yes. She didn't say much else when we interviewed her. She admitted she planned to do it. She said Finch comes every week at the same time. She went to the kitchen and stole a knife and waited for him. When I found your card I thought you might know more about this Finch and be able to shed some light on what would provoke her to do this."

"I believe I can." Ruddy gave him a brief summation of their case and the incident with Robson two days earlier, along with the murders of the Skinner and Cross.

"That explains her strange statement," Echols said. He brought out his field notebook and flipped through to the page he wanted. "When I asked her why she did it, all she'd say was...*I got tired of men taking what I didn't want to give.* Knowing Finch's history now, my suspicion about the statement is confirmed."

The woman who'd been sitting with her head down looked up at Ruddy. Her eyes held that same anger and defiance he'd seen in Robson's.

"I wonder why she didn't come to us and report

him," Echols said, oblivious to her expression.

"I don't wonder. I've seen this twice in two days. She felt the law would not serve her. Whether it would or not didn't matter. The fact she believed it wouldn't made its failure true." Ruddy wished he carried a flask. A shot of whiskey would go down good right now.

"Come by when you're ready and you can read our entire report," Archie told him. "Ready to go?" he asked Ruddy.

Ruddy nodded.

Outside the wind had changed directions from when they arrived. The smell from the river's rotting flotsam and jetsam baking in the hot sun all day blew over. The smell of blood at the crime scene didn't bother him. The smell of blood never did. The sharp vinegary smell in the air of most hospitals, Our Lady of Mercy included didn't bother him. Most days the odors wafting off the river didn't either. He'd lived in London long enough to get used to them. Today, the rank stink was more noticeable than usual.

"Whitechapel really is an abomination to the senses, isn't it?" Archie commented and waved down a cab who'd just off loaded a passenger.

"Yes."

Chapter Thirty

"Two female killers. How extraordinary. Have you ever had a female murderer before?" Honeysuckle asked Ruddy. "The flowers are beautiful by the way."

"Graciela Robson was my first. The bouquet is the largest we could find. Archie and I wanted to show our gratitude. Champagne is on the way to the room too. I stopped at the front desk and requested a bottle."

"I don't understand. Gratitude for what?"

"You talked about poison being a woman's way of killing because it wasn't messy. After we'd explored every avenue for possible suspects, we turned to the only one we never traveled. Could we be looking for a woman?"

"As a woman—"

Ruddy lifted the mass of her dark curls and kissed the base of her neck. "A very lovely woman I might add."

"You should do that to both sides just to be fair." He obeyed and she went on. "As a woman, I'm not sure how I feel about your killer. Part of me feels sympathy for her plight after being abused by the men. That said, the bigger part of me can't grasp the extreme revenge after all these years. Didn't you feel a bit sorry for her?"

Of all the murderers he'd dealt with, Robson

was the most tragic but he couldn't honestly say he felt a lot of sympathy. "What happened to her was horrible. It doesn't excuse taking the law into her own hands. Vigilantism never ends well. She's perfect evidence of that."

There was a knock at the door. The champagne had arrived. The waiter wheeled in a cart with the bucket and a tray of appetizers. "You can go. I'll serve it," Ruddy told the room service waiter. He poured two glasses and set them on the table in front of the sofa before taking his leave.

"We'll enjoy these in a moment. I've something to show you first." He led Honeysuckle by the hand to the armoire where she kept her cloaks and hats. "I saw this when I hung up my hat the other night." He removed a plaid newsboy's hat from the shelf. Then he slid the other items hanging up aside and pulled a blue jacket with a double row of brass buttons out. "This is a boy's coat. As I recall, you haven't a brother."

Honeysuckle's face flushed pink at the sight of the hat and coat. "No, I am an only child. Why do you ask?"

He set the hat on her head and tucked the hair around her face up under it. Then he held the coat up in front of her. "I have seen a hat and coat like this recently. You'll never guess where."

"Oh all right, you made your point." Honeysuckle took the hat off and tossed it back on the shelf. "I know what you said, but I was desperate to see the fight. I wanted to cheer you on if only silently. Can you forgive me? I'll make it worth your while." She offered the last with soft eyes peering up at him through dark lashes in her temptress way.

"Well..."

"Please."

"You're responsible for this." He pointed to his broken nose.

"How so?"

"I glanced over from the ring and saw a young man, you apparently, who looked like your twin brother. The brief distraction got me a right cross on the nose. I'm adding my nose to the list of wrong doings you'll have to make up for." He kissed the top of her breast and then said, "We'll work on some special ways for you to do that."

They moved to the sofa. The appetizer tray had a variety of finger sandwiches and teacakes along with grapes and strawberries, which Ruddy and Honeysuckle nibbled.

"What's your real name?" Ruddy asked in a light tone. Such a melodic name, he suspected it was too perfect. He wanted to know for no particular reason other than curiosity.

"What? Why do you think Honeysuckle Flowers isn't my real name?"

"I've been a detective a long time. I've a good feel for what rings true. Honeysuckle Flowers is too perfect."

"I did pick well. My true name is Helen Fowler."

"What's wrong with that name, why'd you change it?"

"It's not a marquee name."

"Good point. I've another question and I'd really like you to say yes."

Honeysuckle looked wary. She'd expressed a lack of interest in marriage and probably worried that he planned to propose anyway. "I'm listening."

"I'd like to breathe fresh air for a few days. I want to go to Wales before the holidays. I'd like you to join me. Say yes."

"Are you sure? Your family might not approve of my profession."

"I've never been more sure."

"Then yes."

READ THE FIRST IN THE SERIES

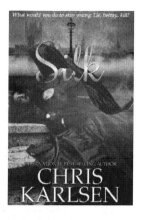

It is the time of Jack the Ripper, the widowed Queen Victoria sits on the throne of England. The whole of London is on edge wondering when or where Jack will kill next. The Palace, Parliament, and the press are demanding the police do more to find him.

In another part of London, rough-around-the-edges war hero, Metropolitan Detective Inspector Rudyard Bloodstone has his own serial killer to find. Inter departmental rivalries, politics, and little evidence to go on hamper the investigation at every turn. In a battle of wills, Bloodstone presses forward following his instincts in spite of the obstacles.

Adding to those problems, away from the strains of the investigation, he is engaged in the ups and downs of a new relationship with a lovely hat maker.

CHAPTER ONE SILK

Dressing the dead required a certain dexterity and patience. William surveyed his work with pride. A pity no one would see his accomplishment. He doubted Isabeau's maid could've done much better.

Sweat beaded his forehead and he used his dead lover's embroidered hanky to wipe his face and the film of perspiration from his chest. The fire in the hearth had gone out while they made love, but even naked, the room was like an oven. He started to pour a glass of wine then thought better of it. Until the body was disposed of and the stage set for explaining her death, he needed to keep a clear head. Instead, he rummaged through the chiffonier hunting for petticoats. No respectable woman left the house without proper underpinnings. A bottom drawer was filled with lace and ribbon-trimmed petticoats. William took the top ones and managed to get them on and tied with far less trouble than he had with the dress.

"Thank God," William mumbled, snickering at the inappropriate application of the phrase. "Now riding boots."

The boot slipped on her tiny foot with ease. He laced it up and had the second one half on when he noticed the ball of stockings on the floor. "Bugger me."

The concept of heaven or hell held no interest for him. On certain holidays, Isabeau droned on about religion and turned a devout Catholic face to the world. If there was anything to her belief, then she was probably gazing on the scene from some perch in Purgatory and laughing. With that grating thought fueling every move, he removed the boot and started over, stockings first.

Finished with dressing her, William threw on the same clothes he'd worn earlier, crept downstairs and headed for the stable. On the way he looked east toward the ruin of the ancient hill fort that bordered his land. Pink streaks lined the distant sky. He'd have to hurry if he wanted to make it to the cliffs before the whole of Tintagel awoke.

He lit a single lantern and carefully placed it to the side where he wouldn't knock it over.

"Sir?" The stable boy stood at the base of the loft ladder rubbing sleep from his eyes, shirt askew and buttoned wrong.

William gave little start. He hadn't heard the boy

stir.

"I can take care of the horses, sir. What did you need me to do?"

"Nothing, Charles. Go back to sleep. I'll saddle King Arthur and Guinevere. Isabeau and I thought it might be nice to go for an early ride." William laid a firm but gentle hand on the lad's shoulder. "Sleep. By the time I—" he corrected himself, "We return, the horses will be ready for feeding and brushing."

The boy nodded and climbed up to his hayloft bed.

Hurriedly working against the rising sun, William tacked up Guinevere, the mare Isabeau rode, and then saddled his big bay hunter. When he was done, he brought both horses round to the far side of the stable and tied them to a rail out of sight from the house.

William dashed back to the bedroom, taking the steps to the upper floor two at a time. Muffled voices came from the kitchen. Of the household staff, cook rose the earliest to begin the day's breakfast preparation. Soon the butler and his valet would be awake. He considered sneaking out of the house but dismissed the idea rather than do anything that might appear suspicious. A ride at dawn's light was out of the ordinary but not so strange as to provoke speculation and clucking by the servants, if he acted normal.

He wrapped Isabeau in a cloak and carried her down the main stairs. With every step, he whispered sweet words to his dead mistress and nuzzled her cool cheek. A smile played at his lips. To any staff member about, it looked like a romantic gesture.

After numerous tries, William secured the body to the mare in a semi-sitting position. Just getting her onto the horse's back turned into a monumental feat and by no means was he a weakling. He took a moment to catch his breath. The short time to sunrise didn't allow for more than a couple of moments. Next he tied her hands to the pommel and her feet to the girth. Isabeau still tipped forward but to anyone they might ride past, the position could pass for a deliberate effort on her part for speed. He'd pony Guinevere on a long line. All he had to do was keep both horses at the same smooth gait, a nice extended canter, or perhaps a measured gallop.

Castle Beach would be his final destination, the easiest spot to unload his baggage without discovery. The route there posed different issues. The foliage of St. Nectan's Glen offered excellent cover and slim odds of seeing other riders. It also added an additional thirty minutes to his journey. The fastest path took him out in the open where he ran the biggest risk of being seen. After a brief mental debate, he decided to use the fastest route and headed straight for the cliffs across the moor.

Guinevere galloped along with King Arthur while William maintained a steady pace, keeping St. Materina's Church in sight and on his right. The church was the midpoint between the cliffs overlooking Castle Beach and Tintagel village proper. The sun had just begun to peek over the horizon when he stopped. Seabirds had already flown from their nests and hovered over the fishing boats preparing to sail out. The absence of gulls, puffins, and other squalling local animal life magnified the roar and crash of the waves against the rocky cliff.

William dismounted and let Arthur graze on the scraggly grass. The fine stallion made an excellent shield as William untied and lifted Isabeau's body from Guinevere. With little effort, he rolled his late lover off the edge of the cliff and watched, grimacing, when her dainty body bounced off a rocky outcropping. True, he planned on packing her back to France, or to another of his associates. And true, he didn't see her death as a great loss, but he wouldn't have wished her bashed on the rocks, even in death. However, this was the most expedient way to rid himself of an inconveniently dead mistress.

It shouldn't have come to this...

****

The ebb and flow of the tide, the rush of water as it churned through the stones embedded in the sandy shore entranced him while the events of the prior evening played in his mind.

"Do you love me, William?" Isabeau pursed her full lips and glided across the carpet with a graceful sway. The sheer gown trailed behind her like a silken mist. She stopped between his knees and faced him.

"No darling. You don't inspire love. You amuse me, which is infinitely better." *You used to anyway.* William took a swallow of the rich claret and swirled the liquid around his mouth and waited for Isabeau's familiar routine. His denial of love always triggered a tantrum.

She'd tested his patience of late. First came the needy question, followed by his honest answer, then the dramatics, the feigned hurt, the pout, the demand for a physical show of desire. *Desire.* It's all there'd ever been between them. Recently, the edge to that passion had grown dull. Even the more unusual aspects of their lovemaking seemed stale, desperate and contrived.

She rubbed her calf against his.

"Don't. I'm not in the mood," he said and moved his leg. "It's a big house Isabeau. Surely you can find something to entertain yourself with other than me."

"I don't want to." Spoiled and demanding, she could be a petulant child when denied. She rubbed the other leg now.

William groaned. He didn't feel like fucking her tonight. He'd risen with the sun and spent the entire day with Harold, the estate manager. They rode the perimeter of the thousand acres that belonged to Foxleigh Hall. Poachers, a constant irritant had become bold over the past few weeks, venturing deep onto the property, shooting badger and deer, even the does, leaving the fawns to die. *Bastards.*

The traps were set—not to attract animal life but human. He'd gone inland to Launceston to hire extra guards, the precaution of distance a necessary evil. In all likelihood, the violators lived in one of the nearby villages, which eliminated using men from the area as possible sentries.

"Just let me sit and enjoy some peace and quiet."

"You're cross. Maybe you should eat." Her winged brows dipped into a furrow of false concern.

"No." Too tired to eat when he returned, he'd waved away the tray of food the maid brought to his private chamber. But Isabeau had no way of knowing he refused dinner since he always ate alone and she never disturbed him. Everyone in the household knew he hated sharing a meal or a table with others present unless a social situation forced him. The sounds people made when they ate disgusted him. Nor did he find idle conversation over food particularly engaging. No witty discussion could compensate for the smacking, slurping, swallowing noises. These offenses were compounded by the glimpses of half-devoured food of folks who felt the urge to speak while eating.

"I'm not hungry. I'm weary. Were you the least bit observant you'd have noticed?" William ignored the sour face she made and laid his head back against the cushions of the chair and closed his eyes. He sat still as stone, holding the wineglass by the globe, not sleeping but resting his eyes.

Close to dozing off, he spread his legs farther apart, so his feet were flat on the floor. The only sound came from the occasional pop of wood in the fire as it burned. The heat from Isabeau's body and the silk of her gown as it brushed his knuckles gave her away as she knelt in front of him. She removed his riding boots and began unbuttoning his shirt. He opened his eyes to watch.

She peered up through thick lashes, her unlined complexion glowed and her moist lips glistened. *The face of a penitent and the morals of a peahen.* A pleasurable combination most nights. She'd deliberately worn the ribbons loose and her gown had slipped from her shoulders. The soft garment split apart below her navel, exposing creamy pink and white flesh. Those thighs, shorter and plumper than an Englishwoman's, produced surprising strength when it mattered, aiding him in burying himself deeper within her.

"I love you," Isabeau said and stretched forward so the tips of her breasts skimmed his wool trousers and the nipples pearled.

"Don't be silly. You love my pounds, shillings, and pence, well, not the pence so much," he clarified with a light chuckle. "You love the jewelry I give you." William picked her hand up and fingered the cameo ring he'd bought her for Christmas. "And, you love the fine clothes, and the sex, but you don't love me."

She pushed off his legs and stood with remarkable speed. With a long sigh, he straightened, ready for the torrent of indignation she'd no doubt hurl at him.

The moue returned, only more pronounced. "How dare you tell me who or what I love. Why must you be so cruel?" Isabeau stomped a barefoot while one fat tear escaped down her cheek. "You break my heart," she added with a dramatic lip quiver. "Why don't we marry? I could be a good wife, a good mother. You could learn to love me. I already know many ways to please you."

"I can learn to play a bagpipe too. That's not going happen either." A lifetime with the temperamental, possessive Isabeau— the thought almost gagged him. William raised a hand palm up in hopes to stay her emotional declarations. "Don't."

"Make love to me. Let me show you how devoted I am."

"Isabeau. I want a hot bath and sleep, in that order."

"Make love to me. I will make you forget your weariness." The gown puddled at her feet as she slid it off. Naked except for stockings and satin slippers, she touched herself, teasing her skin with fluttery strokes. William's cock involuntarily twitched and jumped a little at the tempting sight. *Carnal creature.*

"No, you won't. You'll want to play games, like

you always do," he said low, confident she wouldn't deny the accusation.

She propped a foot up on the arm of his chair, tilted her head and fingered the nest of dark curls between her legs. William sipped the claret and followed the path of her fingers with his eyes. He finished the wine and set the goblet onto the leather top of a side table.

"You like games." Isabeau pointedly shot a glance at the tented front of his trousers. "You especially like me on all fours, tied, restrained and at your mercy, *oui cher*?"

His body warred against him. Part of him wanted nothing more than to lie quiet, but part, wasn't quite as spent as the rest. It had sprung back to life with the minx's teasing and now throbbed for relief.

"True, I like a variety of things. However, were I to forget my tired bones, I'd like to do something completely different this evening." He paused. Isabeau tipped her head, a quizzical expression on her face. William anticipated her curiosity. "Tonight, I'd like to fuck like every other bloody Englishman, with you on your back and me on top groaning and pumping away for a minute or so, then a nice sleep."

A sneer touched the edge of her mouth, then

Isabeau laughed. "You English, you are so uninspired, a pity for your women. My soul cries for them."

"Yes, unimaginative lot that we are, we have somehow managed to colonize much of the world."

She took his hand and led him to her chamber. He didn't object. Upstairs Isabeau unbuttoned his trousers and pushed them down. William stripped out of the legs and held still while she undressed him the rest of the way.

She dropped to her knees and eased the sides of his underwear down to his ankles. He stared at her bent head and wondered how hair that looked so inky in the daylight could reflect so much gold and red in the light of the gas lamps. He leaned forward as she wrapped her warm hand around his cock and toyed with the tip. She wet the end with her tongue then blew on it with her warm breath.

Threading his fingers into her hair, he pushed himself between her parted lips and moaned when she sucked him in further.

When he could take no more, he pulled her up and kissed her. The hard edge of her teeth pressed along the seam of his mouth, painful, almost cutting. She fell backward onto the bed, holding onto his arms and dragged him down on top of her.

She'd done what she said: made him forget his exhaustion. About to explode, William entered her, thrusting, stroking. Isabeau with her incredible sense of drama, jerked her head to the side and scooted away like a crab toward the pillows, dislodging him. "You know what I want."

He panted above her, his arms bracketed her hips. "Yes, I know what you'd like. I told you before we started I had no interest in playing games tonight. I'm tired. Let's be done with this." How dare she do this now, he swore to himself. If he were a different kind of man, a less refined man, he'd force her, roughly if necessary. He'd teach her how unsound it was to ignite a man's baser desires then deny him satisfaction. After tonight, he'd find another lover and send her back to London or Paris, the sooner, the better. "Finish!"

She grabbed a favorite red silk scarf from the stand by the bed and held it out to him. "Do this for me and we shall both finish gloriously." She gave the scarf an impatient shake.

William debated whether to give in to her demand or simply finish himself off. A refusal allowed him to retain the power between them, but he lost much sexual gratification, to give in he relinquished his authority to the rapacious witch.

He suppressed his resentment and snatched the scarf from her hand and sat back on his heels. She lifted her head so he could wind the silk ligature around her small neck. William had to loop it twice to get it snug enough. He gave each end a tug to check the tightness, the amount of play. Isabeau raised her arms above her head, like a slave girl tethered to a pole. She closed her eyes and sighed. Her sooty eyelashes fluttered against her cheek.

He studied the nimble beauty. Would his next mistress be a willing partner of the rarer sexual arts? Isabeau showed him things he'd only heard discussed by some of the men at his club. Strange things, erotic and different, they spoke of rough and tumble love play usually performed by expensive whores. He had several mistresses over the years and numerous liaisons in between. None of his paramours came close to Isabeau in imagination. It's the one thing he'd miss.

She whimpered, and the sound brought him back to the moment. One of her kneecaps prodded his buttocks as she spread her legs. The scent of her readiness inflamed his desire. He trailed his fingers across her belly and she shivered at the touch, tiny goose bumps rose along her pale skin. She grabbed his wrist and laid his hand on one end of the scarf. "Do it."

He wrapped an end in each hand and pulled. His fingers crept up the silk and he tugged a bit harder still. The material pressed deeper into the flesh of her neck. Bright pink dotted her cheeks and radiated down to her jaw. The veins in her temples popped out and pulsed in time to her heartbeat. She moaned, pushed her hips upward and writhed against him. Her soft pubic hair tickled his testicles. Isabeau's unsubtle way of letting him know she wanted him inside her. He obliged.

Her hands encircled his wrists. She tugged hard outward, harder than usual. A choked sigh escaped her. He paid no attention. This was standard. Isabeau always insisted he maintain pressure until she signaled for him to release his hold. In the past, when she reached the edge of consciousness, she'd beat along his upper arms. This time she thrashed her head back and forth, something he hadn't seen before. Her eyes bulged in an unattractive way and she clawed at him. Her nails gouged the skin on his hands, drawing blood.

She hurt him and he wanted to slap her. He almost let go of one end of the scarf to do that. Instead, he pulled tighter. Isabeau tried to insert her fingers into the spot where the material crossed over. Her mouth opened and shut, soundless and fishlike. She swatted at the mattress wildly. Red-faced to the point of being near purple, she bucked beneath him.

She fired his blood with her lack of inhibition. Never had she responded with such intensity. Raw power surged through him, primitive, animalistic. He pumped hard. Ready to climax, William clenched his fists, twisting the scarf one last turn. Odd, feathery touches tapped his biceps, feminine and subtle grazes, and then she went limp. Spent, he released his hold and collapsed on top of her, his heart pounding while he caught his breath.

Isabeau didn't move and her head stayed turned to the side. She hadn't cried out the way she normally did when sated. Perhaps she was disappointed with his effort. He gave the thought a mental shrug. At the end of the day, it really didn't matter. He'd arrange for her departure first thing in the morning.

William rolled over and slung a sweaty arm over his eyes. He tried to decide which was worse, telling her tonight the affair was over or waiting until morning. The idea of doing it after such a rambunctious sexual endeavor seemed bad form, but he wanted to get it over with. He turned onto his side, prepared for histrionics, caterwauling, great tears and verbal abuse.

"Isabeau, look at me. I've come to a decision and it will likely distress you." Nothing. She didn't stir.

"Isabeau?"

He shook her by the arm. Still no response. William let go and her arm dropped listless to the mattress. He raised her arm again and let go. Again, it fell listless. He straddled her and patted her cheeks. Nothing. Her head twisted without resistance first right then left depending on the direction of his pat. He slapped her harder. Nothing. Vacant eyes stared fixed on the ceiling. He bent an ear to her chest. Nothing. William leapt from the bed, snatched a silver mirror from the dressing table, and held it under her nose. Nothing.

"Bitch." William hurled the mirror against the wall. "Bitch, whore," he raged and paced along the side of the bed. "I will not allow you to make my life a nightmare."

****

"This was your doing. I told you to leave me alone." William stood with his hands on his hips and took one last look at the broken female form. He braced his legs wide apart, tipped his head back and drew in several deep breaths of salt air. He loved living near the sea. The dawn held the beginnings of a fine spring day. Too bad he'd spend it and the next several cooped up at his estate, mourning the death of a woman he didn't love. The expectations of polite society grated on the nerves at times like this.

In the east, a sliver of sun appeared. The hour to raise a hue and cry for help had come. He'd stretched his visit to the beach out as long as he dared. Now, he'd ride hell bent into the village demanding help in rescuing his beloved Isabeau.

The clatter of the two horses galloping echoed off the cobblestones village street so it sounded like four. Candles were lit in the hamlet's windows, men and women not already at work came outside to see the cause of the commotion.

"Quick, you must come. There's been a terrible accident." William dropped Guinevere's lead rope and reined in King Arthur hard. The stallion's rear hooves slid on the mist covered stones. William turned him in a circle until the horse found purchase on the edge of a cobble and stopped slipping.

"Please, my lady's mare spooked and thrown her. She's fallen off Trebarwith Strand. I fear she's seriously injured." He directed his plea to several men standing at their gates.

Curious children peered around their mother's skirts at him while men grabbed lanterns and rope. Some of the men ran behind King Arthur on foot, a few had work horses handy and rode. One or two others ran to small boats and would row, paralleling the crowd to the spot where the lady fell. Often victims of cliff side falls had to be relocated by water, when carrying the injured person up the rocks was too dangerous. The women who didn't have infants to feed followed in groups, chattering, eager to witness the excitement.

****

William pressed firm fists into his lower back and arched. The stretch eased the weariness that settled down his spine from the arduous retrieval of Isabeau's body. He briefly considered taking a few minutes to write in his journal but couldn't find the energy. Exhaustion consumed him. The previous day's work on the estate, and the events of the night had taken its toll on his system. While her body lay in the parlor where in the morning it would be dressed one last time, and before collapsing onto bed, he visited Isabeau's chamber one more time. There, on the pillow he'd so often fell asleep on, lay the silk scarf, where he'd tossed it. He picked it up with the intent of burning it in the privacy of his chamber. The silk slid over his palms, through his fingers as he wove it between them. Whisper soft yet deadly, an unusual combination. The thought amused him and he stuck the scarf into his pocket. Rather than destroy the delicate weapon, he'd store it in his bureau as a token of the night, a reminder of the lovely but foolish Isabeau.

He'd ordered the maid to clean the chamber and pack everything. The maid and his valet, Burton, who met him as he left the room, did their best to console him in this dark hour. William thanked them for their efforts. Fully clothed, he lay down and closed his eyes, grateful for such a caring staff.

May 15, 1888

She let it go too long. A ladylike fist banging on my upper arm, our usual signal would have sufficed. Instead, she heated my blood with her wildcat gyrations. The writhing, the intimate press of her swollen folds against me. Inspirational. There'd been no cry, no complaint, only a breathy gasp, that sensual moan. The struggle. The force of her fight. The glassy sheen to her eyes, the way they widened, more and more. Ecstasy. I've never been so hard. I'd have stopped had I known, then again, perhaps not. A moot point. She's dead. An accident, but still...

Journal entry of William Everhard

About the Author
Chris Karlsen

Chris Karlsen is a retired police detective. She spent twenty-five years in law enforcement with two different agencies. The daughter of a history professor and a voracious reader, she grew up with a love of his and books. An internationally published author, Chris has traveled extensively throughout Europe, the Near East, and North Africa satisfying her need to visit the places she read about. Having spent a great deal of time in England and Turkey, she has used her love of both places as settings for her books. "Heroes Live Forever," which is her debut book, is set in England as is the sequel, "Journey in Time." Both are part of her "Knights in Time," series. Her third book, to be released in late 2011, "Golden Chariot," is set in Turkey and she is currently working on another set in Turkey, Paris and Cyprus. Published by Books to Go Now, her novels are available in digital, ebook, and Android App.

"Heroes Live Forever," is available in paperback and "Journey in Time," will be made available in paperback in October, 2011 on her publisher's site. A Chicago native, Chris has lived in Paris and Los Angeles and now resides in the Pacific Northwest with her husband and four rescue dogs. A city girl all her life, living in a small village on a bay was a interesting adjustment. She'd never lived anywhere so quiet at night and traffic wasn't bumper to bumper 24/7. Some of Chris's favorite authors are: Michael Connolly, John Sandford, Joseph Wambaugh, Stephen Coonts, Bernard Cornwell, Julia Quinn, Julie Anne Long, Deanna Raybourne and Steve Berry.

You can find more stories such as this at www.bookstogonow.com

If you enjoy this Books to Go Now story please leave a review for the author on Amazon, Goodreads or the site which you purchased the eBook. Thanks!

We pride ourselves with representing great stories at low prices. We want to take you into the digital age offering a market that will allow you to grow along with us in our journey through the new frontier of digital publishing.
Some of our favorite award-winning authors have now joined us. We welcome readers and writers into our community.

We want to make sure that as a reader you are supplied with never-ending great stories. As a company, Books to Go Now, wants its readers and writers supplied with positive experience and encouragement so they will return again and again.

We want to hear from you. Our readers and writers are the cornerstone of our company. If there is something you would like to say or a genre that you would like to see, please email us at inquiry@bookstogonow.com

62499396R00208

Made in the USA
Lexington, KY
08 April 2017